By the same author

The Hengest and Horsa Trilogy
A Brother's Oath
A Warlord's Bargain
A King's Legacy

The Arthur of the Cymry Trilogy
Sign of the White Foal
Banner of the Red Dragon
Field of the Black Raven (forthcoming)
Drustan and Esyllt: Wolves of the Sea (novella)

The Rebel and the Runaway
Lords of the Greenwood

https://christhorndycroft.wordpress.com/

As P. J. Thorndyke

The Lazarus Longman Chronicles
Through Mines of Deception (novella)
On Rails of Gold (novella)
Golden Heart
Silver Tomb
Onyx City

Celluloid Terrors
Curse of the Blood Fiends

https://pjthorndyke.wordpress.com/

Banner of the Red Dragon

CHRIS THORNDYCROFT

Banner of the Red Dragon
By Chris Thorndycroft

2019 by Copyright © Chris Thorndycroft

All rights reserved. This book or any portion thereof may not be reproduced or used in any manner whatsoever without the express written permission of the publisher except for the use of brief quotations in a book review.

For Maia for her constant encouragement and my parents for their unwavering support.

	Place Name	Modern Name
1	Din Eidyn	Edinburgh
2	Din Peldur	Traprain Law
3	Din Banna	Birdoswald
4	Cair Eburac	York
5	Cadwallon's Lys	Caswallon's Llys
6	Aberffraw	Aberffraw
7	Deverdoeu	Chester
8	Cair Cunor	Caer Gai
9	Cair Guricon	Wroxeter
10	Cair Gloui	Gloucester
11	Corinium	Cirencester
12	Cair Guenta	Caerwent
13	Cair Legion	Caerllion
14	Cair Badon	Bath
15	Londinium	London
16	Crecganford	Crayford
17	Guenta Belgarum	Winchester
18	Cair Uisc	Exeter
19	Din Tagel	Tintagel
20	Cair Dor	Castle Dore

"The twelfth battle was on Mount Badon in which there fell in one day 960 men from one charge by Arthur; and no one struck them down except Arthur himself, and in all the wars he emerged as victor."
- The History of the Britons

PART I

"I will go, I and my teulu," said Arthur, "to seek either satisfaction or bloodshed. And then they surrounded the wood of Clyddon.
- Ystori Trystan

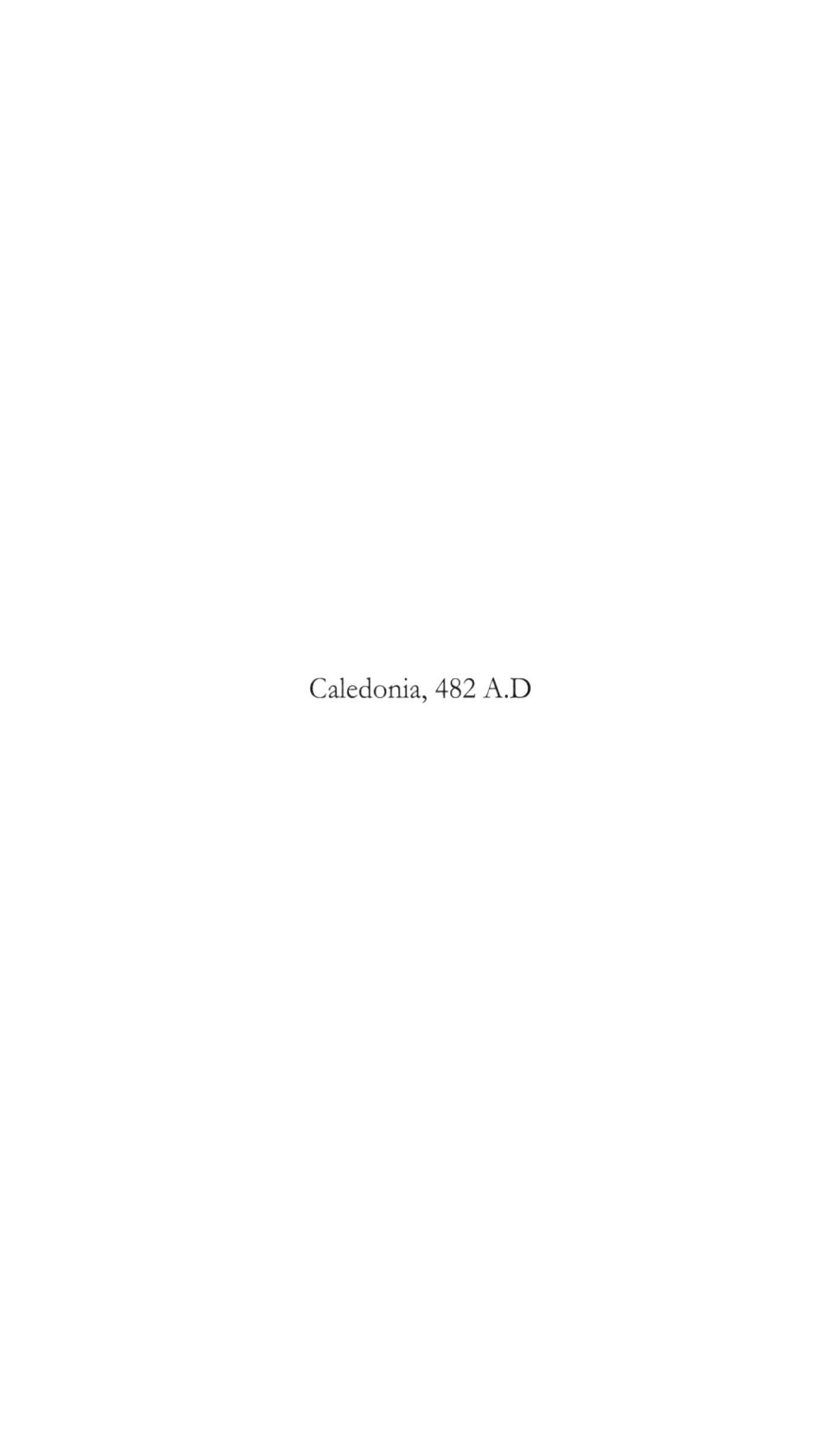

Caledonia, 482 A.D

Arthur

The mist hung over the forests like a shroud. Arthur gripped the reigns of his grey mare Lamrei in his gloved fist, patting her pale neck to sooth her nerves while he fought down his own. Behind him his company stood ready, horses whinnying softly, champing at the bit and scraping at the damp earth with their hooves. Every sound seemed amplified in the muted silence of the forests. The jingle of every harness was like the toll of a bell and every nervous cough a clap of thunder.

He looked out across the wooded valley that lay deep in the Caledonian Forest. Its other side was barely visible in the fog and shade of the tall pines. Somewhere over there Cei was waiting at the head of his own company. Further down the valley waited the combined cavalry of their foster father Cunor and King Leudon, blocking the exit, sealing the trap.

It had been a hard season's fighting. The thick forests of the north concealed an enemy that had dwelt there since the dawn of time, deeply knowledgeable of its paths and valleys, working as swiftly as ghosts in the mist. Blood had been spilt for every inch of ground as the Britons were constantly assailed by small raiding bands sent by King Caw of the Pictish tribes.

The Picts had been united under a high-king before but the fragmented state of the tribes and their incessant blood feuds made it a rare occurrence. The first time had been during the Barbarian Conspiracy of 367 when the Roman garrison at the Great Wall had rebelled. A Pictish confederation under King

Gartnait had swarmed south in an attack coordinated with the Gaels of Erin and the Saeson pirates who plagued the south-east coast. The second time had been during a civil war between Prince Talorc and his aunt Galana who, in accordance with the tradition of matrilineal descent held by some of the tribes, wanted the throne for her infant son. It had been a British army sent by Lord Vertigernus that had crushed Galana's rebellion and placed her nephew Talorc on the throne to rule Pictland from his royal seat at Din Eidyn.

But Din Eidyn had once been the home of the Votadini tribe; a client kingdom of the Romans. Their greatest warlord was Cunedag who had been sent by Lord Vertigernus to reconquer the mountainous region of Venedotia from the Gaels several years earlier. Cunedag had been Arthur's grandfather and although Arthur was but a bastard offshoot of Cunedag's dynasty, he served Venedotia as loyally as any trueborn son.

In the years that followed Talorc's victory over his aunt, the British warlord Leudon set his sights on a northern kingdom of his own and took Din Eidyn from the Picts. In an attempt to legitimise his rule over what had once been the territory of Cunedag's kin, he married into the ruling family of Venedotia. His bride Anna – Arthur's half-sister – had run away from the marriage bed and was now dead yet the kingdom of Leudonion had been secured.

The Picts, never ones to forget an injury, plotted swift revenge on Leudon. Their opportunity came in the form of Caw who banded the tribes together in a confederation with the intent of smashing Leudon's hold over Din Eidyn and driving the Britons back south of Wall. Leudon, cowering in the face of Caw's painted hordes, had sent to his lost bride's family for help. King Cadwallon, newly ascended to the title of 'Pendraig' – high-king of Venedotia – heeded his estranged brother-in-law's call and had sent the Teulu of the Red Dragon north that summer.

Now autumn had come and the treetops had turned golden brown, their leaves stripped away to reveal the skeleton of the forest. The Picts had finally been forced into open battle and Arthur hoped that this would be an end to the war. He was sick of the rain and the mud, sick of the cold, whipping winds and sleeping in rough tents, eating bowls of watery stew and hard tack, day after day. He wanted to go home. For many reasons.

A sound reached his ears; a distant tramping of hooves down on the valley floor. He leaned forward in his saddle and listened hard. He could just make out the sound of the oncoming force as it moved slowly through the trees. It was five-hundred strong according to the scouts. He could see movement; spear tips and blue woad on bare skin. The helmed heads of warriors mounted on their sturdy highland ponies. He turned to Gualchmei.

"Get ready for my signal," he said, and Gualchmei passed the message along the ranks. Spears were gripped tightly and shields were lifted up and down as the warriors prepared their shoulder muscles, revolving their arms in their sockets, loosening up for maximum mobility. The sound of the oncoming Picts was louder now, a low rumbling growl of movement. The trees down in the valley began to sway as the mighty force shouldered its way past. A horn bellowed on the other side of the valley, Cei's horn; the signal to attack.

"'Company!" roared Arthur, holding his spear aloft. "Forward!"

As one, Arthur's company followed their captain down the slope of the hill and into the valley. Earth and pine needles were kicked up by hooves as they gradually picked up speed.

"Keep the line steady!" Arthur bellowed. "As one!"

Trees whipped past them, a fuzzy blur of greens and browns. The enemy was in sight now; a massive force of mounted Picts flanking a column of spearmen. Savage war-hounds strained at their leashes, their ears pricking at the sound of their approach.

Hundreds of heads turned to look in startled surprise at the charging Britons. The hounds bayed and gnashed their jaws and the spearmen tugged on them as they hurried to form a defensive line. But they were too slow and undisciplined. Arthur struck out with his spear as he led his men into their right flank, blinking as a gush of blood spattered the right side of his face. The spearmen went down under the hooves of the Britons and the Pictish cavalry flanks turned in an attempt to hem them in.

Horses whinnied in fear and pain and the war-hounds barked and tore savagely at their flanks. Spears punctured armour and flesh while shields shivered and split under the impact of heavy swords and axes. The Picts, never ones to stay surprised for long, fought back with a furious energy.

Arthur parried a spear stroke and thrust his own iron-tipped shaft into the chest of his attacker, knocking the stricken man from his saddle. He could hear the distant sound of Cei's horn and grinned as the Pictish host turned in shock to face another company of Britons descending the valley on the other side. Caught between two pincers, the Picts fought bravely, refusing to give up any ground to their attackers.

Then came the sound of another horn, deeper, more resonant. It was as if a death-toll had descended from the fog and all in the valley turned to see its source. Emerging from the southern end of the valley was the third cavalry led by Cunor and King Leudon. Above them the banner of the red dragon wavered, nostrils flaring, tail billowing out behind it like a ghastly apparition from the mist accompanied by a roaring of horns. This was the final stroke for the Picts and their captains turned in their saddles and bellowed out the order to retreat.

The Britons roared with triumph and urged their steeds onwards, cutting at the heels of their enemy. They chased the Picts up the valley, slaying any who were too slow to escape their stabbing spears and swinging blades. Arthur heard Cei bellowing to him above the slaughter.

"By Modron's tits, we have them on the hop! Did you see that prince of theirs? We wiped that blue smirk off his face!"

"Hueil? No, I couldn't make him out." said Arthur. Hueil was Caw's eldest son and had led most of the attacks against them throughout the season. "Were you near him?"

"Aye, but I couldn't get a good swing at him. His bastard captains formed a ring about him. But I'll get him next time! They have nowhere to run now. It's only a matter of time."

"Time is something we are running short of," said a voice behind them. It was Cunor, Cei's father, his steed foaming with sweat and his standard-bearer struggling to keep up with him. "We have waited all season for this battle and now that we have these bastards pinned down, winter threatens to take them away from us. I want the heads of Caw and Hueil on poles by the end of the day."

"They'll be heading for the river," said King Leudon beside him. "Caw will most likely be somewhere beyond it with the rest of the confederation. What we faced today was merely Hueil's vanguard. There is a fording point further east."

"Then we must push onwards and cut them off before they cross the river, father," said Cei. "If we stop Hueil reuniting with the rest of the Picts, Caw will be more vulnerable."

"Agreed," replied Cunor. "But beyond that river is unknown territory. I don't want to risk blundering into any of their ambushes."

"The river is wide and deep further west," said Leudon. "If we could push them in that direction, then they won't be able to cross and will be forced to fight."

"Very well," said Cunor. "But we must secure that crossing in case they slip by us. Cei, Arthur, your companies are light and fast. I want you to ride for the crossing as fast as you can. Reach it before the enemy does and hold it until we arrive. With any luck we will be able to crush Hueil between our two forces."

"Yes, sir!" replied Arthur and Cei in unison and they trotted off, hailing their standard-bearers to regroup their companies.

"Follow my lead," said Cei to Arthur as they set off up the valley. "If my company comes across any pockets of resistance, ride yours around on my left flank and engage."

They proceeded northwards and the valley levelled out into flat ground. The forest grew thicker and the two companies had trouble keeping their men in an orderly formation.

"Get those stragglers on our right flank closer in!" called Arthur to Gualchmei. "I don't want anyone vulnerable to ambush!"

The sound of Cunor's horns dwindled into the distance as Arthur and Cei rode on. Soon they could hear the rushing of the river and Cei sent scouts ahead. They reported back with news that Hueil and his company were already in the process of fording it.

"Damn them!" shouted Cei.

"We're too late!" said Arthur.

"We have to cross and cut them down before they regroup with Caw."

"Your father's orders were to wait for him at the ford."

"If we let Hueil reach his father this war could drag on and on! And I don't know about you, but I want that blue bastard's head on a spear before sundown!"

"Cei, we could ride straight into a trap!"

"Arthur is right," said Beduir. "We don't know how large Caw's following is. There could be thousands waiting for us across the river."

"Then that is why we must cut down Hueil before he reaches them! And Beduir, you are in my company, not Arthur's. You do as I say!"

Beduir shrugged apologetically at Arthur and followed Cei as he led his company across the river. Arthur watched in silent disapproval. He knew there was no point in trying to make his pig-headed foster-brother listen to reason when the scent of blood and victory was in his nostrils.

When he was halfway across the river, Cei turned in his saddle to call to him. "Remain on the southern bank and wait for my father if you wish, Arthur. But I'm going to bring back Hueil's head!"

"This is a bad idea," said Gualchmei at Arthur's side. "Both companies are vulnerable divided."

Arthur nodded. "He is a fool, but he is not under my command. Where is Cundelig?"

"Here, sir!" the lead scout replied, trotting over to him. Hebog, his peregrine falcon, sat on his gauntlet, leather hood pulled down over its eyes.

"Take a group of your scouts to the other side of the river and keep pace with my block-headed foster-brother. We can at least watch his back that way."

Cundelig saluted and crossed the river with three of his scouts on their light, fast horses. Arthur waited with the rest of his company on the riverbank, watching the swirls and eddies of the dark water.

Cundelig had barely been gone a few moments before he and his scouts returned, splashing across the ford in great haste.

"Sir!" he blurted. "Cei and his riders have plunged on into the woods in a northerly direction. We spotted a large company of Picts coming from the west and I mean massive. It's a good bet Caw is with them. We only just managed to get back across the river without being seen."

"It was a ruse," said Arthur, panic rising in his gut. "They will be coming up behind Cei. He'll be trapped!"

"Lord Cunor and the rest of the teulu are still on their way," said Gualchmei. "There is nothing we can do."

"The hell there isn't!" replied Arthur. "That's my foster-brother out there. I'm going to get him out somehow. If we can trick Caw's force into coming after us instead of Cei, then we may have a chance to ambush them here at the ford. I'm going to split the company into two units. You shall lead the first, Gualchmei. Ride west as hard as possible and draw Caw's attention. I shall take the second unit and conceal ourselves on that ridge across the river. When the enemy pursues you across the ford, we shall charge their rear."

"Sir," said Gualchmei. "We are a small enough force as it is. Dividing us is extremely risky. Even if we spring a successful ambush, we'll be hopelessly outnumbered."

"We only need to draw them away from Cei. The first party does not need to engage the enemy at all, merely bait them. But we need to move now if we are to prevent them from getting at Cei. Off you go and good luck. And remember, only draw their attention. Do not risk yourselves in combat."

"Yes, sir," replied Gualchmei and he rode off, leading his small group of men across the river.

Arthur waited until the river was clear before leading his own men across. The rise on the other side was thickly wooded and provided excellent cover for his men and their horses. Atop it, he could see the rear of Gualchmei's unit weaving through the trees below, following the river west. As they vanished into the gloom, Arthur felt the haunted wilderness closing in on him. He had less than twenty-five warriors, they were alone and on the wrong side of the river in uncharted territory.

All because of Cei.

It hadn't been the first time his foster-brother had charged into danger without a thought for the consequences. He was a hot-headed, gung-ho oaf. But Arthur loved him and would risk all to save him. It was selfish to risk the lives of his men in doing so perhaps, but there it was.

It wasn't long before the sound of horns calling for chase to be given drifted through the trees towards them. Arthur heard the hammering of hooves and Gualchmei's unit thundered into view, curling around to cross the ford. The Pictish vanguard followed closely, hooves churning the earth and war dogs threading their way in and out, jaws slavering for the kill. They had taken the bait!

The press of infantry hurried along in their wake; hundreds of them dressed in an array of colourful wool, mail, leather and skins. Every inch of bare flesh was either tattooed or painted with the blue dye of the woad plant depicting the sigils and totem animals of a dozen clans.

As the stragglers were wading into the foaming waters, Arthur yelled the order to charge at the top of his voice. They crashed down the slope and the Picts turned, startled at an attack on their rear. But the danger posed by Arthur's paltry twenty-five riders was slim in the face of their superior numbers.

Arthur roared an oath of defiance as they slammed into the rear of the enemy. They cut through the infantry like butter, swinging their great cavalry swords and axes down on unprotected heads, cracking them open like turnips. They drove deep into the enemy ranks so that the shallows of the river wetted the fetlocks of their horses.

Across the river, Gualchmei had wheeled his unit around and was charging the enemy head on, trapping the Picts in the bottleneck of the ford.

Brave lad, thought Arthur. *He is prepared to lay down his life for his comrades.* A retreat south was open to him but he had chosen to die with his teulu. That kind of loyalty could not be bought.

The river turned red and grew bloated with the corpses of the fallen. The Picts were momentarily trapped and many braved the deeper parts of the river. Some made it to the banks while others lost their footing and were swept away by the strong current.

Up ahead, Arthur could see King Caw; a plume of raven feathers cresting an iron helm that wobbled as he hacked and slashed his way through Gualchmei's ranks. Near to him Arthur saw Hueil, roaring defiance and urging the Picts onwards. He must have cut westwards after crossing the ford to bring news to his father while Cei was led on a wild goose chase deep into the forests.

They had no chance of holding them at the ford. Gualchmei's unit was being overrun. The Picts would win through but Arthur did not regret his decision. Drawing the enemy away from Cei and spoiling their trap had been the only choice open to him.

A bellowing roar sounded from the south-west and the Britons cried with joy at seeing Cunor and Leudon at the head of the teulu, riding hard towards the ford. The red dragon standard was as a splash of blood amidst the muted greens and browns of the forest. The Picts saw that the tables had turned suddenly and began pushing against Gualchmei's unit all the harder, not to destroy them now but to break through, to flee.

"We have them!" Arthur cried. "Push on! Cut down their king! Don't let him escape!"

They crossed the ford, threading a path around the sodden corpses that leaked red tendrils into the pinkish water, and climbed the bank to re-join Gualchmei's unit. Cunor and Leudon had slammed into the right flank of the fleeing Picts and battle rang out among the trees.

Arthur led his company into the rear of the fleeing enemy but the battle was over almost by the time they got there. Cunor was wheeling his mighty mount around, waving a bloodied sword in the air.

"You did it, my lad!" he cried upon seeing Arthur. "I don't know how you held that ford against such odds but you did it!" Before Arthur could explain, Cunor interrupted him. "Caw is dead! I saw him hacked down by Leudon's household troops. The head of the tattooed snake has been lopped off! Where is Cei?" he asked at last, noticing his son's absence.

Arthur saw the look of concern cross his foster-father's face. "Cei was not with us at the ford. When we arrived, Hueil and his warriors had already crossed. Cei led his company across the river in pursuit of him while my company remained to wait for you. My scouts brought me word of a large Pictish force coming from the west. It was a ruse to ambush us once we had crossed the river."

"What happened?"

"I split my company and we lured the Picts across the ford and then ambushed them."

"Saving my son," said Cunor, his face grim. "Well were the hell is he?"

"Sir!" said Caradog, captain of the first company, galloping over to them. "Prince Hueil has escaped. He has rallied the remaining Pictish cavalry and they are fleeing south."

"To what end?" asked Gualchmei. "Without their king they can't pose much of a threat to the southern kingdoms. They'll disperse and attempt to sneak back to their tribal lands. It's over!"

"No," said Arthur. "Hueil is as canny a leader as his father was. He'll remain a standard for them to flock to."

"You're right, Arthur," said Cunor. "This war isn't over until I have Hueil's head along with his father's. You must go after them, son."

"Me?" Arthur said.

"Aye. You have the fastest horses. We will finish mopping up here."

"Cei returns!" Gualchmei exclaimed.

Cunor turned an angry face to the ford where his son was leading his company through the water.

"I told you to remain at the ford!" Cunor exploded as Cei drew near.

"Father," Cei protested. "Hueil was within our grasp! I couldn't let him get away! Not when we were so close to winning…"

"Hueil headed west and re-joined his father," said Cunor. They would have bitten you in the arse had it not been for Arthur's quick thinking! You deliberately disobeyed my orders!"

Cei's face reddened. "Father, I…"

Cunor turned to Arthur. "Get going. Don't let Hueil escape."

"Yes, sir," Arthur replied and began rounding up his company.

"Hueil has fled south?" Cei enquired. "Father, let me go with Arthur…"

"No! I want you here with me where I can keep an eye on you!"

Arthur did not wait to hear any more. Water skins were passed around and those who were still fit to ride mounted their horses and set out.

They rode south all afternoon until the sky above the treetops grew blood streaked. The men and the horses were tired yet still they forced themselves on with the knowledge that their enemy would be just as fatigued.

They can't run forever, Arthur told himself as he urged Lamrei on, sympathising with the creature's flagging strength.

They passed through the neck of Albion where the great island narrowed into the tribal territories of the southern Picts, squeezed between two powerful British kingdoms. To the east lay Leudonion with its chief forts of Din Eidyn and Din Peldur. To the west lay the kingdom of Ystrat Clut, ruled by King Caradog; an old Briton who was a little too friendly with the Gaels and the Picts than his countrymen thought decent. This was compounded by his refusal to aid King Leudon in his war against the northern Picts. Eventually, as darkness descended, they were forced to stop and rest.

"Hueil will be doing the same," said Gualchmei. "His horses will be no fresher than ours."

"I want to be ready to move out at first light," said Arthur.

After they had fed and watered the horses and brushed down their sweat-streaked coats, they collapsed around their campfires and boiled their meat. Arthur posted sentries and sent Cundelig and a scouting unit further south to see if they could find out how far away Hueil was camped. With the stars like dust in the black sky, the men began to snore as they sank into a well-earned rest.

Arthur remained awake, staring into the glowing embers of the campfire. His thoughts were of home, of Venedotia and the hair of one woman which burned in his mind as red as the heat of the flames before him.

He and Guenhuifar had grown close over the past two years. Much of Arthur's time had been spent on Ynys Mon with the teulu in their effort to drive away the Gaels. It had been a long campaign but they had succeeded, despite several fresh invasions from Erin along Albion's north-west coast. King Cadwallon, the Pendraig of Venedotia and Arthur's half-brother had rebuilt Cunedag's old lys in the north-eastern corner of Ynys Mon and had made Guenhuifar's father steward of it as he had been of old. Many celebrations had taken place in Cadwallon's new royal seat and Arthur and Guenhuifar had found their eyes meeting more and more often over the heads of the revellers in the smoky hall.

They had enjoyed stolen moments of secrecy and forbidden kisses beneath the moonlight when the autumn wind was peeling the dead leaves from the trees. Whether he was in his bed at Cair Cunor, or in a muddy field facing a horde of howling Gaels or Picts, Arthur's mind yearned for those soft lips and that thick, auburn hair. They had not openly expressed their love to each other but it was there all the same; a glowing ember that smouldered away, biding its time, threatening to burst into flame at any moment.

"Arthur!" called one of the sentries, hurrying over to him. "Cundelig and his scouts have returned!"

Arthur got up and went to the perimeter of the camp where Cundelig was dismounting, his exhausted horse shaking with fatigue.

"Arthur took Cundelig by the shoulder. "You have returned so soon! Are they close?"

"Any closer and we could hurl insults at each other," said Cundelig. "The ground slopes down through the trees over there to the shores of a great lake. Hueil has made camp beneath the shelter of the trees at the water's edge. He commands but a fraction of the warriors we saw him ride away with."

"Where are the rest of them?"

"Deserted? Fled back to their homes? Who knows?"

"Ha!" said Gualchmei, joining them at the camp's edge. "He's a sitting duck!"

Arthur was not convinced. "He must have come this far south for a reason. My guess is that he has sent his warriors out to rally local support. We are in Damnonii territory and we have the Britons of Ystrat Clut to the west of us."

"Ystrat Clut has long been friendly to the southern Picts," said Gualchmei. "King Caradog refused to send his warriors to aid Leudonion."

"And we don't know how loyal the Damnonii are to Caw's confederation but if they rally to Hueil's standard with the support of King Caradog, we could be facing a resurgence here in the south."

"By Christ, we've got to take him and take him now!" said Cundelig. "Else all will be undone!"

"Aye," Arthur agreed. "The lads and the horses need a couple of hours more sleep but I want to fall upon Hueil's camp before dawn. They don't know we have followed them this far and won't be expecting us. Once we have Hueil, we ride east for Din Eidyn. We can hand him over to Leudon's people there and he can be used as a bargaining chip to end this war."

The dawn attack on Hueil's camp went according to plan. Arthur marshalled his cavalry on the top of the slope just as the sky was beginning to pale in the east. They were all still tired, stiff and sore from the previous day's fighting but the sight of the small cluster of campfires down by the shores of the lake was more refreshing to them than either sleep or a good meal. That pathetic encampment was all that stood between them and the end of the whole blasted war.

Arthur gave no orders for horns to be blown. He wanted the surprise to be saved until the very last second. He led them himself, spurring Lamrei down the slope, dodging the trees, spear gripped in his right fist.

As they emerged from the trees in a thunder of hooves, the alarm of the sentries could be heard, but only briefly. They tore through the outer perimeter, skewering and hacking down any Pict who stood in their way. Campfires were scattered by hooves in a flurry of embers and ash. Arthur sent the wings of his company to envelop the camp on all sides, leaving only the lake at the enemy's rear.

The panicked Picts splashed into the shallows and tried to swim for it but Arthur's men dismounted and waded in after them, reddening the water with down-thrust spears. Those who remained on land were captured and herded together.

"Where is Hueil mab Caw?" Arthur bellowed, wheeling Lamrei about as he scanned the faces of the prisoners.

They remained silent but it was a futile gesture. Hueil was known to Arthur and his men. They had seen his blue-painted face roaring at them over the din of the battlefield several times that summer and would recognise it now.

"Here!" said Gualchmei triumphantly.

Hueil was plucked from the gathered prisoners and hauled before Arthur. The woad on his face was cracked and peeling now, tiredness and defeat showing in his wild, dark eyes.

"Arthur mab Enniaun," said Hueil, drawing himself up defiantly. "You have the upper hand today, it seems. The gods take pity on you at last!" He grinned through his blackened teeth.

"Fortunes of war change like the tides," said Arthur. "And today is not your day. Fetch him along!"

"What of the others?" Gualchmei asked.

Arthur glanced at the unarmed Picts who were clustered together like sheep. "They are of no use to us," he said. "Kill them."

The enemy did not scream or beg for mercy as Arthur's men set about their butchery. Such things were the very depths of dishonour for a Pict and they died as Arthur knew they would, fighting with their bare hands until their last breaths. Hueil watched the awful scene without emotion. These were his warriors, his companions. They had done him proud in life and now they did him proud in their deaths.

They ate what they could of the Picts' meagre supplies before setting out east. Hueil was led on a horse, his hands bound behind him, saying not a word.

It was before noon that the scouts came hurrying back with news of a Pictish host approaching from the east.

"Damnonii?" Arthur asked.

"By the looks of their markings, I would say so," said Cundelig. "A thousand strong on foot. They must have marshalled their entire tribe."

"Is there any way around them?"

"If we could make it to the banks of the Bodotria Estuary, we could follow it to Din Eidyn but it would be risky trying to cross that distance so close to their scouts. They have dogs and our horses are tired. We would not avoid an engagement if we were spotted."

"Back north, then?"

Cundelig rubbed his chin. "Possible. But we might run into whatever is left of Caw's warband fleeing south with Cunor on their heels. Even refugees would outnumber us."

"Then there is only one way open to us then," said Arthur. "We go south. To the Wall."

"The Wall?" Gualchmei exclaimed.

"It is quite a distance but we can find safety at Din Banna. They won't be looking for us yet so we have a head start on them."

They turned their mounts in a southerly direction and tried to cover as much distance as possible before night fell. To the south the lands opened up into a vista of rolling moors bearded with purple heather and cut through by flowing watercourses. There was little cover and when they camped that night, Arthur forbade the lighting of fires for they would be spotted miles off. They had no food left and slept in discomfort for only as long as they had to before setting out once more.

At first light Cundelig sent Hebog up and shielded his eyes with his hand as he watched the bird's movements to the north of them.

"Damn!" the scout cried.

"What is it?" said Arthur as he mounted his horse.

"A large host approaching from the north. They've seen us!"

"Ride!" shouted Arthur. "We ride straight for Din Banna and stop for nothing!"

The Wall had stopped functioning as a wall long ago. Unmanned and unmaintained, sections of it had crumbled in leaving gaping holes through which the Picts regularly slipped through to raid the kingdoms of the Northern Britons.

Din Banna was one of the sixteen forts the Romans had built at regular intervals along the length of the Emperor Hadrian's great wall. After the Roman garrison had deserted it, King Gurust of Rheged refortified it and made it the northernmost defence of his new kingdom. Straddling the road that led from west to east, Din Banna was as a rock against the tide, walled on all sides with its old Roman watch towers manned and its granaries full.

Gualchmei called out a greeting as they approached the small wooden bridge that spanned the overgrown ditch at the foot of fort's walls. The great double arched gates creaked open to admit them and once every rider was within the ruined northern section of the fort, they were slammed shut and bolted once more.

Arthur swung himself down from his saddle and heard the relieved laughs and jests of his men at finding refuge. He wished he could share in their relief but they were not out of the woods yet.

"Where is the camp prefect?" he demanded of a nearby soldier.

"Here!" said a short man in scale armour as he strode towards them.

"See that our horses are fed and stabled, they have had a long journey."

"You're Venedotians, aren't you?" the camp prefect said. "What news from the war?"

"All but over and its last engagement is to happen here."

The prefect's face paled. "*Here?*"

Arthur directed the man's gaze to the prisoner who was being lifted down from his horse. "That is Hueil mab Caw. We captured him in battle but were forced to flee south. There is a large band of Damnonii on our trail."

The prefect gawked at him. "You brought Picts to the Wall?"

Arthur looked at him curiously. "I was under the impression the Wall was built to withstand Picts."

"But, but the rest of your teulu? Where is the mighty dragon standard of Cunedag?"

"Mopping things up in our wake," said Arthur. Caw is dead. His son is the last figurehead of the Pictish confederation. That is why we brought him here, where they cannot get at him."

"But Din Banna is severely undermanned! Most of the garrison went with you lot to fight in the north!"

"Nevertheless, a Pictish warband a thousand strong is marching upon us. Bring everybody from the settlement within the walls. Find every bow and spear in the fort and place them in the hands of every person able to use them."

The camp prefect cursed and hurried off to see that it was done. As the frightened villagers began to trickle in through the east gate, supporting the elderly and herding livestock, Arthur walked along the walls and surveyed the defences. Some of the towers had crumbled away but the parapet itself was in good repair. There were even a couple of catapults that seemed to be in working order.

He had barely completed his survey before the horns began to blow from the northern watchtowers. He ran the length of the parapet.

The Picts were emerging from the trees in clusters beneath their banners. They took up a howling war cry intended to intimidate.

"Fewer than a thousand," said Gualchmei as he and Cundelig joined him on the parapet. "Perhaps your eyes are getting tired, Cundelig."

"There are fewer of them because they have divided themselves," said Arthur. "They want to surround us."

His prediction was confirmed as the warning horn was taken up on the west wall and then, after an interval, on the east.

"They have slipped through the gaps in the Wall further along," said Arthur. "They don't want us escaping with their precious prince."

"Shit!" said Gualchmei as he gazed at the horde of woad-painted warriors that chanted and hammered on their shields. "They're surrounding the fort! Can we withstand them?"

"Perhaps," said Arthur. "But we will only last as long as the fort's stores do."

The Picts attacked as one, blowing their aurochs horns to signal an assault on all sides. Arthur bellowed for bowmen to be placed evenly along the walls and he and his men began distributing spears.

"Don't let any of the buggers get their ladders close!" Arthur instructed the terrified soldiers and villagers who lined the parapets. "And hack through any grappling hooks that gain a hold. If even one of those bastards gets up here, our defences will be penetrated and the whole fort may fall."

Arrows sailed out from the fort's walls to disappear seemingly without significance into the mass of warriors below. The catapults hurled stones into the mob but still they came in attempt after attempt to climb the walls with their ladders and hooks. They seemed to be frantic. They knew their prince was within the fort and gleefully hurled themselves at its defences in their effort to free him and save what was left of Caw's confederation.

The assault went on until dark. The catapults ran out of ammunition and hung slack. With the onset of night, the Picts retreated out of arrow range to rest and recover. Arthur ordered the distribution of food. He and his warriors having barely eaten since the previous night, gobbled down hard tack biscuits, bacon and beer. They were dog tired and Arthur ordered them to sleep in shifts until dawn.

The following morning the assault began afresh and the situation looked desperate. They were low on arrows, had few spears between them and the Picts had brought forth battering rams cut from trees during the night, sharpened and fire-hardened to slam again and again at the north and west doors.

"Much more of that and those doors will give way," Gualchmei called to Arthur over the din. "We can't spare extra men to put over the gates else we thin our defences on the walls!"

Arthur nodded grimly. It was only a matter of time. Their fates were tied to that of the fort and before a second night fell the Picts would gain entry and overrun them. He made a decision that he had been grappling with all night.

"Bring me Hueil," he said.

Gualchmei blinked at him and then hurried off to carry out his orders.

The Pict was brought up to the walls and he surveyed his attacking countrymen with an arrogant smile. "You can't win, Arthur," he said. "The Damnonii believe in my father's dream. Every true-born Pict does and will gladly water the ground with his blood in order to see you Britons pushed out of the north for good."

Ignoring him, Arthur grabbed him by his hair and forced him to his knees, his head hanging over a stone in the parapet. "We may all die here," he said, "but so will you. Your countrymen will never hail you as their leader. I'll see to that"

He drew his sword and, as he gripped it with both hands, Hueil turned his head to look at him with wide eyes as comprehension dawned.

Arthur swung down with all his might, once, twice, his blade connecting with the stone on the second blow. Hueil's head tumbled over the parapet as blood gushed from the stump of his neck to wet the stone with gore.

The act had been witnessed by hundreds of Picts and they gave up an ear-splitting cry of rage. Curses burned the air and they drove the attack harder, this time for vengeance for now that Hueil was dead, all was lost to them now. All that remained was a deep desire to bathe in the blood of the defiant Britons.

"Well, that's that then," said Gualchmei in a resigned tone.

"I couldn't let them have him," Arthur replied. "We face the last of their fury now but at least this war is done."

They held out for the rest of the day, using their arrows sparingly. The end was coming but the desire to postpone the inevitable was strong.

A little after midday the Picts on the northern side of the fort dispersed with great urgency. A bellowing of horns drowned out the war chants that had dulled the ears of Arthur and his comrades for over a day.

Mounted warriors burst from the trees, driving the Picts before them. The Britons on the walls went wild as the banner of the red dragon erupted from the green like a burning brand to drive away their attackers. Arthur roared with joy to see Cunor leading the charge with Cei and Caradog close behind amidst scores of their countrymen on Venedotian steeds.

The Picts fled to the western side of the fort but a group of them turned and clustered to the left of the fort's gates, trying to form some sort of defence against the horsemen. As Cunor led the advance against them, the Picts that had fled swarmed around to outflank him.

"They're going to try and blindside him!" Arthur cried. He gripped the stone parapet with whitened knuckles while bellowing as loudly as he could; "Cei! Caradog! On your right flank!"

Caradog had seen them and was desperately trying to drive a wedge between the charging Picts and Cunor. It was too late. They were within spear-throwing distance and a javelin whickered through the air.

Arthur roared impotently as he saw the spear tip erupt from his foster-father's chest in a spurt of gore, its wicked point glinting. Cunor gasped and swayed in his saddle as Caradog led his followers into the Picts and hacked them down. Cei was at his father's side in an instant, seizing the reigns of his horse and supporting him, preventing him from falling.

"Open the gates!" Arthur called. "Let them bring the penteulu in!" He found the camp prefect and ordered him to fetch the surgeon.

Cei organised two columns of riders to protect the gate as it swung open. Leading Cunor's horse, he galloped down the avenue and into Din Banna.

Arthur clattered down the ladder to ground level and rushed to help Cei lift Cunor down from his horse.

"The injury is serious," said the surgeon after a moment's inspection. "He has lost a lot of blood but from what I can see, the barb missed his vitals. I need to get him indoors so that I may treat him properly."

"Help him," Arthur said to two nearby soldiers. He turned to the surgeon. "By the gods, you'd better keep him alive!"

The Picts had dealt the only serious blow there were able to and now most were either dead or were fleeing towards the woods. Arthur ordered the teulu to enter the fortress and the gates were barred once more.

"No point chasing Picts into the woods," he said. "They won't be attacking again in a hurry and we will be long gone by then. Cei, what happened in the north?"

"We won," said Cei. "Caw's warband are raven meat now or else limping back to their tribal lands. Leudon has returned to Din Eidyn with many prisoners. We have a few ourselves travelling with the wagons. We were meant to go to Din Eidyn but when you did not return, father ordered us to ride south with all haste. By the gods, Arthur, you've led us a merry dance! We found the remains of a Pictish camp on the shores of a lake and the waters red with the blood of their slain. We figured you had carried on south but all the way to the Wall, Arthur?"

"We had no choice," Arthur said. "Hueil sent out his riders to muster the Damnonii who gave chase as soon as they spotted us. We nearly didn't make it to Din Banna."

"And where is Hueil?"

Arthur nodded up at the headless corpse that still leaned over the parapet, its arms bound behind it.

"Just as well," Cei said. "He was too dangerous to be allowed to live."

The ravens descended in droves to feast on the awful scene without the fort's walls. Arthur organised food and water to be distributed to all and Din Banna's occupants relaxed into their bittersweet victory.

The surgeon patched up Cunor as best he could but the penteulu was weak and barely conscious.

"We can't stay here," said Cei. "For one thing, the granaries won't feed the teulu for very long and I don't know about you, but I want to smell the mountain air of Venedotia again."

"Can we move him?" Arthur asked, nodding in the direction of the infirmary.

"It will be a slow march, but we must."

"Very well. We spend the night here and tomorrow, homeward." He fumbled at the laces of his cuirass. "Gods, what I wouldn't give for a hot bath, a warm meal and a soft bed!"

Guenhuifar

The herb gardens at the rear of the steward's quarters rippled in the wind, the flowers and petals of bugleweed, yarrow and calendula dancing. Guenhuifar straightened and cursed her aching back.

"That'll do for now," said Guenhuifach. "Take the basket to the kitchens. I'll be along in a minute to prepare them for storage."

Guenhuifar offered a silent prayer of thanks to Modron as she picked up the wicker basket. They had been picking herbs and vegetables all morning. She didn't mind helping her sister but it was dull work. Ever since King Cadwallon had rebuilt the old lys on the north-eastern corner of Ynys Mon and reinstated their father as its steward, their lives had changed dramatically. There were a lot more people about for one thing. Guenhuifar and Guenhuifach had grown up in isolation, living among the ruins, their mother dead with only each other and their father and servant Cadfan for company. Now the lys was a settlement again, teeming with people from courtiers to soldiers to craftsmen and their families. Sometimes Guenhuifar felt deafened by the constant drone of activity and the very air she breathed seemed to be stifled by the various smells of humanity; freshly baked bread, yeast and honey from the brewhouse as well as the stink of the latrines.

Sometimes she longed for the days when there had been nobody about and she had been free to go off on her own, hunting and trapping in the woods, bartering for goods in distant settlements or just climbing the clifftops to enjoy the view of the sea and the mountains of Venedotia which were a purple haze in the distance, unthreatening and dormant.

It wasn't that she begrudged King Cadwallon for bringing Ynys Mon back into the fold of Venedotia. He had expelled the Gaels for one thing and she would never miss their presence. But the buzz of a settlement had always been an exotic experience for her, one that she could dip in to now and again whenever she needed something before returning to the solitude of her home. She had never thought she might end up living in one.

She occasionally slipped away just as she had used to but it was merely for old times' sake. There was nothing she needed beyond the lys's walls. Food was plentiful and traders regularly crossed the straits as well as merchants bringing more exotic goods over land from the port at Aberffraw but occasionally she just needed space to *breathe*.

Guenhuifach seemed content enough with her herb gardens and had made something of a name for herself as a healer, treating all manner of maladies and wounds in the thriving settlement but this had come with a price. Few men wanted to marry a girl who spent most of her time kneeling in the dirt with her hands dirty, steward's daughter or no. And there was the other side of Guenhuifach's work – the side to do with monthly courses, swelling bellies and the feminine mystery of it all – that put the wind up most men. Their father had given up hope that Guenhuifach would marry and so she was left to her work; an arrangement, Guenhuifar suspected, suited her just fine.

While Guenhuifach was as busy as a bee, useful and content, Guenhuifar felt entirely purposeless. Village life bored her. She had blossomed during the hard, lean times when the next decent meal had to be hunted or foraged. She was not used to having everything at her beck and call and worse, people had started to expect certain things from her. She was looked at askance and was tutted regularly whenever she headed off on her own for some quiet reflection. Young ladies were expected to keep company at all times and there were few women in the settlement that Guenhuifar had any desire to spend much time with.

She marvelled at how little people understood of her role in helping Arthur and the others win the civil war. She had killed men! She had shot her arrows into Gaels and rescued Arthur from the Morgens. She wondered how shocked their faces would be if they only knew!

There had been one girl she had once counted as a friend. Nevin was the fifth daughter of a local noble who, her older sisters bearing the brunt of their parent's marital expectations, had been sent to the lys as a handmaid to Queen Meddyf. Nevin was an energetic girl with a slightly vulgar streak and a penchant for mischief. Guenhuifar had initially taken to her but even in those early days she found that they had little in common. Nevin was fascinated with the latest fashions – an interest Guenhuifar could never understand – and was something of a social climber. Before long, Guenhuifar found that Nevin had grown bored with her and moved on to more exciting associates like the young Prince Maelcon and his rowdy companions. *She's bloody well welcome to them*, Guenhuifar had thought bitterly.

The worst of them was Seraun. Seraun was a good deal older and had the reputation of a womaniser. He was a dandy with fine clothes and a nose permanently turned up at anybody who was of a lower social standing than Prince Maelcon (which was everybody). Some noble family on the mainland had offloaded him at court with hopes of being able to say that one of their number was thick with the royal family. Frustratingly it appeared to have worked for Seraun and Maelcon were inseparable, the older a mentor in all things boorish and the instigator of many a jape at some unfortunate's expense.

It was Seraun Nevin had gravitated to. He was good-looking, loathe though Guenhuifar was to admit it and that seemed to be enough for Nevin. That and his noble stock. Their flirting had developed into something more serious and many at court were scandalised at such an open dalliance between two youths. Had their parents been at court, it was generally agreed, a stop would have been put to the whole thing but there were no adults in authority besides Cadwallon and Meddyf who were far too busy to deal with such trivialities. It was just another example of the wild, uncontrolled mischief of the young prince's circle.

As Guenhuifar threaded her way through the vegetable plots and pig runs towards the kitchens at the rear of the Great Hall, she saw that many people were gathering around the hall's double doors. Basket under her arm, she hurried towards the throng, her curiosity aroused by whatever had whipped the lys into such a flutter of excitement.

"It's the Pendraig's son!" said the potter's wife. "He brings news of the teulu's return! The war is over!"

The Pendraig's son. Guenhuifar tried to still the sudden increase of her heartbeat. There were two youths who called Cunor 'father'; one was trueborn, the other a bastard. She desperately hoped it was the latter.

The doors to the hall were ajar and the antechamber was bustling with curious spectators, craning their necks to get a glimpse of what was going on inside. Two spearmen barred the way.

"Back, all of you!" one of them growled. "Let the visitors have their audience with the king in peace!"

Guenhuifar forced her way through the press of bodies to face the spearmen. "Has the teulu really returned from the north?" she demanded. "Are the Picts defeated?"

"There will surely be an announcement once the king has received the representatives."

"Representatives?" somebody called. "Has Cunor not come himself?"

It *was* strange, Guenhuifar had to admit, that the penteulu had not come in person. What did that mean? But the guard had said *representatives*, indicating that there was more than one. Had both Cei *and* Arthur come?

"Please admit me," she said to the guards. "I am the steward's daughter. I count the penteulu's sons as friends…"

"I know who you are, Lady Guenhuifar," said the guard. "But we are under strict orders to admit none into the king's presence until further notice. You will just have to be patient."

"I think an exception can be made in this case, good soldier," said a voice from within the hall. Menw, the king's bard appeared behind the spearmen. "This lady did aid the two lads during the civil war after all. I am sure her father would not begrudge her standing at his side while their news is relayed to the king."

The spearmen grunted and parted their spears just enough for Guenhuifar to slip through. Few would dare contradict a bard of Menw's standing.

"Thank you, Menw," Guenhuifar said as she set her basket of herbs down at the foot of a painted column.

"Not at all, my dear," said the old bard. "I am sure Cei and Arthur will be pleased to see the face of an old comrade."

"They have both come?" she said, hoping that her face did not betray her delight.

"Yes, and they bring news of King Caw's defeat."

She hurried down the side of the hall, concealed by the shadows of the columns, to where her father and several other courtiers were gathered around the throne. Candles flickered, illuminating the swirling designs painted on every column. Behind the throne hung a great tapestry depicting the Pendraig's victory over his treacherous cousin Meriaun in the Pass of Kings not two years previously.

Before the throne stood two youths. Guenhuifar instantly recognised Cei's close-cropped blond hair and Arthur's shoulder-length brown locks. They both looked so thin and weary. Evidently the war had taken its toll on them. As she emerged into the light at the side of her father, Arthur's eyes darted to her briefly, and then back to the king. *He is pleased to see me*, she thought.

Cadwallon sat with Queen Meddyf at his side. "And why was it that Arthur's company alone rode south to apprehend Hueil?" Cadwallon was asking. "Surely two companies would have broken through the Damnonii and the flight to Din Banna would not have been necessary."

"Perhaps, lord," said Cei. "But my father wanted to avoid as many losses as possibly in dealing the remnants of Caw's warband. He considered one company enough and we did not know that Hueil would rally the Damnonii to his cause else my father may have acted differently."

"I see."

The Pendraig's voice echoed in the cavernous hall. Guenhuifar felt her irritation rising at the way Arthur was made to stand before the king as if he were a supplicant instead of a member of the royal family. Cadwallon was Arthur's brother. Half-brother to be sure but Arthur had been instrumental in securing Cadwallon's throne during the civil war. He should not have to report to the king like a common soldier.

"As it stands, King Leudon is celebrating at Din Eidyn and, due to unforeseen circumstances, you have been cheated of that richly deserved celebration." Cadwallon rose from his throne and clapped his hands together as one deciding upon a pleasurable course of action. "We must have a celebration of our own to honour our returning victors! Preparations shall begin immediately but first, I must ride with you to Cair Cunor and speak to my loyal penteulu myself."

"He would greatly appreciate that gesture," said Cei. "And as I said, he offers his apologies that he could not bring you news of our victory in person."

"Nonsense," said Cadwallon. "A man who takes a spear from Albion's enemies must be allowed to rest in the comfort of his own home. A king could not ask for a more loyal penteulu nor a better friend and I would do no less than to ride to him when he is in need."

Arthur approached the dais and held out a bundle of blood-red cloth, neatly folded. "Your standard, my lord," he said. "We have been honoured to carry it before us in battle."

Guenhuifar's father stepped forward to accept it on behalf of the king.

"Thank you, Arthur," said Cadwallon. "You have both done the banner of the Red Dragon proud. Go now and see that you are fed well. I must make the preparations for our journey South."

The court dispersed and servants carried out platters of roasted lamb, fresh loaves, cheese and flagons of mead and set them on the tables. Cei and Arthur fell to with gusto.

"Lord Cunor was severely wounded in battle with the Picts," Guenhuifar's father explained to her as Cadwallon and his entourage exited the hall through the rear door. "He may not live."

"Oh!" said Guenhuifar, suddenly comprehending the severity of the situation. Her heart ached for Arthur's sake.

As her father went to the main doors to announce the news to the assembled settlement, Guenhuifar approached the two warriors who were washing down their food with thirsty gulps of mead.

"My condolences to you both," she said. "Is there any chance he might pull through?"

"Some," said Arthur gravely, meeting her eyes. "But the wound has become infected. The surgeons say that all we can do is pray to the gods."

"Damn the gods!" said Cei with a sudden violence that drew a sharp breath from Guenhuifar more than the blasphemy of his words. "And damn the surgeons! My father has been wounded before. His body is a roadmap of scars. He won't let the lucky throw of a Pictish savage be his end. He'll soon be back on his feet roaring at everybody for fussing over him."

Guenhuifar smiled but she saw that Arthur was not fooled by Cei's bravado and she wanted to comfort him.

"Well, Guennie," said Cei, wiping his mouth on the sleeve of his tunica. "Have you missed us?" He grabbed at her as if to pull her on to his lap. She dodged his clutching hand.

"I've told you not to call me that and I'll thank you to remember that I am no Pictish whore you can manhandle without consequence."

Cei guffawed. "She's become quite the lady in our absence, eh, Arthur? The wild hellcat we first met in the ruins of this place is too good for us now that she's the steward's daughter! We're just common soldiers, is that the way of it, Guenhuifar?"

"And a common soldier is all you'll ever be, Cei," she replied. "Now, if you don't mind, I have work to do. It may come as a surprise but some of us have been keeping this place running while you two have been off playing at soldiers."

She strode over to the pillar where she had left her basket, swept it up in her hand, and left the hall without glancing back at them.

It was later, just as darkness was setting in, that Arthur caught up with her by the grain drying kiln and they were afforded a brief moment of privacy. He took her into his arms and kissed her.

"Gods, I have missed you," he said.

"And I, you," she replied.

This was a dangerous game they were playing. She loved Arthur, she was sure of it. The feeling had grown in the last couple of years just as the young warrior she had first met had grown. No longer was he the quiet, sullen youth living in his foster-brother's shadow. He had become a man. He had killed people, fought battles, led a company and was now a respected captain in the Teulu of the Red Dragon.

And yet he could never be hers, not truly. She had once confided in her father about their feelings for each other and he had subsequently forbidden her to have anything more to do with him. It wasn't that he disliked Arthur, quite the contrary; he thought the world of him, but Gogfran was now steward of the Pendraig's lys. Marriage into a good family was necessary for the daughter of a man of his status and Guenhuifach was generally considered a no-hoper. No matter how likable Arthur was, a landless soldier – and a bastard at that – would never do for Guenhuifar. And besides, there was already a better suitor pressing his claim.

Cei had made it well-known that he had fallen for Guenhuifar and had, on several occasions, spoken to her father on the matter of her hand. Guenhuifar had balked and her father, out of kindness had explained to Cei, in the politest way possible, that he considered his daughter too young to marry and what with the war against the Picts, it was hardly the time to be discussing wedding plans. But now the war was over and the relative normality of peace had resumed. What excuse could Gogfran give now? His daughter was beyond the age when most girls were wed and what's more, Cei stood to inherit Cair Cunor and would be the next penteulu. Her father could hardly refuse such a union.

Guenhuifar looked upon Arthur's war-ravaged face. How she had missed those keen blue eyes! How she had missed the crushing embrace of his battle-hardened arms and those strong lips pressing against hers. She had missed that little half-smile that appeared in the corner of his mouth whenever he was amused. His sensitive nature combined with his rough, toughened exterior made her heart melt. It was as if he somehow did not belong to the world into which he had been born. The war cries, the blood and sweat of battle and the boisterous drinking and merrymaking that followed it; all of these things he was a part of, and yet he seemed distant, beyond it all, as if he were waiting for something, striving for something greater.

"Will you be returning to Cair Cunor tomorrow?" she asked him.

"Yes. As soon as Cadwallon has dealt with the prisoners we brought him. They are due an audience at dawn. Then we ride south."

Most of the Pictish chieftains and nobles who had been captured in the north had been sent to Din Eidyn to be dealt with by King Leudon but a few prisoners had been brought back to Venedotia for political reasons. One of them was Queen Dolgar, Caw's wife. She was heavily pregnant and the matter of her unborn babe – Caw's son and heir – was a knotty problem that would have to be discussed at length.

Another more scandalous prisoner was Queen Meddyf's own uncle, Drustan. Meddyf's grandfather Talorc had been a Pictish chieftain who had lived to a ripe old age and had sired many children on a number of wives. His sixteen-year-old son Drustan was the product of a union that had taken place long after the death of Meddyf's grandmother making him sixteen years her junior.

Talorc had died several years previously and young Drustan had been sent to be fostered by Meddyf's father. She looked on him more as a little brother than an uncle and that abrasion on his pride may have been the reason he had run away to join

Caw's confederacy. Talorc's clan had been the ones who had taken Din Eidyn in the wake of Cunedag's migration to Venedotia. Ever since King Leudon had pushed the Picts back north, Talorc's people had longed for the chance to reclaim it. Not only did Caw's war present the opportunity, but in Drustan they had a prince to follow, and a royal head to crown.

Such lofty dreams had surely stoked Drustan's pride in his family name and, encouraged by Caw's promises of kingship over the old Votadini lands, he had returned to his roots, adorned himself with woad and gone to war against the very people who had fostered him.

Guenhuifar pulled Arthur close and held him as if the winds of fate threatened to snatch him away from her. "I can't stand it when you ride away from me," she said. "I'm always afraid that I will never see you again."

"I'll be back," he replied. "Now that the war is over, I will be returning to Ynys Mon regularly for councils and festivals, just like before the war."

"Arthur," she said, biting her lip, loath to broach the topic. "What if Cunor dies?"

Arthur sighed. "Then Cei will become the next penteulu."

"And then he will ask my father for my hand again. He won't be able to refuse this time. Not the Penteulu of Venedotia."

Arthur was silent. They held each other close in the moonlight, knowing that whatever happened, their time together was running out.

Arthur

As Cair Cunor's gates swung open to admit them, Arthur felt the glow of homecoming warm his heart. This was the fortress he had grown up in, the only home he had ever known. Every barrack block was familiar to him, every studded door and cracked threshold an old friend.

The entire fortress had turned out to greet the Pendraig. Banners hung from walls and windows and the teulu, refreshed from several days' rest, their clothes and armour mended and polished, were lined up on the parade ground. But without the teulu's commander standing alongside them as he often did like a proud father, the whole arrangement felt lacking and leaderless.

Cadyreith, steward of the fortress, approached them as they dismounted.

"Has there been any improvement?" Cadwallon asked him.

"I am afraid not," said the steward. "The surgeons are doing all they can but his fever has not broken. The wound is quite infected and nothing we do seems to bring it down."

"Those dirty, bastard Picts," grumbled Cei. "Live like animals, the lot of them. Their weapons are just as filthy as they are."

"I had best take a look at the patient immediately," said Menw. "Is he conscious?"

"He drifts in and out, his mind wracked with delirium."

While their horses were stabled, they headed into the praetorium where Cunor's quarters were. As they started to climb the stairs to the upper chambers, Cadyreith took Arthur by the arm. "Even more bad news, I'm afraid, lad," he said.

"What is it?" said Arthur, feeling he already knew the answer.

"Your mother is in a bad way. Coughing sickness."

Arthur, his loyalties torn, glanced up at Cei and Cadwallon who had overheard Cadyreith on the stairs.

"Off you go, Arthur," said Cadwallon. "Cunor doesn't need us all trooping in on him. See to your mother."

Arthur nodded his thanks and hurried out onto the central range, following it to the principia where his mother lived in an upper chamber.

Eigyr lay in her bed staring at the ceiling. Her hair was damp with sweat and plastered to her forehead which had taken on a greyish pallor. Her appearance was so changed from the elegance and cold beauty that Arthur had always known her for that he nearly wept when he set eyes upon her. Her servants rose and scurried out of the room to allow the them some privacy. Arthur sat down upon the edge of the bed.

"My son has returned to me," said Eigyr in a weak voice. "Another battle, another war, and yet he still lives. God and his angels watch over him, of that I am certain."

"How are you, mother?" he asked, reaching out to clutch her hand. It was cold and clammy.

"Dying," she replied, with a grim smile.

"No, you're not dying!" said Arthur in urgency. "Menw is here with us! He has come to treat Cunor. When he has a moment, I will bring him here to take a look at you."

"Medicine men..." muttered his mother. "They are at best use on the battlefield, amputating legs or sewing up wounds. They have no power against God's will. They cannot change our fates. No, son. My end is near."

Arthur kissed her hand and fought against the lump that rose in his throat.

"Is fighting back the tears harder than fighting the enemies of Venedotia, Arthur?"

Arthur was silent.

"I am so proud of you, my boy. At first, I was afraid to lose you, but you have grown so much, become so strong. If only your brothers could see you in the same way I do..."

"Mother, stop it," said Arthur.

She was silent for a while and the two of them sat there in each other's company.

"Have you seen Guenhuifar?" Eigyr finally asked.

"Yes, I have," replied Arthur. He had told his mother of the love he bore for the steward's daughter. Ordinarily Cei was the one he shared his secrets with but he could hardly tell him about Guenhuifar without it leading to a quarrel.

"I am pleased that a good woman will be there for you once I am gone. A fine wife for a fine prince."

Arthur sighed. He knew better than to remind her that he was no prince. It was pointless to try and convince her that his love for Guenhuifar was a doomed thing. She would never let it drop. Her obsession would accompany her to her grave.

He sat in silence and listened to her breathing. The small window showed darkness cloaking the mountains to the east. Once she had fallen asleep, he headed back to the praetorium where his own bed awaited him.

Cei had not slept at all. He hadn't even removed his riding clothes. Arthur found him slumped in a chair by Cunor's bedside, the rays of the rising sun shining through the windows, casting him in a golden aura. He had spent the night at his father's side, watching Menw work and then, when the old bard had retired, remained as a sentinel over his father's slumbering form.

"How is he?" asked Arthur.

"He hasn't stirred," said Cei. "Menw got him to drink one of his potions and then put a new poultice on the wound. It seems to have eased his delirium."

Cunor moaned softly at the sound of their voices. Cei knelt at his side. "Don't try to speak, father," he said. "You need your rest."

Cunor waved him irritably into silence. He spoke with a cracked voice through dry lips. "Bring the Pendraig to me. I would speak with him."

A servant was sent to the quarters where Cadwallon was staying and they did not have long to wait before the king was brought to Cunor's bedside.

"You asked to see me, old friend," said Cadwallon, sitting down in the chair Cei vacated for him.

"I would speak to you alone, lord," said Cunor, his eyes indicating that Arthur and Cei should leave.

They glanced at each other and left the room silently. They took a seat on the bench in the hall outside.

"Do you think that he will die?" Arthur asked Cei.

Cei did not answer him and they waited in silence. As boys they would have listened at the keyhole, eager for details of any conversation not meant for their ears. Now, they could not bring themselves to listen. Childhood seemed so very far away these days. All Arthur wanted was to stop time or reverse it to happier days. Eventually the door opened and Cadwallon appeared.

"Arthur, Cunor requests your presence."

Arthur looked sidelong at Cei. There was a hurt expression on his face. Cadwallon seemed to notice it and said; "Cei, your father will speak with you afterwards. But first, Arthur."

Arthur entered the room and Cadwallon closed the door behind him. "Cunor and I have been discussing his successor as penteulu should he die," he said.

Arthur frowned. "Sir, it is not necessary to discuss this right now. You'll pull through this, I know you will." He felt weary at having a second conversation similar to the one he had had with his mother the night before.

"Your father and I have decided," said Cadwallon, "that you shall be the next Penteulu of Venedotia."

There was a moment of silence in the room. Arthur's head reeled. He felt sick to his gut. "But… what about Cei? Your trueborn son…"

"Arthur," said Cunor in a weak voice. "You know as well as I do that Cei is impulsive and headstrong. Time and time again he has let his emotions get in the way of his leadership, putting his own company in danger as well as risking defeat. A cool head is needed to lead the teulu. You have proven yourself to me, Arthur. I have long considered you for the role of penteulu and your pursual and capture of Hueil has made up my mind. You are my successor."

"Do you accept this great honour, Arthur?" Cadwallon asked.

"Yes," Arthur heard himself reply. "With all my heart." Truly he felt he could lead the teulu. Cunor had been an exemplary tutor in leadership. He felt competent yet entirely unready. Everything was moving too fast. He didn't want to lead the teulu because he didn't want the only man he had ever thought of as his father to die.

"What of Cei?" he said. "This will break his heart…"

"Leave Cei to me," said Cunor. "He will come around. He will for my sake."

Arthur was dismissed and, as he left the room, he forced himself to look at Cei. Suspicion showed in his friend's eyes. He tried to not look guilty as Cei rose and followed Cadwallon into the room. The door closed behind him.

Cunor died that night and the fortress sank into a state of mourning. Arthur had not seen Cei and knew better than to force his condolences upon him. He would leave him to stew in his mourning while he dealt with his own.

Cunor's funeral was conducted upon a lonely hilltop within view of the fortress. A procession followed his body up the winding track. Cei and Arthur walked in silence with faces of stone and hearts of lead. They did not speak. Cadwallon followed close alongside Owain of Rhos and King Mor of Rumaniog; both newly arrived for the funeral. The dragon standard that Cunor had served all his life was carried with them, the wind whistling through its mouthpiece mournfully. Behind them, most of the teulu and the inhabitants of the fortress followed, weeping for their lost chieftain.

Menw performed the funerary rites, the wind catching his long hair and cloak and billowing it about him as he did his best to make his voice carry over the sighing breeze. A pit was dug and Cunor's body was lowered down into it, clothed in a white shroud. Gifts from everybody present were placed in the grave with him and the earth was piled on top. Libations of wine were splashed onto the mound and heavy stones were placed atop the grave forming a cairn that would stand the ravages of time for eternity. Before departing, all present came forward to touch the cairn in turn, saying their farewells to the valiant man who had given his life for Venedotia.

Arthur wept unashamedly as the fond memories came flooding back. Cunor had taught him and Cei how to hunt, how to fight and how to conduct themselves with honour and dignity. He had always been there to break up their many fights and had treated him with as much fairness and respect as he did his own son. Arthur cried for him. He cried for Cei. And he cried for his mother who was so close to the brink of being lost to him as well. In succeeding Cunor, he had achieved an honour higher than he had ever dreamed of. Hundreds of warriors would now look to him as their leader. Kings would depend upon him. And yet he had never felt so lonely. The two guiding lights in his world were winking out. The future loomed close like a cold, black shadow.

The funeral feast was held in the great dining room of the praetorium. Menw was called forth to sing a song he had composed in Cunor's honour and the audience listened in rapt silence as his life was related from his youthful exploits to his victory in the Pass of Kings culminating with his battles against the Picts who had eventually claimed his life. There was dancing and drinking and the sound of raucous, drunken laughter filled the cavernous room up to its smoky rafters.

Arthur did his best to show his enjoyment, for a funeral feast was a time for celebration and afforded no room for gloom and melancholy. He sipped at his wine, allowing the strong, spicy drink to blur his senses and numb the pain.

Cei on the other hand was the very picture of drunken debauchery. He guzzled wine at the rate of two men and grabbed at serving girls who giggled and rolled around on the wine-stained floor with him while the other men in the hall roared with laughter.

Arthur could stomach no more and left as soon as it was seemly to do so.

The following morning Cadwallon and his company roused themselves with aching heads to begin the tiresome task of preparing to return to Ynys Mon. Arthur had been told that he was to return with them along with all the captains of the teulu. His inauguration ceremony as penteulu was to be carried out at Cadwallon's Lys. Such a thing could not be done so close to Cunor's funeral and in his own fortress. It would not have been decent to his memory and besides, the presence of all the sub-kings of Venedotia was required for the inauguration of a new penteulu.

As the horses were prepared Arthur visited his mother. Her condition had improved somewhat due to Menw's attentions. Some colour had returned to her cheeks and as Arthur entered her chamber, a servant girl cleared away the empty bowl of broth she had been drinking.

"One of that bard's ghastly concoctions," Eigyr said with a smile. "Tasted vile."

"It will do you good, mother. Menw knows what he's about."

"So, my son is now Penteulu of Venedotia, I hear," she said, unable to keep the pride in her voice from stretching her lips into a wide smile. For a moment, Arthur saw the beautiful woman King Enniaun had once been besotted with. *But her beauty had not been enough to make her his queen.*

"You do not seem pleased, Arthur," she said.

"My father is dead," he replied. "And I don't know if Cei will ever speak to me again."

"Your father died a long time ago, Arthur. Cunor was a good man to us both but never forget that you are the son of a Pendraig. And as for Cei, he will return to you in time. His anger is at his father and at himself, not you."

"I hope you are right, mother."

"Oh, how I wish I could stand by your side at your inauguration! To see my boy pick up the dragon standard of Cunedag. It's yours by right, you know?"

They talked some more and after Arthur had kissed her goodbye, he left her chamber to find Menw climbing the stairs.

"I come to see how she is doing," the bard said.

"She is much improved, old friend," Arthur said. "Thank you."

"Do not get your hopes up, Arthur," said Menw, his face grave. "I have made her more comfortable but winter is coming and I do not have much faith that she will see spring. I will leave instructions for her servants and that sawbones Cunor calls a camp surgeon but you should be prepared to say your farewells when the snows come."

Arthur nodded, gritted his teeth and headed down to the parade ground.

Guenhuifar

The woman's screams rippled through the settlement like a shard of ice shattering in the stillness of the night. Guenhuifar and Guenhuifach hurried from the steward's hall towards the guest quarters, their fluttering nightdresses pale as owls' wings in the moonlight. It was a few hours before dawn.

"It's come early!" said Guenhuifach. "She was not due for another month yet."

When they entered the guest quarters they found two trembling servant women cowering by the door. Dolgar lay on her pallet, her exposed belly glistening with sweat by the light of the hearth. She screamed again.

Guenhuifar glowered at the pale-faced servants. "It's just a woman giving birth," she snapped at them. "Not the end of the world."

"Just?" said Guenhuifach reproachfully. "*Just?* These things should not be taken for granted, Guenhuifar. Many things could go wrong. Oh, if only Menw were here!"

"Well he isn't," said Guenhuifar. "But you are and you have done this before under his supervision without any problems. You'll do fine. Just tell me what you need."

"Linen cloths," she said. "Fetch some from the Great Hall. As many as you can carry."

Guenhuifar hurried off. When she entered the Great Hall, she woke some of the slumbering servants and ordered them to help her. Cloth was found and brought to the birthing bed.

It was dawn by the time the baby was brought howling into the world. There was a lot of bleeding but Guenhuifach was able to staunch it with the cloths. She swaddled the baby, rubbed its tongue with vinegar, and put it to Dolgar's teat. It took the breast well and fed hungrily while Guenhuifach burned the placenta and umbilical cord in the hearth fire.

"Have you thought of a name?" she asked the Pictish queen.

"Yes," Dolgar replied with a touch of sadness. "Caw and I had decided upon Gildas."

Guenhuifach washed her hands and stepped outside to dry them.

"Good work," Guenhuifar said to her as they sat together on the threshold and watched the sun rise. "Menw would be proud."

"Thank you," said Guenhuifach. "Though I don't know what will happen to the poor babe now. Cadwallon won't want the heir to Caw's legacy growing to manhood under his roof. Nor will he want to let him too far out of his sight."

"He'll think of something," said Guenhuifar. "He's not a brute. He'll find a secure home where the lad can be fostered."

Even Drustan, Queen Meddyf's uncle, had been sent away to keep him out of trouble. That had been a scene. The youth had been given a public dressing down in the Great Hall, not by Cadwallon, but by Meddyf herself. She had berated him in front of the whole lys for his treachery and called him an ungrateful wretch. He had stared at her with his sullen eyes and, annoyed by his impudence, she had struck him hard across the cheek.

The blow had drawn many breaths from the assembled lys. To see a proud young warrior struck by his own niece encouraged some sympathy for the traitor, despite his crimes.

Cadwallon had intervened and ordered Drustan to be sent to the court of his uncle, King March of Dumnonia whose sister had been another of old Talorc's many wives. March was a powerful southern ruler who had earned the nickname 'Cunomor'; the Sea Wolf due to his strong fleet and extensive trading connections with Armorica and beyond. There, in the toe of Albion, Drustan would be as far as possible from any further Pictish uprisings should they occur.

"You're probably right," said Guenhuifach. "I am sure a future will be provided for little Gildas." She yawned, setting Guenhuifar off too and the two sisters retired to catch what little sleep they could.

Cadwallon returned two days later. It was a sad procession that rode in through the main gates and all suspected the cause. It was confirmed by Menw who addressed the assembled crowd as Cadwallon entered his hall.

"Cunor has died," said the bard. "Before he passed he appointed his foster-son Arthur Penteulu of Venedotia. The ceremony will take place in two weeks' time."

The surprise was audible. *Arthur, the next penteulu? What of Cei, his trueborn son?*

Guenhuifar struggled to catch a glimpse of Arthur beyond the heads of the crowd. He was too far from her and surrounded by a throng who wished to congratulate him.

She returned to her father's house, her mind wracked with turmoil. Flights of hopeful fantasy flitted through her head and she chastised herself for daring to flirt with them. Could this turn of events truly play in their favour? Could it be possible…?

She was in the gardens with Guenhuifach and a couple of servants when Arthur arrived. Guenhuifar felt her heart skip a beat as she saw him coming up the garden path and she turned to her sister with pleading eyes.

"Oh, very well," said Guenhuifach, rolling her eyes. "Come on, you two. Let us see to the chores that need doing inside."

They headed indoors and Guenhuifar strode forward to embrace Arthur. "I'm so very sorry, Arthur," she told him. "I know how much he meant to you."

"Thank you," he replied. "And thank you for being here for me. I will need you in the days to come."

"Why?" she asked, feeling her hopes rise dangerously high once more.

"My mother is sick."

"Oh no!" she hoped that she masked her disappointment well but truly, her heart ached for his grief. "Will she pull through?"

"Menw thinks it is unlikely, with winter coming on."

She kissed him. "You will always have me, even if I am only ever just a friend."

He held her tight and they enjoyed the silent embrace for a while.

"I suppose now is not the time to offer my congratulations?" she asked him. "Penteulu of Venedotia…"

"Guenhuifar…" he began. "I have come here to ask your father for your hand in marriage."

Guenhuifar's heart soared. "That's wonderful, Arthur!" she hugged him again. He did not respond and she pulled away, feeling that she knew the cause of his trepidation.

"What of Cei?" she asked.

"We haven't spoken. He took his father's death hard and harder still my promotion to penteulu. It should have been him."

"No." She placed her hand firmly on his chest. "Cunor chose *you*. He had his reasons. Cei will come to terms with them eventually. If he has any honour for his father's memory, he will have to."

"I know. I just wish it was all different but then I remind myself of what I would lose if it were. If Cei had been named penteulu then your father could not refuse his offer of marriage and I would lose you to my best friend. But as it stands, I have taken everything from Cei; his father's title and now the woman he loves. If your father will give you to me, that is."

"I have no doubt that he will," said Guenhuifar, "so you may put your mind at ease over that. And as for all the rest, things are as they are, our fates decided by the gods. It does us no good to wish for things to be different. None of this is your fault. Remember that."

Guenhuifar's father was with the king until late that night so they sat together in the steward's hall and awaited his return. It would not do for him to find them alone together so Guenhuifach was summoned to sit with them and they drank a little wine while Arthur regaled them with war stories.

It was evening by the time Gogfran arrived and the torches had been lit. Inside, candles burned and flickered, casting deep shadows. "What's all this?" he said sharply upon entering, his eyes on Arthur.

"Father," said Guenhuifar, "we want to talk with you."

Gogfran straightened. "Very well. In here."

His tone was severe and Guenhuifar couldn't understand what was wrong. He had told her to stay away from Arthur, it was true, but he was the penteulu now. Surely he would not object…?

He led them into a small room jutting off from the hall that was dominated by a large table laid out with parchment, ink and other writing implements. This was his private study. This was also the room that had served as a makeshift infirmary when Arthur and his companions had turned up with a wounded Gualchmei two years ago. Arthur and Beduir had lain their comrade down on that very table for Menw to treat.

He closed the door behind them and went to sit down at his table. Arthur and Guenhuifar remained standing.

"Sir, I have come here to ask you for your daughter's hand in marriage," said Arthur.

Gogfran regarded him in silence.

"Although I am not wealthy, nor have any family to speak of, I can offer her security and some small status as the wife of Venedotia's penteulu. Cair Cunor, while technically Cei's family home, is the headquarters of the teulu and she will be able to live there in safety and relative comfort. She shall not want for anything, I promise you that."

"And what does Cei think about all this?" Gogfran asked. "Is he willing to accommodate my daughter, whose very hand he has sought for himself?"

Arthur cleared his throat. "I have not told him, sir, not without knowing what your answer would be."

Her father's chair creaked as he leant back in it.

"Sir," said Arthur, beginning to flounder. "I love your daughter and she loves me. I couldn't bear to see her marry some other man, even if he were a brother to me as Cei is. I know it would hurt him, his pride mostly, but I would rather lose his friendship than sacrifice your daughter's happiness in a marriage that could only bring her grief."

Her father watched them for a time, studying them. A smile cracked his serious expression and he slapped the palm of his hand down on the desk as if in great mirth. "Arthur," he said, "you are a good man. The very best. I've known that since you first came knocking on my door seeking shelter on that stormy night with the Gaels on your heels. Since then I have seen you grow as a man. I've seen you achieve rank and honour in the teulu and now you command it yourself. I know that my daughter loves you very much and I would be proud to call you my son-in-law. I give you my blessing."

Guenhuifar let out a cry of joy and ran forward to hug her father, kissing his grey beard.

"Thank you, sir," said Arthur. "I will spend my life making sure you do not regret your decision."

"Aye, see that you do!" her father said with mock severity. Then he winked at him. "I had to test you a little, you see. To see where you stood with Cei. I hate to see good friends fall out over a woman but ever since I heard that you were named penteulu I was hoping that you would come knocking, asking for her hand."

He rose from his chair and walked around the desk to clasp Arthur's hand in his own. "We shall announce your marriage at the feast of your inauguration before all the kings of Venedotia. I think a spring wedding will be appropriate, if you two can keep your hands off each other for that long! And now, by Modron, let me have some of that wine! We have a toast to make!"

Arthur

The following morning, Cadwallon decided upon the fate of baby Gildas and his mother or rather, Meddyf did. It was no secret that Meddyf was a Christian and she retained good relations with the bishops and abbots of the southern regions. Abbott Illtud had rebuilt the College of Theodosius in the kingdom of Guenta which had been burned down nearly forty years previously by a Gaelic raid. Youths from across Albion entered its cloisters to learn scripture and live holy lives of solitude.

"Surely this would be a sheltered life of purpose for the boy," Meddyf said. "He would grow up to be a churchman and any thought of retaliation against you for your part in the deaths of his father and brothers would be insignificant to him."

Cadwallon was hard to convince. All knew that which he dared not admit to his wife; that the religion of the crucified god was growing and for a pagan to add to its army of preachers was surely folly. But, with no other solution apparent, he came around to Meddyf's idea.

"Very well," he said. "Little Gildas shall go to into Abbot Illtud's care, far from here. But what of the mother?"

"Let her lead a Christian life too, so that she may share that bond with her son," said Meddyf. "There are several good nunneries which could accommodate her once the boy is weaned."

"Fine," sighed Cadwallon. "I suppose meek churchmen and nuns will present little threat to us."

The arrangements were made and Dolgar and Gildas were accompanied south with funds sufficient for their upkeep.

Although the Teulu of the Red Dragon was made up from warriors from all of the seven kingdoms, the blessing of the other kings was merely a formality. The Pendraig had always chosen the penteulu, ever since Cunedag had chosen his son Osmael, Cunor's father. The other kings were merely required to contribute warriors and to respect their high-king's choice. All were summoned to attend Arthur's inauguration ceremony.

Cei had still not spoken to Arthur and had avoided him as much as possible. Whenever Arthur sat down to his meat in the Great Hall, Cei would leave. Whenever Arthur ran into him in the stables or crossing the main enclosure, Cei would avoid his gaze and walk right past as if he wasn't there.

"He's still grieving," said Beduir. "Give him time. He'll come around to accepting his father's choice eventually."

Arthur nodded glumly. He heard what everybody was telling him but he had a hard time believing it. Especially as he knew that a further blow to Cei's pride was on its way.

His engagement to Guenhuifar had been kept a secret. It was up to the father of the bride to announce it and Gogfran had chosen the inauguration feast. Arthur was eager for it to be out in the open yet he dreaded Cei's response. As Beduir said, he was still grieving and he hated to be the cause of further misery for him.

The kings began to arrive, crossing the straits at the ferry point one by one before riding north to Cadwallon's Lys. First to arrive was King Owain of Rhos. Rhos had never been a kingdom under Cunedag or Enniaun Yrth. It had been Cadwallon who had given his brother a crown as thanks for his loyalty during the war against Meriaun the Usurper. King Mor of Rumaniog had been a close ally in that same war and arrived on Owain's heels. Eifiaun and Usai of Dunauding and Caradogion respectively arrived next followed by Condruin and his father Elnaw of Docmailing.

Their arrival was greeted with nervous anticipation. Elnaw had supported Meriaun in the war and Cadwallon had insisted upon his abdication in favour of his ineffectual son as a precaution against further treachery.

King Etern arrived the following day, aided by attendants. He was an elderly man and the last living son of Cunedag. None of his own sons had survived to adulthood and all of his hopes for the continuation of his line lay in his eldest daughter. He had initially supported Meriaun in the civil war but, through the negotiations of Meddyf, he had switched sides. The marriage of his daughter to Cadwallon's eldest son, Maelcon, had been a condition of the alliance and he was eager to show his face and impress upon everybody the anticipated marriage which was due as soon as Maelcon came of age.

Finally, Cadwaldr of Meriauned appeared, his tardiness clearly a planned petulance. He had never quite forgiven Cadwallon for executing his father but, with Meriauned's teulu decimated at the Battle of the

Pass of Kings, he was in no position to openly defy the Pendraig's rule. Few spoke to him on his arrival and he seemed eager to do the minimal of duties before returning to his kingdom.

The fading sunlight shone in through the windows of the Great Hall and burned the walls and tapestries with its golden flame. The hall was filled to the brim. Arthur waited in a side chamber, dressed in his finest tunica and cloak. He found that he dreaded Gogfran's announcement of his engagement to Guenhuifar more than he dreaded the inauguration ceremony itself. He had approached Cei that afternoon in an attempt to forewarn him. He knew that he would be breaking a taboo by revealing his engagement but he did not want the announcement at the feast to be Cei's first knowledge of the matter. But, as usual, Cei had not wanted to talk to him. He had been watching a sparring session between two of Cadwallon's warriors and had waved Arthur away irritably.

Cadwallon called for the banner of the red dragon to be brought forward and all in the hall fell into respectful silence. Arthur was ushered in and motioned to approach the dais at the head of the hall.

He felt the eyes of everybody upon him as he walked between the benches and trestle tables; the eyes of eight kingdoms upon him but most of all he felt the eyes of Cei, Beduir, Gualchmei, Cundelig, Guihir and all the others. Once his companions, they were now his own men. Would he ever live up to Cunor's shade in leading them? He stopped at the foot of the dais and looked up at the Pendraig.

"Do you, Arthur mab Enniaun, swear to defend the dragon banner of Cunedag and serve Venedotia with your life?" Cadwallon began. "Do you promise to uphold the traditions of our land and protect the honour of the eight kingdoms with every drop of blood in your veins?"

"This I swear," replied Arthur.

"Then kneel, Arthur mab Enniaun."

Arthur did so, bending his knees to rest upon the edge of the dais, humbling himself before the entire hall. The dragon banner was planted before him. He knew what was expected of him. Menw had gone through it with him that morning. Like the hallowed drinking from the queen's cup that accompanied a king's succession, or the arming of a son by his mother upon his becoming a man, a token gesture was required to cement the rites and seal the actions of those taking part.

Arthur drew his knife from his belt and held the blade to the palm of his left hand. He raised his arms so that all in the hall could see and then he drew the blade quickly across it, leaving a thin line of blood that welled up and flowed freely. With this hand he reached out and gripped the dragon banner tightly so that the blood oozed out between his fingers and dribbled down its ash shaft.

"Your blood is now one with the dragon banner," said Cadwallon. "You are bound to its fate by your oath. I, Cadwallon mab Enniaun of the line of Cunedag, Pendraig of Venedotia recognise you, Arthur as its new Penteulu!"

Arthur rose and the Great Hall erupted into cheering and clapping signalling the beginning of the celebrations. Arthur was shown to his seat at the head table, alongside the kings and their queens. As he sat down, he glanced down the length of the white linen decked with dishes and meats and saw Guenhuifar beside her father, beaming at him. Horns and cups were raised in toast of Arthur and he drank deeply, trying to steady his nerves.

Gogfran wasted no time in making his announcement. As the hall fell silent for the third time in Arthur's honour and only the sound of wine and mead being swallowed could be heard, the steward addressed the assembly.

"Friends!" he cried, his mead horn lifted up to the rafters. "We have something else to celebrate this night. It is with great pleasure that I announce my daughter's engagement!"

"Which one?" somebody called out and there was a ripple of laughter.

"My eldest, Guenhuifar," Gogfran replied, ignoring the jibe.

Arthur watched Cei's face as Gogfran's words sank in. It was not at all pretty. Guenhuifar obediently rose from her seat and accepted her father's hand.

"My eldest daughter is engaged to Arthur, our new penteulu!"

The roof of the hall was nearly lifted with cheering and Arthur, hiding his reluctance, rose in response, a forced smile on his face. He felt Cei's eyes boring into him and tried not to meet his gaze. He could sense the hatred directed his way and it was almost unbearable. Once the clamour had died down, the feast continued and there was music and dancing.

Arthur jumped as Beduir clapped his hand on his shoulder.

"Congratulations!" the big man bellowed over the revelry.

Gualchmei stood behind him and handed Arthur a horn brimming with mead. "Well done, Arthur! That was a bit out of the blue! I didn't know that you were courting her."

"Well," Arthur mumbled. "It was sort of a secret. It was only after Cunor and Cadwallon named me penteulu that I was able to ask old Gogfran for her hand."

The other two followed his gaze to where Cei was sitting, nursing his mead, a sour look on his face.

"I'm worried about him," Arthur said. "I didn't want him to find out like this. I wanted to tell him before, but there wasn't time."

"Oh, you know him," Beduir replied. "He's just sulking. Give him a day or so and he'll be back to his usual semi-tolerable self."

"I hope so," Arthur replied and drank some of the mead.

"You did nothing that he would not have done in your stead," Gualchmei offered helpfully.

The night wore on and the flow of mead and wine did not slow. Cei got drunker and drunker and the worse he got, the more lustful, boastful and argumentative he became. Eventually, he clambered onto a table and raised his mead horn high, the liquid slopping over its rim.

"To Arthur!" he cried, echoing a dozen such toasts that night. "My dear foster-brother and best friend!"

Arthur glanced at Guenhuifar who was watching Cei with a worried expression. The rest of the hall might be fooled by Cei's mock joviality but Arthur and Guenhuifar knew better. This was not going to end well.

"Also, to my dearly departed father!" Cei continued. "I was too much in grief to pay him an honourable toast at his funeral, so why not raise our horns to his shade also? To Cunor mab Osmael!"

The hall murmured an embarrassed response and drank to Cunor's shade, wincing a little at the inappropriateness of the situation.

"A son never had a better role model," said Cei, tears welling in his eyes. "He was courageous, honourable and kind. But most of all, he was generous. So generous in fact, that he took in an illegitimate child and its mother, gave them a home and raised the babe as his own."

Arthur glared up at him. He just wanted Cei to stop but there was no way short of hauling him down from the table. And Cei was not finished.

"Who can fault a man so generous that he would hand over his own son's birth right to the offspring of a dead king's hussy…"

"You bastard!" roared Arthur, leaping from his seat and hurling his horn at his foster brother. He didn't care if he was behaving inappropriately but he would be damned if he would let Cei insult his mother's name.

The flung horn hit Cei in the face and showered mead over everyone near to him. Cei stumbled and fell headlong to the floor amidst a clatter of upturned food, drink and crockery. All watched in deathly silence as the drunken man staggered to his feet and faced Arthur, their eyes locked in mutual loathing.

"You can have it, Arthur!" he roared. "You can have it all! I am done with you, with her and with my damned father's memory!"

He turned and stormed out of the hall. Two servants stumbled over themselves to get out of his way. Arthur watched impotently in his wake. As a low murmur was taken up by the feasters, Guenhuifar approached Arthur and held his arm tightly.

"He was drunk," she said. "And still grieving. He didn't mean what he said."

"I'm fed up with people making excuses for him!" Arthur snapped. "Cunor was my father too. I have lost just as much as he has! What right does he have to act like this?"

Cadwallon was just as outraged by Cei's behaviour as Arthur.

"Insolent wretch!" he cried. "How dare he sully the inauguration feast of our new penteulu with his childish tantrums! His grief and jealously should have been left at the door. I've a good mind to strike him from the teulu!"

"Cei is a bull-headed oaf, my lord," said Beduir, hastily intervening. "But he is a fine warrior and loyal to the death. This is the lowest I've ever seen him sink. He will rise up again, lord, I have no doubt of that. He just needs time to cool off. I'm sure if Arthur were to patch things up with him…"

"How can I patch things up with that sore-headed ox?" Arthur said.

"Certainly not tonight," said Menw. "Most inadvisable. Seek him out tomorrow when the drink has worn off and the fresh winds of winter have cooled your heads."

Arthur did not reply, he simply filled another horn with mead and knocked it back. He was determined to enjoy his evening and Guenhuifar's company but deep down he knew that he could never enjoy anything until he had put things right with Cei.

The fishing boat, its hull full of wriggling mackerel made its way back to the mainland where the cliffs rose up to meet the boiling clouds. The sky had begun to blacken and a cruel wind whipped up. Arthur sat astride Lamrei atop the cliffs, his cloak billowing about him as he watched the crew of the small boat jump down into the crashing surf and drag the vessel up onto the sand.

The morning after the feast Cei had been nowhere to be found. The drunken revellers slumbered on the floor of the Great Hall, the smoke of the previous night still thick in the air. Arthur arose early and tried to wash away his hammering headache in a bucket of water.

He searched the lys and asked everybody who was awake if they had seen Cei but to no avail. He then went to the stables and found that Cei's horse was gone. Arthur had saddled Lamrei and ridden out in search of his friend.

Cei grunted as he helped heave the bulging net of fish out of the boat and over to the slimy shacks further up the beach. It was a good catch; one of the last before winter set in and the sea became too rough to fish. Women emerged from the huts and began the laborious task of gutting the fish and hanging them up on lines over smoking barrels.

"What do you want, Arthur?" Cei asked as Arthur walked over to him, leading Lamrei by the bridle. He did not even turn around.

Arthur was aware of the fishermen and their wives gazing at him and the fine mare in dumb awe. "To talk," he said.

"Nothing to say. If you've come for an apology, then you're going to go back disappointed."

"I didn't come for an apology," Arthur replied. "I came to get my brother back. And my friend."

"I have no brother."

"That's nonsense, Cei," said Arthur angrily. "Cunor loved us both."

"Really? I thought that it was pretty clear that he considered you more his son than me."

"Not a day goes by that I am not thankful for his generosity in taking my mother and I in but he loved you more than anything in the world. He would have hated to see this rift between us."

"Then he shouldn't have caused it!"

Their raised voices drove away the fisherfolk who retreated, muttering at the two youths with their horse and their fine clothes. The wind was bitterly cold and whipped about the two figures.

"So what's the plan, then?" Arthur demanded. "Be a fisherman for the rest of your life? Forsake the teulu? Your own family?"

"Maybe. Or I might ride south and find somebody who will pay handsomely for a good sword arm."

"Come on, Cei! Cunor made his decision. It does not mean he did not value you highly as a warrior. Or as a son. He never intended for you to leave the teulu. He would have wanted us to remain side by side because he knew that we were an effective team. I need you Cei. Who else could fill the role of my second?"

"Just forget it, Arthur," replied Cei. "You've won, alright? You've won your title and you've won Guenhuifar. You've taken everything from me, now leave me in peace!"

"It was never a contest!" shouted Arthur. "And neither was Guenhuifar! You know what your problem is Cei? You always let your damned pride get in the way! Cunor knew this and that's why he chose me instead of you!"

Cei roared in rage and swung his fist at Arthur. Unprepared, Arthur took the full force of the blow on the side of the chin and was knocked backwards. He rose up and hurled himself upon Cei, beating at him with his fists. Cei blocked and punched back. The fishermen watched in astonishment from a safe distance. Soon both were bloody-faced and panting with exhaustion.

"I curse the day my father took you and your mother in!" Cei said. "At least you always have her to run to. I have no one!"

"My mother is dying," Arthur said, clutching at his bleeding nose, the tears stinging his eyes. He hadn't planned to bring it up. This wasn't about his mother but Cei's last remark had torn it from him like a fishhook.

Cei's anger was checked for a brief moment. He stared at Arthur in astonishment. "What?"

"She's dying. Menw says she won't make it through the winter. I am just as alone as you, Cei."

"If you're lying to me…" began Cei.

Arthur's expression was the only answer Cei needed. The big man paused, unsure of what to do or say, his anger forgotten for the moment. "How long have you known?"

"Since we returned from the war in the north."

"And you said nothing to me?"

"There was too much else going on. And you were too blinded by your anger to see anything else."

Cei walked forward, his face drained of the hate that had possessed it a moment previously. Arthur's revelation, however reluctant, had kindled the spark of brotherly love that lay deep down inside. That spark glowed and the resentment melted away. Cei's own mother had died when they had been children and Arthur had been there for him, to comfort him as a true brother should.

"I…, I'm sorry," he managed.

Arthur was silent, tears streaking his cheeks. He had not cried for his mother since learning of her sickness but now the sorrow that had made itself a home in his gut rose up and flooded out. Cei grabbed him and the two brothers embraced, their tears drowning their anger.

"Let's stop all of this," said Cei after a while. "It doesn't matter. As you said, my father chose you and that's all there is to it."

Arthur wiped his face on the sleeve of his tunica. "On one condition."

"Name it."

"That you return with me and become my second. Cadwallon is furious and wants you stricken from the teulu but I won't lead it if you are not with me."

Cei sighed. "Done."

They embraced again and left the fishing huts and their gawking owners to climb the dunes to the grassy clifftop.

"Sorry about your nose," said Cei, glancing at the slowly crusting blood on Arthur's upper lip.

"Sorry about yours," Arthur replied.

"You didn't hit it."

"I'm still sorry for you. Terrible thing to be born with. Looks like a squashed turnip."

"So does yours now," said Cei.

"Do you remember the last time we beat each other's brains out?" Arthur said. "I think we were ten years old."

Cei nodded. "We had been swimming in Lin Tegid."

"And you put a grass snake in my boot."

Cei laughed. "And you chased me halfway back to the fortress, flinging stones at me!"

They both laughed. Arthur did not mount Lamrei but led her by the bridle as he walked alongside Cei.

They talked and laughed all the way back to the lys.

PART II

"And the first night Peredur came to Caerlleon to Arthur's Court, and as he walked in the city after his repast, behold, there met him Angharad Law Eurawc."
- Peredur the Son of Evrawc, (Trans. Lady Charlotte Guest)

Venedotia, spring, 483 A.D.

Arthur

Winter set in and the mountains of Venedotia turned white. The northern sea pounded at the coast and the cruel wind whistled down the valleys. The inhabitants of Cair Cunor huddled around well-stoked hearths and bolted their doors to the cold but they could not keep out the spectre of death.

As Menw had predicted, Arthur's mother did not live to see spring. They buried her in the small Christian churchyard that surrounded the nearby chapel in a stone-lined grave. Many came to pay their respects; more, Arthur reflected, than would have come before he became penteulu.

When the rivers began to swell with the spring melt and the hillsides exploded into green dotted with wild flowers, Arthur and Guenhuifar were married.

The praetorium of Cair Cunor was decked out in white trefoils and garlands of spring flowers which hung from every arch and wound around every column. The courtyard and reception rooms were filled to the brim with guests and one of Menw's disciples strummed a melodious tune on his harp.

The old bard presided over the ceremony in the garden before an iron brazier. Arthur and Guenhuifar's hands were bound by a length of silk while the appropriate items were sacrificed to the flames. One of Guenhuifar's childhood tunicas her father had kept in the hope of her eventual marriage was burned, symbolising her transition to adulthood. A splash of wine sizzled on the hot coals as a libation to the gods and a freshly-baked bannock which Arthur and Guenhuifar each took a bite from was then tossed into the brazier. Modron was called upon to bless the happy couple and the garden erupted into cheering and clapping as the newlyweds kissed.

Then came the presentation of gifts and neither Arthur nor Guenhuifar had been on the receiving end of such kindness and generosity before. A magnificent plated shield was presented to them by King Cadwallon and Queen Meddyf. King Owain gave them a gilded horn decorated with mythological scenes from the tales of the bards. Gold and jewellery were heaped upon them by the other guests along with other items beautiful in their craftsmanship.

It was deep into the night by the time the feast ended and Arthur was glad to finally be alone with Guenhuifar. In their newly-painted chambers she lay on the bed looking up at him with those wonderful green eyes, a smile playing on her mouth. His heart pounded in his chest with the knowledge that they were finally free to love each other with no boundaries or limitations, no guilty secrets or half-snatched kisses in secluded moments. They were man and wife now, free to do as they pleased. He unfastened his cloak and lifted his tunica up over his shoulders, baring his naked chest in the candlelight. Guenhuifar smiled at him before pulling him down to lie with her while the light in their window burned until dawn.

With May came one of the cornerstones of the pagan year; *Calan Mai*, the may festival of spring, light and rebirth in honour of the sun god Bel. Every May since taking the throne, King Cadwallon had summoned all the sub-kings of Venedotia to his lys to begin the season with a council. It helped to keep communication open in a family whose members had grown somewhat distant in recent years.

As penteulu, Arthur's presence was also required and he and Guenhuifar reluctantly left the home they had so recently made their own to voyage to Ynys Mon so that he might take his place alongside his royal brothers and cousins.

Cadwallon's Great Hall was decorated with marsh marigold, hazel and rowan and, according to custom, the hearth lay prepared but unlit. Later, once darkness had descended, a burning brand would be carried from the great bonfire on the nearby hilltop to relight the lys's hearth as a symbol of the waxing power of the sun.

There had been a buzz of rumours in the days leading up to the council that Cadwallon was to present a pair of ambassadors from some southern kingdom, although who they represented or what their aim was, none could confirm.

Arthur looked around at the faces of his cousins who each ruled a portion of Venedotia under his brother's high-kingship. He had never dreamt that he would ever be counted among their number but here he was, his voice as relevant as any of the others. With a brief pang of sorrow, he realised that this was what his mother had wanted for him all his life. Now that he was here, she was gone.

There was a murmur of voices and all rose as King Cadwallon entered the hall with Menw at his side. The dragon banner was carried by a standard bearer and placed behind the throne. It was the two unknown men who walked in with Cadwallon who caused the most interest. They had short hair and no beards – unusual in that part of Albion – and their cloaks and garments were much more Roman in style than the attire of the northern kings. Cadwallon sat down in his throne and his two companions took their seats in the chairs that had been placed to the left of him.

"Greetings to you, Kings of Venedotia," he began. "I welcome you to this council, my third as Pendraig."

At this, all took their seats. The council had begun.

"The year that has past has been turbulent," said Cadwallon. "It has been with great sorrow that we lost our penteulu, Cunor mab Osmael, whose spirit journeyed to Annun after winning a great victory over our enemies in the north. But let us welcome his successor, Arthur mab Enniaun."

There was a polite murmur and Arthur found himself nodding an embarrassed acknowledgement.

"I wish to start this council by presenting two guests of mine," said Cadwallon, indicating the men who sat to the left of him. "They have journeyed far from their homeland to request an audience with me and I have chosen to present them to this council. Please welcome Marcus Leptinus and Claudius Caecilius of the Borderlands."

There was an interested muttering at the mention of the much troubled Borderlands. That thin strip of disputed land was all that separated the Britons of the west from the Saeson barbarians to the east. The man called Marcus Leptinus stood and addressed the council.

"Kings of Venedotia," he began. "Dragons of the North. It is with great honour that I am allowed to stand here before you. Your reputation and that of your ancestor Cunedag mab Etern resounds in every corner of Britannia."

"Bloody southerners," whispered King Efiaun, who sat next to Arthur. "They all think that they are Roman Senators with their Latin names for everything."

Arthur smiled but said nothing.

"News may have reached your kingdoms of the plight of the Borderlands," Marcus continued. "Since the departure of the legions, we have been overrun by barbarian invaders from all sides. You, who have fended off the Gaelic wolves and the Pictish savages with such heroism need not be reminded of this. But there is an enemy which threatens the south with a ferocity unparalleled. The *Saxonii*, or Saeson in the common tongue, have long plagued us with their looting, their ravaging and their bloodlust. For many years now, we Britons of the south have held these dogs at bay under the leadership of Ambrosius Aurelianus."

There was a stirring among the council members. The name of the great war-chief of the Borderlands had indeed reached the ears of the Venedotian kings. Ambrosius Aurelianus was nothing short of a living legend in Albion. His exploits and battles were told of throughout the land and he had held a check on the Saeson for at least two generations.

"Two weeks ago, Aurelianus was defeated in battle and he was captured by a Saeson chieftain called Aelle. He is currently being held in a town called Cair Badon. This was a devastating blow to us as the Borderlands are effectively lost and the Saeson menace threatens the kingdoms of Dumnonia and Guenta."

"And you wish us to send a party to free him, is that it?" piped up King Efiaun of Dunauding.

Marcus glanced at him. "We have heard of the famed Dragon-Army and its successes against the age-old Pictish threat. We now ask that you lend us your spears and join us in our battle against the new enemy."

There were knowing chuckles around the circle of kings.

"Didn't you southerners already send a similar request to the Roman armies in Gaul to help you with your Saeson problem?" asked King Cadwaldr of Meriauned.

"Yes," spoke up Marcus's colleague Claudius. "The now defunct Council of Britannia did send a letter to Aetius of Gaul, but that was many years ago. He replied that he had his hands full with the Huns and sent Bishop Germanus in his stead. The result was... less than satisfactory."

Several of the kings laughed at this and the ambassadors sought a new way to approach their audience. "The council we speak of was ruled in those days by the lord Vertigernus, the very same who was a friend to the founder of your dynasty. It was Vertigernus who persuaded Cunedag to relocate to Venedotia and repel the Gaels."

"Don't talk to us of those days, boy," said King Etern of Eternion, his voice dripping with condescension. "Some of us here met *Lord*

Vertigernus and let me tell you, if he is an example of southern kingship, then I'm not surprised that the south is overrun by barbarians."

There was much guffawing and Claudius coloured with indignation. He sat back down, helpless. Now it was his colleague's turn to try and win the kings round once more.

"The point my companion here is trying to get across to you, is that the Sais threat will not simply dissipate once they have control of the south. When our territories fall Aelle will soon set his sights on the rest of Britannia. Soon the Saeson will be making their way across the mountains to knock on your door. Would it not be wiser to confront them now before they grow any stronger?"

"You underestimate the difficulty in penetrating the mountains," said King Etern. "Even if the Sais pigs manage to break through your defences and march across Albion, they will not know the mountain passes of the northern lands. Remember, it took the Romans years to get all the way up here to conquer the Venedotii, the Ordovices and the Decanglii. And even then, they were not able to keep the tribes fully under control. And these Saeson lack the discipline and unity of the Romans. I think you exaggerate the danger they present to us, southerner."

"Even if we choose to send our teulu south," said King Owain of Rhos, "how can we be sure that we will have any chance of halting them? How big is this warband of theirs?"

"We do not know the full size of Aelle's forces as we have never encountered him at his full strength," said Claudius. "But our estimates put their number in the thousands."

"Thousands?" cried King Elnaw of Docmaeling. "The Teulu of the Red Dragon is a hundred-and-fifty riders! Even counting auxiliaries, it numbers a mere three-hundred. We wouldn't even dent them!"

"It is true that we are outnumbered," replied Claudius. "But Venedotia has cavalry! Aelle's men march on foot and the south has long suffered for the want of good horses. Your intervention could turn the tide and if we rescue Aurelianus, more will rally to his banner. We have been fighting the Saeson with inferior numbers for years. By raiding convoys and ambushing foraging parties we have been able to keep them at bay. All we need is one final, united push against them otherwise all of Britannia is doomed to Sais conquest."

"I think we should let Arthur speak," said Cadwallon, who had been listening to the discussions with a furrowed brow. "After all, he is our penteulu and if we decide to send the teulu south, he shall be the man to lead it."

Arthur cleared his throat at Cadwallon's indication and fumbled for the words to say.

"This youth?" asked Marcus, barely disguising his shock. "Forgive me, High-King, but I had been under the impression that the Dragon-Army was led by someone a little, well… *older*."

"It was," replied Cadwallon. "But he died. This is his foster-son and my own half-brother who has proven himself against Pict and Gael numerous times. He has my full support and confidence in leading the teulu."

Arthur felt all eyes upon him and he coughed before addressing the council in as loud and clear a voice as he could muster. "If the council decides to send the teulu south, then it can rest assured that I will lead it to the best of my ability. As for my personal opinion, well, I agree with Marcus that this Aelle must be stopped as soon as possible before he grows too strong."

"He may be too strong already, Arthur," said King Owain.

"If that is the case, then I am prepared to die fighting him so that the rest of Albion may ready itself for the storm to come. My father – Lord Cunor, I mean – always taught me that it is better to perish fighting your enemy rather than live under his boot. I promise you that if we are to go south, you can know for a certainty that the banner of the red dragon will witness much slaughter and butchery before it falls under the Sais advance."

He sat back down. Marcus and Claudius looked at him with surprised admiration. The council was silent in thought. He had impressed them. For all their dismissal of the ambassadors' request, the kings of Venedotia were a proud lot and did love a good warmongering speech.

It was put to a vote and it was a close-run thing. Ultimately, more hands were raised in favour of sending the teulu south than were raised against the notion and so it was decided. Arthur would lead the Teulu of the Red Dragon south to fight the Saeson and, if possible, rescue Ambrosius Aurelianus.

Several other matters were attended to before the council adjourned. Queen Meddyf and her handmaids swept into the room marking the beginning of the festivities. Dusk was approaching and pinpricks of light began to appear in the hills as farmers lit the great bonfires in honour of Calan Mai. Cattle would be driven through the flames and the light of Bel would purify them, ensuring fertility and protecting them from disease.

On the hilltop nearest Cadwallon's Lys, the servants had been building the fire stack for three days. As evening fell, all gathered around it, king and commoner alike, to witness its lighting. Pavilions had been erected and trestle tables groaned with food the kitchens had been preparing all day. Barrels of mead and wine were rolled out and broken into.

The great bonfire roared and crackled, sending glowing embers whirling up into the evening sky on a plume of black smoke. The revellers danced and capered in its light like leaping shadows to the drumming and piping of Menw and several bards-in-training.

Arthur sat with Guenhuifar at a trestle table while a parade of men, from kings to warriors, came to wish him luck in the war to come. Marcus and Claudius sat at their table and Guenhuifar was keen to discuss the people and customs of the southern kingdoms with them. The two ambassadors were apparently accustomed to a more toned-down Calan Mai in the Christianized south and were sipping their mead and looking around at the loud and boisterous antics of their northern countrymen with a mixture of horror and titillation.

"Tell me, sirs," Guenhuifar said loudly as a dancing couple whirled past in a flurry of sweat and bare skin, "what of southern women? Have I any need to be concerned about my husband's fidelity when he is away at war?"

Cei and Beduir laughed out loud and Arthur coloured with embarrassment.

The two ambassadors seemed miffed by her question. "Most are good Christian women," replied Marcus. "Not that I am casting a shadow on the modesty of pagan women, you understand." He began to flounder under Guenhuifar's critical eye. "But I do not think you have cause for worry."

"Tell me about the Saeson," said Arthur, eager to change the subject. "What language do they speak? Latin?"

"Not a bit of it," said Claudius. "Although they come from the continent, their ancestors never came under the dominion of the Roman Empire, much like the Gaels and the Picts here in Britannia. They are a barbarous people. Their chief god is a one-eyed brute called Woden. They also worship some kind of thunder-god."

"Rather like our Taran," said Menw.

"Their savagery is unmatched," added Marcus. "I have seen them march into battle waving banners made from human skin and beating on drums fashioned from skulls."

Cei whistled. "It's going to be an interesting war."

"And their leader?" asked Arthur.

"He calls himself King Aelle of the South Saeson. A brute of a warlord. We're not too sure when he came to these shores but there was already a large number of Sais tribes in the south. All it took was somebody to unite them."

"So there are different factions then?"

"Oh, yes. They are not a united people by any stretch of the imagination. They come from a variety of different homelands with different languages. The Angles, the Saxons and the Jutes are predominant but there are also Frisians, Danes and Franks all wanting a piece of the action too. It must have been a mighty feat for Aelle to unite any of them at all for they hate each other as much as they hate us."

Arthur sipped his mead as he contemplated the days ahead. He was about to lead three-hundred men into a foreign, predominantly Christian land against an enemy he had never encountered before who apparently made trophies out of human body parts. Cei was right. It was going to be an interesting war.

There was a whoop of laughter and heads turned to see Prince Maelcon and his companions guffawing as one of them fell off his bench to sprawl on the grass. He'd been at the mead. Maelcon was only twelve and the friends he had surrounded himself with were brats from noble families who hoped to curry the future Pendraig's favour. Queen Meddyf hurried over to them and chided them for supping mead.

"This is the future you're fighting for," Guenhuifar said to Arthur in a low voice. "Spoilt children who know nothing of war and never will."

"Don't begrudge them that," said Arthur. "Let them hold onto their innocence for as long as they can. War has a way of bringing out the worst in us."

Few nights had gone by that he had not seen the faces of the Picts he had ordered slaughtered by the lake. *Unarmed prisoners.* A couple of years ago he wouldn't have thought himself capable of such atrocities. But as he had said, war changed people. Some nights he saw Hueil's corpse laughing at him; a remarkable feat for a headless man.

"What's wrong?" Guenhuifar asked him.

"Oh, pay me no heed. All this talk of war is just getting me down, that's all."

"I thought all warriors craved battle."

"War is more than battle."

A burst of applause and cheering rippled through the crowd as two figures emerged from a pavilion dressed in the ceremonial attire of the festival. They were both naked except for short loincloths, their faces masked by elaborate headdresses. One was in the shape of a ram and between its great curling horns, a golden disc reflected the light of the bonfire like a shimmering image of the sun. The other man wore the shaggy head of a wolf. A silver crescent moon was mounted between its ears and long, grey fur fell down over its wearer's shoulders.

A table was dragged before the bonfire and the crowd cheered as both men leapt upon it and faced each other. Armed with sticks of rowan, the two men played out a mock battle on the table top, striking and parrying until the sweat glistened on their torsos.

Their audience clapped and stamped out a rhythm as the battle between summer and winter, light and dark was acted out before them. Eventually the golden ram struck down the black wolf who landed with a crash on his back. A flaming torch was handed to the ram-headed man who brought it close to his defeated opponent's chin, singing away some of the fur; a symbolic act depicting summer driving away winter. The victor raised the torch high into the air and took off his mask to reveal himself as King Cadwallon. The crowd roared with applause. The Pendraig lifted his foot off the black wolf's chest and the defeated man removed his headdress. Arthur recognised the man as one of Cadwallon's household guard.

Beaming with pleasure at his reception, Cadwallon stepped down from the table and tossed his golden headdress to an attendant. A horn brimming with mead was handed to him and he drank greedily, quenching the thirst the mock fight had elicited.

Guenhuifar nestled into the crook of Arthur's arm and laid her head against his shoulder. They watched the flames of the bonfire, basking in the red hot glow of its embers.

"I have spoken to Cadyreith," he told her. "He will be at your full disposal in the months I am gone. He is well-used to running Cair Cunor and you can learn all you need to know from him. If you have any problems, just ask him to intervene."

"Is it acceptable for the lady of the household to be its steward's apprentice?" Guenhuifar said and he could tell by the tone of her voice that she was troubled by her imminent responsibilities.

"You have been doing fine so far," he said.

"It has barely been three weeks since I crossed its threshold as your wife. Now I am expected to order people about who were born within its walls and lived there all their lives. What if I disappoint everybody?"

"What is it Guenhuifar? What do you fear?"

"I just don't feel ready to step into my role as lady of the house, that's all. Especially without you by my side. I would be much more comfortable if I remained here with my father until you return."

Arthur considered this for a moment. "You are lady of Cair Cunor now," he said. "Even Cei has to follow your orders, though don't tell him that. It is expected that you will rule the roost while I am gone."

"I just don't feel ready…"

He felt her tense body in his embrace and wondered at how vulnerable and insecure she seemed, this fiery, woman he had loved and feared in equal measure. *How responsibility crushes even the bravest of hearts*, he thought. "All right," he said. "You shall remain here if it is your wish. When I return from the south, we shall cross Cair Cunor's threshold together once more."

The night wore on and as the eastern skies began to pale with the coming dawn, Menw plucked a burning log from the bonfire. The final rite of the festival was at hand. All followed him back to the lys in a great procession of drums and bells.

Every hearth, candle and torch in the lys and its surrounding settlement had been put out the previous day. Now, all awaited the lighting of the hearth in the Great Hall. From that fire, each household would kindle their own hearths so that each and every home would be purified and blessed by the light of Bel.

Once the logs were crackling merrily in the Great Hall, the revellers bedded down on the rushes of the floor and began to sleep off the effects of the heavy celebrations. Arthur and Guenhuifar retired to the steward's quarters and Guenhuifar's old bed, exhausted and glad to be alone each other's company while they could.

The following weeks were a whirlwind of activity at Cair Cunor. After a civil war and two campaigns against the Gaels and the Picts, the fortress was well-used to preparing for war but this time the scale was grander, the tension stronger. None knew how long the teulu would be away and the odds were stacked so high against them that there was no guarantee that they would ever return at all. Arthur knew that nobody felt this more than Guenhuifar. Proud as she was to see her husband lead the teulu, he knew that she was pained to see him depart on so perilous a mission so soon after their marriage. Despite being kept extremely busy organising the stockpiling of supplies, the ordering of the companies and the equipping and training of the men, Arthur made a point of spending every spare moment he could with Guenhuifar.

"It feels as if the gods jest with us," she told him. "To allow us to finally be together only to throw another war, another enemy in our path. Will it ever be over? Will Albion ever run out of enemies?"

"Only the gods know that," Arthur replied. "I know it seems unlikely but I believe there will come a time of peace. We shall have to fight hard for it, but there must come a summer after the winter. A dawn after the dark. When I am done fighting Albion's enemies, I will return to you and we shall enjoy those days together."

But no matter how long they savoured their time together, the days seemed to fly past and the moment of Arthur's departure reared up suddenly like a beast from the depths of the ocean.

Hengroen, the white foal Arthur had rescued nearly three years ago was now broken and trained for battle. He had spent hours upon hours with the young horse, going through his paces and riding him in the valleys of Venedotia. As he brushed his gleaming coat in the stables, he whispered into his ear; "Now is the time, Hengroen. Now we shall ride together."

He was aware of Lamrei peering at them from her stall and felt guilty. "You shall come too, Lamrei," he told her. "I will have need of you both."

The mountains of Venedotia disappeared in the early morning mist as the teulu marched eastwards and many heads turned to watch the familiar peaks of their homeland vanish, not knowing how long it would be before they would see them again.

Marcus and Claudius rode with Arthur and advised him on the customs of the south as well as imparting their knowledge of the enemy. Menw rode with them too. Some questioned the presence of an old bard on the war trail but Arthur would not have ridden forth without him. Cei and the others understood. It had been Menw who had guided them on their perilous mission to Gaelic-held Ynys Mon three years ago. The bard's knowledge and wisdom were invaluable.

They made for the town of Deverdoeu, once Deva Victrix; a Roman legionary fortress, which was now an important outpost of the Kingdom of Powys. There had long been enmity between Powys and Venedotia but the sudden emergence of Caw's Pictish confederation and the subsequent war had necessitated a brief respite in hostilities. The teulu had passed through Deverdoeu on their way to the north and had received food and shelter. Arthur hoped that they would receive similar hospitality this time.

They spent the night in the old barrack blocks without incident and the following morning, they turned south and followed the Roman road to Caer Guricon; the royal seat of Powys. King Ridfet accommodated them with surprising hospitality and Arthur got the feeling that the Powysians were keen to see the back of them. *Let the Venedotian's fight their wars far from here*, seemed to be the feeling. *The further the Teulu of the Red Dragon is, the better.*

The green hills of the south stretched out before them, dappled by the sunlight streaming through the clouds. The sky to the south was leaden. War beckoned with its gnarled and scarred claw.

Peredur

Sunlight filtered down through the trees in wide beams, penetrating the jade world beneath the forest's canopy. Insects buzzed and the air teemed with the life of early summer.

It was hot under the splayed branches and sweat trickled down Peredur's neck, willing him to lose his focus. He gripped his hunting bow, the string pulled taught to his ear, as he squinted down the length of the shaft at his prey.

A noise barely audible to his ears disturbed some crows high in the treetops and they broke forth, cawing and flapping. The hart raised its horned head in startled surprise and was off like a flash, taking great bounds into the undergrowth.

Peredur relaxed his bow and straightened with a sigh. It was one of those totally uncontrollable variables that can make or break a killing shot. He would be lucky if he would get another chance at the deer. He swore under his breath and then quickly regretted it. His mother strongly disapproved of swearing.

He wandered in the direction the hart had taken, his bow over his shoulder. He knew this part of the forest like the back of his hand. It was his home – rather his entire world – and always had been. Yet he had never ventured beyond the small stream that wound its way through the forest. He could hear its trickling now, the sound that marked the border of his existence. Beyond the stream lay the Evil.

"Never, never go beyond the stream," his mother had warned him. The world beyond was filled with evil men who worked the deeds of the Devil. Those men had claimed the lives of his father and brothers. He was safe as long as he never crossed that current of water. God would protect him so long as he followed her instructions.

For all of his fifteen years Peredur had lived in fear of what lay beyond the stream. Only once had he dared to stand on its bank and peer across at the dark shadows under the trees on the other side. He had seen some movement in the dim light, probably a deer (or so he had tried to convince himself) but had fled back home with his heart in his mouth nonetheless. Since then he had stayed well away from the stream, preferring to hunt in other parts of the forest. But he was close to it now. He could hear its trickle singing to him in its eerie voice. The hart had gone in that direction and so must he.

As he cut a path through the trees he drew in the woodland scents through his nostrils. He loved the sounds and smells of the forest in summer. He had wandered the hidden paths of that jade kingdom all his life and was well versed in its lore. He knew the names of all the different plants and their purposes, be it culinary or medicinal. He knew what birds' nests to plunder for eggs and he knew which of the mushrooms that grew in the silent and dark places were edible and which drove you mad and sick. Not that his mother approved of mushrooms of course. They sapped their strength from dying and decaying things and were therefore in league with the Evil.

The stream was close now and Peredur could see it winking through the trees, a sliver of fluid crystal cutting through the green. He felt a great sucking at his soul as he approached its tranquil banks, as if the other side was pulling at him, beckoning him to cross. *It does that, the Evil*, his mother had told him. *It tricks and tempts you like the serpent in the Garden of Eden.* It had tricked his father and now he was dead.

On the other side stood the deer, water dripping from its flanks. It had seen him and it gazed across the water with its wide, black eyes, reading his intentions. Was this too a trick? The devil was horned, after all, as were the wicked pagan gods who had ruled Albion before the coming of the word of Christ. The beast lost interest in him before turning and vanishing into the forest.

He had lost it. No venison tonight. His mother would be angry. Her illness often confined her to her bed but it did not blunt her sharp tongue or her hard hand. But what did she expect? Peredur felt a rare flare of rebellion. She forbade him to hunt beyond the stream and yet she berated him if he did not kill enough deer or trap enough rabbits. Even mushrooms were forbidden at mother's table. A hunter cannot hunt in a small area of woodland all his life. He needed more space! Her rules were stifling him.

"The Good Lord will provide," were her words, but it was neither her nor the Good Lord who was out every day with a bow, spear and knife, stalking and tracking be it rain, snow or sunshine.

He looked over at the dark patch of forest beyond the stream where the hart had vanished. In fact, all the animals he hunted came and went as they pleased. They were God's creatures as much as he was. Why then, were there different rules for him? It didn't make any sense. If he shot that deer, who would know which side of the stream he had killed it on? Certainly not mother because he wouldn't tell her.

But what of the Evil?

He had his bow and his long hunting knife. He would be prepared for any tricks or malevolence against him. He nocked an arrow to his string. He would cross, he decided.

He didn't know how he would feel when he emerged from the stream upon the other bank but once he was shaking the water from his boots, he was surprised to feel absolutely nothing. No hideous demon rose from the stream to consume him. Nor did the twisted and gnarled trees extend their black arms to scratch and maul him. In fact, this side of the stream seemed exactly the same as the other. The sun was still shining and he could even hear birdsong high above him.

His courage growing, he ventured a little further into the woods but he made sure he could always hear the reassuring sound of the stream behind him. Old Garth, his mother's servant, had once told him a story about an enchanted forest where the trees moved to confuse lone travellers who became lost and were never heard from again.

The ground swept down into a valley and at its bottom a silver river shimmered in the afternoon sun. Great clouds of dust rose up from it and Peredur realised that it was not a river at all but a road.

A road! He had heard of them of course, but never in his life had he seen one. But what a colossal monster rippled down it! It clanked and groaned under its own weight, stirring up the dust in great plumes like dragon-breath. He had heard of dragons too. Excitement filled his gut, competing for space with sheer terror.

His curiosity won out and, as stealthily as he could manage, he crept down the slope towards the road. He could not return home and continue with his mundane life with the knowledge that he had seen an actual dragon and had not taken a closer look.

The trees provided ample cover and as he approached, he lost all fear of being heard so great was the noise coming from the road. Clanking, grinding, jingling and stomping, all was a deafening roar that would have put Peredur in mind of the sea had he ever heard it.

He was level with the road now and from behind a low fern, he peeped out. His eyes grew wide with sudden astonishment. The long and shimmering thing was not a single being at all, but a massive column of men on horseback. They wore armour of iron and leather. Helms glinted in the sun, some plumed with vibrant colours. They carried spears, shields, swords and axes. Banners of every colour and emblem fluttered high above them in the gentle breeze and the bellow of a great aurochs horn sounded truly like the roar of a dragon.

Peredur's whole world had been shaken. He had only ever known his mother and the two servants who lived with them in the seclusion of the forest. It had never occurred to him that there could be this many people in the whole world. And now he was seeing them all march past in all their splendour and grandeur.

To him they were beautiful. Everything that was glorious about the world that had been forever beyond his reach was summed up by that synchronised stomping and glittering of polished iron in the sun. He looked at the faces that marched past. Pride and fierceness were etched onto every one of them. These were men with a purpose, a calling. These men were going somewhere, to glory and beyond. These were more than men, these were... what did mother call them? That's right - *Angels*.

He froze as one of the stern and powerful faces turned to look at him. He had been seen! He cowered, and wished that he could flee, but that would do no good.

"Hello, lad," called out the warrior in a friendly voice. "Have no fear. Come on out of there."

Slowly, Peredur rose from his hiding place and crept out into the blazing light of the sun. A dry ditch followed the road and stood between him and the marching army.

"How's the hunting in these parts?" enquired the warrior.

"Not too bad," Peredur found himself answering, his voice barely audible over the clamour.

"Good. We have many bellies to fill."

Several of the warrior's friends had stopped to examine him. A man on a massive stallion trotted up. He was not much older than Peredur but his hard eyes and scarred jawline was proof that he was a good deal more worldly and weathered.

"Who's this?" he asked, looking down at Peredur, his long dark hair spilling down beneath his helmet.

"A local lad. Hunter by the looks of him," answered the first man.

"Well, boy," said the rider. "Are you any good with that bow?"

"I catch a lot of rabbits," said Peredur, gazing up at the face that was almost silhouetted against the sun. "And the occasional deer."

"Ever shot a man?"

Peredur shook his head, horrified.

"It's not so very different. Fancy joining us to give it a try? We need bowmen."

Peredur gulped. Join them? It was out of the question of course. Mother would never hear of it.

"Is there to be a battle, sir?"

"Oh yes. The Saeson have invaded the Borderlands. Haven't you heard?"

Peredur didn't know what the Saeson were and he had never heard of the Borderlands.

"I am Gualchmei," continued the warrior. "I follow the banner of my lord Arthur, Penteulu to the High-King Cadwallon of Venedotia. We march south to war! Join us!"

And with that he trotted off, his men falling in behind him. Peredur stayed where he was, his feet rooted to the ground as he watched the army stomp past.

Daylight had begun to fade by the time the last of the army had vanished into the distance and the dust began to settle. He sighed gently. His whole life had been changed by that afternoon's events. He had seen the angels of the Lord march through the big, wide world on their holy mission. The thought of returning to the little dwelling in the forest and never setting eyes upon such magnificent beings again sickened him. He could not even tell anybody what he had seen, for he had crossed the barrier between his world and theirs. But he had seen no evil that afternoon. He had seen goodness and valour and glory. And he desperately wanted to be a part of it.

Darkness was descending as Peredur heard the bleating of his mother's goats from their enclosure that he had built for them last summer. As he entered the clearing where his home stood, he looked around at the surroundings that had been all he had known in his short life. The house, the stables, the chicken huts. All the sounds he had grown up with; the bubbling of the spring from which he drew water every day, the snorting of the pigs and the scratching and clucking of the chickens. All of this felt as nothing after what he had witnessed that afternoon.

He had always felt that he had not been born to live the life of a simple farmer and hunter but today was the first time he had *known* it. He was noble born, or so he had been told. His father had been a high-ranking man in Eboracum, a large town in the north, in days gone by. He had been killed in battle along with several of his sons the year Peredur had been born. His mother fell sick with grief and fled Eboracum with her new born and two servants, taking what valuables they could carry. She had sought a secluded spot in a lonely forest to raise her remaining son and there Garth and Emlin had built the house.

As he always did when he passed the barn on his way to the house, Peredur thought of his father's armour sitting on its rack within, covered with an old cloth. Once, his mother had caught him lifting the cloth to sneak a look and had beaten him soundly for it. Weapons and armour were tools of the Evil. He wondered then why she kept his father's armour and sword at all but he had never found the courage to ask her. She missed his father a good deal, he knew that.

He entered the sickly atmosphere of the house and hung up his bow. He could hear his mother coughing violently as always and went into her room to see her. Emlin was mopping the sweat from her brow with a rag.

"Have you not brought back venison as you promised me?" were her first words to him upon noticing that his tunica was not blood-stained and his hands were clean.

"I promised you nothing mother," he replied. "I said I would try, but the deer crossed the stream where I could not follow it."

Her eyes bulged in their sunken sockets and she wheezed for breath. "You went near the stream?"

"Yes."

There was a silence.

"Mother, I don't think the land beyond the stream is evil," he said, feeling uncharacteristically defiant.

"Oh, no?" she replied with a sneer. "The world beyond claimed your father and your brothers. It took them from me. I took a vow in the presence of God Almighty himself that I would keep you from its evil."

"Did that vow include lying to me all my life?"

"How dare you!" she tried to rise to strike him but fell back in a spasm of coughing.

"I'm sorry mother," he cried, overcome with repentance and knelt at her side. He took the cloth from Emlin. "I disobeyed you, mother. I went beyond the stream today." He couldn't hold it in any longer. His mother was the one person he had ever loved and the guilt at betraying her had welled up inside him.

He had expected her to fly into a rage and strike at his bowed head but instead she simply lay there, staring at the ceiling. A single, heavy tear rolled down her cheek and soaked into the pillow.

"God forgive me," she whispered. "What did you see?"

"I… I saw a road. And men riding it. Hundreds and hundreds of men, all in armour and marching with coloured banners flying high above them. One of them spoke to me. He said he served a man called Arthur and that there was a great battle coming."

His mother squeezed her eyes shut in pain. She gasped for air. "You… you wish to join them don't you?"

Peredur paused. There was no point lying to her. "Yes, mother."

"False illusions of glory and valour inspire vanity in men which is an offence to God! I sought to protect you from the evils of the world by raising you here, in seclusion. Would you betray me now?"

"Mother! I will never betray you!"

"You already have, boy."

"No! You cannot force me to remain here in a prison all my life! I want to see the world, mother. I want to meet people and taste life! But you want me to stay here and be a farmer. Well, I'm not a farmer. And neither was my father."

"Your father was a fool! And his foolishness spread to your brothers and the Lord took them all from me! I will not allow you to follow in their footsteps."

Peredur rose from the bed. "You can't stop me."

She screamed at him as he left the room and flung the covers from her in a rage. As he left her, she hurled herself at his turned back and beat at it with her fists. He spun around and grasped her wrists in his hands, noticing for the first time that he was so much stronger her then her. Her face paled and she sank to her knees. He released her and she fell to the floor, sobbing.

Garth and Emlin gazed at the pair, open-mouthed.

"I'm sorry, mother," he said. "But I am leaving. I will return one day, I promise. I love you."

He left her weeping and went out to the small chapel that Garth had built next to the house. He entered it and knelt before the crude crucifix that hung on the wall depicting the son of God who had been executed by the Romans in a land far to the east. He prayed for God's forgiveness for wounding his mother and then he swore a vow in the presence of God, as his mother had done many years ago. He swore that he would do all that he could to become the warrior he felt destined to be.

Then he went to the barn. Light trickled in as a single bluish beam from a gap in the thatch, illuminating, as if in some holy image, the cloaked figure of his father's armour. The cloth covering it was old and blackened by mould and cobwebs. With a single sweep, Peredur whipped it back and then coughed and hacked while the dust settled.

There it stood. His father's armour. Breastplate, greaves and helmet. A great round shield hung at its side decorated with an eagle device. On the other side hung his father's sword. Peredur reached out and lifted the weapon from the rack. It was heavier than he expected but then again, he had never held a sword before. He couldn't imagine how anyone could swing it around and cleave metal, flesh and bone. He drew it from its sheath and found the blade gleaming, not even flecked by rust after so many years. He looked at his reflection in the blade.

"You'll want to keep that well-oiled," said Garth behind him. Peredur jumped. "Look, young master, are you sure you don't want to stay here for a few days before setting out? You're acting awfully fast. Your mother… she's not well…"

"I need to catch up with Arthur's army while I have the chance," Peredur replied. "And my mother has never been well. That will not change."

"Then let me give you some advice, sir. If that army you saw is heading south, then they are probably headed for Isca Silurum. It's the closest town that can support a force of that size and is called Cair Legion in the common tongue. You can take a shortcut to the road by following the stream instead of crossing it. It curves east before crossing the Roman road that leads to Cair Legion."

"How do you know so much of the outside world Garth?" Peredur enquired.

The loyal servant coughed once and flushed. "I uh, occasionally slipped out for a day or two without your mother knowing sir. But never for anything less than an emergency, mind. There was the time you had the fever if you'll remember, sir, so I…"

"It's alright, Garth," said Peredur with a smile. "You don't have to explain yourself to me."

"No, sir. Thank you. One other piece of advice though. Take old Amren with you. He'll carry that armour no problem and if you find you don't need him, well you can use him to barter with. And speaking of bartering…" He lowered his voice and produced a small leather pouch that jingled as he handed it to him. Peredur opened it and looked inside. Within were many items that glinted in the dim light. "Your mother's jewellery, sir. She doesn't put much stock in finery anymore – you know how she is on the matter of vanity – and I don't reckon she'd miss them any time soon. You can exchange it for items like food, clothing and shelter. Everything has a price in the world. You will need it but use it sparingly for it is mighty hard to acquire wealth and there will be people who will wish to steal it from you or trick you into giving it to them."

Peredur hugged Garth and felt a lump rise in his throat. "All my life you have treated me well," he said, willing himself not to cry. "You and Emlin have been my only friends. When I was just a baby, the two of you left your homes and came with my mother and I to this place so that I would grow up in peace and security. You built this farm with your bare hands and provided a home for a child and his mother who had none. You taught me how to hunt and skin animals and I always laughed at your stories, although now I can see that some of them had a ring of truth to them. Emlin was always there with a warm hug and soothing words when I scraped my knee or fell out of the apple tree. For all these things I am grateful and I hope that I can find some way to repay you one day."

Garth's eyes grew a little wet though he did his best to hide it.

Old Amren the donkey twitched his ears and swished his tail as Peredur saddled him with his father's armour and shield, two hunting spears, his bow, a quiver of arrows, a leather sack containing bread, apples, cold meat and a skin of last autumn's ale.

"Steady, Amren," he soothed as the old donkey stepped back and forth and tried to shake himself free as he fastened the straps. "I hope your old legs are up to this."

Once the complaining donkey was all set, Peredur put on a summer cloak and fastened it so it fell down over his body, covering the purse Garth had given to him and his long hunting knife.

Garth and Emlin stood at the farm gate to see him off with tears streaming down their faces. Weeping too, Peredur turned to wave at them before he disappeared into the forest and let the wide world swallow him.

Arthur

The villa had once been a grand affair, the home of some nobleman and his family in happier times. Now it lay dilapidated and ruined. Grass grew high around the base of its walls and creepers wound their way around the pillars of the galleries. A tree blown down in a storm had torn a great hole in the tiled roof and leaned against its walls like a drunken old man.

"This will do for the night," said Arthur as they looked at it from a distance.

They had crossed the great curve of the Afon Sabrina that swept around to the south-west before it emptied into the Sabrina Sea and were passing through the endless green hills and wooded valleys where southern Powys met the northern fringes of Guenta.

They should make Cair Legion the following day. The usefulness of a legionary fort with enough barrack blocks to house five-thousand men was an attractive prospect. The word was that Cair Legion was still occupied and indeed thriving with trade from Dumnonia and even distant Armorica but Arthur had no idea how they would be received there. King Ynyr ruled from nearby Cair Guenta and Marcus and Claudius couldn't give much of a picture as to what he was like.

They hobbled their horses in the overgrown gardens at the front of the villa and while Cei and Beduir set the men to the foraging of food and firewood. Arthur and Menw ventured up to the main building.

The floor in the entrance hall was a mosaic depicting capering lions in a border surrounding a star. The cracked plaster on the walls had once been turquoise and a broken statue of some ancestor, caked with moss, stood in the far corner beneath the gaping hole in the roof. The remains of campfires on the floor in the central room showed evidence of other visitors since the villa's original inhabitants had left. Corridors lead off from the main room to bedrooms, a kitchen and a bathhouse slick with green slime.

"I don't like these old Roman houses," said Menw. "No warmth."

"We'll soon get a fire going," replied Arthur.

"It's not the temperature," the bard replied. "There is no soul here. Probably never was." He glanced at the moss-encrusted statue. A beetle crawled across its cheek and dropped to the floor.

Arthur saw his point. It was a far cry from the roaring fires and cosy halls of the British strongholds that were so filled with song and cheer. He wondered if all houses in the south were like this; empty and forgotten, their very stones gradually being reclaimed by the earth.

Cold and ruined though it was, the villa offered a change from sleeping in the woods, on beds of brush. Arthur and his captains commandeered the central room and the men were billeted in other rooms as well as the dilapidated washhouse next to the gardens. Menw, still unhappy about the villa chose to sleep up on the rear gallery where he could see the stars.

Arthur joined him on the gallery after their evening meal. The back of the villa faced an overgrown orchard and a thick cluster of hawthorns and tangled vines suggested some sort of structure beneath the foliage.

"Probably a temple," said Menw. "Trust the Romans to lock even the gods up in their damnable square houses."

Arthur left him muttering to himself and went down into the main room where the men were bedding down by the glowing embers of the fire. Tiredness weighed heavily on each of them and soon they drifted off to sleep.

Arthur dreamed of apple trees. He saw an orchard and knew that he had been there before. The trees were heavy with ripe, red fruit.

He knew the girl would be there even before he saw her.

But she was no longer a girl.

As he turned to face the figure that stood in the tail of his eye, he found himself looking at a woman in the fullness of adulthood. That it was the same person as the girl he had seen in his fevered dream three years ago was beyond a doubt. Those same green eyes and that burning hair – both so much like Guenhuifar's and yet somehow different – were unmistakable.

"You've grown," he said.

She smiled. "So have you."

She wore a light and floaty dress the colour of fresh blood that flowed down from her shoulders, clinging to her curves.

Then they were running; he chasing her, or was it the other way around? Through the trees he caught brief glimpses of red gossamer and the flame of her hair. The blood swam in his temples as if he were drunk. She toyed with him, letting him catch up with her only to vanish with a laugh to some other part of the orchard. On and on they chased like fox and hare. The woman finally stopped and turned to face Arthur. He gasped with exertion while she had not even broken a sweat.

"You are far from home, Arthur, son of the Pendraig."

"Yes. I have come to drive the Saeson back."

"You will need help."

"Whose help?"

She smiled again and turned slightly to the left. Behind her stood a structure that had not been there a moment previously. It was a Roman construction of bricks and plaster.

"Seek it out, Arthur," she said. "Seek out the tools you need to fulfil your destiny."

Arthur awoke with a start. The glow of the fire was low and the shadows were long across the cracked and flaking plaster of the walls. Beyond the collapsed roof he could make out the stars twinkling in the black sky. He judged that he had only been asleep for a couple of hours. Something had woken him but he had no idea what. Unable to fall asleep again he rose quietly, buckled on his sword belt and walked across the room.

The others still slumbered peacefully despite Cei's loud snores. Arthur made his way out into the grounds at the back of the villa. The air was chill and the sky clear. He pondered the meaning of his dream. Only once had he seen the woman before. He had been washed up, half drowned on the shores of

Venedotia after falling into the straits. Following that dream he had rescued Hengroen from a hawthorn bush. It was a sign, Menw had said. A sign that he had become a man. The white foal was Mabon, son of Modron. He was a gift from the goddess. Arthur had not been so sure. He had often debated the value of a dream borne of an overindulgence of seawater and the terror of near death.

But now she had come to him again. *But to what end?*

He thought of the Roman temple in the dream and then remembered the overgrown structure Menw had pointed out that day. The orchard was black beneath the night sky but he could still make out the clump of bushes and vines that denoted something hidden.

He made his way over to it and cut away some of the foliage, working in a circular motion until he found the entrance. Green double doors had once formed the portal to the inner sanctum but now only one remained and that hung slack on broken hinges. Arthur hacked away enough dead brush and thorny growth in order to gain access.

He stepped into the temple's interior and waited for his eyes to grow accustomed to the dimness. Moonlight shone in through a high window and illuminated plastered walls painted with frescoes of vines, rivers and lush growth. A sunken pool occupied the centre of the room, its surface a skim of algae. On the other side of it stood a stone statue of a goddess wearing a crested helmet and holding a spear. A shield carven with the face of a gorgon rested on her hip. She gazed down at him with lifeless eyes.

He sighed. He didn't know why he was here, chasing the words of a dream. This temple was a shell of what it had once been. Anything valuable would have been removed long ago. The last couple of generations of the villa's inhabitants had most likely been Christians and had all but forgotten about this pagan shrine on their lands, letting it vanish from sight in a heap of undergrowth.

He walked around the pool to examine the gorgon device on the goddess's shield. As he approached it, he felt a slab move under his feet. He looked down. The flagstone he was standing on wobbled up and down as he shifted his weight.

He knelt and ran his fingers around the edge of the stone. It was heavy so he drew his sword and slid the blade in under it. He levered it up and was able to shift it to one side with a grating sound that echoed deafeningly in the confined space.

The earth below was soft and damp. He dug into it with his hands and scooped out as much as he could into a small pile. He was not more than a foot down when his fingertips found something hard. *Something hidden.*

He began to dig in earnest, piling up the soil around him. Several objects were buried beneath the loose flagstone and it occurred to Arthur that the pagans who had used this temple had buried some sacred objects to stop them falling into the hands of looters or Christians. They had probably counted on coming back for it one day but had never done so.

The first object he removed was a leather pouch that felt heavy with coin. A further bundle revealed a silver priest's staff, a ceremonial cup and a pair of silver votive plaques inscribed in Latin.

After some more digging, his hand closed around a long, thin object wrapped in heavy cloth. It took him a few tugs but eventually he was able to draw it out. He unwrapped it, pulling at the rotten twine that bound it together. Several layers of mouldy cloth and filth fell away before he uncovered an oiled animal skin. Wax sealed the package and he cut into it with his knife.

That he had found a sword had become apparent to him several layers ago but when he finally set his eyes upon the weapon, he knew that it was a very special sword indeed.

It was an early Roman spatha; one of the long cavalry swords that had replaced the trusty gladius as the need for mounted troops rendered the old ways of legionary warfare obsolete. The scabbard was of red leather, studded with garnet and gold. The hilt was fashioned into the image of a woman and two snakes entwined around her thighs formed the handguard, with head on either side of the blade.

He drew it slowly from its scabbard. It slid out noiselessly, the unwashed sheep's' wool that lined it having done its job in protecting the blade. There was not a single rust-fleck on its long, glimmering length. It caught the light of the moon and sent a flash across the temple's interior.

Before he left the temple, he replaced the loose flagstone and hid the objects behind the statue. All except the sword. He felt a connection to it, a possessiveness that had consumed him since he had first grasped its hilt. He took it back to the villa with him and slept with it under his blanket, never letting go of the hilt all night.

The following morning, while the men were saddling the horses, Arthur led Menw down to the temple. It looked a little less eerie in the bright light of morning and seemed like a sad old thing, as if it had been robbed of something.

"And how did you say you came upon the idea to ransack this old place?" the bard asked him with a quizzical eye.

"A dream," he told him.

"Modron?"

"Perhaps."

Arthur led him into the temple and Menw gazed up at the face of the goddess. "Hmm," he said pensively. "Sulis Minerva most likely. A local deity once worshiped in this part of Albion. She is the spirit of water springing from the earth among other things, hence the sacred tank before us. Now, what about this treasure trove you've found?"

They inspected the items together. The leather bag contained mostly silver denarii from the reign of Emperor Honorius. Menw read the inscriptions on the votive plaques.

"Let's see; 'To the goddess Sulis Minerva from Quintus'. Hmm. I was right. And the other; 'To the goddess Sulis Minerva, Gaius Calpurnius Atticus willingly and deservedly fulfils his vow'." His eyes wandered to the sword Arthur wore buckled to his belt in place of his old one. "And I do believe you found something else last night."

Arthur drew the blade and held it up for the bard's inspection.

Menw's eyes lit up at its magnificence. "That truly is a sword of kings," he said.

"But what was it doing in the temple?" Arthur asked.

"Swords are often sacrificed to water goddesses or to the Great Mother herself, but they are usually ritually bent or destroyed before being cast into a lake. No, this sword was hidden as treasure. Why a sword, you ask? Why anything, really. Why cups and plates? But there are no inscriptions on it… Strange."

"The hilt is in the shape of a woman,"

"Yes, I noticed that."

"The goddess?"

"Perhaps. I think this sword was *made* as an offering to her and was kept in this temple as a charm."

"Would you think ill of me if I took it?"

Menw smiled. "You want it, don't you?"

"Aye. It seems a shame to leave it here amidst the ruins."

"What exactly did the goddess say to you in your dream?"

"She told me to seek out the tools I needed to fulfil my destiny."

"Then I think you have your answer."

"You mean, she meant for me to find it?"

"This sword has been waiting for something. I believe it has been waiting for you, Arthur. You have a great war ahead of you, what better tool than the sword of a goddess?"

Arthur looked up at the blank expression of the goddess on her plinth and then at the gleam of the blade he held. "I will call it… *Caledbulc*," he said after some deliberation.

"*Hard-splitter*," said Menw. "As good a name as any."

As they approached Cair Legion from the north, it became apparent that a group of riders was keeping pace with them although remaining at a cautious distance.

"Warriors of Guenta," said Marcus. "Keeping tabs on our progress."

Arthur sent Cundelig and Guihir out to assure them that they were not an invading force but the group rode off in an easterly direction before contact could be made.

"Most likely heading for Cair Guenta," said Marcus. "King Ynyr will be most interested to hear of our arrival."

Cair Legion stood upon the banks of the Afon Usg which washed out into the Sabrina Sea. Originally a legionary fort, the vicus had sprung up to the west of it, supplying it and in turn, earn a living from the presence of a large number of soldiers, hence frequency of wine shops and brothels. The town was walled and boasted an amphitheatre and a harbour.

There was a large hill that rose above the town on its north-western edge. A British fort had once stood there in the days before the Romans but all that remained now was a series of ditches grown over with grass. It was here that Arthur chose to make camp and plan his next move.

"The Saeson are in control of the lands just across the Sabrina Sea," said Marcus. "Guenta will be the first British kingdom to fall should they cross those waters or march around to the north where the river narrows."

"And what of Cair Badon?" Arthur asked "Is it heavily fortified?"

"It was abandoned many years ago," said Claudius. "Little more than ruins. What the Saeson make of it all I have no idea. Aelle's left his son in charge there; a man called Cymen. If Aurelianus is still being held there, then there must be a large Saeson presence to prevent anybody trying to rescue him."

"Why is he being held at all?" asked Cei. "I would have thought that this Aelle would have wanted to do away with his greatest threat as soon as possible, not keep him locked away in some deserted town daring somebody to attempt a rescue."

"He may wish to hold him against any incursions into his new realm by the other British kings," said Marcus. "A man such as Aurelianus is invaluable to Albion's cause. Few will risk his life by crossing the Sabrina."

"This Aelle seems to be a cunning dog," said Arthur.

Beduir poked his head in through the tent flap. "Sir, there is a delegation here from the town that wishes to speak with you."

"That will be the magistrate," said Marcus. "Come to pay his respects. Or to demand yours. I advise against expecting too much from Magistrate Nectovelius."

Nectovelius had the short hair and shaved cheeks common in the south. He wore the fine clothes of the aristocracy and gold decorated his wrists and fingers. Evidently trade had not been too disrupted in Cair Legion. He had brought a small guard with him, clad in mail and ridge helmets in the Roman style.

The two parties faced each other outside Arthur's tent, the wind rippling through the camp, whipping at tent flaps and the dragon standard that had been planted in the ground nearby.

"Greetings, Artorius," said the magistrate of Cair Legion in British, although keeping the Latinised form of Arthur's name. "Welcome to Isca Silurum. I am Nectovelius, magistrate of the town and the outlying lands, subject of King Ynyr."

"Greetings, Nectovelius," replied Arthur.

"I thought it common courtesy to pay my respects to the man who has brought his army from so far afield to do battle with our enemies," said Nectovelius. "But tell me, Artorius. How long are you planning on staying with us?"

"We're not too sure," Arthur said. "It all depends on how quickly we can rescue Aurelianus and drive the Saeson out of the Borderlands."

"With the greatest respect," the magistrate said with a small smile, "that may take some time. I'm not sure that you fully realise the state of things here. Right across the water is an army the like of which this land has not faced since the Romans first landed. Speaking of numbers, how many of you are there?"

"We near one-hundred and fifty in cavalry. Horses too of course, and about the same in auxiliaries. Then there are the camp followers;

blacksmiths, armourers, whores, you know how it is. This includes a number of new recruits we have picked up on the way; country lads with a blade or a bow to their name, keen to do their bit and earn a crust. We near five-hundred, all told."

"Five-hundred!" gasped the magistrate. "Then surely you can see the problem you present."

"Problem? No, not really."

"Well, five-hundred men will require an awful lot of food. And then there are the horses, as you said. We simply cannot accommodate you. No, I think that it would be best for you to turn around and take your army back home. There is nothing to be done here. Nothing at all."

Arthur looked from Nectovelius to his captains who all shared his surprise. He was not sure that he had heard the man right. "Turn around?" he exclaimed. "We were asked to ride to your aid by Marcus and Claudius here, soldiers of Aurelianus. I would have thought that you would be grateful to have us here with a Sais warband sharpening their knives on the opposite bank!"

The magistrate glanced at the ambassadors, his expression disapproving. "Yes, well these two men are soldiers, not politicians. They overstepped their mark in calling upon your aid. You see, as far as we in Isca Silurum are concerned, the Saeson are welcome to the lands across the river. I can assure you that the Sabrina served as a very good barrier against the Romans for quite some time."

Arthur sighed. "I have heard such excuses before, magistrate," he said. "In my homeland they talk of the mountains that protected them against the

Romans. Here you talk of the river. Both kept out the Romans, it is true, but only for a while. Don't you see that you are only postponing the inevitable? Once the Saeson grow in strength they will cross your great river or march around it and into the streets of your towns, burning and looting as they go. Now is the time for action. You asked me to leave. Well here is my answer; I refuse. We shall stay. For as long as it is necessary. Cair Legion will offer a good base for my forays across the river and the old Roman barracks will provide ample housing for my men and many more who wish to join our cause. In fact, I have been giving thought to rebuilding the fortress that once stood on this hill. It would provide a secondary defence against any Sais incursions. Of course, that would require additional supplies and materials. I think we may be here for some time."

The colour drained from Nectovelius's face. "Re... rebuild the fortress?" he spluttered. "You can't be serious! How are you planning to find resources?"

"Oh, I think we can manage," replied Arthur with a cool air. "We have manpower enough. I think we can bring in both food and timber from the surrounding countryside. I'm sure the locals won't kick up a fuss. Our presence here is for their own safety, of course."

At this the governor grew suddenly angry. His pale face turned red and he bellowed at Arthur. "You can't make a difference here! If you cross that river the Saeson will massacre you! They outnumber you ten to one – you haven't a hope! And if you do decide to cross, I will enjoy hearing of your defeat from safety of my home on *this* side of the river!"

And with that he turned smartly away from Arthur and mounted his horse. They watched him descend the hill, his guards trotting along behind him. Marcus and Claudius looked apologetically to Arthur.

"I told you not to expect too much from him," said Marcus. "He has long sat in the lap of luxury and has never been a soldier. He cares little for those across the river and is content to leave them to their fate."

"He's a damned coward!" said Cei.

"Never mind," said Arthur. "We don't need his help. I am surprised Aurelianus allowed such a miserable wretch to remain in office."

"Gone are the days when a vicus was under direct control of a military commander," said Claudius. "Aurelianus has billeted his troops in the fort many times, but the vicus is under the jurisdiction of the magistrate. Nectovelius is King Ynyr's man and he is good at what he does; controlling trade, which is all Ynyr expects from him."

"Nectovelius is a greedy weasel," added Marcus. "He grows fat on the profits of others' misfortunes. Aurelianus depended upon him for supplies and reinforcements, but they always came at a high price. The month before we were defeated, Nectovelius refused to send several sacks of grain that Aurelianus requested. Almost as if he knew he would not be getting the money for it."

"Yes," said Arthur, rubbing his beard. "I am beginning to see how things work in the southern kingdoms."

Peredur

Peredur gazed into the flickering flames of the campfire, inhaling the glorious smell of cooked chicken through his nostrils. The stars shone from their homes in the heavens and the moon was a slim crescent of silver, its reflection shimmering in the gentle ripples of the Afon Usg.

The day had been exhausting mentally as well as physically. Peredur had followed the stream down rocky brooks and flowing currents as it wound its way through the forest just as Garth had told him. It seemed to go on forever and he had begun to wonder if the old man had been mistaken and that he would never join up with the road that led down to Cair Legion. Eventually, the stream widened into a river and Peredur's eyes widened with it as it kept getting bigger and bigger and the opposite bank grew farther and farther away.

He saw many different birds he had not known had existed fishing along its banks. Unseen creatures swam up from the murky depths to snap at insects leaving only expanding circles of ripples behind. The river sucked the water into its flow as if it were a humongous and greedy snake and he felt sucked along with it.

He had followed the bulging swell of the river, mesmerized by its movement, until darkness settled and the first stars began to peep out at him from the inky sky. Amren began to drag his hooves and pull at the rope indicating that he was tired and Peredur realised how exhausted he was too. They had been travelling for a full day from dawn to dusk with very few breaks so excited had he been by his new and ever-changing surroundings. Hunger and weariness took its hold and he looked around for a suitable place to spend the night.

Through the dark shade of the trees he could make out the glimmer of a campfire and heard the low murmur of voices. A new curiosity gripped him. People! The first people he had encountered in his entire life besides his mother, Garth and Emlin. He made for the light, his heart pounding and his mind reeling at what he might say to them. For the first time in his life he was overcome with shyness.

The voices stopped abruptly as he approached and two men rose up defensively. A challenge was shouted out in the darkness and Peredur identified himself and his business. The two men took a good, hard look at him and Amren before abruptly changing their attitude and inviting him to sit with them by their fire.

The eldest of the two was called Bevon and his face was marked by a long scar that ran down his forehead and ended halfway down his cheek, splitting his eyebrow in two. The eye was a pale, milky colour and Peredur wanted to ask him if it was blind, but he thought that this might be a rather rude thing to ask. Bevon's companion was called Maelduin. He hardly spoke and his face was mostly concealed by a long fringe of greasy black hair that hung down in front of two steely blue eyes that gleamed with cunning.

"'Where are you heading to, boy?" asked Bevon as Peredur warmed himself by the fire.

"To Isca Silurum," he replied, exhilarated to be having a conversation with a complete stranger for the first time.

"Never heard of it," replied the man after a brief moment of concentration.

Peredur's heart sank a little at this and he said; "I'm told that it's a big town not far from here. Its other name is Cair Legion."

The two men looked at each other.

"It's *other* name?" said Maelduin. "So you speak Latin?"

"Yes. Why, don't you?"

Bevon smirked at this. "Latin is for churches and noblemen's letters to their fancy lovers. Are you a nobleman?"

"No, but my father was. He was the military commander of Ebura… Cair Eburauc."

"Was he indeed?" said Bevon, exchanging another look with his companion. "And where is he now? Walled himself up in his villa with lots of silver, I suppose. Most of them have these days."

"No, he died in battle with my brothers when I was a baby."

"Oh, I see," said Bevon, a barely concealed look of disappointment on his face. "So, tell me, boy, what business do you have in Cair Legion?"

"I seek the camp of the lord Arthur. Have you heard of him?"

Bevon nodded solemnly. "Him and his army marched through here not long past, tearing up the whole countryside. Northern heathens most of them. Little more than barbarians. Nothing left to steal after his lot raided every farmhouse between here and…"

A sharp kick from Maelduin silenced him and the topic was hastily changed.

"So you're on your way to join them then are you?" asked Bevon.

"Yes. My father was a great warrior and I hope to become one too. That's why I have his armour with me. It's all I have left of him."

"Armour eh?" asked Bevin, his single eye twinkling. "I bet the armour of a commander would be fine gear."

"I suppose so," replied Peredur uncertainly. "I have his sword and shield too, but I can't really use them yet. I've had no training. I'm sure Arthur's men will give me some."

Bevon grinned and passed him a skin of something that sloshed invitingly. "Have some mead, lad."

Morning broke over the Afon Usg, a thin mist rising up from the water and creeping into the wooded glade where Peredur slept. The first birds of the day began to chirp in the treetops and he stirred gently before opening his eyes. His head throbbed and his mouth tasted dry.

He sat up and looked around. Smoke curled up from the burnt-out campfire. The clearing was deserted. He remembered talking long into the night with his two new friends and drinking lots of their mead. He didn't remember falling asleep, nor did he recollect Bevon and Maelduin leaving. A sudden flush of horror overtook him. Amren was gone. Along with his father's armour!

He cursed himself for a fool as he strode down to the banks of the river, looking this way and that for any sign of the thieves. Garth's words resounded in his head; *people will wish to trick you*. He had been tricked out of the one thing he valued in the whole world; his heritage and his birth right. And he had made it so easy for them!

Rage boiled up inside of him and he took pleasure in imagining what he would do to the two villains if he ever caught them. But it was a hopeless task. He had no idea when they had left him slumbering like a drunkard. They could be half a day's journey ahead of him. Tears welled up in his eyes and his throat ached with grief. He had lost his father's armour to the first people he had met in his entire life! He was no warrior. Already he had broken his vow and lay wretched before God. What would he do with his life now? He felt so utterly alone. He had not one friend in the whole world. Even old Amren had been taken from him.

The sun rose to its peak in the sky and blazed down with hot fury upon the riverbank. Sweating and thirsty, Peredur stopped for a drink at one of the many small wooded inlets that were tucked away in the shade. As he knelt down to splash the cool water on his dusty face and neck he heard voices coming from behind a thicket a short distance away. Wary of who he might be getting involved with now, he crept stealthily into the thicket and peered between the branches.

What he saw made his blood boil in his veins. There, in a secluded clearing, shaded from the midday sun, sprawled Bevon and Maelduin. They were drunk and laughing at some private joke. Peredur suspected that the joke was on him. Worst of all, Bevon appeared to be wearing his father's helmet, his ugly features grimacing with mirth beneath the glimmering iron. Amren stood nearby, flicking his tail at flies, not seeming to care who owned him these days.

A curse caught in Peredur's throat as he burst from the thicket, eyes blazing with rage. The two bandits scrambled to their feet in astonishment but the enraged boy was already upon them, his hands fixed around Bevon's neck like a vice, knocking him back to the ground. The stolen helmet bounced away from them. Bevon's single working eye bulged in its socket as Peredur squeezed with all his might, crushing his windpipe.

Maelduin snatched at Peredur from behind, locking his arms around his elbows. Peredur ran backwards and rammed him against a stout tree trunk, knocking the wind out of him. Bevon was already on his feet and had pulled a long knife from the recesses of his greasy tunica, brandishing it wickedly.

Peredur dropped to the ground and picked up a large flat stone. He hurled it at Bevon. The stone glanced off the man's forehead, opening up an ugly wound that spurted blood down the unscarred side of his face. Wiping the blood from his vision, Bevon just had time to see Peredur hammer into him, knocking him to the earth, the knife spinning out of his grip. Peredur picked up the stone from where it had landed and cracked it across Bevon's face once more.

The man howled in pain but Peredur was not deterred. He was consumed by rage. Again and again he smashed the stone into the ugly skull of the man beneath him, mutilating it even further, the glorious feeling of vengeance coursing through his body.

Behind him, Maelduin got up, gasping for breath. Appalled by the butchery of his comrade, the thin, dark man took to his heels and vanished into the forest.

Peredur screamed his wrath at the world as he slammed the stone into Bevon's face for the last time. Sobbing with exertion and horror, he rolled off the limp and bloodied corpse to lie weeping beside it. Nearby, Amren stood swishing at flies, watching the turn of events with mild interest.

A long time passed before Peredur was able to lift his head up from the tear-soaked earth and confront what he had done. The man who had been Bevon was unrecognisable. The whole front of his face had been completely caved in and all that remained was a pulpy red mess. Peredur's stomach rose up to his throat and he turned quickly to vomit.

His whole body shaking, he desperately tried to say a prayer for the dead man, villain though he was.

He had taken a life.

That simple fact throbbed in the darkest reaches of his soul and it burned like the fires of damnation. He had taken a life and it hadn't even been in self-defence. It had been in anger. It was the worst of all the sins and he was forever dammed because of it.

How could this have happened? He had been a simple farmer who had lived with his mother and had always done his best to abide by God's commandments. One day in the outside world and he had degenerated into a murderer, a fool and a coward.

So this was what his mother had been trying to tell him! The Evil lurked everywhere. And it was so seductive! He had let himself be fooled, let himself become Satan's henchman by giving into vengeance. How he had failed her!

He buried Bevon there in the secluded glade on the banks of the Afon Usg. He said several prayers for the man's soul and asked God to overlook some of the sins the thief may have committed in life so that he might enter the Kingdom of Heaven. He even offered his own place in exchange as punishment for being Bevon's murderer but he knew it was a futile gesture. He was doomed to wander the earth with the weight of his sin upon his shoulders.

Afterwards he piled rocks upon the grave and marked it with a wooden cross. The glade was so still and silent and Peredur felt as if everything was watching him, waiting for him to do something. His father's armour lay nearby where Amren was grazing. He understood. He was being given a chance in life to make up for what he had done, and by the Virgin Mary he swore, he would do just that.

Arthur

Construction had begun on the hillfort in earnest. Arthur had dispatched men to fell timbers and had even recruited labour from the local workforce. Many seemed eager to help despite the opposition of their magistrate. They seemed to regard the arrival of Arthur and his teulu with a mixture of curiosity and cautious optimism. The nearness of Aelle's horde had them deeply concerned and, as Arthur had said, a secondary military installation could provide a better defence should the Saeson do the unthinkable and cross the Sabrina.

But on the third day, the unthinkable did happen. Arthur had sent scouts east to take a look at the point where the river narrowed. The Roman colonia of Cair Gloui straddled the Sabrina and was home to a rather small and destitute population. Originally built to settle veterans of Rome's legions, those venerable warriors had long since passed on, and their descendants were now farmers with little experience in warfare.

The scouts returned with news that the Saeson were on the move. A large force had descended upon Cair Gloui and the inhabitants had fled into the countryside in terror.

"They have crossed the river and are now camped on its north bank," said Cundelig. "Hundreds of them."

"Do you think they intend to march on Cair Guenta?" Arthur asked him.

"Most likely. They are armed for war."

"Then we must drive them back before they penetrate any further. Relay my orders! Saddle the horses! We move out before noon."

The lightning-quick mobilisation of the teulu left the labourers who were working on the hillfort gawping about themselves, unsure of what to do. Arthur had no time to leave any orders in his absence; construction on the fort would have to be picked up when they returned. *If* they returned. The Saeson were notoriously lacking in cavalry and that gave the Britons the edge but Cundelig had said there were hundreds of them. How outnumbered were they?

As they skirted Cair Guenta, Arthur sent messengers to King Ynyr to warn him of the approaching threat. He was still unsure of what Ynyr thought of a northern teulu encamped in his kingdom and there wasn't time to find out.

The lands surrounding the mouth of the Afon Sabrina were dense with forest. That was alright for Cundelig and his scouts on their fleet horses, but a large teulu tramping along the road was slow and vulnerable to ambush.

Arthur sent out a vanguard led by Cei. Any sign of the enemy and Arthur could count on Cei to charge. Stealth was impossible with so many men. Hit them hard and hit them fast, those were their orders. Arthur would bring up the rear as quickly as he could at the first sign of trouble.

Trouble was sighted soon enough. The first Arthur heard of it was the blowing of horns from the vanguard.

"Cei has found them!" Arthur cried, kicking Hengroen into a gallop. "Follow me close! Prepare for combat!"

They thundered down the road and found Cei and his company not far off, looking bewildered.

"What happened?" Arthur demanded, reigning Hengroen in.

"We saw a column of their infantry," Cei replied, "idly heading down the road towards us. At the first sight of us, they turned tail and fled back the way they had come. We chased them but they cut off into the forest before we could split a single skull."

"Trying to lure us into an ambush," said Arthur. "You did well to stick to the road. Our horses can't pass through this foliage without becoming divided and isolated."

"Do we continue?"

"Aye, we have no choice. We can't start heading off into the forest looking for them. If they want us, then they must come to us."

They continued onwards with Cei leading the van out for a second time. The men were nervous. Trees grew close on either side of the road and they knew now that the enemy was near. Of all the places to ambush a column of cavalry, this was the perfect spot.

Arthur was worried he was a fool for pushing on, knowing that the inevitable was just around the corner. But he could not turn back. The Saeson had crossed the river. They were in his territory now and he could not leave them to rove unchecked. They had promised the people of Guenta their protection. To return without blood on their swords would damage their reputation irrevocably.

Again, the sound of Cei's horns reached them through the stillness of the forest and again Arthur brought up the rear expecting to come upon Cei's company under attack. But, once more, he found them idle on the road, horses panting and foamy-flanked.

Cei was furious. "Why don't the bastards make their move? All this cat-and-mouse nonsense!"

They were near the banks of the Afon Sabrina now. Through the trees they could see the small settlement that had sprung up on the northern bank. No smoke rose from the thatched roofs; those cold hearths had been abandoned many days ago. Beyond, the Roman bridge spanned the sluggish waters and the walls of Cair Gloui could be seen in the distance. Dust churned up by the retreating Saeson hung in the air.

"Do you know, I do believe they are trying to lure us across the river?" Arthur said to his men.

"I think you are right, sir," Beduir replied. "Do we pursue?"

"No. This ruse had a purpose and I will not ride blindly into enemy territory. Besides, if Aurelianus is still alive then I won't do anything to put his life in danger. No, these Sais dogs will have to do better than that to draw us into open combat. We ride back to Cair Legion. There is something altogether unsavoury about this business."

Arthur's suspicions were confirmed when they rode into sight of Cair Legion. Smoke rose in a column and hung in a fug over the town.

"Something burns!" said Cei.

"It's coming from the hillfort!" said Beduir.

They rode at a fast gallop across the fields but Arthur knew it was too late. He had been tricked. They all had been. In their absence somebody had put the torch to the wooden foundations of his new hillfort. There was nothing left. Rage boiled inside him.

"Do not dismount," he told his captains. "We ride into town."

"What, all of us?" asked Gualchmei.

"Every last one of us," he replied firmly. "Carry the dragon standard before us and carry it high. I want all to see us coming. Nectovelius most of all."

The entire town flocked around them as they made their way up the main street, eager to see what these mad northerners were up to now. Arthur led them right up to the iron gate of the magistrate's villa. Within the courtyard, several guards who had previously been playing a game of dice on an upturned barrel scrambled to their feet in alarm at the appearance of the approaching warriors and rushed to pick up their spears.

"Open the gates in the name of Arthur, Penteulu of Venedotia!" bellowed Cei at the top of his voice.

At this, more guards stumbled out of a small barrack block clutching their weapons and joining their comrades in a sloppy defensive line behind the gate, their alarmed faces comical under their dull helmets.

"I don't think they're going to let us in," said Gualchmei in mock outrage.

With a motion from Arthur, Cei and Beduir advanced upon the gate and tied ropes around the iron railings. They tied the other ends of the ropes to their saddles. As they urged their horses on a few steps, the ropes pulled taught and the whole gate was plucked from its stone pillars and came crashing to the ground.

The magistrate's guards looked on in helpless horror as Arthur and his companions trotted into the courtyard and dismounted. Cei handed the reigns of his horse to a terrified guard and smiled at him.

"We won't be a minute," he said and the man and his comrades looked on as the strangers disappeared into the villa.

Terrified servants directed them to the stout, oak door of the magistrate's office and Arthur walked up to it and hammered on it three times. There was the panicked sound of shuffling feet within and then silence. Cei turned to him.

"Arthur?"

"Yes please, Cei."

Cei hefted a large war-axe which he had brought especially for the occasion down from its shoulder strap and swung it at the door with mighty force. After three blows the door buckled on its hinges and fell inwards with a loud *boom*. Arthur strode into the room. Nectovelius, who had chosen to confront the intruders sitting at his desk as if interrupted in some administrative task, exploded in rage.

"You have no right to burst in here, you heathen oafs! Have you no sense of decency?"

Cei and Beduir marched around his desk to stand on either side of him and, gripping one arm each, heaved the magistrate out of his seat and hauled him into the centre of the room where they deposited him roughly on his knees. Arthur walked around the desk and took a seat in the governor's recently vacated chair.

"Magistrate Nectovelius," he said. "I am relieving you of your office."

"By what authority?" demanded the magistrate, still on his knees.

"I need no authority to oust a tyrant and a traitor," replied Arthur.

"But you can't do this!" the magistrate protested. "You are just a bunch of northern bandits and thugs no better than the Saeson! This is robbery! Kidnapping! I am King Ynyr's man and you shall answer to him for your crimes!"

"Yes, I've been meaning to have a discussion with him on the administration of his kingdom," said Arthur. "And I'm sure he will be interested to know what you've been doing with the power and position he entrusted you with."

"Look at this," said Marcus, who had been rifling through the piles of papers that littered the governor's desk. "Trade invoices. And look where the supplies have been going. He's been selling food and weapons to the Saeson!"

"I may sell to whomever I like!" squeaked the magistrate. "You can't possibly understand the situation here!"

"I understand that you are a fat merchant who hides behind the position of magistrate," bellowed Arthur. "And I recognise you for a traitor and a coward!"

The magistrate scrambled to his feet and pawed at his robes, trying to arrange himself into some form of respectability. "*You* dare to call me traitor?" he answered. "You, the son of a northern cattle-herder! Insolent whelp! I will not take orders from you and neither shall this town! We have seen your like before and we have seen them meet their end!"

No doubt the magistrate would have continued his tirade had not Cei, at a glance from Arthur, seized the man with his powerful arms and marched him over to the window and hoisted him up. A brief look of terror crossed Nectovelius's ruddy face as he seemed to hover in the air before Cei sent him tumbling out.

They heard his body hit the tiled roof below with a tremendous crash and the people in the street looked up to see their former magistrate roll off the edge of the roof in a shower of tiles to land with a sickening crunch on the paved street.

"Perhaps he had some courage after all," said Beduir, peering out of the window at the bloody mess below. "I would have expected him to grovel at your feet rather than insult you."

"Brave or stupid," said Arthur, still sitting in the magistrate's chair. "These people are soft and unused to violence. That will soon change."

"What are your plans?" asked Claudius.

"Cair Legion shall be our base of operations for the time being," replied Arthur. "We can billet the men in the old Roman barrack blocks while work on the hillfort continues. And I want to set up some kind of training camp for new recruits."

"Are you thinking of expanding the teulu?" Cei asked.

"What we saw on the outskirts of Cair Gloui was but a reconnaissance force. Our enemy has far greater numbers. We need some kind of centre for attracting new warriors. Send out the word, offers of glory and plunder, that sort of thing."

"The old Roman arena might be a good place for it," said Beduir. "Big open space, plenty of seats for spectators. We could hold tournaments there maybe."

"Good idea," replied Arthur. "Cei and Caradog shall be in charge of that. Gualchmei, take a group of men and investigate the granaries. Find out how much food we have. Then send out some foraging parties."

As his captains set about their duties, Arthur sank back in the magistrate's chair and poured himself a cup of Nectovelius's wine. He sipped it slowly and looked around at the cracked walls and stacks of parchment that littered the room. He could hear the cawing of gulls wheeling over the Sabrina Sea and the bustle of a town resuming its business after the brief interruption. He smiled. This place would do nicely.

Peredur

Anything Peredur had previously imagined about towns was instantly dismissed from his mind as he approached Cair Legion. The whole busy mass of buildings looked like a cancerous growth amid the serene countryside. The River Usg was an oozing slither of muck and slime. The splendour of the Roman architecture had decayed into crumbling plaster and dirt-streaked masonry.

The first thing that hit Peredur's senses as he entered the town was the smell. The scent of freshly baked bread carried on the wind, tantalising his nostrils. Cooking meat and smoked fish lingered in the air making his empty stomach rumble in complaint. But there was also the unmistakable stench of human and animal filth, sweaty, unwashed bodies and decomposing waste, souring the air with its pungency. The river slithered past shabby houses, a thick, green scum clinging to its surface giving off a stagnant odour made all the more palpable by the midday sun.

Town life was an utterly new experience for Peredur. He was totally unused to the hot press of human bodies and found himself apologising to everyone who bumped into him as he dragged Amren down the mud-caked central street. Beggars pawed at him for scraps of food and various street dealers tried to sell him unusual items; jewellery, clothes, tools, religious artefacts carven from wood, dried fruit and preserved meat. Two women, their faces brightly painted, approached him, grinning through the gaps in their teeth. One of them pulled down the top of her tunica, displaying a pair of plump breasts which she proceeded to stroke and caress. Aghast, Peredur staggered backwards, bumping into Amren before hurrying along on his way, leaving the two women muttering behind him.

In desperation, he resorted to asking passers-by if they knew of Arthur and where to find him.

"Shove off!" said the first man, elbowing his way past.

The second and third attempts yielded little better.

An old man sitting in the shade of a wine shop chuckled at him. "Come to try out for his teulu have you? You youngsters are all the same. So quick to get yourselves killed. Never seen this town so busy since them northerners came. Every young lad for miles around has descended on us over the last few days. Off to fight the Saeson they say. Off to save Albion from the heathens! What tickles me is that this Arthur is little more than a pagan barbarian himself! I tell you, it's a fine state of affairs we're in when a northern savage has to come down here to fight our battles for us!"

The man grinned and squinted at Peredur under his hand which he had held up to shield his eyes from the sun. "Well then lad, I suppose there'll be no stopping you whatever I say, same as the rest of them. I daresay you can find your heathen hero in the old amphitheatre. Word has it he's testing the mettle of you would-be warriors in the very place the Romans used to feed young men to the slaughter in the pagan times. Not much has changed is all I can say. Turn right down the street that crosses this one and you'll spot the amphitheatre. What's left of it that is, and that's not much."

Peredur thanked the old man and went on his way, hearing him muttering under his breath at the foolishness of youth.

The amphitheatre was not hard to find, in fact Peredur needed only to seek out the crowds who swarmed about the circular structure. The arena had eight entrances, several of which were blocked by rubble. The walls were in the same shabby state as the rest of the town and parts of it had crumbled away completely. People filled the seats that rose tier upon tier around the circle of hard-packed earth that had once soaked up the blood of gladiatorial combat to watch the spectacles. It was as if the Romans had never left.

Peredur headed down one of the entrances and stopped in the dark tunnel to don his father's armour. As he walked out into the light of the arena, a group of men turned to stare in startled surprise at the extraordinary figure who strode proudly towards them. Their faces could not have been much different if one of the Caesars had returned from the grave to stalk their streets.

Peredur beamed with pride. His father's armour was a little loose-fitting but he was sure his muscles would fill it out once he began his training. He smiled inwardly at the townsfolk's expressions of surprise. He bet they rarely saw true warriors. He remembered his first day beyond the stream when he had set eyes upon Arthur's army. Now he was one of them. Well, almost. He hoped that the gaping children that were tugging at their parent's tunicas and pointing with bulging eyes were experiencing that same feeling of uplifting awe that he had on that day.

The sound of wood clacking on wood reached his ears along with the exciting chattering of the spectators. Several groups were arrayed around the arena, each demonstrating a particular skill; spear, sword or archery. Stern faced men who were presumably Arthur's warriors were watching them keenly. The townsfolk who filled the seats of the amphitheatre were yelling out encouragement to friends and family members. When a potential warrior was deemed good enough, one of the observers would hand him a wooden token and direct him to one end of the arena where many men stood already looking pleased with themselves.

Peredur watched the activities for a while, wondering which he should try out for first. He was good with a bow but he did want to spend his life at the back of Arthur's ranks giving support to the true warriors who fought out in front. Spear throwing too was an option, but again it was hardly the glamorous role he had imagined himself filling whenever he listened to Garth's tales about mounted men charging into battle, slaying enemies on either flank, hooves churning the earth and banners fluttering in the wind.

But there did not appear to by any category for horsemanship. Not that he had a horse to enter with anyway. He had a feeling that old Amren would not do much charging into battle no matter how many carrots he fed him.

He tied the donkey's reins to one of the metal rings that were fixed into the circular wall. As he stepped away he tripped over the reins and fell flat on his belly with a crash. Embarrassment burned his cheeks and he heard several spectators in the nearest seats roar with laughter.

Scrambling hastily to his feet, he picked up his shield and looked about. *Good.* None of Arthur's men appeared to have noticed. He did his best to look unaffected as he strode over to the group of men who were sparring with wooden foils. They turned to stare at him as he approached and he recovered some of his lost pride as he saw what they were wearing. Most of them had no armour at all and those that did wore crude constructions of boiled leather that only protected the most vital parts of their bodies. A few had swords, but again they were simple affairs and paled in comparison to his father's gold hilted blade.

He joined their ranks and watched as a youth about the same age as himself sparred with one of Arthur's warriors. Their wooden blades clicked and clacked as they struck and parried, fighting for space on the small circle of ground. The youth showed some skill and held his own against the seasoned warrior but even Peredur could see that the older man was holding back, waiting.

Then it came. The boy took a wrong footing and then, quick as lightening, the warrior slashed out, knocking the wooden sword from his opponent's grip. The disarmed boy ducked a whistling blow and rolled in the dirt, scrambling out of the man's line of attack. He made for his weapon where it lay on the ground but was too slow. The warrior's boot caught him in the belly, sending him sliding across the earth, doubled over in agony. When he opened his eyes, the man was holding the dull point of his blade over his exposed jugular, a victorious grin on his face.

The small group clapped in polite respect as the victor helped the beaten boy to his feet.

"You show some skill but you must learn to choose your moment. Don't risk attacking if you are unsure of your footing."

The boy nodded in appreciation, still wincing from the kick to the ribs.

"These skills will be honed in battle; the true testing ground of any warrior," continued the man. He handed him a wooden disc engraved with some design Peredur was unable to make out. "Go and join the other recruits over there. In a while someone will take you to the fort on the hill where your service in Arthur's teulu will begin."

The youth beamed with joy, his aching belly forgotten. He ran to collect his belongings before hurrying off to join his new comrades.

"Who's next?" asked the warrior, twirling his sword around expertly in his grip.

Several men raised their arms but the man's gaze fixed on Peredur, a smile forming in the corner of his mouth.

"What about you?" he asked. "That's some impressive equipment you have there. Care to put it to the test along with yourself?"

Peredur nodded eagerly and, feeling everyone's eyes upon him, stepped forward into the circle. Before he was ready the man tossed a wooden foil to him. Peredur tried to catch it but fumbled and dropped it to the ground.

"Can't even catch a sword!" bellowed a voice in great mirth. The group turned to see an ogre of a man stride towards them, bull-necked and arms bulging like tree trunks. Sweat glistened on a shaved head and ruddy complexion. "A warrior's got to have good reflexes. What's your name boy?"

"Peredur, sir."

"I'm Cei," said the big man snatching the sword from his companion's hand, taking his place in the circle opposite Peredur. "And you might say that I'm Arthur's second in command. Quality control, that's what I'm in charge of today. I'm here to see that no rubbish gets through the nets and into Arthur's ranks. Because let me tell you boy, we need warriors to fight the Saeson, not peasants who fancy a bit of looting. Where did you steal that armour?"

"I didn't steal it," replied Peredur in a clipped tone. "It was my father's."

"Looks more like your great-grandfather's," mocked the big man. "I only asked because you clearly don't know how to wear it or keep it in good condition."

Peredur stiffened. "I am the son of a great warrior and I hope to become one like him someday. I wear his armour to honour his memory."

"Then why are you wearing his breastplate back to front?"

Peredur risked a quick glance down at his chest and paled in horror. The man was right. Smooth iron greeted his view instead of the moulded muscular form that now adorned his back. His face reddening, he struggled to unbuckle his armour, fiddling with the straps while Cei and the other men howled with laughter.

"Don't bother to put it back on," said Cei, wiping a tear from his eye. "A real warrior doesn't rely on fancy armour to win battles. He relies on his wits and his skill. Come, fight me!"

Peredur placed his armour upon the ground and removed his helmet. He bent to pick up the wooden foil and had barely straitened before Cei swung at him, knocking the blade from his hand and planting a heavy boot in the centre of his unprotected chest. He stumbled backwards, the wind knocked out of him.

Cei laughed and helped him up. "Try again, and this time be ready."

Now Cei waited for Peredur to attack him. Testing the weight of the foil, Peredur lunged forward, hacking and slashing at his opponent in a whirlwind of energy. Cei blocked every single blow effortlessly. Once Peredur's energy was spent, Cei let him rest his hands on his knees, panting and heaving for air. Cei yawned in a mock fashion of boredom, provoking snorts of mirth from the group. In anger, Peredur rose up and took a savage swipe at Cei only to sprawl forward as the big man stepped neatly out of the way, catching his left forearm as he did so.

Peredur grimaced in pain as Cei twisted his trapped arm around behind him and held him in a tight hold so that he was utterly powerless. The warrior leaned close and spoke into his ear so that he could smell his hot breath.

"Useless, boy, utterly useless. I've seen pig farmers show more skill with a sword than you. Warrior's son? Pah!"

And with that, he released Peredur from his grip and sent him sprawling with a stout kick to the rear. Peredur sprung up and turned on his tormentor, whirling his blade for one final attack. But Cei was ready and in two stokes knocked the foil from his grip. The third stroke was a brutal uppercut that clipped the underside of his jaw. Stars spinning behind his eyelids and blood spurting from behind his teeth where he had bitten his tongue, Peredur fell backwards and landed heavily on the hard earth. He was just conscious enough to hear Cei's stinging words in his buzzing ears.

"Get lost, peasant! If your father was of the same stock as you, then I'm not surprised he is dead and his armour is left to rust in the hands of his incompetent son!"

Peredur rolled onto his belly, sick with pain and emotional turmoil. All the fighting spirit had drained from his body like the blood that oozed sluggishly from his chin and mouth. The only thing he could concentrate on was getting away, away from the arena, away from the humiliation and the pain. Away from himself.

He crawled to where he had left his father's armour, knowing that everyone was watching him. Somehow he summoned the energy and the courage to stand up and lift the armour. It felt ten times heavier than he remembered.

The group turned their attention to the next contestant as Peredur limped away, shamefaced and broken. He untethered Amren and together they wandered out of the entrance they had come in through.

Nobody in the streets of Cair Legion noticed the pain in the eyes of the young boy with the bleeding chin as he pushed his way through the crowds and out of the town with his faithful donkey trailing behind. It was a busy day and he was just one boy vanishing into a world of thousands.

PART III

In spite of that, Trystan said nothing; and Arthur sang the fourth englyn:
"Trystan of exceedingly prudent manners,
love thy kindred, it will not bring thee loss;
coldness grows not between one kinsman and another."
- Ystori Trystan (trans. Tom Peete Cross)

Guenhuifar

Barely a month had passed before the Great Hall of Cadwallon's Lys was prepared for another feast. This time it was to celebrate the thirteenth birthday of Cadwallon's eldest son and heir, Prince Maelcon.

Gifts arrived from all of Venedotia's sub-kings although, unlike Arthur's inauguration ceremony, their actual presence was requested rather than required. Several of Cadwallon's closer associates made their way to Ynys Mon for the second time that year and these included his brother Owain, King Mor of Rumaniog, King Efiaun of Dunauding and of course, the venerable old King Etern of Eternion along with the daughter who was Maelcon's betrothed.

Princess Tarren of Eternion was a fair, marginally pretty girl but there was a doe-eyed simplicity in her eyes. Far from the quick cunning of Queen Meddyf, the future queen of Venedotia seemed to exude dullness of wit and Guenhuifar could well imagine that this rankled with Cadwallon as much as the fact that the union had been a condition for Etern's support in the civil war.

Tarren and Maelcon sat together at the high table and did their best to ignore each other. Guenhuifar couldn't blame Maelcon's reluctance at being forced to marry his own aunt but he was truly no great catch himself, future Pendraig or no, with his surly nature and poor manners. He had to be called to table like an errant child and practically prised from the company of his boorish companions who were enjoying watching a wrestling match outside. Nevin and Seraun were there but were no longer on speaking terms, Guenhuifar had noticed. Their scandalous affair had been cut short by something and many assumed that Queen Meddyf had finally intervened and reprimanded her handmaid for carrying on with one of her son's playmates. But Guenhuifar was of a mind that it was more due to Seraun's womanising ways. It was no secret that he had been sniffing around other prospects and he didn't limit himself to noble stock either. More than one serving maid had been surreptitiously accused of spreading her legs for him.

"Guenhuifar!" called out Queen Elen of Rhos as she moved across the crowded hall.

Guenhuifar shuddered. Of all the ladies at court she had been forced to associate herself with, Elen was the one who irritated her the most. Queen Meddyf was agreeable and her handmaids – even Nevin – were tolerable but Elen was a wet blanket, always finding something to complain about.

"Isn't the sea rough for this time of year?" said Elen. "I was as sick as a dog on the way over here. But I suppose you took the ferry and were spared the ordeal of a coastal voyage."

"Actually, I have been here since Calan Mai," said Guenhuifar. "There is not much call for me at Cair Cunor and I am quite grateful for the chance to spend some time with my father and sister."

"Oh, silly me, I had forgotten that this is your real home. Have you heard from that husband of yours?"

"I have not, although the season is still young."

"It is so dreadful when they are away at war, isn't it? I am just glad that my own husband's campaigning days are behind him. He may only be good for drinking and singing these days but at least I can keep an eye on him." she threw a wink at King Owain who was talking to Guenhuifar's father nearby.

"What's that?" Owain said, overhearing. He moved to slip a hand around his wife's slender waist. "I wouldn't be too sure of that, my little pretty. Arthur is the envy of many a man, riding off to war after war. I have half a mind to ride south myself to join the excitement."

"You shall do nothing of the kind," Elen replied. "The teulu was formed so that kings like you would remain where they belong. At home with their wives."

"Even so," said Owain, "I miss the old days and hate to think that my last battle was behind me. I would give much to be alongside your husband now, Guenhuifar. The thrill of battle is something no woman can understand." At this he gulped down the last of the mead in his cup and stifled a belch.

"Oh, I am sorry my dear," Elen said, touching Guenhuifar's arm gently. "You must be missing him awfully and we stand here talking about battles and war. No more! Tonight is a night for celebration!" She snapped her fingers at a servant girl who hurried over to refill her cup.

King Etern was enjoying himself. As father of the future bride, he was already accepting congratulations from sycophantic nobles. Cadwallon and Maelcon watched from the high table with rigid faces.

Guenhuifar slept uncharacteristically late the following morning. It was Guenhuifach who woke her with her clattering about in the main hall as she made breakfast. She looked relieved to see Guenhuifar emerge from her chamber, rubbing the sleep from her eyes.

"Oh, good," she said. "You're up."

Guenhuifar had the feeling that her sister's business had been intended to wake her. "What's up?" she asked, sitting down at the table.

"There was an attempt on King Owain's life last night," Guenhuifach said, placing a bowl of porridge before her.

"What?" Guenhuifar exclaimed, ignoring the steaming oats before her.

"An assassin sneaked into his chamber while he was dead drunk. Elen apparently awoke and her screaming saved her husband's life although she was wounded by the assassin. He fled but Cadwallon's guards shot him down. The whole lys is in an uproar! I'm surprised you were able to sleep through it."

"Where is father?"

"In the Great Hall with Cadwallon and Meddyf."

Guenhuifar rose and returned to her chamber to dress herself, her breakfast forgotten. She headed outdoors towards the hall. Upon entering, she found her father on his way out, his face grave.

"You have heard?" he asked.

"Yes. Is Queen Elen all right?"

"More or less. She threw herself over Owain and the assassin's knife caught her shoulder. Her screaming woke Owain and he was able to disarm the intruder."

"Guenhuifach said that he was shot trying to flee."

"Yes, that is what I have just been discussing with the king. He gave strict orders for the assassin to be taken alive. Somebody felled him with an arrow in his back but nobody knows who it was. We have interrogated the guards who were sent out and none of them have owned up to it. Cadwallon is livid."

"I imagine he is. The name of the assassin's employer would have been wrung from him one way or another…"

"There's more. A ring was found on the dead man's body. A ring with the seal of Eternion."

Guenhuifar was speechless for a moment as this sank in. "But surely Etern would not be so stupid as to…"

"We don't know," her father said. "Cadwallon has ordered Etern and his entourage to be confined to their quarters."

"He's keeping them prisoner?"

"He has no choice. The evidence implicates him."

He left to address the people outside. Guenhuifar entered the hall and approached the dais where Cadwallon and Meddyf sat with Owain. All had grave faces.

"Ah, Guenhuifar," said Meddyf. "You have heard the news? If only your husband were here. We would be in a much better position should matters deteriorate any further."

"Do you really think it will come to war, my queen?" Guenhuifar asked.

"God forbid it!" said Meddyf. "But with the teulu gone, we are vulnerable."

"Etern's followers would not dare attempt an attack while I hold their king and princess prisoner," said Cadwallon.

Meddyf rose. "I need some air," she said. "Guenhuifar, shall we walk together and leave the men to their talking?"

"Yes, my lady," said Guenhuifar.

They exited the hall through the door at the rear of the dais and followed the wall of the building around to its eastern side where the sun warmed it.

"What are your thoughts on the matter, my dear?" said Meddyf.

"I find it hard to believe that Etern would try to have Owain killed over a mere quarrel," Guenhuifar replied.

"You think there is a third party trying to lay the blame at Etern's door?"

"The ring found on the attacker's body just seems a bit too convenient for me. And then there is the unexplained killing of the assassin, effectively silencing him. Somebody might be trying to cause a rift between the kingdoms."

"I'm inclined to agree. But I cannot for the life of me imagine who would wish to do us such harm."

"If this situation does indeed lead to war, then whoever it is may seek to capitalise on it and manoeuvre their way onto the throne."

"But who?"

"King Cadwaldr would be the prime suspect," said Guenhuifar. "Meriauneth was ruined by the civil war and Cadwaldr surely resents Cadwallon for executing his father."

"Possible," said Meddyf. "There is also King Condruin of Docmaeling to consider. Or his father, rather. Old Elnaw still lives and rules through his son by all accounts. It's certainly understandable if he hates my husband for forcing him to abdicate."

They spotted Elen leaving the guest quarters and waving to them with her uninjured arm. A bandage, spotted with blood, was wrapped around the other.

"Elen!" Meddyf reprimanded her, shortly. "You should not be up and about!"

"Oh, I just couldn't lie around in bed all morning with the servants fussing over me. I haven't slept a wink! I keep seeing that awful man standing over us and the knife in his hand! Oh, gods!" Tears welled in her eyes and she seemed to fold in on herself. Meddyf caught her.

"You must rest, Elen," said Meddyf. "You are perfectly safe now. The man is dead and our husbands will not rest until they find out who sent him."

"But what if they send another assassin to succeed where the first one failed?" said Elen.

"It is not certain that Owain was their true target," said Guenhuifar.

Elen looked at her through her tear-streaked face. "What do you mean? The man knifed me in his attempt to get at my husband!"

"Guenhuifar and I have just been discussing the possibility that the true aim of the attack was to tear a rift between Etern and my husband," said Meddyf. "The ring found on the man's body seems a little too convenient."

"But why?" asked Elen in desperation.

"That is what we must find out," said Guenhuifar.

The day proved to be frustrating and uneventful. Cadwallon and Owain remained in the Great Hall, interrogating every guard who was on duty the previous night. There were so many questions to be asked. How had the assassin got in? How had he known where to find Owain's chamber? And most of all, who had killed him? Guenhuifar had a few questions of her own and she desperately awaited the approach of dusk.

When the evening meal was underway in the Great Hall, she made her excuses and left, her food barely touched. With most people at their meat in the hall or by their own hearths there would be few wandering about the lys's precinct in the waning light of dusk. Now was the time to find out what she could about the mysterious assassin.

The body was being held in one of the outbuildings awaiting burial the following morning. A guard had been placed there during the day but Guenhuifar was pleased to see that he had been called away. She approached the door and turned to make sure she had not been seen before entering.

The small outhouse stank of death. It had been a warm day and the flies had managed to get in. They buzzed angrily at being disturbed and took off into the thatch as Guenhuifar approached the body.

It lay stretched out on the floor of the hut, its pale face ghostlike in the gloom. It wore simple garments; a dark green cloak over leather breeches and a grey woollen tunica. He was a man in his twenties with close-cropped black hair and a fine stubble on his cheeks. An old scar marred the left side of his cheek and half of the ear was missing. His cheekbones and chin seemed prominent. That could have been because he wore the taught, sunken visage of death Guenhuifar was not sure. She hadn't seen many dead bodies before.

There was little else within the small confines of the room save a bench upon which several items had been laid out. Presumably the dead man's belongings. Guenhuifar walked over to the bench and picked over the objects. Whoever the man had been, he had required little in life. There was a leather purse containing a stale crust of bread, a rust-stained tinderbox and some sort of talisman inscribed with a triple spiral motif. Its owner had probably considered it an item of good luck. It hadn't done him much good.

There was no sign of the dagger he had tried to use on Owain, or of King Etern's ring. Both were too valuable to be left lying around in an unguarded hut. But there was another item on the bench that had not belonged to the dead man; a broken arrow with grey goose fletching. Dried blood coated half of the shaft.

Guenhuifar glanced at the dark patch on the dead man's woollen tunica where the arrow had punched through his chest from behind. The arrowhead was missing and the wood was splintered where it had been snapped off. She slipped the broken arrow into a fold in her dress and then, after a moment's consideration, picked up the talisman and hid that away too. She doubted either would be missed. The dagger and the ring had clearly been considered the only evidence worth preserving. These other items were junk and would be either buried with the body or thrown away.

As she left the hut she questioned what she was doing. She felt outraged at what had happened and that surprised her. She looked around at the wooden palisade and the lime-washed buildings, halls and storage huts and remembered how this place had looked not three years ago. She remembered the crumbling ruins and mouldering thatch, home only to the rats and the owls. She remembered the loneliness of childhood but it had been *her* childhood. The buildings may have been repaired, the people may have returned and a king might dwell in the Great Hall but this was *her* home and it always would be.

She had initially found it hard to adjust to the hustle and bustle of the Pendraig's court springing up around her ears but after three years, she felt for the first time in her life, that she was part of a bigger world. The Gaels were gone and her father, who had been a broken man for as long as she had known him, was now a man restored in both body and mind. Prosperity, health and happiness were theirs and now somebody was trying to tear all that down. Somebody wanted war. As if the barbarian hordes that roamed Albion were not enough, some bastard actually wanted another civil war in Venedotia.

Well, she was not going to let that pass. Arthur had his own war to fight in the south but she was not about to fail in her wifely duties by letting the hearth grow cold. If somebody was intent on working evil in Venedotia, she was intent on finding out who and putting a stop to them.

Arthur

Arthur's reorganisation of Cair Legion was going well. The food situation had initially presented something of a problem but there was plenty of game to be had in the surrounding forests and fishing boats brought in a surprisingly large catch from the Sabrina Sea once they had been organised into some sort of efficiency.

King Ynyr had predictably shown up at Cair Legion's gates with a large band of warriors once the news of his ex-magistrate's fate reached Cair Guenta. Arthur had ridden out to meet them and dispel the need for hostilities before inviting him into his villa to talk.

He found Ynyr to be a likeable sort. His family had been part of the old Roman aristocracy for generations and it showed in his dress and manners. He was no more a warrior than Nectovelius had been and Arthur began to wonder why the Saeson had not taken the west years ago. Then he remembered Aurelianus.

"That man was our only hope," said Ynyr glumly. "Without his leadership I fear that the day when we must retreat further west is not far off."

"Retreat to where?" Arthur asked. "To the sea? To Erin? My teulu is outnumbered, it is true, but Britons do not outnumber Saeson in Albion. If only we could unite against them we might stand a chance of survival, even victory."

Ynyr studied Arthur keenly. "I like you, Arthur. You have a positivity about you that we forgot long ago. What would you have of me?"

Arthur set his wine cup down on the small table and leaned in close. "Give me complete command of Cair Legion," he said. "As it was in the old days; a vicus ruled by a military commander. With the fort on the hill and the granaries and barracks full in the town, I can turn Cair Legion into the last British bastion against the Saeson. I need men, as many as you can spare from your own teulu as well as whoever can be recruited from the countryside."

"You intend to march into the Borderlands and attempt to oust the barbarians?"

"Aye, but first I intend to free Aurelianus and restore him to his rank and position as figurehead of the British resistance."

Ynyr looked deep into Arthur's eyes as if trying to see some weakness in his resolve. When he found none, he smiled gently. "Done," he said.

It was too risky to commence a full-scale invasion of the lands across the Sabrina so Arthur called his captains to a meeting in the villa to discuss their options. Claudius began with a brief talk on the defences of Cair Badon.

"These Saeson are not town-dwellers by nature. They are more accustomed to wooden halls and small farming communities. But Cair Badon does have a walled perimeter and we can assume that Cymen will have every gate watched. There may also be small groups of guards in the buildings and farmlands surrounding the town. Getting close will not be easy."

"That is why I propose to send a small group of warriors across the river," said Arthur. "We should be able to reach the walls of Cair Badon undetected."

"We?" asked Cei.

"I intend to lead the party myself," replied Arthur.

This caused a certain amount of outcry from his captains.

"Is that wise?" asked Caradog. "Surely, as Penteulu, you should remain with the bulk of the teulu and not venture off behind enemy lines without protection."

Arthur smiled. "Thank you for your concern, Caradog but the only protection I require is the protection of my friends."

"So we are going with you then?" asked Cei.

Arthur nodded. "The party shall consist of myself, Cei, Beduir, Gualchmei, Cundelig, Guihir and Menw."

"Old friends reunited eh?" said Cei.

"Aye. The same group of warriors who journeyed to Ynys Mon three years ago to retrieve the Cauldron of Rebirth will now rescue Ambrosius Aurelianus from the clutches of the enemy."

"Seven is indeed a fortuitous number," said Menw. "It should bring us luck. If Modron blesses us."

"But as I am sure you remember, Arthur," said Cei, "all did not go exactly to plan on Ynys Mon three years ago."

"No, but we won through all the same," Arthur replied. "As Menw said, luck should be with us once more."

"This is all very well," said Beduir. "But can we please talk tactics? How are we to get through the guards and the barred gates?"

"I have been discussing this with Marcus and Claudius," replied Arthur and he pulled a piece of blank parchment from a stack and dipped a quill in ink. "As you will have heard, Cair Badon was built by the Romans on the site of a sacred spring. This spring was expanded into an elaborate bathing complex with an attached temple." He drew a rough square on the parchment. "This represents the central bath house and this…" he drew another square jutting off from its southern side, "represents a smaller bathhouse. There is a drain that leads from it beneath the town and empties into the river." He drew a long line leading away from the bath house and connected it with a squiggle representing the river. "It is through this drain that I propose to gain entrance. We will then be able to search the city for Aurelianus."

"He is probably being held within the old basilica," said Claudius. "That's the only properly defensible place. It has a gate and a wall so getting in will not be easy."

"And what happens once we free Aurelianus?" Cei asked.

"Caradog will lead the teulu up the banks of the Afon Sabrina and cross it near Cair Gloui, breaking through any enemy lines that might be encamped there. We shall head north and re-join it on the old Roman road that leads to the ruined town of Corinium."

"You are giving me complete command of the teulu?" Caradog asked in astonishment.

Arthur placed his hand on his captain's shoulder. "I know you are up to the task, old friend. Cunor trusted you with his life before either Cei or myself were able to hold a spear."

Caradog smiled, a hint of tears showing in his eyes.

"There is a problem with this plan," said Marcus. "Had you proposed to do this when the Romans were still present at Cair Badon, then no doubt you would succeed. But since they left, the drains have been poorly maintained and the rising water level has flooded the town. Most of the drainage tunnels will be submerged."

"We are good swimmers," said Arthur with a grin.

The following day Arthur and his companions made their way along the northern bank of the Afon Sabrina. They would not try to cross at Cair Gloui in case it was too heavily defended. Instead, Arthur had sent Gualchmei ahead to procure a fishing boat for their purpose.

They descended the banks to the old disused ferry point and saw a small boat with a square white sail bobbing up and down in the water. The horses were taken back to Cair Legion while the companions boarded the small vessel and shoved off, letting the current carry them out into the sweeping curve of the river. The wind caught the sail and Beduir steered them towards the opposite bank which was high and grassy in the distance.

They sailed in silence, each of them contemplating the dangers that awaited them on the other side of the river. The sunlight darkened suddenly as a cloud obscured the sun and Arthur and his friends felt the chill all the more when they remembered their expedition to Ynys Mon three years ago. Once again they were setting off in a boat for hostile shores and the sense of history repeating itself was felt by all of them.

They made landfall and concealed the boat on the mud beneath a rocky bulge in the cliffs. Arthur and his companions set out along the cliff top towards the point where a tributary flowed out into the swelling waters of the Sabrina. As they followed the winding river from its mouth further and further into enemy territory, Arthur began to get a sense of what Ambrosius Aurelianus had been fighting back all these years. The land was in ruins; a ghost land of deserted fields and smouldering villages, all that was left in the wake of Sais looting parties. They saw few farmers or village folk, and those they did see were always on the move. Bands of families bore what few belongings they still owned and carried starving children too sick to even cry anymore. Arthur nearly wept to see the hopelessness in their eyes, the expressions of a beaten people with nowhere else to go, nothing else to do but keep moving, eating what they could poach or steal until the cold hand of death eventually claimed them, one by one.

Aurelianus had been their protector, their banner of hope against the black tide that had been lapping at their shores all their lives. With him gone their worst fears had been realised as the full impact of the Sais savagery had hit them. The sights hardened Arthur's soul and made him feel all the more resolute that their mission must succeed.

Darkness had fallen by the time the small group rounded a bend in the river and set their sights on

Cair Badon. Deserted houses scattered the fields that surrounded the dirty white walls of the town. Collapsed roofs and crumbling masonry were all that was left of a once thriving community. A trackway followed the river and led into the town through the large, square gatehouse with its rounded archway. A winking light could be seen atop the gatehouse indicating the presence of a guard.

"We should enter the river here," said Arthur, "rather than thread our way through the outlying community. We don't know how many Saeson might be crawling about the outskirts."

They were near a crumbling old bridge that crossed the river to the farmland on the opposite side. The water was cold, even for spring and the current was surprisingly strong. Up to their middles in the river, the seven companions slowly made their way upstream, clutching at the moss and dank earth of the riverbank for support, out of sight from any watchful eyes in the houses beyond.

"How far to the drain, Arthur?" asked Cei in a whisper.

"We should be nearing it soon. Ah! Here we are!"

The drain was larger than Arthur had thought but Marcus had been right; the level of the water had risen so much that only the top of the drain was above the water. There was a tiny gap between its surface and the red brickwork, just enough to allow the companions to breathe as they made their way through the drain and into the bath house. Arthur reached down and felt about in the scummy water that flowed out of the drain. His hands grasped some sturdy metal bars set into the brickwork.

"Damn!" he hissed. "A grate is blocking the entrance!"

"Let me see," said Cei, wading forward to inspect the blockage. He tugged at the iron bars and they loosened just a fraction. He unstrapped his axe from his back and wedged its head between the iron and the stone. "This should do the trick." Using his axe as a lever, Cei heaved with all his might until the veins throbbed in his temples. With a sudden crunch, the grate gave way, forced from its fitting in the brickwork. Cei heaved it away from the tunnel and let it sink down to the riverbed. "After you, Arthur," he said with a grin.

The tunnel was too low to stand in but by crouching, the companions could waddle their way along, their necks craned upwards to reach the small pocket of air between the water and the curve of the ceiling. It was a world of total blackness. The water was still and stagnant, its flow long since cut off, indicating a further blockage.

Arthur could feel the slimy brickwork under his fingertips as he inched himself along at the head of the party and every so often, he felt his boots brush past unknown objects in the darkness. He did not want to imagine what sort of debris had collected in the tunnel over the years. Occasionally his face brushed against the ceiling and he gagged as the cold, slimy tendrils of algae tickled his mouth and nostrils.

The tunnel seemed to go on forever, its gaping darkness suffocating the thoughts of the party. The only sound was the sloshing of the water and heavy breathing. They did not talk, their concentration fully occupied by the task of keeping their faces above the stinking water, desperately hoping that it would soon come to an end.

Arthur felt the ceiling slope down to touch the water – a result of the uneven brickwork – and in a panic, he realised that they had run out of air space. He stopped and struggled for space as Cei bumped into him from behind.

"Stop, damn you, all of you stop!" he spluttered. "The water meets the ceiling here. We are cut off!"

"How close are we?" Cei asked. "Perhaps we could swim the distance."

"I'll check," said Arthur, "but give me some space first!"

There was some sloshing about as the men backed up a little to give their leader some room. Arthur took a deep breath and sunk his head below the stagnant water. Pushing with his feet he worked his way along for a bit, reaching out at the ceiling with his hands, feeling for air. There was none and his lungs began to ache so he turned back and resurfaced.

"Well?" asked Cei.

"No good," Arthur replied, peeling a slimy strand of algae from his face.

"Then we're stuck."

"We have come quite a way so far," said Menw from behind Cei. "I would guess that we are near the bath house."

They were silent in the darkness whilst they considered this. The bath house may very well be a few yards away but if they found the tunnel blocked they might not have enough air in their lungs to make it back.

"It's worth a shot," said Arthur. "As Menw says, we have already come so far. But we must move fast and efficiently. We cannot afford to hinder each other or cause a bottleneck. I shall go first. Cei, you count to five and follow me and so on. Is that clear to everyone?"

Six voices murmured their confirmation in the blackness. Arthur then filled his lungs as deeply as he could and dived.

He pawed at the walls and kicked with his legs, propelling himself forward as fast as he could through the murky water. On and on he swam, every so often rising to the ceiling to see if that pocket of air had miraculously reappeared but he was met only with the hard, clammy brickwork, still submerged. His lungs soon began to crave air, and he could feel his heart beat in his chest under the strain but still the tunnel stretched on.

Suddenly he bumped into something. He tried to manoeuvre around it but couldn't and he was hit by the horrific realisation that the way was blocked. He desperately clawed at the debris that had piled up in the tunnel. His lungs were bursting and he was acutely aware of the fact that Cei and the rest of his companions were swimming up on his heels and would soon be upon him, colliding in the small confines of the tunnel.

Slimy, half decayed things slipped through his fingers as he dug. He felt loose bricks, caked with foulness move under his fingers and clouds of dislodged dirt and grit rise up to prickle his face.

Somehow he managed to push his way through the blockage and he rose up, flailing for air. His face broke the water and he gasped at that sweet, glorious air.

He was no longer in the tunnel that was for sure. The sound was totally different. An ominous, cavern-like echo greeted his ears indicating a much larger chamber. He wiped the muck and slime from his face and bobbed up and down in the water, gazing up at the walls and ceiling of the room he had resurfaced in.

It was like the bath houses he had seen in Cair Legion and Deverdoeu but in a much greater state of decay. The walls and square pillars were thick with slime, obscuring the red paint and white plaster that had once decorated the chamber. The water level was much higher than it should have been and the edges of the bath itself were far beneath him in the flooded room. Moonlight shone in through the broken lattices set high up in the walls.

Cei rose to the surface next to him with a burst of water and a loud bout of coughing. One by one the rest of his comrades resurfaced, gasping for air and pulling slimy algae from their faces. They swam over to the entrance to the chamber and felt the floor rise up under their knees in a series of steps. They staggered to their feet and leant against the grimy walls for support. The water nearly came up to their middles.

They waded out of the eastern baths and into the main chamber. The sight that greeted them knocked them all speechless. The chamber was enormous. Twelve mammoth pillars rose up out of a murky sheet of water to support a cavernous roof. Ivy coiled up the pillars, serpentinely reaching for the crossbeams and timbers that hid in the darkness above. The roof was damaged in many places and the moonlight shone in, reflecting off the black water. The whole place was a temple of stillness and silence; a ghost of its former self when the people of the town had once frolicked in its water, laughing and splashing. Now nothing was left of those days but the grimy walls and pillars of this ruined building.

"Did you ever imagine such a place?" said Beduir in awe, looking up at the tendrils of plant life that dangled from the high roof, perfectly frozen in the silver moonlight.

"Keep away from the centre of the room," said Menw. "Paving stones line the great bath but one wrong step and you might find yourself taking a deep plunge."

"Which way is out?" asked Cei.

"The sacred spring is just through there," said Arthur pointing between the pillars to a doorway on the other side of the room. "We can get out into the temple precinct and then move on to the basilica."

They waded their way along the colonnades, watching their footing as they went, ever wary of the massive sunken pit in the centre of the room that lay hidden from view. The doorway led to a corridor and three windows were set in the northern wall, the water nearly reaching their sills. They looked in on a vaulted chamber that enclosed an irregular-shaped pool. Plinths and statues surrounded it, festooned with plants.

"The sacred spring," said Menw. "People used to stand here and toss offerings to Sulis Minerva through these windows. Beyond lies the doorway to the temple precinct."

They lifted themselves up onto the sill of the semi-circular central window and slid down into the water on the other side. Arthur looked up at the statue of the goddess to whom the baths had been devoted. She looked little different to her image in the temple of the villa in which he had found *Caledbulc*. Unconsciously, his hand dropped to its hilt as if in honour of the goddess who looked down on them, her face covered by the moss of ages.

They passed between the plinths and made their way through the doorway into the moonlit courtyard beyond. To the left of them rose the steps to the temple itself; a ruin now with much of its masonry robbed to refortify other parts of the town. The great altar stone still remained in the courtyard.

Beduir unwrapped the oil-skin package of spears and handed them out while Gualchmei strung his bow and uncovered his quiver. Arthur led them through the columned entrance of the temple precinct to the street beyond.

"The arena lies ahead," he told his comrades, "and next to it is the forum and basilica."

As they rounded the corner they found themselves facing a group of Saeson coming down the street towards them.

"Have at it!" cried Cei and before the enemy could comprehend what they had seen, Beduir's spear whickered through the air and skewered one of them in the chest.

Arthur drew *Caledbulc* and swung it at a charging Sais, cleaving his large, round shield down to its boss.

The man dropped it and slashed at Arthur with one of the long-bladed knives the Saeson were known for. Arthur had the greater reach and *Caledbulc* split his skull like a ripe fruit.

Cei dodged an axe-blow from a heavy set man and waited until his opponent was off balance, sidestepping to connect his own axe with the back of his helm, cleaving through iron and bone. Feeling naked and vulnerable without their shields, the Britons used their lighter footings and agility to battle the guards who, although smaller in number, refused to give up any ground.

Beduir rammed his sword point into the throat of one of the warriors, felling the man instantly. Arthur cut another's legs from under him and stabbed down into the man's chest. Guihir and Cundelig cut in and out of the fray with short, stabbing movements to the groins and throats of the enemy.

Soon the Sais guards were no more than corpses on the cobbles, their blood running in rivulets between the stones.

"Keep on the move," said Arthur. "We can't afford to take on every guard that crosses our path."

They jogged at a brisk pace down the street and passed the ruined amphitheatre; its crumbling stones and deserted benches ghostlike in the darkness. The basilica rose up at the end of the street, a large, oblong building with a curved roof much like the bath house. The square colonnaded forum lay before it with high walls and a solid looking gate barring the entrance. Beyond it they could make out the flickering torches of the men who were guarding Aurelianus.

"How do we get in?" asked Cei in a low whisper. "Call for the porter?"

"Some of the neighbouring buildings are very close to the forum's walls," said Arthur.

"If we can get up onto the roof of one of them, perhaps we can jump to the portico."

The building directly next to the basilica had been some sort of administration office at one time. Fortunately it was now empty but for detritus and rats. The companions made their way in through a side entrance, out of sight from the forum, and headed for the top floor. The stairways were cluttered with rubble and broken masonry. A gallery overlooked the street and the overhanging roof was just low enough to reach.

The warriors unbuckled their weapons and Arthur scrambled up onto the roof. Cei passed up the weapons to him one at a time and then the rest of the companions heaved themselves up.

The roof offered a stunning panorama of the town. They could see the fortified walls encircling them, dotted by pinpricks of light. Many guards patrolled the perimeter. They could see the great curved roofs of the baths a few blocks away, silent and sombre under the stars. Somewhere in the streets below a company of guards hurried by, sounding the alarm and shouting orders in their barbarous tongue.

"Our handiwork has been spotted," said Menw.

Below them, the tiles of the colonnaded portico that surrounded the basilica could be seen. The jump was not far, but impossible to do stealthily.

"We jump together," said Arthur. "As soon as you have your feet, drop down to the forum on the other side and then run like hell towards the basilica. Watch your backs though, we don't know how many guards are in the forum."

They lined up along the roof's edge and peered down. Arthur took a deep breath and leapt. He hit the tiled roof a second before his comrades did and the noise must have been heard several streets away. A hundred tiles shattered under impact and slid to the street below in a shower of terracotta. They scrambled up the roof on their hands and knees, dislodging even more tiles before sliding down on the other side and dropping to their feet in the forum.

They pounded the stones as they made their way towards the massive pillars of the building ahead of them, aware of the alarmed shouting coming from the portico behind. An arrow zipped passed Cei's ear and skittered off the stonework of the basilica wall. The comrades ducked into the shadows the columned entrance and whirled around, drawing their weapons.

Several guards who had lit a camp fire under the vaulted ceiling of the basilica leapt up at the sight of the intruders; their roasted chicken and mead forgotten in the face of attack. Swords clanged and echoed off the stone pillars as the two companies met. Arthur slew a man with a single sword stroke and turned to face the guards from the portico who had caught up with them. Blood spattered a nearby pillar as Cei swung his axe against the side of a man's helm and another guard sank to his knees with Gualchmei's dagger in his belly.

"To the stairs, quickly!" bellowed Arthur.

Their footsteps resounded in the lofty hallway of the basilica as the companions headed towards the wide staircase that led to the rooms above the cloisters that lined the nave.

Guards spilled out of every door and archway and Arthur's arms ached with the effort of swinging his sword while his hands were numb from the vibrations of clashing blades.

"Too many of the buggers," shouted Beduir over the noise.

"Are we close do you think?' said Cei. his grim face spattered with blood.

"One more stairway," answered Arthur as he parried a savage sword thrust and head-butted his opponent.

They made for the stairs but found their way blocked by the gigantic frame of a huge Sais who stood on the top step, spear in hand. He hoisted his weapon and aimed it at Arthur's chest. Before he had a chance to throw it, the short blade of a gladius erupted from his chest, glistening with blood. The man gasped for air and his eyes rolled up to gaze at the ceiling in muted shock.

The blade disappeared back through the wound and the man pitched forward, assisted by a heavy kick from behind, to roll down the entire flight of steps and land heavily at the feet of the astonished companions.

They looked from the corpse to the top of the stairs. The man who stood there was a figure from a forgotten age. A moulded cuirass encased a powerful, stocky body crowned with a polished helmet topped by a red horsehair crest. This matched the red cloak trimmed with wolf fur that hung down over large shoulders, fastened with a bronze broach. A stern face looked out from under the helmet with dark, intense eyes and an unkempt grey beard hung from his square jaw. The man had seen sixty winters at least but there was an iron-hardness to him that looked as if it had kept death at bay for many years and would for many more to come.

"Who the hell are you lot?" the man demanded.

"General Ambrosius Aurelianus?" Arthur asked.

"The same."

"I am Arthur mab Enniaun Yrth."

Aurelianus's feathery eyebrows lifted in recognition of his father's name.

"I am the Penteulu of Venedotia," Arthur went on. "We are here to rescue you."

"Penteulu of Venedotia, eh?" Aurelianus said. "Not that I wish to appear ungrateful, but Venedotia's strength seems a little lacking of late if six men is all you have to command."

"My teulu is currently crossing the Afon Sabrina, drawing Aelle's attention," Arthur explained. "I thought it best to employ stealth in rescuing you."

"Very good. How do you plan to get out of here?"

"We entered through the bath house drains," said Arthur. "But it would take too long to return that way and it is probably cut off by now."

"Yes, every guard in the town will be alerted to your presence by now," Aurelianus said. "I heard your ruckus from my cell on the top floor. My gaoler's attention was taken up by it and I saw my chance to brain him with my chamber pot. I found my armour in the adjacent room. If I am to die in this godforsaken town, then I will die a Roman, with a sword in my hand."

"Is there any other way out?" asked Beduir.

"I suggest we make for the western gate. The Sais scum will be too busy combing the streets for you. They will have left a minimal guard at best."

"It's worth a try," said Arthur.

The gatehouse stood at the end of the street they were on; a pearly-white arch against a black backdrop of night. A torchlight illuminated the helms of two guards, spreading their shadows on the stone wall behind them.

"Rush them!" said Arthur. "It's our only chance!"

The guards at the gate whirled around, alerted to the oncoming Britons. An arrow sung through the air, shot from one of the arched windows above the gate and narrowly missed Beduir.

The companions flung themselves to the walls of the buildings that lined the street for cover. They were nearly at the gate now. As one, they charged. Arthur saw the brief look of terror in the faces of the two guards as they were overrun and watched, impressed, as Aurelianus moved like a panther, his gladius flashing in the night, spilling Sais blood with the fluidity and ease of several decades of combat experience.

The heavy oak door was now all that stood between them and the world outside and the Britons hurled themselves against it, swinging it open with all their might. They could hear angry shouts and heavy footsteps behind them and, one by one, they slipped through. Turning briefly to heave the mighty door shut on their pursuers, they headed off into the outskirts surrounding Cair Badon.

"There is still a good distance between us and safety!" cautioned Menw as they ran down the muddy track that led between ramshackle houses and deserted farmyards.

The cry of alarm had been taken up at the western gate. Torchlights flickered in the darkness behind them as the search was taken up.

"We cannot outrun them, Arthur," said Aurelianus. "I'm a little long in the tooth for night runs across country."

"Down to the river," said Arthur, sheathing *Caledbulc*. "Perhaps we can outwit them instead."

The river flowed nearby and just as they were climbing down the muddy slopes to slip into the cold water, a group of Saeson appeared from behind a ruined barn. Arthur motioned to his men for absolute silence. Slowly, he edged through the water to a point where the riverbank overhung the water. The companions squeezed together beneath the grassy knoll and listened. The heavy footsteps of their pursuers came closer.

Arthur got the feeling of a hairy Sais face peering down at the river from above and thanked the gods for the shelter of the overhang. The Saeson muttered something to each other in their own, unintelligible tongue and then moved on, their footsteps gradually receding.

The crumbling bridge stood nearby, ghost-like under the moon. Arthur and his companions moved silently through the river towards its grimy pillars. Once they were past the bridge, they clambered up the riverbank, hidden from anybody who might be looking westwards from the town.

"Well, you're a rag-tag group of rogues," said Aurelianus, as Arthur helped him out of the water. He glanced at Menw. "And you look like you've seen almost as many winters as I have."

"Menw mab Teirguaed at your service, bard to the Pendraig of Venedotia."

"A spear-wielding bard, no less," said Aurelianus, impressed. "You have my thanks, all of you. I had all but given up hope in there. But my men! Do you have any word of their whereabouts, or if any survived the battle of Guenta Belgarum?"

"We have Marcus and Claudius in our company," said Arthur, "and many more of your soldiers have come to us at Cair Legion. We are re-forging what you once wielded."

Aurelianus smiled and it looked like it was an uncommon occurrence for him. "Then take me to them, Arthur, mab Enniaun. We have great plans to make!"

Peredur

The tavern was one of the seedier ones Peredur had visited in the last few days. The whole place stank of sweat and stale beer. The cracked stone floor was masked with big clots of dirty sawdust and the tables were sticky under his elbows. Several other customers lounged about on the benches and stools, their grim faces illuminated by the flickering candlelight and the pale morning sun that crept in through the tiny square window.

Most of them were travellers like Peredur. Some of their trades were obvious by their dress – fishermen, cattle drivers, hunters and farmers – but Peredur was less sure of some of the others. Scarred faces and barely concealed weapons marked several out as warriors or mercenaries. Possibly bandits too, Peredur thought, consciously placing his hand over his purse.

A large pitcher of beer stood in front of him which he used to top up his leather drinking jack when it got empty. His head was swimming with the effects of the fermented barley, its taste clinging to the back of his throat. He had only begun drinking that morning to dull the pain of his hangover from the night before. Unused to the effects of alcohol (and he was sure his mother would have disapproved sternly), the last few days were a fuzzy blur in his mind. It had been enjoyable when he first started; that first gulp slipping down his throat, washing away the bitter taste of disappointment and humiliation he had suffered in the arena at Cair Legion.

He had been travelling for three days, paying for lodging with some of the items from the purse Garth had given him. A pearl necklace, a gold brooch and tonight, an intaglio ring of red jasper engraved from behind with the image of a noble woman. The innkeeper's eyes had bulged when he had handed to him and Peredur was concerned that he had paid the man too much. But by then it was too late and the ring had quickly disappeared into the man's apron before the pitcher of beer and a plate of bread, eggs and cheese had materialised in front of him.

After leaving Cair Legion, Peredur had followed the Afon Usg north. He had come across a small monastery and one of the robed brothers had taken pity on him, asking him in for a bowl of watery broth. They had talked and Peredur had even confessed his murder of the bandit. The monk patted his arm gently and told him that God would forgive all sins so long as his heart was truly set on repentance.

Peredur remained in the monastery for two days and paid his way by helping out in the garden and doing odd jobs around the grounds. He gave serious thought to staying there on a more permanent basis. After all, here was something of a sanctuary from the world that had rejected him. Here he was closer to God and what better place was there to repent for his sins? Food and shelter were readily available and none of the tasks the brothers set him were beyond his competence.

But still he burned inside. He knew that he could not stay forever. Sooner or later his conscience would force him to resume his path in the outside world. The monastery, like his childhood home, was just another hideaway from the world. He could not redeem himself in the eyes of God by playing the coward and remaining within the comfort and safety of those stone walls. Early on the morning of the third day, he fetched Amren from the stables and continued north.

The morning passed and customers came and went, the tavern getting more crowded as the sun burned its noon heat on the thatched roof. By early evening the place was heaving and Peredur was barely conscious. Someone knocked him and he irritably decided that it was time to get some sleep.

He staggered out into the yard where a few chickens clucked about, unworried by the drunken roaring coming from the tavern. He wobbled a few steps and splashed through a puddle. A mangy old dog looked up at him as he passed and gave a low growl. The first few stars were glimmering in the sky, barely seen through the wavering treetops that encircled the roadside tavern.

He shared his lodgings with Amren. The barn was warm enough with plenty of straw for bedding. The roof was split by gaping holes and Peredur was glad that it was not raining. He flopped down on the pile of straw and sank into his usual nightmares.

He awoke to the sound of hushed voices that crept in through the cracks in the walls of the barn. His head hammered and he wished he had a jug of water to hand so that he might empty it over his throbbing skull. Why did people have to whisper so loudly?

He sat bolt upright. Who would bother to whisper in a tavern yard? *Thieves no doubt.* Amren stood on the other side of the barn twitching his ears at the approaching footsteps. In the dim moonlight that seeped into the holes in the roof, Peredur could see the bundle of his father's armour, the hilt of the sword protruding from the heap.

He dived for it just as the barn door was booted open. The sword eluded his grasp as three figures stormed the small interior and set upon him with heavy hands, dragging him to his feet. Amren brayed in noisy protest and Peredur found himself forced to his knees, his hands tucked behind him and bound with rope.

A large shape filled the entrance to the barn. Peredur looked up and saw a tall man staring down at him, hands on hips. A smaller, fatter man who Peredur recognised as the innkeeper hovered uneasily behind the first, watching the proceedings.

"Look at this, my lord!" said one of the burly intruders with a low whistle. He had whipped the blanket away from the heap of armour, revealing the dull metal with its tattered plume and gold hilted sword. "Quite the bandit we have here!"

"What is your name thief?" asked the big man in the doorway.

Peredur was silent. One of his captors struck him across the face. "Manners, boy! My lord asked you a question."

"He did not," replied Peredur insolently. "He asked a thief his name. I am no thief."

Another savage cuff to the face sent Peredur's head reeling backwards.

"I am not in the mood for mirth, boy," said the big man coolly. "I want to know where you stole this."

Peredur squinted at the gold ring with the red garnet intaglio the man held under his nose. "It was my mother's," he said truthfully.

"Oh, fetch him along!" said the man irritably. "I shall continue his interrogation at my leisure in more suitable surroundings."

Peredur was hauled to his feet and dragged out. He could hear Amren snorting angrily as strange men laid hands upon him. The innkeeper shuffled out of the way as the procession made its way to a group of horses in the yard.

"I… ah…" the innkeeper stammered. "Are we agreed that my debt to you is paid off?"

"That depends upon the outcome of this matter," the big man replied. "If I find out that you had anything to do with the boy's acquisition of the ring then you would do well to disappear before my men come knocking with a hangman's noose in their hands."

The fat man gulped and scurried back to his tavern. '

A length of rope was tied around Peredur's middle and fastened to the horse of one of the warriors. Another man led Amren who had been saddled with Peredur's belongings. The big man hoisted himself up onto his mare and led them all away from the tavern.

Peredur staggered and stumbled as he tried to keep up, almost falling every time the rope was yanked taut by the man who rode ahead. He took no notice of the blackness of the countryside that enveloped him. He no longer cared. This new turn of events was just another meaningless step to stumble over in his miserable existence. He would have cried again if he hadn't already spent all his tears. Now he just felt numb, numb as the cold night sky that loomed overhead.

They arrived at a villa complex deep in the countryside. Its grounds were well-tended and lamps burned in several windows. Peredur was taken to a reception room and placed on a chair in the centre of the room. He looked about at his surroundings.

Tapestries concealed flaking red paint on cracked plaster. In the corner a brazier's leaping flames cast flickering shadows across the room. A table stood in front of him. Dripping tallow oozed from candles to form pools of slowly hardening wax upon the oak between the debris of a nobleman's office; a golden drinking horn, a stack of parchment scrawled on with a spidery hand, a wax writing tablet, a knob of sealing wax and a small knife. In the centre of the table, dwarfing everything else, rested the large elbows of the big man. Peredur followed those bulging forearms to powerful fists which gripped a pair of ugly looking pliers.

Peredur tried to move but his guards had secured him to the chair with rope.

"Please sit still," said the man holding the pliers.

Peredur obeyed.

"Now then, boy," continued the man. "You are within the walls of my villa. Outside this room stand ten of my best warriors. There are a further twelve in the courtyard and on the gate. Escape is impossible so do not insult me by even considering it. You have some questions to answer. I wish to know where and how you came by this ring." He held up the object once more for Peredur's inspection. "Before you answer I feel I should warn you off any attempt at mocking me or passing me false information. As I hope I have already made clear, you are my guest for the foreseeable future, and the degree of comfort in which you spend it is entirely up to you." This last sentence was punctuated by a sharp click of the pliers. They were dull, Peredur noticed, and he imagined that the red stains were not only rust.

Peredur waited, trying to choose his words carefully but he quickly came to the conclusion that there was nothing else to tell the man other than the truth.

"The ring belonged to my mother," he said once more in utter misery.

There was a slow sigh from the man holding the pliers. "Very well," he said, eying Peredur with a steely gaze. "I shall assume, for the sake of argument, that you are either telling the truth or are a complete fool and proceed from there. Who was your mother?"

Peredur looked up at the beamed ceiling. A tear welled up in the corner of his eye and he sighed. "She was everything to me, my whole life. But now I am utterly alone. My father was the commander of Eboracum but he was killed in battle with all of my brothers the year I was born. My mother, wishing to protect me from the evil in the world took me to a secluded location in the forest with two of her servants. There we lived in peace and happiness. But I destroyed all of that because I disobeyed her. I crossed the stream and became tainted by the Evil that dwells beyond it."

Peredur sobbed. He was not even talking to the man before him anymore. He was confessing everything to himself and to God. The man at the table watched and listened in stunned silence.

"I left her and my home," said Peredur once he had composed himself a little. "I set with my donkey Amren and my father's old armour for all the damned good it would do me. I made my way to Cair Legion where I heard that Arthur the warlord was training his army. But I killed a man on the way; a bandit who tried to rob me. I smashed his face in with a rock, damning myself forever as a murderer. When I got to Cair Legion I tried to join Arthur's army but I made fool of myself. I was beaten black and blue by a brute named Cei who insulted my father, a slight which I shall neither forget nor forgive. I left then and wandered the roads for days, drinking myself into a stupor and sleeping in barns, paying my way with the jewels and gems that had once belonged to my mother. Last night I took refuge in a roadside tavern and paid for the night with that ring you hold. I am a wretched and sinful creature who deserves no less than whatever you plan to do to me. So perhaps you now understand how I care so little for your threats. I am forsaken anyhow."

The man watched him in silence for a while, his eyes studying him hard. He lay the pliers down upon the table and picked up the ring. In a soft voice he said "You gave this in exchange for a tankard of beer and a single night's lodging? Were you born simple boy?"

"By your words I take it that the item was too costly for such a purpose. Well, sir, I am unwise in the ways of the world, for I am naught but a newcomer. I do not know the value of things and there is the reason."

"You have told me an interesting story, young traveller," the man said. "In return, allow me to give you a story in exchange, a story of this ring in fact. Years ago it belonged to a fair and beautiful woman of a noble family. Her marriage was arranged to a young man who was a soldier of some rank in some town in the north. She liked the man and felt that in time she could learn to love him as was required of her, but she wept to leave her home and family behind. On the eve of her wedding, her brother, who loved her dearly, gave her this ring that had been handed down through the generations of their family, as a token of remembrance and of his love for her.

"The woman left and her brother never saw her again. Years later he learned that she had borne her husband many sons and that they had lived in happiness in the north for a time. But it had not lasted. The Picts had invaded from beyond the great wall and while the rest of Albion cowered and dithered over what should be done, word spread that the courageous commander of Eboracum had ridden out into battle, flanked by his eldest sons, his banner a standard of defiance against the heathen.

"All were slaughtered and the Picts plundered the land with sword, axe and torch. Upon hearing this, the brother of the fair lady rode north, desperate to find her and return her to safety. He found her home empty and the town in a state of turmoil. He asked those who had known his sister for any news, and they told him that she had been seen leaving the town with a cartload of her belongings, accompanied by two of her servants. In her arms they said, she carried her single remaining son who was no more than a baby.

The brother spent the following year searching the countryside for his sister and his nephew but he could find no trace. He had no choice but to assume the Picts had butchered her and her babe, and they, like the ring he had given to her, were forever lost to him."

The room was silent but for the crackle of the brazier and the occasional flutter of the candles.

"If I untie you, young man, will you give me your word of honour that you will not try to flee?"

Peredur nodded.

His bonds loosened, Peredur rubbed some life back into his limbs, still unable to take his eyes from the man who sat before him. The words fought for space in his mouth each demanding to be spoken first. He had so many questions but did not know how to begin to ask them.

"My name is Edlim" said the man before him. "I am known hereabouts as Edlim Redsword."

"I am Peredur," Peredur managed in a croaky voice.

Edlim nodded thoughtfully. "Peredur. I believe your story. I also believe that your mother was my sister and that I am your uncle. Whatever divine plan brought you to me I suppose we shall never know but you are welcome to remain here for the time being.

We have much to tell each other. Would you like some wine?"

Peredur nodded. Through all his misfortune and misadventures, all of his sin and misery, he had ended up in the company of a member of his family, the first such member apart from his mother, that he had ever met. As they talked long into the night, warmth glowed inside of him, encouraged by the wine that stung his palate and warmed the deepest recesses of his soul, he thanked God for delivering him. In the warm eyes and smile of Edlim, he knew that he had at last found a little acceptance in the cruel world that so alienated him. And once again he wept, although this time, the tears were not borne of sadness, but of joy.

Guenhuifar

Guenhuifar's first action was to find out who had made the arrow that had killed the mysterious assassin. There had to be a dozen fletchers on Ynys Mon alone and each had their own trademarks and styles. If she could find out where the arrow came from, she might find out who had purchased it. It wasn't much to go on, but it was a start.

She borrowed an arrow from one of the king's guards and compared the fletching to the broken shaft she had taken from the hut. Although were both fletched with grey goose feathers, there were some distinctions. The binding at the nock of the broken arrow was of tendon or sinew whereas the nock on the guard's arrow was bound only with glue. In addition to this the fletching on the broken arrow was slightly longer and the 'cock feather' was set at an obtuse angle to the groove of the nock as opposed to the right angle of the guard's arrow.

Guenhuifar knew that the cock feather was always of a different colour to the two 'hen feathers' so as to be easily identified. When an arrow was nocked to the bowstring, the cock feather always pointed away from the bow to minimise the brushing of the hen feathers against the bow when the arrow was shot.

Guenhuifar frowned. The arrow was far from distinctive and it could have been made anywhere in Albion. She had always bought her own arrows from Banon the fletcher at Aberffraw. He might have some ideas on where this one was made.

She gave the arrow back to the bemused guard and returned home. In the chest at the foot of her bed she dug out a green tunica, a light cloak and a pair of men's breeches that she had tailored to fit her figure. At the bottom of the chest she found her old boots; castoffs from her father which she had mended and adjusted to suit her feet comfortably. As she dressed herself, she felt as if she was slipping back into an old skin long neglected. It had been a long time since she had dressed in her common hunting gear and she realised with a pang of nostalgia that this was what she had worn when she had voyaged across the straits with Arthur and his companions to embark upon an adventure that would change her life forever.

Hidden in the thatch above her bed was her bow and a quiver of arrows. As she strapped the quiver on, she took a look at the fletching of one of her own arrows and noted that, like the guard's arrow, its cock feather stood at a right angle to the nock. Old Banon probably sold to Cadwallon's men as well as to her. *Good for him.* She liked the old fletcher and was pleased that the return of the king's lys to Ynys Mon had profited local businesses.

She left the hall through the back entrance and made her way across the herb gardens. She could see her sister kneeling over some bush, cutting away with her sickle. There was nobody else about but Guenhuifar drew the hood of her cloak up all the same and hurried over to her.

"I need you to cover for me," she said, squatting down next to Guenhuifach.

Her sister glanced at her in surprise. "What on earth are you dressed like that for?"

"As I said, I need you to cover for me. I'm going away."

"Where? For how long?"

"I don't know. I want to get to the bottom of this attempt on King Owain's life."

"Father and Cadwallon are already looking into that!"

"They have no clue! I need to ask around. I had the run of this island before Cadwallon rebuilt the lys. I have contacts in Aberffraw and other places. Somebody must know something."

"But you're not thinking of going off alone?"

"Why should I not? I did all right on my own when I used to hunt game in the lean months or when I gathered herbs for you."

"But... you're a lady now," Guenhuifach protested. "And a married one at that! Leave it to the men, Guenhuifar, I beg of you!"

"The men are too taken up with the political wrangling and powerplay this has caused," said Guenhuifar. "They may miss vital clues as to the true identity of our enemy. Say you'll cover for me when father notices I'm gone, please? I only want to ask a few questions and then I'll come right back. Promise."

Guenhuifach sighed. She had always been the good girl, the one who never lied or did anything unexpected. But she had on occasion covered for Guenhuifar during her wilder escapades. "Fine," she said. "But promise me you'll be safe?"

"Always. And thank you."

She rose and left Guenhuifach with her herbs. By following the palisade of the settlement, she was able to reach the east gate without being spotted. The gate was guarded of course, but several traders were making their way in with their goods from Aberffraw or the ferry point down south. As wains loaded with wicker cages, bolts of cloth, pots and amphorae squelched through the mud, Guenhuifar slipped between them, her face hidden by her hood from anybody who happened to be looking her way. She made for the woods to the right of the trackway and vanished out of sight from the palisades.

By the gods, it was good to be running free once more! It had been so long since she had been alone with nothing but the birdsong in her ears and the fresh winds of the wild in her lungs that she felt almost drunk with exhilaration. She followed the coast west, cutting south once she was well clear of Cadwallon's Lys. Aberffraw was on the other side of the island and it would take her most of the day to traverse the distance.

Aberffraw was little changed since she had last visited. Ringed by earthworks, the port town sat on the muddy banks of a small river that flowed out into the Gaelic Sea. It was bustling with business just as Guenhuifar remembered it. The colonnaded entrance of the old Roman administrative building which had been converted into a tavern looked over the sprawling marketplace where goods were brought up from the harbour to be bartered and sold. It was there that Guenhuifar knew she would find old Banon.

He hadn't changed either. His bald pate surrounded by wispy white hair bobbed over his work as he fletched another arrow to add to the bundles on the trestle table before him. A striped canvas canopy shaded him from the heat of the afternoon sun.

"Don't you ever stop working, Banon?" Guenhuifar asked with a smile as she walked over to his stall.

He glanced up at her in surprise. "Can't afford to, lass... I mean, *my lady*,"

"Knock it off, Banon," she chided. "I'm still the same Guenhuifar."

"So I see," he said, looking her up and down. "I thought you had traded your breeches and bow for frocks and slippers."

"For the most part I have. But frocks and slippers do me no good beyond the company of kings. I needed to pay you a visit."

"Out of arrows? What do you find to shoot at these days?"

"I've still got some of your best in my quiver. No, I wanted your opinion on a rather special arrow."

Banon set his work to one side as Guenhuifar took the broken shaft out of her quiver and handed it to him. He examined it intently, running his expert hands up and down the stained shaft and riffling its fletchings. "Not one of mine," he said at length.

"No, I gathered that. Can you tell me whose it is?"

His beady eyes looked up at her. "Have you any idea how many fletchers there are? My competition is no small thing, I can tell you that much."

"I know and I wouldn't ask you if I had anything else to go on. I must find out who made this arrow. Have you heard about the attempt on King Owain's life?"

"Aye, nasty business. Is that what you are mixed up in?"

"Just trying to find some answers. This is the arrow that killed the assassin. We don't know who he was or who sent him but I was hoping you might point me in the direction of his killer's preferred fletcher."

Banon turned his attention back to the arrow. "It's good workmanship, I'll give you that. Are you sure your man was from Ynys Mon?"

"No. Not at all sure."

He whistled. "You could be casting your net a little wide. There are a couple of other fletchers on the island. Vericus plies his trade in the settlements of the south-east but he mostly sells to customers on the mainland. I don't think this is his workmanship; it's too fine. Look at this colouring on the nock crest. That's done with care. Vericus provides arrows for soldiers and household guards. His workmanship is pretty standard. Quantity over quality."

"Who else is there?"

"Well, there is a fletcher north of here who used to turn out some pretty good arrows although I've no idea if he is still in business. I haven't seen him or any of his workmanship in some time. Could be worth looking up. His stuff used to be pretty good. I wouldn't put this arrow past him."

"Where can I find him?"

"Well, as I said, I don't know if he is around anymore but he used to live on the southern shores of Lin Alaw. Used to supply the settlements on the northern part of the island."

Guenhuifar thanked Banon and bought a few of his arrows to fill up her quiver. She made sure to pay him more than they were worth for his help.

She ate at the tavern and said hello to a few old acquaintances before heading north, following the Afon Alaw inland. Dusk was approaching and she made a small camp on the riverbank and slept under the stars, enjoying the warm summer night and the twinkling constellations spread on the velvet above.

The following morning the great lake of Lin Alaw came into view. This was the very centre of the northern part of the island. Guenhuifar traversed its length from west to east and came across the small settlement of roundhouses, the smoke of morning cookfires hanging above the thatched roofs.

It was not a settlement she had visited before and she was treated with suspicion on arrival. It had only been a couple of years since the Gaels had been driven away and it was natural for the local populace to be a little on the wary side concerning armed strangers, but she was alone and the villagers were more curious than hostile.

"I want to buy some arrows," she said. "Is there a fletcher here?"

"Aye, we have a fletcher and his wife," said an elderly man who seemed to be in a position of some authority. "Where have you come from?"

"Aberffraw."

"Long way for some arrows. Don't they have a fletcher there?"

"Yes, but I want some good arrows. I was told your fletcher makes the best on the island."

"That's as may be," said the elder. "He does enough business, I'll say that."

"May I see him?"

"Second house on the left when you get to the lake's shore."

Guenhuifar thanked him and without too much trouble, found the fletcher. It was quite an industry he ran for so small a settlement and she found that encouraging. Such good business must rely on customers from far afield.

The fletcher himself was busy at his trestle table, shaving and shaping arrow shafts. Behind him were racks and racks of completed arrows along with a couple of bows and a target presumably for testing out the wares. Two women worked nearby, plucking the feathers from a pile of dead geese.

"Hello," Guenhuifar said, approaching them.

The three of them looked her up and down, the contrast between her face and attire registering mild surprise.

"What can I do you for?" the fletcher asked.

"Looking to buy some arrows."

His eyes glanced to her full quiver. "Seems to me you've already got some. That old Banon's handwork down in Aberffraw?"

"The same. It was Banon who told me about you, actually."

"Now why would that old fool send trade my way?"

"Well, it's a special kind of arrow I'm after." She showed him the broken arrow.

"One of mine," he said after giving it a quick glance. "I can let you have as many as you'd like but I'm not cheap."

"Who else do you sell to?"

"What do you want to know that for?"

"I want to know whose arrow this was."

He narrowed his eyes and glanced again at the bloody shaft in her hands. "I don't want no trouble," he said. "I make and sell arrows. What they get used for is none of my business."

"I'm not here for trouble," Guenhuifar said in a tone she hoped would set the man's nerves at ease. "I just want to find this person. If you can point me in the right direction, I promise you I won't tell anybody."

He looked about nervously as if expecting somebody else to appear at any moment. The wind was quiet and the waters of the lake were still. Only the sound of distant industry in the village could be heard. "There's a gang or something who buy from me regularly. I don't know any names but a man comes here once a month or so and buys enough of my stock to equip a good band of men. He doesn't say much about what they do but robbers or mercenaries is my guess. He's dressed like a warrior and is a pretty tough customer. That's all I know!"

"Good. Thank you. And you have no idea where this gang operates from?"

"I already said, I told you all I know! Now, are you going to buy some arrows or not?"

"As you noticed, my quiver is already full but here is something for your time," she drew out a few broken bits of silver from her purse and gave them to the man. He scooped them up and pocketed them in a flash, turning his attention back to his work.

Guenhuifar walked away. Whoever this gang was, they were obviously mean enough to put the wind up the fletcher. She knew she wasn't going to get any more information here, but she had to somehow find out more about this gang.

She returned to Aberffraw and made her way to the tavern. It was a large two-storeyed construction with an atrium that served as the tavern floor and enough rooms upstairs to cater to private parties, business transactions and other more carnal arrangements. Custenhinn was the man who owned it; a disgraced member of an old aristocratic family and Guenhuifar knew him of old.

She pushed her way through the early evening drinkers and climbed the staircase to the upper rooms. She found Custenhinn attending to some paperwork in his office. He was a man in his middle years, hair and beard greying with the onset of old age. He wore a green tunica trimmed with gold thread and a heavy medallion around his neck.

"I see the daughter of the Pendraig's steward is gracing my tavern with her presence," he said, looking up from his paperwork with a smile. "Does your new husband know you are so far from his hearth, alone and wearing clothes most unbecoming a penteulu's wife?"

"You are as well-informed as ever, Custenhinn," she replied, sitting down unbidden in the chair opposite him. "That's good. I am here for information. And some wine if you have any to hand. My throat is parched from my travels."

Custenhinn smiled and poured some of the wine from the jug on his desk into a clean cup and passed it to her. He poured some for himself and they raised a toast to old times.

"What business can I help you with, Lady Guenhuifar," Custenhinn said, licking the wine from his moustache.

"The business of murder."

Custenhinn coughed on his second sip of wine. "Marriage into the nobility has not curbed your bluntness. But you know that I am a merchant. I deal only in the business of trade. If you wish some poor bugger ill then surely your husband or your father have people on hand who are suited to the task?"

"I do not require anybody murdered," said Guenhuifar coolly. "I wish to identify a man who has already committed the act."

Something dawned on Custenhinn and his face paled. "You are here about the assassination attempt over at the lys! And you came to me seeking information? I can assure you, my lady, if I am under any suspicion I will gladly answer questions in the presence of the Pendraig himself…"

"You are under no suspicion, Custenhinn. And the Pendraig has no knowledge that I am here."

Custenhinn looked a little relieved at this and he sank back into his chair.

"While news of the assassination attempt may have reached your ears, you may not know that the assassin was himself killed by persons unknown while fleeing the lys. He was felled by this." She placed the broken arrow on the desk between them. "I have traced the fletcher who made this arrow and he tells me that he sells regularly to a gang somewhere on the island. He knows nothing about them. I was hoping that you might."

"A gang?" Custenhinn said. "There are a few gangs on the island and we get some tough customers coming over from the mainland to do business. Not that I know such men personally, you understand."

"This gang would have to be a cut above the usual thieves and thugs for hire. They use expensive arrows. Some sort of group of assassins perhaps?"

"I can assure you that I am not acquainted with such types…"

Guenhuifar decided to try a different tack. "Custenhinn, if this mystery is not solved then there may very well be civil war again."

Custenhinn watched her in silence.

"Nobody wants that, surely?" Guenhuifar said. "Bad for business, am I right? And you needn't think that war would be confined to the mainland. When the Pendraig rebuilt the lys, he both saved and cursed Ynys Mon. We may have got rid of the Gaels, but any future hostilities will lead to attempted invasions of our island. You did all right under Gaelic rule, and I don't blame you. We all had to make do the best we could. But another invading force might be keener on the fire and sword approach rather than long-term rule. How do you think your businesses would fare if that happened?"

Custenhinn swallowed.

"And on a more personal level," Guenhuifar continued, "things would go very badly for anybody who was found to have held back information regarding the attempted murder of the Pendraig's brother."

"Now wait just a minute," Custenhinn exclaimed. "You presume too much. Whatever I do know, I know nothing of this plot against King Owain."

"Well, let's start with what you do know."

"There *is* a gang, like you said. Assassins. Knives for hire. That's all I know about them. I don't know where they are based or any details about their work."

"How do you know anything about them at all?"

He looked uncomfortable. "This is a place of business. Everybody on the island comes through my doors at one time or another, save the Morgens. We get all types in here. Including the occasional assassin wanting to discuss a job."

"*I* want to discuss a job with one of them."

"You? You're mad! You should be at home tending to your husband's hearth."

Guenhuifar slammed the palm of her hand down on the table, making Custenhinn jump. "Don't tell me what to do again," she told him.

Custenhinn sighed. "This is very dangerous."

"If all goes to plan and this nasty business is cleared up, then I will personally put in a good word for you at court. If King Cadwallon hears that you were instrumental in uncovering the plot against his brother, he may look rather favourably on you and your business interests."

Custenhinn's face brightened a little at this. "Very well," he said. "I know a man who has dealt with them in the past. I shall arrange a meeting. It will take a day or so to set up."

"Fine. I shall take a room here. I am weary and hungry from my wanderings. And I know the chicken here is good and the ale is palatable."

The birds twittered in the trees above the creek, their chirruping voices carrying across the still water of the Afon Ffraw. Sunlight dappled the river, filtered through a screen of green as it passed through leaf and branch, a lazy, sluggish light that oozed rather than shone with all the vigour of a summer afternoon.

Guenhuifar gazed across the water at the opposite bank. Custenhinn's man should have been here by now. It was well past noon. If he suspected a trap then he wouldn't show at all. She held the reigns of the dapple grey she had hired at Aberffraw. Her breeches and weapons had been left at the tavern and she was dressed in a simple long tunica and shawl which veiled her hair.

She began to wonder what the hell she was doing. She had identified a band of assassins on Ynys Mon. If she was smart she would return to the lys and inform Cadwallon of her findings. But she was still not sure that these assassins were the ones who had attempted to kill Owain or who had paid them to do it, let alone why. She wanted to find out more before she handed it all over to Cadwallon.

A rider approached from the north-east, following the river from the reedy waters of the lake that fed it. He was dressed in dark, muted colours befitting a man who spent much of his time out of doors. A quiver of arrows and an unstrung bow hung from his saddle and a heavy sword was strapped to his belt.

"Are you my saviour?" Guenhuifar called out in a voice dripping with a forced helplessness she was entirely unaccustomed to. *All part of the act*, she told herself.

"For the right price, I can be," the man replied, trotting up to her. He had a deep, smooth voice that sounded like it was rarely used. His hair and beard were dark with a few flecks of white like snowflakes and his face was the weathered type that made it difficult to pin an age on.

"I am Enfis," Guenhuifar lied.

"Morien," the man replied. "I understand you have a problem with a creditor."

"Yes. Since my father died, I have been more or less on my own and I fear that unscrupulous types are trying to take advantage of me and lay their hands on my fortune."

Morien looked her up and down and then smiled. It wasn't a pretty smile. "What is your trade?"

"Silk from Parthia. The last of my father's stock. I am seeking to retire and have found a buyer for the whole lot. But my father ran up extensive debts and, as I said, some have tried to take advantage of me and claim more than their share. I am no pushover when it comes to haggling – father taught me his business well – but I am no match for thuggery. These people will stop at nothing and will strip me bare if given half the chance! Oh!" She dabbed at her eyes with the hem of her shawl. "I'm making rather a mess of this, aren't I?"

Morien narrowed his eyes at her. "You are completely on your own?"

"Goodness me, no. I have servants whom I intend to pay handsomely and send on their way once the goods are sold. They are currently with the stock at my father's warehouse in Aberffraw."

"Yet you ventured out here alone to meet with a stranger?"

"I simply had no choice! Father died only last month leaving me with three servants and a whole lot of debt. I couldn't trust one of them to procure me the help I needed and…"

"You're doing the right thing, lass. I'll see that this fellow is no longer a problem. For my fee of course…"

"Of course! Once the silk is sold, I will have the funds to pay you."

"*Once the silk is sold?*" Morien raised an eyebrow at her. "I'm sorry, we require payment up front."

Guenhuifar bit her lip. "Of course. I do have some silver and other valuable objects in my father's chest at Aberffraw. I could pay you out of that, but you would have to accompany me there."

Morien frowned. "Where am I to deal with this unscrupulous creditor?"

"He plagues me at my place of business. Is Aberffraw too populated for you to do your work?"

"Not at all. But the risk is greater and that will make the fee higher."

They spent some time haggling over the price and Guenhuifar did her best to live up to her claim of being a good business woman. Once the matter was settled, they mounted their horses and followed the river south-west towards Aberffraw.

It would be dark before they reached the town and Guenhuifar suggested that they camp for the night and reach Aberffraw in the morning. "I have a roasted chicken and a skin of rather good wine," she said as invitingly as she could. He may get the wrong idea but that wouldn't matter. Soon enough *he* would be answering *her* questions.

They made a small fire by the river and sat opposite each other. Guenhuifar passed Morien half of the chicken which he tucked into ravenously. She passed him the wine skin and watched as he gulped down a few mouthfuls. He noticed her watching him and offered the wineskin back.

"No thank you," she said. "I don't much care for wine. I brought it as I thought you might like some refreshment."

"You come well prepared," he said, gulping down more of the wine. "And optimistic that I would accept your offer."

She said nothing and watched him empty the skin down his gullet. The stars were out and they lazed by the fire, waiting for sleep to come. Morien gazed at her across the glowing embers. "You're a curious one," he said.

"How so?"

"You seem a simple, kind lass with a good heart. But you've taken a great risk in coming out here to meet me all on your own."

"I told you, I have no choice. My father's servants are good people but they are lackwits. They would be too frightened to meet you."

"You're not frightened?"

"Should I be?"

He smiled and Guenhuifar cringed on the inside. He was drunk now and not for the first time that day she questioned her wisdom in going through with this plan. He could try and rape her. She was betting on his eagerness for a full payday and hoped he would resist temptation and carry out the job she had presented to him instead. If not, she had prepared herself in *other* ways. She touched the dagger beneath her tunica to reassure herself of its presence.

He yawned and that gave Guenhuifar hope. "Gods, I'm tired," he said. He lay back and rested his head on his rolled-up cloak. Within a few minutes, he was snoring.

Guenhuifar waited until she was sure that the drugged wine had taken its full effect. Then she rose and crossed softly to him. She nudged him with the toe of her slipper. He didn't stir. The drug had been a sleeping draught she had purchased from the healer woman she knew in Aberffraw. It was fast-working, the woman had told her. She had not been lying.

She walked around to the man's head and bent down to loop her elbows under his armpits. With some effort, she dragged him over to a tree and propped him up with his back against its trunk. Then she went to the saddlebag of her borrowed horse and drew out a length of rope. She wound the rope around Morien and the tree, tying it with the best knot she knew. Then she went and sat by the fire and waited until dawn.

Morien stirred several times as the rays of the rising sun touched the tall pines. Guenhuifar drew some water from the river and doused his face with it. He spluttered and groaned before falling back asleep. *Damned drug!* She wanted to get this unsavoury business over and done with so she could return to the lys with the name of whoever had tried to have Owain killed.

It wasn't until the morning sun was high over the trees that Morien opened his eyes and looked about, groggily. He tried to move, found that he couldn't, and was suddenly more awake.

"Rise and shine," said Guenhuifar, squatting near him.

"Huh?" His eyes rolled in their sockets as he tried to focus on her. "Why am I tied up?"

"Because I don't want you running off on me."

"Why'd you tie me up?" he repeated.

Guenhuifar sighed. "Listen, *assassin*. I have tied you up because I want some answers. I want to know about your gang, where you operate from and what sort of jobs you pull."

"Who are you?"

"More than I seem. Now, tell me where your base is."

"Never."

Guenhuifar swallowed. She had known there was going to be some resistance. What she didn't know was if she had it in her to overcome it. She drew her knife and looked at the blade as she tested its point with her thumb. "Please don't force me to remove bits of you."

His eyes flashed with a defiant anger. "You're mad! Do you know what you're up against? How many of us there are?"

"No, why don't you tell me; how many of you are there?"

"Fuck off!"

She pointed the tip of her dagger at his left eyeball. "How many?"

He glared at her, white-eyed, stubborn in his terror. His lips were pressed together tight. Beads of sweat rolled down his forehead.

She lowered the knife and stood up suddenly, sick to her stomach. Surely Arthur would not have any compunctions about torturing a Pict or a Gael to get information? Not when lives depended upon it. She hated herself for not being able to go through with it and yet she also hated herself for following a path that led her to the point where she was about to maim somebody.

She walked down to the river's edge and breathed the air deeply as she watched the shadows of the current rippling over its stony bed. Morien was right. She *was* mad. What was she thinking? This was a job for men, men like Arthur and Cadwallon. She should have returned to the lys as soon as she had learned that a gang of assassins was operating on Ynys Mon.

The worst of it was that she was now at an impasse. Things had escalated beyond the point of no return. If she cut Morien loose he would kill her. If she left him where he was it would be as good as murder. The more she thought about it, the more she realised that she had to go through with it. She *had* to torture him.

She turned and went back to her prisoner, steeling herself for what was to come. As she pushed through the bushes her heart stopped when she saw the tree. Her rope lay serpentine on the ground, severed by something sharp. Morien was gone.

She could have screamed curses at the sky. How could she have been so stupid not to check him? Of course he had blades concealed about his person. He was an assassin! And now he was loose with a hot vengeance for her hide.

She looked about frantically. Her horse grazed nearby, its thick lips nibbling at the grass. She hurried over to it, the thought of galloping back to the lys as fast as she could in the forefront of her mind.

A rough hand seized her from behind. A blade was pressed against her throat. A hot voice smelling of sour wine and roasted chicken hissed into her ear.

"Now then, pretty one. *I* shall be asking *you* some questions."

Arthur

Caradog and the teulu had played a game of cat and mouse with the enemy, drawing them and then retreating, luring and running, always avoiding contact. Now that Arthur had returned to lead them, the teulu knew that open battle was not far off.

The entire teulu buzzed with excitement at the rescue of the legendary general. When they had seen their penteulu and his most trusted companions hurrying across country with Ambrosius Aurelianus in their company, filthy, exhausted but beaming with victory, they were elated. Even though none of Arthur's men had met Aurelianus, they knew his name and they knew what he meant to Albion.

They camped with their backs to the chalk downs north of Cair Badon. Arthur and his companions, scrubbed clean and wearing fresh clothes, discussed their next move over a well-needed meal. People kept slowing their pace as they passed by to get a better look at the living legend.

"Who leads the Sais warband?" Aurelianus asked.

"His son, Cymen, we think," replied Caradog.

"The scouts report that Aelle is still far to the east," said Cundelig.

"He will still be rounding up more chieftains to swear him allegiance," said Aurelianus. "When he returns, he will be stronger than ever."

"Then we must act fast to destroy his foothold in the west," replied Arthur. "As we speak there will be Sais scouts on their way to Aelle to report our presence here. I want to take Cair Badon before he has a chance to march on us. We can fortify ourselves behind its walls and draw on supplies from Cair Legion."

"You saw its fortifications," said Cei. "We would lose most of the teulu trying to get through its gates."

"Cymen and his band are still combing the downs for us," said Caradog. "If we can draw out the rest of them from the town, we might be able to defeat them on the field."

"That is my plan," said Arthur. "Cymen has no cavalry. We could ride all over him."

"Then why on earth would he come chasing after us?" said Gualchmei.

"Because he's a fool," said Aurelianus. "I know Cymen. He is overeager and impulsive. If he sees the slightest chance to win a victory and earn some of his father's favour, he will jump at it. If it had been up to him, we would have never lost Guenta Belgarum but Aelle is a far more cunning advisory and was able to keep a check on his son's tearaway tactics."

"Even so," said Arthur. "We must honey the trap a little. We can't risk them fleeing at the sight of our cavalry. We must hide our horses from them. They must see only our spearmen and bowmen and think they have caught a portion of the teulu unawares."

"A wise enough plan," said Aurelianus. "But you need to decide upon a suitable location to spring the trap."

"One of the wide valleys would be perfect," said Arthur. "If we can lure Cymen into a trap then we can seal it by springing the cavalry on him from above."

Aurelianus smiled. "You northerners with your valley warfare," he said. "No wonder Suetonius Paulinus had such trouble subduing your ancestors in the old days. There is a hilltop not far from here where the trees grow thick on the southern side and curl around to its eastern edge. If you position your troops atop that hill and force the enemy to march up it to meet you, your cavalry can make their way around under the cover of the trees and strike them on their left flank."

"Good," said Arthur. The old man's experience of the enemy and knowledge of the land was going to be a great advantage to this campaign. "Then we move south before nightfall. For the time being, get some sleep. We all need it."

"What I need is a good dip in a river," said Beduir, sniffing his long, damp hair. "I still stink like a sewer rat."

A chattering flurry of blackbirds burst from the treetops and up into the sky. Arthur spotted them from atop the hill where he sat astride Hengroen. He knew they had been disturbed by the movement the cavalry through the trees and hoped that the enemy had not noticed them.

Before him stretched rows and rows of spearmen, backed by the bowmen. The view down the slope was impressive. The river curved through the valley and wound its way through the hills, vanishing past the line of trees on their right flank.

Aurelianus turned in his saddle to speak to Arthur. "May I make a suggestion?"

"By all means."

"Move your bowmen closer to your front lines."

"Will that not endanger my own men?"

"Have them draw back when the enemy gets within throwing range then order a low volley of shafts downhill from your spearmen. The Saeson will be holding their shields high to protect themselves from arrows and their middle sections will be vulnerable."

Arthur nodded and gave the order for the bowmen to march forward a few paces. At the bottom of the hill, the spear tips of the approaching enemy could be seen rounding the bend in the river.

"I am glad you are with us, general," Arthur said. "Your experience is invaluable."

"Were it not for you, I would not be here at all, Arthur," the old soldier replied. I thought it was all over when I was captured by Aelle. You have given me a new lease of life; a chance to finish what I started."

"*Can* it be finished?" he asked as they watched the enemy's advance.

"In our lifetime? God knows. But that is no reason for us to stop trying."

The Saeson had begun to climb the steep hill. They numbered about two-hundred; an equal match for the men who held the hilltop but no match for the cavalry that lurked in the trees on their left flank.

Arthur peered down at Cymen's host. Great round shields were carried by the front lines, decorated with geometric patterns in vibrant colours. Behind them bearded faces snarled and chanted war songs in the Sais tongue. Some wore iron helms, fierce eyes peering through loopholes and flaxen hair spilling down over bulky shoulders. Above them a banner wavered, decorated with some kind of wolf insignia and adorned with a sun-bleached ram's skull.

A small company of mounted men brought up the rear; Cymen and his personal guard. The were accompanied by a thrumming rhythm on skin drums.

"The Sais war ethic is based entirely on honour," commented Aurelianus, showing none of the tension that had gripped Arthur and his men atop the hill as the enemy marched ever closer. "The Romans had their discipline and the Britons rely on their hit-and-run tactics but the Sais chieftain holds bravery higher than any other virtue, almost to a suicidal level. He will throw as many men as possible against the enemy despite the odds for death is something they do not fear."

"They don't fear death?"

"No, to die in battle is the best death they can think of and the ultimate honour. They believe that warriors who die with their swords in their hands go to some golden hall in the sky where they will feast with the gods until doomsday."

Arthur nodded but said nothing. He was too tense to discuss pagan theology. The enemy was close now, their round shields overlapping at the front forming an effective wall against assault. They were almost in range.

"Bowmen ready!" bellowed Arthur. A horn was blown and nearly a hundred arrows were pulled back on strings with a synchronised creak, their iron tips pointed up at the sky.

Arthur raised his arm. The front line of the enemy struggled onwards up the grassy slope, the sunlight glinting off their helms. He dropped his arm and arrows whistled through the air, singing as if in joy at their release. The sky was marred by a hundred black streaks as they rose and fell downwards upon the enemy. Cries of alarm echoed throughout the Sais ranks as the darts hit their marks, piercing mail, leather and flesh. The great wooden shields went up and the noise of arrows striking wood was like a heavy rain.

Atop the hill the bowmen nocked more arrows to their strings and drew back. Again the sky was clouded with flying missiles and again the hillside resounded with the hammering of iron tips against shields. There were a few screams of agony as lucky arrows found their marks but for the most part the oncoming host was barely slowed.

Arthur turned to one of his standard bearers. "Tell my captains to begin the charge."

The youth galloped across the hilltop, his coloured standard fluttering, to where he would be visible from the trees below. Arthur sent another volley singing through the air and then pulled his bowmen back.

"Spearmen!" he yelled out to the front ranks. "A volley! Keep it low!"

The two front lines of infantry hoisted their javelins up into an overhand grip and hurled them with all their might at the first line of the enemy. The missiles zipped down the hillside and plunged deep into the enemy ranks, working their way in below the upraised shields. Iron punctured flesh with sickening thuds and the screaming taken up was almost unbearable to the ears. Almost the entire front line of troops stumbled and fell, bellies, legs and groins pierced by iron-tipped lances of death.

Arthur drew *Caledbulc* and yelled the command to advance. As one, the line of infantry picked up their long spears and marched forward to meet the enemy, picking up speed as they descended the hill. The two sides clapped together like two large waves in the middle of a stormy ocean. Shields slammed against shields and spears worked their way in through the chinks in the lines, seeking out unprotected limbs and torsos. Arthur sat up in his saddle, neck craning to see what was going on further down the hill.

"Relax, Arthur," said Aurelianus with a smile. "I wish I were down there too, but this type of battle is between two shield walls. We have to settle for the position of spectators."

Arthur gripped Hengroen's reigns as he watched the slaughter. The two sides were at a complete standstill with neither giving up a foot of ground to the other. Suddenly, a great bellow rolled out across the hillside. From the trees on the eastern side of the hill Cei, Beduir and Caradog led their companies out of the forest and thundered across the grassy slope towards the enemy's left flank.

The battle was over in an instant. Turning in horrified surprise, the Saeson had no time to form a defensive flank and fell like wheat beneath the hooves of the Britons. Pressed on two sides, they faltered and fell back, at last giving up some ground. At the rear of the enemy host, Cymen and his commanders wheeled their mounts around and ordered the retreat.

"Their leaders are getting away!" bellowed Aurelianus. "They shame their gods! After them! No

Sais escapes this day!" He urged his horse into a gallop and took off down the hill, red cloak billowing.

Arthur marvelled at the old man's energy and lust for slaughter and kicked Hengroen into a gallop.

Cymen had left himself too little time to flee. In the confusion, the frightened horses turned and got in each other's way in their attempt to escape. Aurelianus led the charge around their right flank. The Britons surrounded the enemy leaders and, one by one, brought each of them down, their horses whinnying in fright as they rolled and kicked, their riders struck from their saddles.

Arthur hailed Cei, Beduir and Caradog across the field of slaughter but it was already over. Every one of the Sais commanders was dead.

"Victory!" yelled Cei in triumph and the cry was taken up by the whole hillside; a great cheering clamour rolling up to the clouds.

"Which one is Cymen?" Arthur asked Aurelianus as they inspected the corpses that lay strewn across the bloodied grass.

"Here he is," replied Aurelianus, indicating a bloody corpse that had been rolled on by one of the horses and half crushed. The man's face was a mask of horror and his body was riddled with holes where a spear had struck him again and again. "His father is going to be most upset."

Behind them, Cymen's wolf standard had been knocked down and his men were stamping it into the mud, shattering the white ram's skull into hundreds of splintered fragments. Some men had begun to chant Arthur's name as their bloodied spears and swords stabbed at the air. Aurelianus smiled at him.

"The day is yours, Arthur."

They rode immediately for Cair Badon and found it emptied. They rode through deserted streets and looked upon a town frozen in time. It must have been an impressive sight in its day but now its grandeur was decayed and its streets haunted by the whispers of memory.

Arthur immediately gave orders for the gates to be repaired and for the walls and towers to be manned. The only place large enough to accommodate the teulu was inside the ruined amphitheatre. A makeshift camp was set up on its sands, surrounded by the crumbling benches that rose tier upon tier seemingly to the sky. Menw advised Arthur to drain the bathhouses to reduce the risk of fever and work began on clearing all the debris and stagnant water that they had swum through on their first visit to the town.

Arthur and his captains took lodgings in the basilica along with Aurelianus and his own men. The Saeson had left some stores and these were broken into eagerly for the men were hungry and keen to celebrate.

"That is some sword you have there," said Aurelianus. They were eating in one of the upper chambers that looked out over the sprawling tents in the amphitheatre where the lights of cookfires twinkled like stars and the sound of singing drifted up to them. "Where did you get it?"

"Funny you should ask," Arthur replied, drawing *Caledbulc* from its scabbard so that Aurelianus could inspect it properly. "I found it in a villa on the journey south. It was hidden in a temple to Sulis Minerva along with a few other bits and pieces."

"A fine blade," said Aurelianus, testing the weapon's balance. "And the workmanship! I'd say this was the sword of somebody rather important. A king perhaps."

"Menw thinks it may have been made with the goddess in mind and kept in her temple as a perpetual offering. It looks as if it has never been used or at least if it has, I'd like to meet the man who can burnish the nick and scrape off a blade entirely."

"Perhaps your bard is right. Who knows what the old pagan customs were?" He remembered himself and glanced at Arthur from beneath his long white brows. "I understand they still flourish in the northern fringes of Albion."

"Yes, Christianity has not found such a secure foothold in Venedotia as it has in the south. I have seen swords thrown into lakes at the funerals of great warriors but never anything so fine as this."

"You are a pagan?"

Arthur considered his words before answering. "I am no Christian if that is your meaning. I was raised with the customs of my people, taught devotion to Modron, the Great Mother. But…"

"But what?"

"I am unsure of my true path. Sometimes I feel the Great Mother speaking to me, other times she is silent."

"That can be said of my god too," said Aurelianus with a grim smile. He sighed. "For years I always believed that only the power of Christ could defeat the pagan barbarians at our gates but I suppose the sword of another pagan might be just as effective. After all, I don't seem to have achieved very much after forty years of war. Christ in Heaven, forty years! For what? The Saeson are now deeper into the west than they have ever been!"

"Come now," said Arthur, feeling a touch of sympathy for the old general. "Your name is spoken with awe across the island. It means hope to those who have none. You have held the barbarian wolves at bay for two generations. Many have lived because of you."

Aurelianus looked to him, his tired eyes grateful for his effort to cheer him. "And now, this old wolf grows grey and long in the tooth. The enemy smells its ailing strength. What for Albion when I am gone?"

"Albion will fight on, in your name."

"Then it needs a leader."

Arthur understood what Aurelianus was getting at and he was deeply flattered. And also terrified.

"I was once the *Comes Britanniarum*," said Aurelianus. "One of the last commands of Roman Britannia, created by Theodosius after he saved us from the Barbarian Conspiracy." His eyes gazed into the flames of the brazier as he remembered days long passed. "My command was of a mobile field army – cavalry mostly – charged with the island's defence. I reported to the head of the Council of Britannia for there was such a thing in those days. His name was Vertigernus." At this his face darkened as if tasting something bitter.

"I have heard of Vertigernus," said Arthur. "It is said that he was the one who persuaded Cunedag and his sons to relocate to the west to fight the Gaels."

"Yes, he knew your grandsire, as did I."

"You knew Cunedag?" Arthur asked.

"I was a very young man at the time. Vertigernus held Albion in his grasp and his influence stretched from Dumnonia to the lands of the Votadini. He was very good at manipulating fire to fight fire. The old roman tactic of *Foederati*; using one lot of barbarians to fight another. He wasn't always successful though."

"The Saeson," said Arthur.

"Yes. They were led by two brothers in those days; Hengest and Horsa." He almost spat their names out, such contempt they summoned in his gut. "Vertigernus used them to fight the Picts and it fell to me to lead them in that war. They were insubordinate animals and I was glad to be shot of them as soon as the war was over. Vertigernus had promised them land in Cantium and that should have been the end of it. But Vertigernus was a lecherous old dog and he lusted after Hengest's daughter. He would have traded all of Albion for that Sais witch."

"Vertigernus's sons and I wrote to the mighty Aetius of Gaul, asking him for aid but he was too busy keeping the Huns at bay. The only help that came was a wily old bishop. Germanus was his name and he helped rid us of Vertigernus and we cast his wretched treaty with the Saeson to the flames."

"What happened?" Arthur asked.

Aurelianus seemed to be grappling with something that had lain buried deep within for many years. It threatened to break to the surface and Arthur wondered how the old man had kept something of such magnitude under control for so many years. Tears started in his eyes and he wiped them away quickly, looking away from the flames. "We lost. We lost Cantium and Hengest and his spawn set down their roots. Now we all suffer for Vertigernus's treachery and our own weakness."

Aurelianus lapsed into silence, his voice spent.

"You are still our *Comes Britanniarum*," Arthur said.

Aurelianus shook his head. "The old Roman commands are dead. They call me *Dux Bellorum* now; the Leader of Battles. An informal title, nothing more."

"But you hold it as if it were the most sacred office in the Roman Empire. Official title or no, the people of this island look to you as their protector just as they did in the days of Vertigernus and the Council."

"And now they must look to you, Arthur. Give them hope as I once did."

"Hope they have. But can we beat them?" It was a question everybody had been avoiding but he had to ask it.

"I honestly don't know," Aurelianus replied. "When we beat Cymen we beat only a small vanguard. As we speak, Aelle is planning his vengeance, gathering as many Saeson clans to his banner as he can. It will not be long before he marches on Cair Badon. You do well to refortify the town, but we cannot sit out a siege. And it will do no good to retreat further west, Aelle will bring fire and sword to Cair Guenta, Cair Legion and all the rest of them. This is where we must make our stand, our *final* stand if needs be. You have cavalry, that is good, but they are useless behind these walls."

"I agree," said Arthur. "I must lead them on the field, but we will be hopelessly outnumbered. Is there nobody else we can call on for aid?"

"Yes. King Marcus Cunomorius of Dumnonia; the *Sea Wolf*. He has ridden under my banner before. He has access to the fine horse markets of Armorica where he has extensive territories. The Gaels plague his coastline and trade routes which is I assume, why he did not come to my aid when I was captured. But no matter. You must go to him, Arthur and convince him to join us. He must send for as many horses from Armorica as he can."

"Marcus Cunomorius…" said Arthur.

"They call him March in the common tongue. He is a hot-tempered bugger but a good fighter and we need his horses if we are to beat Aelle."

"Then I will ride west and speak with him."

"I suggest you leave tomorrow for time is short. God knows how many days we have until Aelle will be upon us."

As soon as it was light Arthur began making preparations. "I'm taking Beduir and his company," he told Cei. "You and Caradog shall remain here with Aurelianus. When word gets around that he is free, more will come to our cause. Get them trained up as you did at Cair Legion. Keep up the reinforcement of the town. Make this place a fortress that can withstand a storm."

"You know I'll whip the buggers into shape," said Cei.

"Establish a supply route with Guenta. We need grain and horse fodder. The granaries here are in not too bad a shape. See how well you can stock them."

"You can count on me, Arthur. Take care down in Dumnonia. They're mad bastards by all accounts."

Arthur laughed. "If they are mad enough to fight alongside us, that will be good enough for me!"

They rode out before noon and took the road south-west towards another deserted town called Cair Uisc. From there they headed across rough tracks into the toe of Albion; a country of bleak moors dotted with wind-blasted tors.

King March held his court at Cair Dor on the Afon Fowydh. Far from a grand Roman town of stone and terracotta roofs, Cair Dor was a truly British ringfort. A banked ditch enclosed thatched roundhouses and Arthur was reminded that Roman culture, like its roads, had not extended this far into the south-west. He was also reminded of home and did his best not to think of Guenhuifar.

They camped on a hilltop in plain sight and Arthur sent Gualchmei and a small detachment down to Cair Dor to inform King March of their presence.

It was early evening when they returned. "He was drunk," Gualchmei said. "Drowning his sorrows after losing something of a civil war."

"Civil war?" Arthur asked. "Here in Dumnonia? Aurelianus never said anything about that."

"It's been a rather recent upset. Do you by any chance remember a young Pict we brought back as a hostage from the north? A sulky little bastard called Drustan?"

"Yes, now that you mention it. Wasn't he the son of Talorc, the chieftain who was set to rule the Votadini lands had Caw's confederation been successful?"

"The very same," said Menw. "And uncle to Queen Meddyf."

"Now I remember!" said Arthur. "He was sent down south as a political hostage!"

"To his uncle, King March," said Menw. "March's sister was one of Talorc's many wives."

"It's all gone a bit sordid, I'm afraid," said Gualchmei. "King March has recently married some Gaelic princess in an effort to bring the marauders to heel. That worked out all right, until Drustan ran off with her."

They gaped at Gualchmei.

"Are you telling me," said Arthur, "that treacherous little swine has seduced the Queen of Dumnonia and started a civil war?"

"That's more or less the size of it. There has long been political division in Dumnonia you see, and Drustan was able to exploit it to his advantage. He now rules the Cornubians from Din Tagel; March's most valuable port on the northern coast."

"Cornubians?" Arthur enquired.

"Dumnonia was a sub-province thrown together by the Romans," Menw explained. "It was originally two distinct tribal territories; that of the Dumnonii and the Cornubii. The Dumnonii were evidently the superior, thus the kingdom's name but the rivalry has continued to this day it seems."

"And Drustan has split the kingdom down its old tribal lines," said Gualchmei. "Now he sits on March's trade routes with Gaul, Armorica and a few distant places I've never heard of."

"Lands as far as Constantinople trade with Dumnonia, I've heard," said Menw. "I can well imagine March is seething."

"Will he meet with me?" Arthur asked Gualchmei.

"Yes. He is very keen to receive you. I think he hopes for your intervention and sees a chance to get Din Tagel back."

"I'm not here to get bogged down in a civil war," said Arthur. "Our time is limited. I just need those horses of his."

March was a tall, broad-shouldered man with black curly hair and clothes that revealed his far-reaching trade links. Eastern influence was abundant in his silks and the gold crucifix that hung about his neck was Byzantine in style.

"Greetings, Arthur mab Enniaun, Penteulu of Venedotia," he said as Arthur dismounted in the main yard of Cair Dor. "Welcome to Dumnonia. I hear you bring tidings of victory from the east."

"Indeed I do, King March," Arthur replied. "We have struck the first blow in the war that will drive the Saeson back to where they came from. Ambrosius Aurelianus is freed and Cair Badon is currently being refortified to hold back the tides of darkness."

"I regret that you stood alone in your task but I fear these are troubled times for Dumnonia."

"They are troubled times for all Albion, sire. But together we may yet see the light of dawn."

"You propose a union? An alliance in arms?"

"It is my deepest wish to call as many British kings and leaders to Venedotia's dragon banner as I am able. The Saeson are strong but they have always faced us when we are divided by quarrel and blood feud. The only way to defeat them is to unite against a common enemy."

"I am glad you think so," said March with a small smile. "Aurelianus has long called for unity and I have often fought alongside him but the other rulers in these parts have been unable to look beyond their own interests. Come, let us drink to our union indoors!"

He led them into his great roundhouse with was luxuriantly painted and decorated with tapestries. Over their meal they discussed the troubles afflicting Dumnonia and what must be done to resolve them.

"I'm sure you understand that I want my nephew dead for what he has done," said March around a mouthful of olives.

"And your wife?" Arthur enquired.

March sighed. "Esyllt is the daughter of a powerful king over in Erin. Our marriage brought an end to a generation of bloodshed between our two peoples. I cannot so easily discard her nor punish her too severely despite what she has done. I don't want King Crimthann of the Laigin knocking on my door with accusations that I have mistreated his daughter."

"Then you are prepared to take her back."

March sighed and patted the table softly with the palm of his hand as if wrestling with an irrevocable truth. "Yes, damn her, I want her back."

"How well defended is Din Tagel?" Beduir asked.

"Ha! That's the bugger of the whole thing! My traitorous nephew only managed to steal the most impenetrable fortress in all Dumnonia from me! It sits on a peninsula connected to the mainland by a narrow neck of rock. You could throw a thousand men at it and all would be slaughtered in that bottleneck. No, a direct assault won't work else I would already have retaken it. We must lure Drustan out somehow."

"Haven't you already tried that?" asked Arthur.

"Yes, but he is too cunning to fall for any trap. He knows I want his head."

"Perhaps he would agree to a temporary truce," said one of March's lords who sat by his side. "The word of a neutral third party might yield some concessions on his part."

"Yes," said March in an innocent tone that seemed rather overdone to Arthur's ears. "An intermediary might serve as a magistrate in the matter."

"You wish me to intervene," said Arthur.

"As a neutral third party, of course," said March.

"Why would Drustan listen to me? Even if he knows who I am, he is not likely to think kindly of me for my part in the defeat of the Pictish confederacy."

"He knows this stalemate can't go on for ever," said March. "He may be prepared to listen to reason."

"There would have to be terms," said Arthur. "Concessions."

"There is a limit to how much ground I am prepared to give," said March, his eyes suddenly flashing with defiance. "Even if I let him live, I can't have him wandering free making a mockery of me."

"What do you think he would settle for?"

"Nothing short of my bloody wife, I should think!" snapped March.

"And that is something you are not going to yield to him, even if he gives up Din Tagel?"

March was thoughtful. "No. Already I wear the cuckhold's horns in the eyes of my people. Esyllt must be returned to me."

"With respect sire, we do not have time for this," said Arthur. "Every moment we waste, Aelle grows stronger. I came here to ask for your help in fighting the Saeson. Aurelianus says you have the best horses in Albion. We need a strong and large cavalry to defeat Aelle."

"Alas, my cavalry is in Armorica," said March. "I have long faced resistance from those who resent my rule there and now Drustan, God curse his name, has even voyaged to Armorica personally to stir up yet more hatred of me. Even some of my own bannermen have switched their allegiance to him, no doubt bribed by some of the wealth he is leeching from my trade routes at Din Tagel. Even if I could rally some of my cavalry, I have no way of getting them here. All my boats fit for the transportation of horses are in the southern portion of Armorica, harboured in ports controlled by Drustan."

Arthur closed his eyes in frustration. This was exactly the kind of thing that had made Albion weak in the face of her enemies. "So, what you are telling me, is that I cannot have your horses unless Drustan is brought to heel."

"That's more or less it."

Arthur wanted to slam his fist down on the table in anger but he was able to keep a check on his rage, remembering that he was the guest of a king. "Then it seems that we shall have to have words with this Drustan mab Talorc."

Gualchmei was proving himself to be quite the honey-tongued emissary and so Arthur dispatched him to carry his invitation to Drustan at Din Tagel. The ruling, if Drustan accepted it, was to take place in the forest that stretched between Cair Dor and Din Tagel. Arthur and March set up camp there with their retinues and they were joined by two holy men; Abbot Petroc and Abbot Piran who oversaw small monasteries in the west of the kingdom, in the part now known as Cornubia. They were not at all happy about its new designation and remained loyal to March.

"He's a pagan savage," said Petroc.

"And she's an adulterous whore," added Piran, not sugar-coating his words leading Arthur to assume that March had spoken of his wife to them in similar terms before.

They looked on Arthur and his men with an uneasy caution. It was clear to them that yet more 'pagan savages' had been admitted to the fold but they refrained from objecting, given their desire to see Drustan and his whore ousted from Din Tagel and the western portion of Dumnonia returned to March's rule.

"The church has wholly condemned both Drustan and Esyllt," said March. "He has even proclaimed himself king of this rebel state. There was talk of excommunicating him but he is a pagan so what can be done?"

"Not my area of expertise," said Arthur. "You do realise that this discussion is eventually going to boil down to you offering him Din Tagel in exchange for Esyllt, don't you?"

March snorted. "If I can get my way, I'll have both back from him! And if he is stubborn, well, let us just say that your arrival is most timely. Your teulu at Cair Badon may be a most persuasive factor in the negotiations"

"I told you, we don't have time for a war. I seek only a quick resolution or a compromise that gives us access to the horse runs and markets of Armorica. This feud over your wife can wait until we have sent Aelle back east with his tail between his legs."

The following morning, reports reached them that a large host had marched south from Din Tagel and camped on the edge of a moor beyond the reach of the forest. Gualchmei was sent to establish communication and rode back into camp bearing Drustan's message. "He agrees to discuss terms but will not enter the forest for fear of his life."

"Craven!" said March and he was joined by the jeers of his men.

"Will he speak with me?" Arthur asked.

"Aye, remembers you and wishes to renew your acquaintance."

Arthur turned to March. "Let me go and meet with him alone. It will allay his fears of an ambush."

"Fine," said March. "I trust in you, Arthur, to negotiate on my behalf. But I have the final word on any agreements."

"Of course, sire."

Arthur, Beduir, Gualchmei and Menw, along with a small guard, rode north out of the forest to the camp up on the moor. It was a cluster of tents and pavilions and the Cornubians turned out in numbers to meet the delegation.

It was not hard to pick Drustan out. He had a beard, thick and full for a lad his age and his hair was long, bound by a simple crown to fall back in a loose tail that reached to the middle of his shoulders. He was a stark contrast to the clean-shaved and short-haired southern Britons that surrounded him. He said nothing as Arthur and his retinue approached and looked down on them with a mixture of scorn and triumph.

"Drustan mab Talorc," said Arthur. "I hope you are well. You seem to have used your banishment to your advantage."

"Corner a lamed wolf and he will still fight," said Drustan. "But if you turn your back on him he will lick his wounds and recover his strength."

"I wish I could say that I came bearing the best wishes of your niece," said Arthur, "but Queen Meddyf has no knowledge of what has occurred in Dumnonia. I myself only learned of it upon my arrival."

"And so my uncle sent Venedotia's butcher to do his dirty work," said Drustan with a wry smile.

"He just wants his wife back," said Arthur.

"No. He wants Din Tagel back and my head on a pole. He shall have neither."

"What's your plan then? Wall yourself up on that peninsula forever? March wants to break this stalemate but not nearly as much as I do."

"You? What do you care of Dumnonia's troubles?"

"I assume you have heard of the threat from the east."

"Aelle? March will face him long before I do and who knows? Perhaps both will be weakened enough for me to claim the rest of Dumnonia and consolidate our defences indefinitely."

"Hmm. A canny plan but a flawed one. Aelle will march west before the summer is out. You have March's cavalry tied up in Armorica. The Saeson will sweep into Dumnonia's western lands with ease. March will be defeated and you will be next but by that time there will be no one to help you."

"Help me? Who offers me their help now? You, Arthur?"

"Yes. I have retaken Cair Badon. I have rescued Ambrosius Aurelianus and sent the Sais dogs running back to their master. I am the last defence of the West. But I cannot hold the Sais tide without your help. We must work together now else all will be lost come harvest."

"It sounds like you are more interested in becoming my ally than helping my uncle get his wife back."

Arthur did not allow his face to betray a single emotion or motive. "This war is bigger than March's pride and his petty feud with you. I will do whatever it takes to win it."

Drustan smiled at this and invited Arthur and his companions into his pavilion for meat and drink. Arthur was surprised upon entering to see a woman seated on a chair bedecked with furs at the head table next to Drustan's empty chair. She was fair and beautiful and wore a circlet of silver; the crown of a queen.

"Allow me to introduce you to Queen Esyllt of Cornubia," said Drustan as he led them to the head table.

"You brought her with you from Din Tagel?" said Arthur. "Isn't that a little risky?"

"She is Cornubia's queen as I am its king. We decide its fate together."

"And when I heard that the mighty Arthur, penteulu of Venedotia had arrived in the south," spoke Esyllt, "I wanted to see the man himself." She spoke British well although with a strong Gaelic accent.

Arthur knew he was being flattered. What would a Gaelic princess know of him? And in that bout of flattery, he knew that Drustan wanted his friendship despite his surly attitude. Why else bring his queen down from their peninsula fortress? He clearly hoped that she would win Arthur over with her beauty and her honeyed tongue. And yet, there was a little hostility in Drustan's voice and manners, almost as if he was daring Arthur to challenge his rule.

"March wants his wife back above all things," said Arthur as they sat down at the table and food and drink was brought out by servants. "He is willing even to forsake Din Tagel in order to get her."

"Din Tagel is a fortress," said Esyllt coolly. "I am a woman. I will not be bought or bartered as if I were a lump of sea-blasted rock or a crown of cold metal. I am Drustan's and he is mine. Some things cannot be negotiated."

"I understand that," said Arthur. "Indeed, I respect it. But you must see March's predicament. He is the laughing stock of his own kingdom. Not only have you dishonoured him, you have crippled his power by taking Din Tagel and disrupting his influence both in Dumnonia and Armorica. Something must be done in order to break this stalemate."

"Must it?" asked Drustan. "Tell me, Arthur. Why is it that you are so keen to negotiate when it comes to British matters and yet, if a Pict claims sovereignty over an area his ancestors ruled, you seek only bloodshed?"

There it was again; a deep resentment in the young Pict's eyes that threatened to cast peaceful negotiation to the wind and invite war instead.

"I know that you blame Venedotia for the defeat of Caw's confederation," said Arthur. "But his ambitions stretched further than reclaiming the Votadini lands. In a year, perhaps two, he would have turned his eyes south, to the lands below the Wall. King Cadwallon saw fit to nip that in the bud. I am sorry that you felt you had to be involved."

"I was *born* involved," said Drustan, his eyes spitting fire. "My father was Lord of Din Eidyn, king between the Wall and the Bodotria estuary. That was to be my kingdom; I was to be a king! But you changed all that. I don't blame Venedotia or King Cadwallon. I blame *you*. It was your cavalry charge that decimated our ranks in the Caledonian Forest. I saw you myself, butchering my men with your red sword!"

Esyllt's hand reached out and rested on Drustan's forearm, restraining him, reminding him of what was at stake and Arthur saw who the real power in Cornubia was. She wasn't about to let her lover's hot head ruin things.

Arthur held Drustan's gaze. "And, denied your birth right, you sought to claim another kingdom." His eyes glanced to Esyllt. "And found the means to do so."

Esyllt glared at Arthur and he laughed. "Don't misunderstand me, I do not judge you for what you have done, although March wants me to. I care not for Dumnonia's politics. I just need its allegiance. Ambrosius Aurelianus tells me that March has access to the finest of war stallions and brood mares but it seems that you now hold that game piece. What would it take for you to open up the ports in Armorica and ship over two-hundred of the best horses?"

Drustan narrowed his eyes. He seemed impressed by Arthur's bluntness and willingness to cut to the chase. "Recognition of our sovereignty," he said. "And he must divorce Esyllt."

Arthur grimaced. "He may find those terms a little hard to swallow. And so too would the church."

"Nevertheless," said Esyllt. "Those are our terms."

They were invited to stay for the evening and drink was poured liberally while the harp strings were strummed. They all got a little drunk and as Arthur watched Drustan and Esyllt lolling in their fur-clad throne, she popping morsels of food into his mouth and he nuzzling her neck, he knew that he saw something more than just ambition and rebellion. He saw love; a forbidden love he had experienced himself in those early days with Guenhuifar.

Menw spoke into his ear, disturbing his reverie. "Think carefully which side you are backing in these negotiations. There are advantages and disadvantages in supporting either."

"Who said anything about supporting a side?" said Arthur. "I am merely a peacekeeper; an intermediary."

"But sooner or later you will be called to give your judgement," said Menw. "Both March and Drustan want to use you and your military power as a lever in the negotiations to get what they want. And don't try to fool me, young man. I know that you will do what is necessary to get those horses. If you support March's claim, then it will mean bloodshed and it might be hard to explain to Queen Meddyf back home if it became known that Venedotia's penteulu had supported a war against her young tearaway of an uncle. On the other hand, if you decide in Drustan's favour, both March and the Christian church will condemn you. You must choose at some point, Arthur. Just make sure you choose wisely."

They awoke with aching heads and the heat of the day did nothing to help. Arthur sought water and doused his head in a butt to refresh himself.

"Gaulish wine gives one the worst hangovers," said Drustan, exiting his tent and stretching his long limbs in the sun. Through the tent flap, Arthur could see Esyllt's naked form curled up on the furs as she slumbered.

"I must return to March," he said. "And tell him of my decision."

"And what is your decision, Arthur of Venedotia?"

Arthur rubbed his temples. He knew that he had made his decision even before the discussions of the previous night. "Drustan," he said. "Get me those horses."

Peredur

Peredur's uncle had been shocked to learn that his sister's son did not even know how to hold a sword correctly, let alone use one.

"Do you mean to say those dolts my sister employed didn't even teach you the basic means with which to defend yourself?" he had exclaimed.

"Garth and Emlin were simple house servants," Peredur had explained. "They were good people but they were not warriors. Mother wanted me to have nothing to do with warriors or battle."

Edlim had thrown up his hands in despair and Peredur soon found himself embarking upon a rigorous routine of martial training and exercise. He rose early every morning and ran several miles in the hills that surrounded Edlim's villa, returning to wash and eat a simple breakfast before a long morning of sword and spear practice.

Edlim's master-at-arms trained him, first teaching him the simple cuts against a wooden post to get used to the weight of the weapon, then later rehearsing an array of stances, blocks and attacks with wooden, weighted foils. Sometimes Edlim himself stepped in and they sparred together until the sweat ran down their brows.

Peredur learned how to fight in a shield wall as well as in single combat against adversaries wielding swords, spears and axes. He had strong arms from a life of toil at his mother's farm but he was also light on his feet and learned the fast moves and stances with surprising ease. It was hard work and each evening he collapsed into his bed, his muscles screaming with fatigue and his eyelids feeling as if they were weighted with lead like the wooden foils they practiced with.

Edlim was impressed with Peredur's archery skills and admitted that there was little to teach him in that department, indeed his nephew had a few things to teach him. When the time came for Edlim to evaluate his young ward's skill upon a horse, Peredur was forced to admit that he had never even sat upon a horse let alone ridden one. When his uncle had finished choking upon his appalled shock, he hastily added horse riding to the already considerable list of things to teach his nephew.

Peredur took to his tuition with all the eagerness and enthusiasm of a child devouring a honeycake. He had longed for the chance to learn the skills his father had excelled at.

He noticed that his body was changing day by day. His muscles had taken on a more defined look and had hardened over the past few weeks. His chest grew deeper and his shoulders wider and he could no longer see his ribs thanks to the wholesome meals provided by his uncle's kitchens.

They spent their evenings in the hall, sharing stories about Peredur's mother. Peredur listened with fascination as his uncle recalled a girl far removed from the bitter, melancholy woman who had scolded and berated him throughout his childhood. As he looked around at the walls of what had been her childhood home, he began to see her in a wholly new light. It was a given that she would come and live with them and Edlim had dispatched riders to fetch her along with Garth and Emlin. Soon they would live in the villa as a family reunited.

For his part, Peredur felt that his arrival in his uncle's life had brought some closure to a pain Edlim had felt for many years. The mystery of his sister's fate had finally been resolved, long after he had given up hope. Peredur got the feeling that a huge void in his uncle's life had finally been closed and for that solace, his uncle was grateful.

But Edlim's riders returned bearing sorry news. Garth and Emlin rode into the villa complex wearing long faces and when Peredur saw that his mother was not with them, he feared the worst.

"She died not two days after you left," said Emlin, hugging Peredur tight.

"She died because I left her!" he said, tears streaming down his cheeks.

"No! You must never believe that!"

"She was a sick woman, lad," said Garth. "We all did what we could for her but had you stayed, her days would have been short anyway."

Edlim was also sorely grieved to lose his sister a second time, and before he could even see her one last time. He gave Garth and Emlin positions on his staff and they gradually reacquainted themselves with being around people, just as Peredur had had to.

Villa life was an exhilarating, fascinating and often confusing new experience for Peredur. Raised in the quiet seclusion of the forest, all around him was suddenly noise and clamour; the creaking of iron-bound wood, the smell of sweat and leather, the heavy blows of the blacksmith's hammer upon glowing steel, and of course the shouting. Everyone shouted in Edlim's villa. The guards shouted, Edlim shouted and the servants shouted. They shouted when they were angry, they shouted when they were happy and even their laughter was loud.

He found that he was well-liked by his uncle's men who were always ready with a smile and a polite bit of conversation whenever he passed them. Several of the servant girls giggled to each other and flashed him smiles whenever he passed and one had even winked at him causing his face to burn with embarrassment. Women were something of a mystery to him. He liked them (especially their hair and the way their chests wobbled when they walked) but he could never think of a single thing to say to them and so preferred to steer well clear of them altogether.

On the whole, life was good. He had found something of a family in the home of his uncle. His heart glowed with the happiness that acceptance had brought. But deep inside, there was a gnawing guilt. He still prayed for the soul of the man he had killed, and despite his best efforts to convince himself that he was doing the right thing in staying with his uncle, he had not forgotten the vow he had made in the presence of God that he would not rest until he had joined Arthur's teulu.

Edlim smiled at this and told him that he was pleased with how far he had come from the inept and lost youth he had first met. He also said that there was nothing wrong in killing a man who stole from him and if he was going to get on his knees and pray for the soul of every man he slew, then his life would rapidly begin to resemble that of a monk.

In an effort to teach his nephew some vital lessons in life, Edlim let him attend some of the many matters of business that occupied his days. Peredur understood that his uncle was some sort of local nobleman who collected tribute and offered protection to businesses and homesteads. There were also some other more complicated business transactions involving trade that Peredur did not fully understand but his ears pricked up one time when Arthur's name was mentioned.

"He's some northern warlord come down here to help old Aurelianus against the Saeson," said the merchant with whom Edlim was sharing a jug of wine one sunny afternoon in the colonnaded portico. "Word has it he took Cair Badon from Aelle's son and sent the Saeson running back east."

"They'll be back," said Edlim.

"Oh, aye, this Arthur is counting on it. He's fortifying the town and demanding weekly shipments of grain from Guenta. He must have King Ynyr convinced he's Christ resurrected if that old fool is prepared to send that much grain into the borderlands."

"Perhaps this Arthur shows promise," said Edlim, glancing at Peredur. "At least my nephew seems to think so."

When the merchant had left, Edlim took Peredur to one side. "I know you want to go galloping off to Cair Badon and join Arthur," he said, "but please consider remaining with me for a while longer. You have learned much in the way of fighting, but you have far more to learn about how the world works."

"You mistake me, uncle," said Peredur. "I have no wish to join Arthur's teulu until I have drawn an apology from his man Cei and humiliated him as he humiliated me."

Edlim looked at him with an expression that showed he did not fully comprehend his intentions but respected them nonetheless. "That's good, lad. Strengthen yourself as Arthur strengthens Cair Badon. War will come soon enough along with your chance to avenge your father's honour."

A few days later a nun visited the villa. She sought an audience with Edlim and he and Peredur received her in his office.

"You may perhaps remember your neighbour, Sylvester," said the nun.

"Yes, I haven't heard from him in some time," said Edlim.

"That is because he is dead, God rest his soul."

"Oh? That is a shame. Who runs the estate now?"

"That is, in part, why I have come to you. I and my sisters live in a small nunnery on the edge of the late Sylvester's land. We always had good relations with the family but there was ever a black cloud on the horizon. His name is Heubarth; a wicked villain of a man who owns land to the south of Sylvester's villa. He has long coveted the hand of Sylvester's daughter but Sylvester would never hear of it. Now that he is dead, Heubarth has made his move."

"What's the villain done?" Edlim asked.

"He holds Sylvester's daughter and foster brothers hostage within their own villa. He commands a large body of thugs and they will not let anyone in or out. Even food is denied them."

"He starves them?"

"As good as. My sisters and I carry some food to them for Heubarth's thugs dare not touch us. We do what we can for them but have little enough as it is and I fear that they are running out of time."

"And Heubarth won't let up unless this girl agrees to marry him," said Edlim.

"Yes. But she is stubborn and so are her foster-brothers, God protect them. They will hold out until death claims them, I fear. Or until somebody does the charitable thing and intervenes on their behalf…"

Edlim smiled. "The charitable thing? You have come to the wrong man if you seek charity. I am a businessman. And it sounds like this Heubarth commands a considerable force. I could muster no more than twenty fighting men and they would need a better cause to fight for than some girl's honour."

"What better cause is there than to save one of God's children?" asked the nun, her voice audaciously frosted with criticism that surprised Peredur.

"No, I am sorry," said Edlim. "There is very little I can do save give you some advice to carry back to this girl of yours."

"And that advice is?"

"Marry the bastard. Then her family can eat."

The nun left them, frowning with disappointment.

"Uncle, it sits ill with me that we have the power to help a young woman in distress and we do nothing because there is no profit in it for us," Peredur said once the nun had left.

"Does it? You are a sensitive lad, Peredur. Perhaps that is my sister's fault. But really, what can we do? Go to war with our neighbours? We have war knocking on our door as it is without stirring up yet more trouble."

"This Heubarth sounds like a neighbour we could well do without."

"True enough. But I have too few men to hurl at him. How many must die so that one girl can marry whom she chooses?"

"Perhaps a more subtle plan may get the job done without any lives being wasted."

"How?"

Peredur was silent. He had hit upon something, a crude idea of a plan that would require much hammering out. "Let me think on it," he said. "In the meantime, could you do me a favour, uncle?"

"Of course."

"Find out as much as you can about Arthur's grain supply between Guenta and Cair Badon. When is it expected? How large is the guard escorting it, things like that."

Edlim raised his eyebrow at Peredur. "All right. I can't see what you're up to, but all right."

Two days later, Peredur rode out of the villa complex on one of the fine Iberian horses from his uncle's stables. He wore a simple tunica and breeches while his father's armour, expertly polished and restored by his uncle's armourer, was carried by a grey mare he led behind him. He travelled south-east, following the landmarks his uncle had identified for him to the lands of the recently deceased Sylvester.

He saw the villa from a distance. Nestled in a small valley, it was similar in appearance to his uncle's although it looked a little more run-down. The fields were barren and there was no wall surrounding the villa proper. Peredur wondered how Heubarth stopped food from getting in but there did seem to be an armed presence in the cluster of roundhouses on the villa's southern face.

Peredur rode over to the settlement and was immediately challenged by a pair of brutish warriors who were lounging about.

"Who the devil are you, young stripling?" asked one of them, eyeing the covered bundle on the back of Peredur's grey mare.

"My name is Peredur and I seek employment."

"Employment as what? The chief's bugger-boy?" They laughed at this bit of wit but soon stopped when they saw that Peredur was neither fazed nor amused.

"I am a warrior," he said. "And I will test the mettle of any man here to prove it. As it happens, I have some important information your 'chief' might be interested in."

"What sort of information?"

"Let me speak to the chief and you might find out."

"Bugger off."

"Fine. I'm sure there are other lords and landowners hereabout who need good sword arms. Doesn't Edlim Redsword live in these parts?"

"Just a minute," said the slightly cleverer of the two guards. "What have you got under that cloth?"

He eyed the grey mare again, curiosity getting the better of him.

Peredur reached over and flipped up the corner of the cloth. "My armour," he said.

The jaws of the two guards dropped.

"Well, if your chief isn't interested in my services or my information about a large shipment of grain passing nearby in a couple of days, I suppose I'll be off."

"Not so fast," said one of the guards, laying a hand on the bridle of his horse. "Maybe the chief would like a word with you."

They escorted him away from the settlement and across country to a crude house that was a mockery of a Roman villa. It was constructed entirely of timber and instead of terracotta tiles, it was roofed with wooden shingles. Warped wooden pillars supported a gallery and there were a dozen or so grubby outbuildings.

They waited outside the doorway to the main building while somebody who apparently had the role of a porter, went inside. He promptly emerged and indicated that they were free to enter.

They went indoors and up a staircase to what seemed to be a bedroom. The windows were shuttered, keeping in the fetid smell of body odour and sex. A man stirred on a pallet of skins before getting up, leaving a slumbering woman to roll over and curl up on her other side.

The man walked over to a basin and doused his face with water. He was bare to his breeches, his body hard, muscular and scarred. He was not an old man, but he had seen a lot of action. Wiping the water from his eyes, he turned to stare at Peredur.

"This is the lad who wants employment, is it?"

"Aye, chief," said one of the guards. "You should take a look at his armour. Proper Roman stuff."

"Are you Heubarth?" asked Peredur.

"Aye, that I am. How came you by my name?"

"It seems to be well-known in these parts. And a warrior looking for employment knows that the biggest wolf-pack will offer the largest pickings."

"You look a little young to be a warrior," said Heubarth.

"I have been trained since the cradle," lied Peredur. "My father was a great warrior in the service of a northern king. It is his armour I now carry."

"I am told you have some information about a grain shipment."

"Aye. There is a warlord in the south who thinks to take on Aelle and his Saeson. He has made Cair Badon his base and supplies it from Guenta. There is a large wagon train of grain and horse fodder making its way down from Cair Gloui two days from now."

"And I can trust this information, naturally."

"I am willing to lead the ambush myself," said Peredur. "So that you know my word is good."

"Lead?" asked Heubarth, narrowing his eyes at him. "Lead my men? No, boy. You will come with us and you will follow my orders. And if there is any hint of a trap or treachery, I will personally ensure that you will be the first to die. Slowly."

The ambush consisted of twenty riders concealed in the wooded ridge by the side of the road. Heubarth led the riders himself. They were armed with a variety of weapons, tools and crude objects fashioned to inflict maximum blunt force.

In the two days leading up to the ambush, Peredur had done his best to make himself one of the gang. Although there had initially been talk of putting his martial skills to the test, nothing had come of it for Heubarth had been too busy preparing for the outing. Peredur had proved himself in a few wrestling matches with the men and he thanked God for a life of farming and labour that had given him a strong build and Edlim's training that had given him the skills needed to overcome his opponents.

They waited for most of the morning before the slow progress of the wain came into sight. It was drawn by two mighty aurochs, their long, curved horns bent to the road as they pulled it along. A company of six riders escorted it their plumed helms and round shields denoting professional soldiers from Cair Guenta or Cair Legion. Ten foot soldiers marched in back of the column, bows and crossbows over their shoulders and on their backs.

Peredur chewed his bottom lip nervously as they approached. This was a risky plan that could go awry in so many ways. He feared for the lives of the men escorting the grain. While they were not Arthur's men, they were affiliated with him and he did not want to see any of them killed. But he could hardly tell Heubarth to go easy on them lest he suspect anything.

When they were almost within bowshot, Heubarth gave the signal and they rode down the wooded slope as one, threading the trees and charging onto the road, ten in front of the wain and ten behind.

The horses of the mounted guard reared up and whinnied in fright while the footmen turned this way and that, unslinging their bows and fumbling for arrows.

"Stay your weapons!" roared Heubarth. "Throw them down and you will live. Resist and die!"

The captain of the mounted guard looked ready to charge but thought better of it when he compared his sixteen men (of whom ten were on foot) against the twenty hardened thieves on horseback who surrounded them. At a signal from him, weapons clattered to the road's surface.

Peredur breathed a small sigh of relief as the subdued men were sent back west to explain to their master what had happened. It had been as he had hoped; they cared too much for their own lives to put up a fight. Why should they die so that some warlord got his grain?

Heubarth's men were jubilant upon inspecting their haul. "There is enough grain here to feed us for a year!" one of them exclaimed.

"If you want to live on grain alone," said Heubarth. "No. We keep some for ourselves and find a buyer for the rest. There are plenty of starving families in this part of Albion. We are sure to get a good price!"

The men laughed and Peredur swore to himself that he would die before he let Heubarth and his gang of rogues grow fat by extorting the desperate.

The success of the raid had lifted Peredur in the esteem of Heubarth and his gang. They slapped his back and promised him a celebratory drinking session as soon as they got back.

The crude granary on Heubarth's land was too small and rat-infested to hold the grain. Instead, the sacks were kept on the wain in a disused stable. Peredur enquired as to what was to be done with it next. He got his answer the following day.

"We have a much more secure place for the grain further north," said Heubarth. "You will come with me. I have some friends to check in on."

They rode north with the wain and Peredur smiled inwardly when he realised that they were approaching the villa of Sylvester.

The road led past the small settlement Peredur had first approached. It seemed to serve as some sort of guard over the villa. They were admitted with a grudging respect by the villa's occupants. Four young men met them on the steps to the villa proper and, by their frowns, Peredur could tell that they resented this impromptu visit. A young woman stood behind them beneath the portico. Her dress had once been fine but it was now soiled and patched in places. Despite this, Peredur could see that she was very beautiful. Hair, black as a raven's wing, fell down over her slender shoulders and the contrast of her red lips against her pale complexion reminded Peredur of hot blood spilt on fresh snow.

"Greetings, neighbours!" said Heubarth, swinging himself down from his saddle.

"What is the reason for this visit?" asked one of the four lads.

"Do I need a reason to visit the home of my love?" Heubarth asked, flashing a grin at the woman at the top of the steps. Her eyes spat fire at him and she vanished inside.

The attention of the four men was focused on the wain and Peredur could almost see them salivating at the thought of what it might contain. Heubarth followed their gaze and smiled. "Yes," he said. "We have been rather fortunate. This convoy of grain fell into our hands and I knew that the only safe place for it was within the secure walls of your villa. Take it around the back boys! The grain was not our only stroke of good fortune. I thought perhaps I should introduce you to our newest member and quite a find he was too!" He rested a hand on Peredur's shoulder. It was all Peredur could do not to shrink from it.

"Do you seek to torment us?" asked one of the four youths. "You bring enough grain to our villa to feed an army while you starve us half to death?"

"Oh, you do me an injustice, Aeron," said Heubarth. "I brought it here not only to keep it safe from marauders, but to share my good fortune with my future in-laws!"

"A bribe then," said another of the youths. "You seek to starve us into desperation and then buy our foster-sister from us with grain!"

"Can I help it if the harvests have not been good?" said Heubarth. "What little grain there is is quickly gobbled up by strong fighting men who need their strength to ensure the safety of others…"

"Men like yours, you mean," said the brother called Aeron. "I suppose you deny holding all the food in these parts for yourself."

"I take what I can for myself and my men," said Heubarth. "If your foster-father had made adequate provisions for his offspring, you might not find yourselves in the predicament you are currently in. Take this grain as a measure of my charity but know that I would be willing to share on a more permanent basis if your foster-sister would look a little more favourably on my offer of marriage."

There was nothing to be done and the four brothers went back inside, leaving Heubarth to strut about as if he were lord of the villa. He made arrangements with the servants for the billeting of his men for the night and even invited himself for dinner.

As the men sought out their rooms on the ground floor, Peredur put a question to Hefin, one of Heubarth's men.

"Does the chief really want to marry that girl?"

"Oh, aye," said Hefin. "He's had his eye on her since they were both children. But if you ask me, its the land he wants more." He gave Peredur a conspiratorial wink. "Old Sylvester's land was always more profitable than Heubarth's."

"What was all that about starving the family?"

"That's just Aeron letting off steam because they're going hungry. It's true what the chief said; there is little enough food to go around. Best it goes to the fighting men who are willing to protect weaklings like Aeron." He patted his chest with inflated sense of pride as if to indicate that he was such a man. "The chief regularly pays them a visit. He sees them as his charge ever since old Sylvester died."

"The girl is Sylvester's daughter?"

"Aye. Angharad is her name. She was Sylvester's only child but after Angharad's mother died, he married some chit from the east. She was a widow with four lads to her name. Old Sylvester took them in. None of them can fight worth a damn, though."

"Why doesn't the chief just take the land by force? We are more than strong enough for those four and whatever servants and tenants they can muster."

"I've often wondered the same thing myself. Perhaps he is truly in love with the girl. And he knows as well as any, that if he took her land by force, she'd rather die than marry him. She's as stubborn as a mule, that one. So he plays the waiting game."

They dined in the main hall that night and the whole scene had a forced air to it. Angharad and her four foster-brothers sat on one side of the long table while Heubarth, Peredur and the others sat opposite, the length of oak between them set with only the simplest of dishes along with some loaves hastily made from the grain they had just delivered.

Peredur sat opposite Angharad and she spent most of the meal staring at her plate, doing her best to ignore the unwelcome guests. Aeron spotted Peredur gazing at her and spoke sharply to him.

"That's some fine armour you were wearing when you rode in. How is that a lad no older than myself has such fine armour?"

"Peredur here is the son of a northern lord," Heubarth answered for him. "A warrior trained form birth."

"What does the son of a northern lord do with a band of common thugs?"

"Aeron!" Angharad rebuked sharply. It was the first word Peredur had heard her speak and it was one of warning laced with fear. She clearly wanted no trouble between her hot-tempered foster-brother and Heubarth, however much she might despise him.

Heubarth looked ready to take offence at Aeron's insult and Peredur hastily interjected. "My father was killed by the Picts and our lands were taken. With no money or property left to my name I rode south seeking employment."

"Have you had much success?"

"Some. Everybody needs protection in these lawless times. I have fought for many a petty nobleman and earned good payment. But it is a restless life. One day I will return to the north and rebuild my home. If the Picts have left anything worth rebuilding."

Halfway through the meagre meal, two nuns were admitted to the hall. They carried a basket of loaves between them. One of them, to Peredur's horror, was the nun who had brought the case of the family's plight to his uncle. Would she recognise him? If she did his whole plan would be blown open and his very life would be in danger.

"Ah!" said Heubarth. "Our holy sisters are keeping up their acts of charity, I see!"

"We do what we can to relieve the suffering of God's creatures," said the nun Peredur recognised. Her eyes roved the faces of those seated at the table and froze for a heartbeat as she spotted Peredur. It was a heartbeat only and she continued her survey of the room without batting an eyelid.

Good, thought Peredur. *She has some sense.*

"Your efforts are a little redundant tonight, I am afraid," said Heubarth. "As you can see, we have bread and ample grain for the foreseeable future."

"Speaking of which," said Aeron, "just how much of your grain supply were you planning on giving us, Heubarth?"

"Oh, I am sure I can support you for as long as you agree to be supported," said the bandit with a smile. The answer was obvious to all at the table. Heubarth would withdraw his patronage at a moment's notice if he did not get what he wanted. "No, I shouldn't think your charity is required from now on, sisters," he said to the nuns.

The nuns deposited the basket of loaves on the table all the same and turned to leave. Angharad nearly rose form her seat, watching them depart with great sadness in her eyes.

The meal was almost over and Peredur made his excuses and left the table early. He hurried out into the villa courtyard and saw the black habits of the nuns flapping like bat's wings in the darkness as they made to fetch their ponies from the stables. He caught up with them and they glared at him in shock, unsure of his intentions.

"You remember me?" he said to the nun who had visited his uncle.

"Yes," she said, summoning some resolve. "You were the quiet lad in Edlim's household."

"His nephew," Peredur replied. "You and I have a common goal."

"I hardly think that is likely," said the nun.

"Call it charity if you will but I am trying to help the young lady of this household throw off her oppressor."

"You have a funny way of helping her by joining Heubarth and eating her food at her table while her people starve."

Peredur glanced over his shoulder at the open door to the villa. He could hear Heubarth laughing at some jest and the sound of movement as the awkward dinner came to an end.

"Listen to me very carefully," he said. "Today Heubarth captured a wain of grain heading from Guenta to the warlord Arthur at Cair Badon. Have you heard of him?"

"Yes. He is a pagan by all accounts. Some think he is to be our saviour against the Sais savages but I can't see how…"

"Never mind that!" said Peredur. "Can you get a message to him that his grain is currently being held at this villa?"

"I do not keep company with warlords, sir, pagan ones less so."

"Could you do it if it meant the freedom of Angharad?"

She studied him closely. "Perhaps. I could try. Cair Badon is over a day's ride to the south, but I may find somebody willing to carry a message."

"Do it! Only make sure it is done quickly. I don't know what Heubarth's intentions are. Arthur must make his move against him before the grain is sold or moved elsewhere."

The nun regarded him curiously. "I don't know what you are planning, young man, but I see that you are in earnest in your desire to help this household. For that God will surely thank you."

"Never mind that," said Peredur, the colour rising on his neck. "Just get going and get a message to Arthur as soon as you can that his grain is here!"

The nun nodded and joined her companion who looked eager to leave the villa complex. Peredur watched them lead their ponies through the gate and down the road before he turned back to the villa.

The kitchens and storerooms may have been bare of food but there was still plenty of wine and mead and Heubarth and his men were keen to celebrate their victory. As Angharad and her foster-brothers climbed the stairs to their beds, Peredur briefly showed his face for the sake of appearances before he too retired to his chamber.

With the door bolted, he stripped to his tunica and laid his things out on the chair by the bed. He checked the window to make sure it was large enough for him to squeeze through. Tonight was the night he would put the second part of his plan into action. The appearance of the nuns had been an unforeseen circumstance that had made him quickly rethink his plans. It was running a risk but if he could bring

Arthur's vengeance down on Heubarth, he might just be able to solve Angharad's predicament.

All the same, he would have to leave with the grain tonight as planned. He knew where he would hide it; a safe place where it would not be found until he had drawn the attention of Arthur and brought about a reckoning with Cei. Only then, once he had beaten and humiliated Cei, and proven to Arthur that he was a fit warrior for his band, would he give the grain back to Arthur.

Heubarth would be enraged by the theft of course. Peredur just hoped things wouldn't get too fraught here for Angharad's family before Arthur arrived looking for his grain.

As he stood by the window, he heard noises coming from somewhere above. People were whispering – a man and a woman – and he realized that it was coming from a room or gallery on the upper floor. He couldn't make out much of what was being said but by the voices he believed it was Angharad and Aeron, arguing about something. He seemed to be threatening her while she remained defiant. Her resistance to his threats however, crumbled and Peredur could hear the emotion making her voice crack. Eventually the voices faded as the pair moved deeper into the building and out of earshot.

He bedded down to sleep and must have dozed for a while before he was awoken by a faint rapping at his door. He listened. The villa was silent. Heubarth and the others must have gone to their beds or else lay passed out drunk in the dining room. The knocking came again.

He rose and crossed to the door. He opened it and found himself looking on the pale face of Angharad, her dainty features illuminated by the oil lamps in the corridor.

"Can I speak with you?" she asked, her tone deadly serious.

"Of course," he replied, opening the door wide enough to admit her and then becoming horribly self-conscious that he was naked to the waist.

"Close the door," she said. "I would speak with you in private."

He obeyed but not before checking the vacant hallway for any lurking foster-brothers that might be spying on them. It crossed his mind that this was some sort of strange prank at his expense. He turned around to find Angharad seated on his bed, her tattered dress stretched tightly over her knees. "Come," she said. "Sit with me on the bed."

He plonked himself, not as gracefully as he would have wished, next to her on the ruffled sheets. The bed's wooden frame creaked noisily and he felt his face colour.

"I hope you will understand that I am a little curious," she said. "Why is it that such a lion of a warrior is keeping company with gutter rats like Heubarth?"

"Gutter rats?" said Peredur. "Heubarth is looking out for your best interests."

"He is looking out for his own interests. And I am one of them."

"You despise him."

"Yes. I loathe him. I would much rather have a real man with a pure heart." She placed her hand on his thigh.

Peredur's heart pounded. He had a fair idea where this was going but he had difficulty accepting it. It felt too much like a dream, or worse, a trick. Were her foster brothers waiting just outside his door, ready to pounce on him as soon as he laid a hand on their ward?

"You may take me tonight if you wish," Angharad said, bringing her face closer to his, her black hair dropping down over one side of it, ruining the perfect symmetry. Everything was ruined; the goodness, the innocence and Peredur's world threatened to fall apart in a glorious maelstrom of destruction. And, much as it surprised him, he loved the thought of it. He could feel her hot breath upon his check, those ruby-red lips parting a fraction, her wet tongue moving slowly behind them.

Peredur was disturbed to find his thoughts drifting to his mother. What had she said about women? She had told him to beware, she had told him that most were whores; demons in woman form. She had told him that they tricked men by using their sexual appeal, tricked them out of their money out of their souls. Was this a trick? What else had his mother said about women?

He couldn't remember what she had said. To hell with his mother! He no longer cared. He was in a room, on a bed with the most beautiful woman he had ever seen and she was offering herself to him on a plate.

But why? That was the thought that nagged at him like a grey moth fluttering around inside his skull. Why was she doing this? Was she really attracted to him?

She had moved away from him now, still holding his attention with those jade eyes that burned like crystal sunlight in deep forests. She lay down on the bed, bringing her legs up, her dress riding up around thighs, skin as smooth and creamy as milk. She beckoned him with her eyes.

"Take me," she said. "Take me now."

"Wh... what?"

Her body relaxed. The room seemed to drop a few degrees in temperature. Her wonderful eyes screwed up tight and she covered her face with her hands. Peredur wondered what new game this was but then realised with a sudden horror that she was weeping. The game, if it had ever been one, was over. She brought herself up to the edge of the bed and dropped her bare feet down to the stone floor.

"Oh, I'm not very good at this," she sobbed between her hands, the tears steaming behind them.

"I... thought you were rather good," said Peredur, not sure if this was the right thing to say.

"Forgive me. It's just that we are so desperate. *I* am so desperate to escape Heubarth. I thought that I could seduce you into helping me."

Peredur thought for a moment, remembering the ugly scene he had heard from his window not an hour ago. "Did your foster-brother put you up to this?" he asked quietly.

She looked up at him, the charcoal on her eyelashes running down in streaks, marring her beautiful features. "Yes. It was Aeron's idea. I had a horrible feeling that it wouldn't work, but he made me try…"

The feeling of awful disappointment washed over Peredur like an icy-cold tide. So, she had not been attracted to him at all. It *had* been a trick. He could almost feel his mother's gloating triumph gazing down at him. She had been right. As always. He felt as small and insignificant as he had done that terrible day in the arena at Cair Legion. He was an insignificant fool, used and laughed at by the incomprehensible world had stumbled into. But he could not bring himself to be angry with Angharad. She was desperate, it was true, and she seemed almost as embarrassed by the whole thing as he was. No, he could not be angry with her. Her foster brother on the other hand…

"I feel so foolish," muttered Angharad.

"Don't," said Peredur, rising from the bed. "You were doing whatever it took to ensure the survival of your family." He was surprised by sudden conviction in his voice but an anger had been awakened inside him; a blazing anger at Aeron, at Heubarth, at the callousness of the world that treated someone as wonderful as Angharad so brutally.

"So," she said, looking up, almost fearfully at him. "You're not going to…?"

"It would be a sin," he said. "We're not married."

She blinked at him. "You are a strange boy, Peredur. So righteous and full of virtue that it is as if you are from an entirely different world. I doubt there are many men like you in Albion."

"My father was a highly-respected warrior," said Peredur proudly. "When I took his armour, I swore that I would do all that was in my power to earn it. I swore that I would not tarnish his name by succumbing to the same evils that claimed his life. I swore this before God."

She smiled a little sadly. "God seems to have forsaken this household."

"Do not lose your faith, Angharad. You are a good and kind woman and before these terrible days are over, God will aid you. Of this I am certain."

"We have grown so desperate that our faith lies only in the aid of mortals. My foster-brothers hoped you would be the one."

"What do *you* hope for?"

"I... I don't know. They see a strong warrior from a noble line and think this will be enough to defeat Heubarth. I see you more clearly, I think. I see your fine armour but I also see a kind but sensitive boy. I worry that you might not be enough to beat Heubarth for he is a brutal man fed and nurtured on violence his whole life."

"There are other ways to defeat a man than with violence," said Peredur and he knew he was trying to fool himself as well as Angharad. With a pang of shame he remembered that he was planning to use Arthur and his warriors to defeat Heubarth while he ran away. And even if he saw his plan through to its fruition, it could only culminate in direct combat with Cei. He had no subtle plan to beat Arthur's champion. It always came down to violence at the end of it.

"Might I stay here with you tonight?" she asked him. "I know that nothing will happen and I appreciate your integrity. But my foster-brothers, Aeron in particular, will be furious that I failed them. Might we let them think that I succeeded?"

"And have them think I am the lowliest of men to take your maidenhood in exchange for betraying Heubarth?"

"Then you truly mean to keep your allegiance to him? You won't help us?"

He sighed, wanting to tell her what he was planning, to tell her who he really was, and that help would soon be coming but knew that he couldn't. "I am sorry, Angharad. I cannot help you. But if you still wish it, of course you may stay the night."

They lay on the bed together, her right arm hugging his waist, her face resting on his chest, raven hair brushing his skin while the oil lamp in the corner burned low.

"Have they always pushed you around?" he asked her. "Your foster-brothers, I mean."

Her head stirred. "I was ten years old when they came here with their mother. They were all young men and I was still a girl who had just lost her own mother. My father did his best to make the boys feel part of the family, but Aeron has always been a bully. The other three are frightened of him and will go along with whatever he says."

"But he does not dare stand up to Heubarth."

"No. He is, at heart, a coward."

They lapsed into silence and after a time, Peredur felt Angharad's breathing deepen as she drifted off to sleep in his arms. He lay awake for a time. He had plenty to worry about. Her staying the night had scuppered his plans to make off with the grain but he couldn't bring himself to resent her. He only hoped that those nuns would get his message to Arthur and that Arthur would march on Heubarth before tomorrow evening. What he would do then was something that would require careful consideration.

He refused to burden himself with worry now. For tonight, at least, he would try to sleep easy and forget all his troubles. Through the window he could see the stars burning in the night sky with a brilliance he had never noticed before. The cool night air and the blossoms in the gardens smelled sweeter than ever before and he lay for a long time, listening to the soft breathing of the woman who slumbered in his arms. Despite the danger he was in, despite the challenges he faced, he was truly happy in her presence. Happier than he had ever been before.

With the dawn came the sluggish light of late spring, seeping through the windows, hauling its shadows across the stone floors of the villa. Peredur awoke to find Angharad gone, her side of the bed cold.

He got up and hurried over to the door. The sun was well on the rise and he could hear Heubarth's groggy voice barking orders at his men somewhere within the villa. He cursed.

He left his room and found Angharad in the atrium discussing some item of domestic business with the head cook. Aeron lounged on a stone bench.

He looked up at Peredur with a smile as he entered. "Sleep well?"

"Not too bad," Peredur replied.

Aeron held his gaze, the smile still on his face. "You must be the only one of Heubarth's men who doesn't have a sore head this morning. You all but emptied our wine cellar last night. I only hope our contribution was worth it. And I don't just mean the wine."

Peredur crossed the atrium towards the dining room where the rest of his comrades were making short work of whatever breakfast had been rustled up. Aeron leapt up and barred his way. He spoke to him, keeping his voice low.

"What's the plan then, warrior? Will you challenge Heubarth in front of all the others or is it to be a knife in the back? I would have done the job myself, but I have no guarantee that the rest of his men won't tear me to shreds. Are you sure they'll follow you once Heubarth is disposed of?"

Peredur seized Aeron by the collar of his tunica and drew him close so that he could hiss into his ear. "Not one more word! I will choose my time and my method. Any more jabbering from you might offset the whole thing."

He released Aeron and the man stumbled out of his reach, his face outraged at being treated so within his own home. But Angharad was right; he was too much a coward to do anything about it.

And speaking of Angharad, Peredur shot her a glance which she quickly deflected before vanishing into the kitchens with the head cook. She had obviously been spinning some tall tales for Aeron.

The lad practically thought Peredur was ready to murder Heubarth over breakfast.

It couldn't play out like that of course. Peredur had nothing like the backing of the rest of the gang. He would leave Heubarth for Arthur while he continued with his own plan and hope that things worked out for Angharad.

After breakfast, Heubarth sent a couple of his men out to find a buyer for the grain. The rest of them milled around the villa, sunning themselves and gambling in the shade of the colonnades. Peredur kept his eye on the stables where the grain was hidden. There was no way he could get to it and move it out of the villa without being spotted. His plan depended upon a timely diversion; a diversion he was not at all sure would ever come.

But come it did, as dusk was settling over the hills and the woods surrounding the villa. The first Peredur knew of it was the shouting of one of Heubarth's men in the grounds south of the villa.

"A host approaches! Armed men on horseback!"

Everybody threw down whatever they were doing and ran to the front of the villa. In the distance, dust was being kicked up by an approaching body of horsemen, banners waving overhead. Peredur squinted but couldn't make out the red dragon banner he had seen that day in the forest or later at Cair Legion.

"Who the devil?" asked Heubarth.

"Marauders?" said one of his men.

"They're well-fitted out if they are," said Heubarth. "And I would have heard of it if another band bigger than ours was causing trouble in these parts. No, this is some foreign warband by the looks of things. Fall back to the villa! Bar the doors!"

His face was pale and for the first time since meeting him, Peredur saw fear in Heubarth's eyes. The iron-bound door was heaved shut after the last of the straggling servants slipped indoors. Everybody retrieved their weapons and Peredur ran to his room to put on his father's armour.

Angharad's foster-brothers dawdled about until Heubarth roared at them to rustle up some bows and arrows. They hurried off and returned with a handful of hunting bows, two crossbows and half a dozen quivers of arrows.

Heubarth sent some bowmen to man the windows and galleries on the upper floor and told Aeron to get Angharad behind a bolted door.

"You will hold them off, won't you?" Aeron asked him.

"There's a bloody lot of them and few of us," said Heubarth. "We'll try and pick as many off as we can but they will breach the door sooner or later."

"She's yours if you save us," said Aeron, his voice dripping with desperation. "Angharad, I mean. She's yours."

"Damn you, Aeron!" Angharad spat. She drew back her hand and struck him hard across the face. He reeled backwards, blood starting from his bottom lip. He gazed at her dumbly for a moment before a cold fire flickered in his eyes.

"I've a mind to take you up on that, Aeron," said Heubarth. "But for now, get her out of here!"

Aeron reached for his foster-sister but Peredur stepped between them. "I'll take her," he said. And before Aeron could object, he took Angharad by the arm and led her away.

"What are you up to?" she asked him as they hurried across the atrium, dodging panicking servants who scurried about looking for places to hide.

He led her through the kitchens and stopped at the back door. He held her by the shoulders and looked into her eyes. "If I asked you to run away with me, now, tonight, would you do it?"

"Run away with you? My villa is under attack. My foster-brothers face death…"

"Only if they resist," he said. "The host that marches on us is the host of Arthur. I sent for him."

"*You* sent for him?"

"I told him his grain was being held here."

"But why would you…?"

"He will not harm your foster-brothers or your servants. He is no bloodthirsty reaver. He is here only for his grain. He will kill Heubarth if he resists him, but he will leave your villa standing and your people alive if they do not stand in his way. I leave tonight with the grain and I am asking you to come with me. I love you, Angharad. I do not know the path my future will take, only that I want to walk it with you at my side."

"I… I don't understand. You say that you love me yet you brought Arthur here and then you tell me you plan to steal his grain..."

"I can't explain it to you now. I have personal business with Arthur, or more correctly, his captain, Cei. Heubarth was a means to an end but when I met you I knew that I could not leave you in his hands. That is why I brought Arthur here. He can dispose of

Heubarth but also provides the distraction I need to get away. Well, Angharad? Will you come with me?"

"No." Her face was wracked with emotion but still defiant. "You say you love me, well I don't know with any certainty that I do not love you. But this is my home. My place is here with my foster-brothers."

"Even though they have used you to their own ends? Even after Aeron promised you to Heubarth despite your wishes?"

"Yes. Whatever fate this Arthur brings to us, I must meet it alongside my people. If your trust in him is true, then you will have saved me from Heubarth forever. I don't understand your plans, Peredur, but perhaps, one day you will return to us and I may reconsider your offer of walking by your side. But if you are wrong, and Arthur is not the man you believe him to be, I will not run from him and leave my home to his vengeance."

Peredur swallowed and felt a little ashamed. Angharad was braver and nobler than he had given her credit for, perhaps braver and nobler than he was. But time was running out. Already he could hear the blows of the attackers on the front door echoing through the villa. If he was to leave, it had to be now.

"I will return to you, Angharad," he promised. "One day, when I have done that which I need to do, I will return."

She kissed him on the mouth and his heart raced as those blood-red lips touched his own, burning him with a flame that he knew he would feel the scar of forever. "Go, then Peredur and complete whatever quest occupies your heart more than your love for me. I will be waiting for you."

She turned from him and vanished from the kitchens to seek her refuge. Peredur could hear the shouts outside as Arthur's men tried to break in. He prayed to God that his faith in Arthur was well-founded. If it was not, Angharad's soul would be on his shoulders and he knew that it would be a burden he would never be able to bear. He turned and exited the villa through the kitchen door and felt the cool starry night on his face.

The grounds at the rear of the villa were black under the night sky. He hurried over to the stables and found them deserted but for the great wain and the two snorting aurochs in their stalls.

With some difficulty, he dragged the massive beasts out of their stalls and hitched them to the traces of the wain. He led them out of the stables and onto the rough pathway that led north from the villa. Before the villa's outbuildings were behind him, he scrambled up into the seat atop the wain and took the reins.

He turned and looked down at the villa's roofs beneath he night sky. Its southern side was bathed in orange from the torches of Arthur's host. He could see groups of horsemen galloping around the villa, circumventing it to find another way in. He had escaped just in time.

I'll come back for you, Angharad, he said to himself. *One day, when this is all over, I'll come back for you.*

PART IV

"516: The battle of Badon, in which Arthur carried the cross of our Lord Jesus Christ on his shield for three days and nights and the Britons were victors."
- The Welsh Annals

Aesc

The tide lapped its tongue along the shores of the isle of Thanet, washing the feet of the white cliffs. King Aesc of Cent watched as the vessel made its way from the mainland to the island stronghold that had been his family's home for over three decades.

King Aesc had seen nearly fifty winters. He was tall and had been considered handsome in his youth but now the snow of age streaked his hair and flecked his beard. Every summer of peace seemed a precious thing to him for he knew that in the winter months, old scars would ache like bad memories.

The vessel was beached and a sturdy, broad-shouldered man dressed in fine mail and wolfskins jumped down into the surf while his men hauled the boat up onto the sands. He had dark mane of shaggy curls and a thick beard to match. His face was lined and scarred, aged by the violent life he had led, so that he looked much older than his thirty-odd winters.

Aelle, thought Aesc.

That the self-proclaimed King of the South Saxons should pay him a visit in the middle of campaigning season did not bode well. The thought that he might have been defeated did not bear thinking of. If the Welsc – as their people referred to the native Britons – had won a victory large enough to send Aelle running east with his tail between his legs, it would not be long before they would be pressing the advance into Cent with old grievances on their minds.

Aelle had landed on the southern shores of Britta several years ago and had quickly earned a following despite lacking a single drop of noble blood. He was a commoner who had won his fame through brutality and violence back in his homeland. His name was spoken with trepidation among his people ere he set foot on British soil.

He had wasted no time in achieving further renown by storming the old Roman shore fort of Anderitum and slaughtering every Briton within its walls. Over the past few years, the various Saxon tribes of the south coast shuffled under his banner and began to resemble something of a kingdom with Aelle as its self-appointed king.

He had been a threat to Aesc in the early days. Ever hungry for more land, Aelle had first pushed eastwards until the South Saxons were rubbing shoulders with the Jutes of Cent. Several battles had been fought but, though he was a vicious fighter, he was unable to take on the established and well-organised kingdom of Cent, oldest of all the Germanic kingdoms in Britta. So, Aelle had turned his attentions westwards and pursued a war of conquest against the lands of the Welsc.

"King Aesc!" boomed Aelle, his arms spread wide in an overly familiar gesture of affection. Aesc did not feel that he could refuse and allowed himself to be embraced by this bear of a man, wincing slightly as he heard his joints crack under the strain. "*Hwaet*, my friend! How goes things in the east?"

"*Hwaet*, Aelle. Things go as they have gone these past ten years. We live in peace and grow fat off plentiful harvests."

"Fat?" Aelle patted Aesc's belly playfully. "There's more fat on a wren! I must send you some of the wine, meat and grain we have looted from Welsc settlements! The fruits of this land, I tell you, await only those who have the courage to pluck the apple from the tree!"

The hearth fire burned low that night as the two kings supped mead and discussed war. "I had that bastard Ambrosius Aurelianus beaten," said Aelle. "But my good-for-nothing son managed to lose him before he lost his own life."

"My condolences, Aelle," said Aesc. "I had not heard. Was it Cymen?"

"Aye, my firstborn." Rare emotion brought forth by the drink dampened Aelle's eyes and he hammered the arm of his chair with his fist in frustration. "I'll bear him no grudge. He paid for his failure with his life and we shall embrace in Waelheall when my time here is done."

"I can't understand why you kept Aurelianus alive and in one of their westernmost towns," said Aesc, unable to keep the criticism out of his voice. Aurelianus had long been the chief enemy of his people and he had been secretly glad of Aelle's successes in the west. *Anything to keep his greedy mind occupied.*

"I thought to use him as a bargaining chip to squeeze some recognition of my rule out of those Welsc bastards," said Aelle. "And that town was a veritable fortress! I'll never know how they manage to get him out. A small group sneaked in, I am told, and escaped with Aurelianus before my son knew they had been infiltrated. There is a new warlord come down from the northern hills to test my mettle. Arthur, they say his name is."

"Arthur?" Aesc said. The name was strange to him, exotic and a touch savage.

"Some hill chieftain the Welsc kings have paid to fight their battles for them. He has strong numbers. And cavalry too. He calls support to him like flies to shit."

Ah. There it was. The reason for Aelle's visit.

"What is the state of your stables?" the King of the South Saxons asked, subtlety a skill beyond him.

"Mostly empty," Aesc replied. "There are some mounted men in the fyrds that guard the fringes of Cent but there is little need for horses on Thanet or even in the coastal settlements on the mainland."

"How many riders could you muster from your fyrds?"

"Perhaps a hundred or so. But I hope I should never have the need to leave my borders unprotected."

"A hundred," said Aelle, doing nothing to mask his disappointment. "What of the white horse of Cent? The symbol of your father and uncle? What happened to Cent's brave riders?"

"They grew old and retired to their farms." Aesc did not like the reproachful tone in Aelle's voice. This war of conquest was Aelle's business, not his. He had learned to live in peace with the Welsc. Many served in his fyrds and even his queen, Aeronwen, was a Briton. For Cent, the days of conquest were behind them.

That war had been fought a generation ago by his father Hengest and his uncle Horsa. Exiled from their home in Jute-land across the North Sea, they had landed their three ships on these sands to carve out a new home for themselves. Gradually, through much bloodshed and sorrow, the old Roman territory of Cantium had become Cent; kingdom of the Jutes.

"There is not a Saxon, Angle or Jute on this island who does not hold the names of Hengest and Horsa in the highest honour," said Aelle. "Truly, they founded something great in Britta."

"There were Saxons, Angles and Jutes in Britta before my father and uncle arrived here," said Aesc.

"But they were leaderless! It was Hengest and Horsa who showed them what could be achieved, just as I seek to show my men what can be done when we unite!"

"The south-east of Britta is still a patchwork of tribes who bear grudges like old women and pursue blood feuds that began back in our homelands across the sea," said Aesc. "There are near a dozen different dialects and some are even taking up the worship of the White Christ. We are far from united."

"But we are many," said Aelle. "And we are strong. Every spring, boatloads of young hotheads looking for plunder land on these shores. These are the hungry wolves I have bolstered my army with. They need leadership and they deserve a kingdom, just as you and your family did."

"A kingdom we won," said Aesc. "But it came hard to us. You seek only conquest, pushing first east, then west. Where will it all end? Do you seek to claim the whole island?"

"If I can." There was a gleam in Aelle's eye that suggested he was not entirely joking. It caused a cold streak to run through Aesc's body.

"My father had similar designs," he said. "And it cost him dearly." He grew misty-eyed as he cast his mind back through the decades to when he had been a youth. "I remember the day he fully understood the price he had paid. We had beaten the Welsc at Crecganford and pursued them to Londinium. When we arrived we found the town all but deserted. As we stood on the road that led west and saw the approaching host of Aurelianus, my father knew he was beaten at last. He could go no further. My sister Hronwena, whom my father had married to the lord Vertigernus in exchange for Cent was forever lost to us. That day broke him."

"That day was many years ago," said Aelle. "We are far stronger than the hosts your father led but only if we work together. Will you join me, Aesc? Will you fight for a glorious future for our people?"

"You don't know how like him you sound," said Aesc. "But the men of Cent learned long ago that Britta is too large, its tribes too many, to be conquered."

"Your father carved out his own future here," said Aelle. "Help me carve out my own. Aurelianus is defeated, replaced by some stripling with a few hillmen to his name. The borders of my territory stretch almost to the sea that divides the northern kingdoms from the lands of the West Welsc. If we can drive a wedge between them, we will have broken them! Join me, Aesc. Join me and together we can defeat this Arthur and secure a safer future for all of us. Besides, if the South Saxons are overrun, do you really think Arthur will stop there? He will push the war eastwards until every scrap of land the Welsc have lost has been reclaimed. We are not the only ones who remember the names of your father and uncle. But the Welsc do heap the same acclaim on them as we do."

The fiery determination in Aelle's eyes told Aesc that here was a dangerous man who would not take no for an answer. Could he really afford to make an enemy of him? And besides, everything he had said was true. If this Arthur was not broken, there would be no stopping the wrath of the Welsc.

He thought of his son, Octa, already ripe to succeed him. He was a good lad, fair and wise but he had grown up in peace; a peace bought by his forefathers and paid for with their blood. Perhaps that price had not yet been paid for in full and Aesc had no desire to take his seat in Waelheall and leave his son to face the consequences of Aelle's war alone.

He cursed. He wasn't interested in conquest, only ensuring peace. And the only way to do that might be to smash this Arthur utterly. He had an uncomfortable feeling that Aelle had started something that could not be stopped.

Guenhuifar

The room was bare and had clearly been used for holding prisoners before. A water jug and chamber pot were its only furnishings other than the pallet of dirty straw in the corner of the room. Guenhuifar looked out of the window at the heather-clad slopes of the island's lone mountain. It was topped by the ruins of a Roman signal tower.

Morien had led her on her horse with her hands bound up the south-west coast to a small cove where a skiff had been hidden. The horses had been loaded onboard and he had sailed them across the narrow strait to what was known to the locals as the Isle of the Dead.

The small island off Ynys Mon's western coast was largely uninhabited and with good reason. Since time immemorial it had been used as a burial place and tombs and standing stones dotted the island. Few dared live in such close proximity to these gateways to Annun and even the Morgens kept to their sacred lake in the western fens.

The Isle of the Dead had been avoided by all except the Romans. Having reached what would become the westernmost point of their empire, they sought to watch over the sea that stood between Albion and the unconquered Gaels beyond. A signal tower had been built on the island's highest point and a small fort on its eastern side to serve primarily as a naval base for the *Classis Britannica*; Rome's provincial naval fleet. The fort had been abandoned several decades before the last of the legions had departed

Albion and had presumably lain vacant until Meluas had commandeered it as his gang's headquarters.

It was into Meluas's hands that Morien had delivered Guenhuifar.

He was a man of middling years with long black hair worn in a plait down the centre of his back. A patch covered his left eye where the tip of a scar peeked out. He had remained seated at his desk as Morien forced Guenhuifar down on a stool opposite him. They were in the fort's north-west tower which served as Meluas's personal quarters. He eyed her curiously as Morien laid out her personal effects on the desk for his perusal.

"And this is the lass Custenhinn said wanted some debts annulled?" said Meluas.

"Aye," Morien replied. "And then she drugged me and attempted to torture me into telling her all about the Brotherhood of the Boar."

The 'Brotherhood of the Boar', Guenhuifar gathered, was the name of Meluas's little gang of cutthroats.

"Let's see," said Meluas as he picked over the objects on the desk before him. "A dagger, a broken arrow, some silver bits… what's this?" His finger hovered over the strange talisman she had taken from the dead assassin. His face indicated that he knew exactly what it was.

"Looks like one of those symbols the Morgens use," said Morien.

"Aye, it's the trinity knot of Modron," said Meluas, displaying a deal more spiritual knowledge than Guenhuifar would have expected from a gang leader. "I've only ever seen it used by the Nine

Sisters." His eyes looked up at Guenhuifar under darkened brows. "How did you come by it? Or are you one of those damned Sea-born yourself?"

"I am no priestess," said Guenhuifar. "I took that talisman from the body of the man who tried to assassinate King Owain of Rhos."

Meluas and Morien glanced at each other. "You came from Cadwallon's Lys?" Meluas asked her.

"Yes. And you have as good as told me that you and your little gang of villains were involved. What was the deal; kill your own assassin and frame King Etern by planting his ring on the corpse? It was a little obvious, I must say."

"I don't know what all this about King Etern is," said Meluas, "but you are in way over your head, little lady. What's your name?"

"Guenhuifar." She saw little reason in lying to him. They would probably kill her no matter what she said.

"The steward's daughter?" Meluas said. "Old Gogfran's brat?"

Guenhuifar was silent. Meluas and Morien shared a moment of mirth. "What on earth are you doing chasing assassins across the island? Haven't you just married Cadwallon's new penteulu? Why trade the warm hearth for the wild heath?"

Guenhuifar was silent. Meluas had a point and she knew it. She had charged off on her own private mission and she was not wholly sure of her motives. Did the apprehension of the killer mean that much to her? Or was she running from something? Putting something off by following hunches and leads across the island? All it had led her was straight into the lion's den. Was she frightened? Of course she was. Meluas was well-informed about events on the other side of the island, indicating to Guenhuifar that she may be dealing with more than the leader of a local gang of thugs.

"Why, Guenhuifar?" said Meluas. "Why have you, of all people, sought us out? Surely the whole lys is up in arms trying to find out who tried to kill Owain."

Again, Guenhuifar was silent. She had said enough and would give these two bastards nothing more.

"We'll use more persuasive measures to loosen your tongue tomorrow," said Meluas. "For now, please enjoy the hospitality of our home. We have so few visitors you understand and the men get lonely. Take her to her quarters, Morien."

Morien lifted Guenhuifar off the stool and dragged her towards the door. He turned before leaving and spoke to his master; "If she's truly the daughter of Cadwallon's steward, she might fetch a fat ransom."

Meluas nodded but said nothing as Morien hauled Guenhuifar away. She was not the fool Morien was and neither was Meluas. There would be no ransom. She knew where this bloody brotherhood had made their lair and Meluas was not about to let her leave it alive.

The fort was walled on three sides by stone ramparts which ran down to the water's edge, enclosing a landing beach. The tower Guenhuifar had been locked in was one of four that guarded each corner of the fort and a ditch ran parallel to its three walls. The fort was a ruin. Most of the roofs on the storehouses, barrack blocks and stables were gone and the perimeter wall was in serious need of repair. Meluas and his gang had fortified the only buildings they needed and left the rest to its ghosts.

Here on this isle of tombs and standing stones was where the gang of assassins called their home; this crumbling fort of a bygone era beyond the bounds of civilisation, beyond the bounds of the *living*.

As Guenhuifar gazed out at the bleak, treeless landscape, all she had learned over the past few days shuffled itself into some sort of order in her mind. Meluas had not denied being involved in the murder of the assassin but he seemed oblivious to the attempt on Owain's life and the framing of King Etern. The two assassins, it seemed, had been hired from two separate groups. Perhaps the Brotherhood of the Boar had been called upon to tie up any loose ends. Who then, had sent the first assassin? He had carried a talisman worn only by the Morgens, according to Meluas. Had he been a disciple of the Nine Sisters? Were they meddling once more in Venedotia's affairs?

She was not going to find out a prisoner in this fortress. Escape had crossed her mind several times in the past few hours but the odds were stacked against her. She was locked in the south-west tower and the drop to the ground below was considerable. Then she had to get back across the strait to Ynys Mon. Several vessels were beached on the sands at the fort's eastern side but getting to them without being spotted would be difficult.

She leaned over the sill and looked down. The fall would kill her. She needed some sort of rope but there was nothing, no bedding, no…

But wait…

Further down the wall, ivy was snaking its way up the dry stonework from the tangled undergrowth at the foot of the wall. The ditch that ran the perimeter of the fort was choked with brambles, ferns and nettles after many years of neglect. The Romans would have kept it clear but Meluas's confidence in the fastness of his stronghold could be his undoing. *If she could only reach it…*

She would have to climb down the face of the tower for a few feet, searching for footholds and handholds in the dry stonework before she reached the ivy and even then she was not sure the green vines would support her weight. If she fell it would all be over. But if she stayed, she would probably die tomorrow after many hours of torture. The more she thought about it, the more she realised that it was her only choice.

Refusing to dwell on the implications of failure, Guenhuifar climbed up onto the sill and swung her legs over. Slowly, she twisted and lowered herself, her slippers scraping the stones for purchase while her knuckles showed white as she gripped the sill with all her strength. Inch by inch she lowered herself down from the window and clutched at the stonework, hands grasping dark, cobwebbed holes.

She was committed now. She had not the strength to climb back up through the window. The only way was down and the relative safety of the ivy suddenly seemed a long way away. She took her time choosing her holds on the wall face, ever conscious of the strength waning in her arms. If she went too fast she might misjudge a footing but if she went too slow, she risked losing the strength required to hang on. It was a fine balance.

Finally the green leaves of the top of the ivy crawler brushed her slippers. She eased herself down into its tickling foliage and grasped at the fibrous vines. They were strong and held her weight without complaint. She breathed a sigh of relief.

It was easy going for the rest of the way and she reached the ground in good time, sinking into the tangles of growth at the foot of the fort's walls. It was a hard fight to follow the southern wall down to the waterfront and every bramble and thorn clawed and tore at her clothes as she pushed her way forward.

It was high tide and the waves lapped at the shattered end of the wall, forcing Guenhuifar to wade into the shallows to skirt it. The harbour on the other side of the wall seemed to be deserted but she knew it was visible from the walls and buildings of the fort that overlooked it. Several vessels ranging from small coracles to large skiffs capable of ferrying men and horses across the strait were beached on the dark sands.

Keeping low, she hurried along the beach and ducked into the shadow of a large hulk. Peeping around the curve of its hull, she could see the light of a fire at the top of the beach where the first ruined buildings of the fort stood. The figure of a lone lookout could be seen huddled there. She lamented the absence of her bow. One arrow was all she needed to clear the way for her escape but there was nothing for it. She had to hope the lookout did not spot her.

She needed a small boat that required only one rower to cross to the mainland and she settled on one of the coracles. It would be faster and considerably less effort to sail across but that would take much more preparation and the whole fort would be roused by the time she had got the boat out of the harbour.

Crawling on her belly, she made her way to the nearest coracle. It was only a flimsy thing of hides stretched over a wicker frame but it looked watertight and there was a paddle resting against the crude seat inside. Shuffling around to the side that faced the water, she began to drag the vessel down towards the waves.

With the water lapping around her middle, lifting her dress up in big pillows around her, she knew the time had come to get in and paddle like mad. Hauling herself up, she rolled unceremoniously into the tiny vessel. The coracle bucked and rocked and she seized the paddle and used it to steady the craft.

There came a shout from the beach indicating that the sudden theft of one of the boats had been noticed. She took great digs at the water, alternating side to side, powering the vessel out over the breakers and into the bay. Up ahead she could see the low line of the mainland and her courage balked at the distance she would have to cross.

More shouting from the fort. She risked a glance over her shoulder and could see a line of men hurrying along to the beach to the boats. She was about to have company.

She quickened her pace, controlling her breathing and ignoring the screaming pain in her shoulders. The waves tossed the coracle up and down and side to side and she fought to steady it and put as much distance between her and the Isle of the Dead as possible.

When she had judged that she had crossed half the distance, she took another look behind her. Three boats had set out from the harbour; two rowing vessels and a larger sailing craft that, now it had caught the wind, was making good progress.

She turned her face back to the coastline ahead and gritted her teeth, forcing herself to paddle faster. *Pain is nothing*, she told herself. *Escape is everything.*

The coast approached at an agonizingly slow rate and Guenhuifar refused to look back again. She forced every ounce of her focus into crossing that last stretch of water and reaching land before her pursuers caught up to her. Her arms were numb with pain and her hands burned with blisters, blood seeping between the knuckles.

Eventually she felt the grinding of the shallows beneath her skin keel and she immediately dropped the paddle which felt as if it had been forged to her hands and dived out of the coracle. Gasping and spluttering, she hauled herself up out of the surf and forced her exhausted body up the beach towards the trees. She had to get out of sight.

She could hear the shouts of her pursuers as they beached their own craft and the splashes of them jumping down into the shallows. They were close but she had made it! Ynys Mon with all its woods and hollows, its hills and deep streams stretched before her. She could lose them but she was so very tired!

She cut a south-easterly direction, following the coast and dived into the shadows of the pine trees. Looking back from the cover of the branches, she could see Meluas's men pressing onwards through the long grass, seeking her out. They headed in her direction but they did not have a fix on her.

She hurried on through the woods and the trees thinned out as they met the muddy banks of the Afon Alaw. She splashed across it, her clothes already sodden, and emerged in the long grass of the opposite bank. It was slow going wading through the thick growth and she knew she would never outrun her pursuers that way. Instead she found a dip in the ground and sank down into it, concealed from view.

As she lay there, cushioned by the soft grass, she listened for the approach of Meluas's men. She could hear distant shouts but they drifted away, indicating that they had no clue in which direction she had gone.

She didn't know how long she lay there, her damp and exhausted body held in the embrace of the tall grass. Every part of her screamed with pain and fatigue, especially her hands which were slick with blood.

She awoke with the light of dawn warming the fields and marshes to the east. Rising groggily, she realised that her makeshift bed had been so comfortable that she had slept the entire night through.

Her whole body was stiff and her hands were crusty with blood and newly swollen blisters. Melaus's men had most likely given up the chase and returned to their lair. The long grass swept away to the east and dipped down to marshes and lakes. It was there, Guenhuifar knew, that the Morgens dwelt, custodians of their sacred lake. And it was to them that she must journey next.

She made her way down to the reedy fens where pools and lakes mirrored the clouds. Her underclothes were still damp from her swim the night before and she felt the chill despite the warmth of the rising sun on her face.

She had journeyed to the lake of the Morgens once before; to rescue Arthur from the clutches of his half-sister Anna, the high-priestess. Anna was dead now and the Morgens claimed to be behaving themselves. Still, she had hoped never to visit this place again. *Yet here I am*, she thought, as she stared down at the thatched roofs of the settlement that supported the priestesshood.

Goats trotted out of her way as she approached. Villagers paused mid-task to eye her with suspicion as she followed the muddy trackway between the houses. They were simple folk, wholly given over to the service of the Nine. Jaws hung slack and idiot stares gazed uncomprehendingly. Guenhuifar wondered what drugs the Morgens had boiled up in their cauldrons to blast the sense from their skulls.

No challenge came and none barred her way as she passed through the village. There were no guards here; the Morgens relied on fear alone to keep intruders away. She reached the shore of the sacred lake and to her left stood a portal; a timber trilith cut with niches into which human skulls had been set. The effigy of a raven was perched atop the lintel.

She passed through the portal and felt as if she had crossed the barrier between worlds. Up ahead stood the great roundhouse of the Morgens and it was aflush with colour. Banners wavered in the slight breeze off the lake and they had been dyed a blood red. Red streamers and feathers hung from the thatched overhang where many other objects of bone and dried twisted things the nature of which Guenhuifar could not discern turned in the breeze.

There was nobody about and Guenhuifar realised with a sick feeling in her gut, that she was going to have to enter the roundhouse and face the Morgens in their own dwelling.

The door posts were carved with many symbols and marked especially with the triple spiral the copy of which she had taken from the dead assassin. It occurred to her now that Meluas still had the talisman and she had nothing material to show the Nine Sisters.

She pulled back the hide apron that covered the doorway and peered in. The interior of the roundhouse was dark. Smoke curled up from the central hearth and vanished through the hole in the thatch which admitted the only light into the cavernous interior. As she squinted, Guenhuifar could see several shapes laying around the hearth covered in skins and woollen blankets. As she pushed her way through the apron, the forms stirred and, one by one, the Nine Sisters rose from their slumber, like the dead reanimated.

"Who comes?" asked a cracked and aged voice.

As Guenhuifar's eyes adjusted to the light, she began to see the faces that peered at her through the gloom. White eyes stared out of masks that looked like blood but it was dried, cracked and peeling. They all wore gowns that had perhaps been white once but had been dyed red. *With blood?* Guenhuifar wondered.

"Who comes into our sanctum uninvited?" the old voice asked once more.

"I am Guenhuifar," she answered them. "Daughter of the steward of Cadwallon's Lys."

"What business have you with us?" asked another of the voices.

"I seek answers."

"Does it concern the Great Mother?"

"I… don't know. I think so. Not many nights past, there was an attempt on the life of King Owain of Rhos. The assassin was killed as he fled by a member of the Brotherhood of the Boar."

Breath was sucked in through several sets of teeth. "The Brotherhood of the Boar are defilers," said one of the women. "They desecrate the Isle of the Dead with their presence, showing no respect to the souls who dwell there."

"Just as the Romans did," said another.

"And like the Romans, so shall they pass from existence."

"The dead will remain. It is their island."

"Yes," said Guenhuifar. "Look, the man who tried to Kill King Owain wore a talisman; a pendant marked with the triple spiral."

There was a moment of silent contemplation. Then; "do you have this talisman?"

"No. It was taken from me by Meluas of the Brotherhood of the Boar. He seemed to think that such talismans are worn only by yourselves."

"Anyone can carve such a talisman," said one of the Morgens. "It does not mean that we carved it."

"Then it is possible that somebody is trying to implicate you in the assassination attempt?"

The Morgens said nothing and Guenhuifar took their silence as agreement.

"Why would anyone do that?" she asked. "What would they have to gain?"

"You are asking us the wrong questions," came the reply. "Or you are asking the right questions of the wrong people. Either way, we cannot help you."

"But you must try!" Guenhuifar felt desperation constricting her soul. She had come so far, been through so much, she could not bear to find herself at the end of the trail with nothing to show for it. "Is it possible that somebody acquired one of your talismans? Have you given one to somebody in good faith?"

"Child!" came the rather stern reply. Fingers reached up to touch objects tucked behind red robes. "These talismans are worn only by the Priestesses of Modron. We do not *give* them away."

"There is one," said another voice and the heads of her eight sisters turned and for once, Guenhuifar was able to see which one of them was talking. "An outcast. A failed priestess."

"Who?" Guenhuifar asked.

"Virginity is central to a priestess's service to Modron. We may lie with no man, nor may we be taken against our will and remain in the order. This happened to one of our number, many years ago."

"She was raped?" Guenhuifar knew of whom they spoke. The priestess who had been raped by Enniaun Yrth had turned up at his door nine months later with a babe in her arms. That babe had grown up to be Anna – Arthur's half-sister – and had brought bloody civil war to Venedotia as high-priestess of the Morgens. Anna was dead. Nobody knew what had become of her mother.

"We did not cast her out through any vindictiveness. It is just our way. All of us must remain pure."

"What happened to the woman?"

"She too lives on the Isle of the Dead."

"Is she a member of the Brotherhood of the Boar?" Guenhuifar's heart skipped a beat when she considered that her quest might lead her back into that nest of vipers.

"No. She lives on the south of the island with a small group of wretches. She is accepted nowhere else and so she cares for those who, like herself, are outcasts."

"What is her name?"

"Cerdwen."

"Then it is to her that I must go."

"Perhaps. The path set before us by Modron is often difficult to discern. But you are wounded. The skin hangs from your hands in strips. Hungry too, we don't doubt. Remain here and rest yourself. Gather your strength before the next leg of your journey."

Guenhuifar did as they suggested and was glad of the reprieve. They bathed and salved her hands before wrapping them in linen strips and fed her well on broth, dark bread and fish. She slept in their roundhouse, nervously at first, for she had never considered the Nine Sisters to be allies of anybody but themselves, but they had won a little of her trust and she was so very tired. She slept long and deeply on a wolfskin pelt and awoke with the dawn light on the next day.

After a breakfast of fresh bannocks and goat cheese she prepared to set out. One of the Morgens came to her and spoke in private. Guenhuifar wondered if this one was the high priestess.

"Why is it that you chase death with such perseverance?" the Morgen asked as she draped a shawl around her shoulders. The woman was old but it was difficult to see much of her true features for her face was obliterated by dried blood and her hair hidden in the hood of her red cloak.

"I don't know," Guenhuifar answered truthfully. "At first I just felt angry, angry that somebody was trying to destroy the things my father and my husband had fought so hard for. But then I found that I was enjoying myself. I felt free, as I have not felt in several years."

"What would you be doing if you were not chasing answers into the unknown?"

Guenhuifar sighed "As wife of Venedotia's penteulu I have my duties, it is true, but… I do not feel ready for them."

The Morgen nodded. "Duty is a burden we know only too well. You are running from something, Guenhuifar. Do what you have to do but know that running will only carry you as far as the edge of the world. Once you get there, you will be faced with a choice; turn back or run off the edge, into the void."

Puzzled by the old priestess's words, Guenhuifar left them and made for the coast where the southern portion of the Isle of the Dead almost touched the mainland of Ynys Mon. A slim body of water separated the two islands and all but vanished at low tide. She sat down in the long grass and gazed at the opposite bank as she waited for the tide to draw out and reveal the sandy flats that she intended to cross.

As she looked at the wavering grass of the isle, bleak beneath the scudding clouds, she considered the Morgen's words and wondered if she should just turn around and go home. Here, she truly was at the end of the world. She must either turn back or cross over to the Isle of the Dead and confront whatever she found there. All her questions and wanderings had led her to this point. Did she have it within her to see this thing to its conclusion?

As the waters were sucked out by the tide it felt as if the veil between worlds was swept away. Guenhuifar made her decision. She could not turn back now. The way forward was open and if she gave up out fear she would never forgive herself, not when she was sixty years old, tending the hearth at Cair Cunor, with Arthur old and grey by her side and whatever children Modron saw fit to bless them with were fully grown. All of that happiness would be sullied forever if she betrayed herself now.

She rose and descended the dune to the wet sands below. She cut a zig-zag path across the emptied strait, following the highest of the flats and avoiding the deep pools left by the tide. Eventually she was forced to get her feet wet and then wade across the last stretch. Her dress was torn and soiled and her slippers little better than bundles of rags strapped to her feet. She longed for the boots and breeches she had left in her room at Custenhinn's tavern at Aberffraw.

It did not take her long to cross the island to its western side where, according to the Morgens, their disgraced priestess had made her home. She passed several burial chambers, grown over with grass and a couple of standing stones carved with swirling patterns by a people long forgotten. The cliffs on the isle's west coast fell away sharply to the booming surf below and it was in a shallow dell that a crude settlement stood overlooking a small cleft in the clifftop.

Nothing more than a drystone wall surrounded the settlement and this only on its northern side. Half a dozen tumbledown structures of stone and thatch were clustered together and some people could be seen milling about, planting, repairing and doing other odd jobs about the place.

As Guenhuifar approached, a man herding some scraggly goats hailed her. She put up her arm to shield her eyes from the sun and gasped as the man's face became clear to her. It was marred by horrific sores that glistened with seepage. The man was a leper! Startled, she took a few paces back and the man grinned at her through loose teeth before shepherding his flock in behind the stone wall.

"Don't mind him," said the voice of a boy who was repairing the wall further along. "He's harmless. They all are."

He was not more than thirteen and was dressed in a sheepskin jacket and rough spun breeches. A tangled mop of black hair crowned his narrow face and his lean forearms bulged as he lifted another rock onto the wall.

"Is this a leper colony?" Guenhuifar asked him.

The boy shrugged. "Not only for lepers. All sorts; lepers, paupers, criminals. If you've come seeking somebody, you'll go home disappointed. They all gave up their names when they came here, and their pasts. They've found a spot at the edge of the world where none of that matters to them anymore."

"You speak as if you are not one of them. Do *you* have a name?"

The youth pushed a tendril of hair away from his eye and nodded. "Medraut."

"Well, Medraut. I am told there is a woman who cares for the folk here. Name of Cerdwen."

"Aye, that's my nan. She's mistress here. If you've business with us, you'd best take it up with her."

My nan. Guenhuifar examined the boy closer. The dark hair, the deep brown eyes, the slim but lithe build. Arthur had been sixteen when she had first met him but she imagined that he had not looked much different than this boy in his younger years. Cadwallon too, for that matter.

"May I speak with her?"

Medraut nodded. "Follow me."

He led her through the settlement to a small roundhouse that was better built than all the others. It sat over the cleft in the clifftop and the lintel above the door was carven with many swirling designs.

As Medraut leaned past Guenhuifar to pull the hide apron to one side, she caught a glimpse of the pendant nestled against his hairless chest behind the flaps of his sheepskin jacket. It was the identical twin of the talisman she had taken from the dead assassin.

The answers, whatever they are, are here.

"Nan?" Medraut spoke into the gloom.

Guenhuifar could hear running water from within and then a voice spoke; "What is it, boy?"

"Woman here to see you, nan."

"What's she want?"

"Didn't say."

"Show her in, then."

Medraut nodded at Guenhuifar and stood aside as she slid in through the hide apron.

The source of the trickling water sound became apparent as her eyes adjusted to the gloom. In the centre of the room was a stone-lined pit that looked to be built into the cleft in the rock. Water bubbled up from some underground source. Above the pit stood three statues of women carven from driftwood. They were cruder than the statues to goddesses Guenhuifar had seen previously and were decorated with necklaces and armbands of coral and shell. This wasn't a house. It was a temple.

The woman who sat at their feet, her own legs hanging over the edge of the pit, not quite touching the water, was old. A hooded cloak of thin, tattered material half veiled her face as she turned to examine Guenhuifar.

"What do you seek here, child?" she said.

"The talisman your grandson wears," said Guenhuifar.

"What of it?"

"I have seen it before."

"Then you have met my former sisters. Did they tell you where I was?"

"Yes. And no... I have seen it somewhere else. On the body of a dead man."

A brief moment of surprise – *and perhaps sorrow?* – registered on the wizened face before the old woman turned quickly away.

"You know who he was, don't you?"

"He is dead, then?"

"Yes. He tried to murder King Owain of Rhos. Another assassin killed him as he fled. Did you send him?"

"No. He went of his own free will. I could not keep him here. I raised him as a babe, you see."

"Your son?"

"No. Some other poor wretch's. He hasn't been the first orphan I have taken in. The talisman you spoke of; I give them to all who live with me here. I fashion them myself. It is the Great Mother's symbol." She gazed up at the unreadable faces of the three statues who towered above her.

"For their protection," said Guenhuifar.

The old woman smiled. "They see me as their priestess, the ones who live here, and who am I to disappoint them? I was once one of the Morgens until my own sisters cast me out!" She spat out the words, showing that time had done nothing to dilute the bitterness.

"Because King Enniaun raped you," said Guenhuifar. "The babe you had... it was Anna, wasn't it?"

Cerdwen's eyes flashed up at her, a sudden anger there. "Who are you? Why have you come here digging up the past?"

"My name is Guenhuifar. I am the daughter of King Cadwallon's steward."

"Pah! You serve the family who ruined me and my daughter! Have they sent you to finish the job?"

"No. I am here of my own accord, I swear it. I seek only the motive behind the attempt on King Owain's life. Please tell me what you know. Who was he?"

"He was nobody. Nobody you or your kings and princes would be interested in. He was abandoned by a nobleman's daughter who had him out of wedlock and I took him in and raised him to be a man. But he had a fierce heart and life here chafed at him. He left seeking his place in the world. Wanted to find his family, he kept saying. I told him that we were his family but we were never enough, not for that one."

"He became an assassin."

"Then I suppose he never did find his family. Employment comes hard to those the world has turned its back on. With no skills but what they can do with their own hands, what else can be expected of them."

"I am very sorry. You have no idea who might have hired him?"

"I heard no more from him after he left this place."

Guenhuifar sighed. That was that. It was over at last. She had finally reached the end of the trail and she was met with failure. There were no more leads. Here, in a colony of outcasts at the edge of the world, she had run out of places to run. The only way open to her was back home.

"The boy outside," Guenhuifar said, unable to shake him from her mind. "Medraut. He is Anna's son, isn't he?"

Cerdwen narrowed her eyes at her and the corner of her mouth turned upwards almost as if in mirth. "That's a whole different sack of frogs you're poking now."

"I see a resemblance..." she almost said *to my husband* but she was not sure she wanted to tell this woman too much about herself.

"He is the seed of that family through and through. His father was his mother's cousin."

Guenhuifar tried to mentally trace Arthur's complex family tree and found several candidates stepping forward.

"Meriaun of Meriauneth," Cerdwen said, solving the puzzle for her. "As high-priestess of the Morgens my Anna hooked him like a carp into her plans. It was a mad scheme, I told her so, but when she came to me after fleeing her marriage to King Leudon I found that she had a hatred of that family stronger even than my own. She wanted to destroy it in the purest way possible; by birthing its ruin from her own loins."

"I am to blame for part of it. I was the one who pushed her and pushed her to become a priestess, filling her head with every bit of knowledge I had. It was just us two in those days, eking out a living here by this sacred spring. I wanted my revenge on my sisters and knew the best way to get it was to manoeuvre my daughter into their order so that my own spawn, the reason for my disgrace, would one day rule them."

"She copied the idea from me, I suppose. She began laying the foundations when Diugurnach and his Gaels took Ynys Mon thirteen years ago. Anna already had designs on King Meriaun for he was both the strongest and the weakest of the Venedotian kings and suited her purposes perfectly. The arrival of Diugurnach and his cauldron from Erin provided her with the opportunity and she put her plan into action."

"She seduced Meriaun?" Guenhuifar asked. She felt cold all over as these revelations sank in. What awful plots and twisted designs had been hatched on this island!

"As soon as she fell pregnant she began negotiating a treaty between Meriaun and Diugurnach. It took years to put together for all had to be cloaked in lies and deception. Meriaun was willing to give a portion of the mainland to the Gaels in exchange for their help in winning him the throne. But they knew that even together they were not strong enough to defeat old Enniaun Yrth. They bided their time, watching and waiting as the old bastard grew older and sicker. And all the while Anna and Meriaun's son – Medraut – grew up here, with me."

"Did the Morgens know?"

"Ha! That was the most beautiful part of it. Anna strung those crones along as she did everybody else. They would have cast her out of the order as they had done me. No, Medraut was birthed here and given over to my care while Anna continued as high-priestess. The seed had been planted. We awaited only the fruition of Anna's plans so that Medraut, might arise from the ruins of civil war and rule Venedotia. Meriaun would have been dispensed with once he had served his purpose and my Anna would rule through her son."

The old woman lapsed into silence. There was nothing left to tell. Guenhuifar thought back on the events three years past. All the planning, all the insidious scheming and deception, it had all been swept away by Arthur, by Guenhuifar, by a band of youths who, in their eagerness and without the faintest idea of what they were destroying, had undone it all.

Guenhuifar backed out of the hut. She felt sick to her stomach. Of all she thought she might find here at the end of her trail, she had not been prepared for this.

The sun was setting and the ocean looked like beaten gold. Medraut was still working away on his wall, piling one stone on top of another. Guenhuifar wondered how much he knew about it all. *Does he know that he had been intended for something far greater? Does he know that he might have traded wall-building for ruling seven kingdoms?*

He seemed a nice boy and she felt her heart break with the knowledge that he had been born of such evil and was doomed to live out his life as an outcast because of his mother's ambitions; an acorn from the old oak, carried far away to dry and arid soil. Yet still he grew.

Modron plotted cruel fates sometimes.

Arthur

'Enraged' was something of an understatement regarding King March's reception of the news that Arthur had cut a deal with Drustan. How predictable, he had raged, that a pagan would side with another pagan against all that was proper and decent under God. Cursing him for a damned turncoat, he had ridden back to Cair Dor with his entourage, abandoning Arthur with his fellow 'family outcast'.

"Looks like I shall be your host for the foreseeable future," said Drustan with a grin. "Come, let me show you what Din Tagel has to offer!"

They rode north and reached the coast just as the sun was sinking. All was aflame with gold. They crossed a narrow neck of land that led to a hump of rock, encircled by a wicker palisade. Thatched buildings rose tier upon tier and the spire of a church pricked the sky from the highest point on the peninsula.

They dined in the Great Hall and Arthur marvelled at the exotic foods and trappings Drustan paraded before him as he played the part of the conquering hero. Olives and dates were plentiful and they ate dishes of meat and fish spiced with saffron and garum off red table wear from Byzantium while Gaulish wine was poured liberally into glass Iberian goblets.

"Do not think my uncle will take this insult lying down," Drustan said as he and Arthur discussed their plans over yet another amphora of wine. "He will be plotting his revenge as we speak."

"But what can he do, in the end?" Beduir asked. "Our teulu is less than a week's march from here. We would crush him if he tried any funny business."

"Oh, he won't be blowing the war horn just yet," said Drustan. "He is no fool. But he is treacherous. Beware a knife in the back, that's all I'm saying. It would be best to smash his resolve while we have the chance."

"I am not here to enforce a regime change," said Arthur. "Your business with your uncle is your business. As far as I am concerned, two kingdoms exist here in Albion's toe; Cornubia and Dumnonia. I am interested in peace between them not war but do not think that I won't call my men from Cair Badon to intervene if there is any hostility. From *either* side. We cannot let ourselves become further weakened by feuding than we are already."

"Fair enough," said Drustan, swallowing another gulp of wine. "I'll play nice for the time being."

"I am glad to hear it. Now, tell me more about the situation in Armorica."

"It is much the same as it is here; a peninsula kingdom split into two tribes. Dumnonians and Cornubians have been settling there since the old days with the Dumnonians on the northern side and the Cornubians on the southern. The Cornubian lords are led by Gralon who rules from Cair Ys; a fortress on the southern coast that is constantly under threat of erosion by the sea. Jonas is another Cornubian lord whose seat is Cair Ahes in the mountains. I have befriended both of them and they look kindly on me for championing the cause of their people back in the old country."

"They no doubt hope it is indicative of your support in the new country," said Menw.

"Aye," Drustan smiled. "Their courage has doubled since I took half of March's kingdom. Jonas in particular has often risen in revolt against March but to little effect. If they could only band together they might have a chance…"

"I told you I am not interested in regime changes," Arthur insisted. "Particularly not in Armorica. You are friends with this Gralon of Cair Ys, yes? How many horses does he have?"

"Some, to be sure, but he will not likely want to send them over to Albion to fight in a war he has no stake in. Not with the situation in Armorica as it stands."

"Then it is to the horse fairs we must turn," said Arthur. "I am told the summer fair of Darioritum has some of the best horses from Gaul and Iberia."

"Old Roman town, Darioritum," said Drustan. "I have heard the same. But horses don't come cheap. How heavy is your warchest?"

"A little light," Arthur admitted. "We Venedotians are not gold hoarders as these southerners are. We live off the land and have foraged what we have needed until now."

"That's what I thought," said Drustan. "I can lend you some wealth but even the coffers of Din Tagel might not be enough to cover the amount of horses you are hoping to buy."

"Then we shall have to dig into the land for a little gold," said Arthur with a grim smile.

Word reached them that March had departed Cair Dor and headed to his lands in Armorica along with his teulu and what was left of his fleet. He had effectively abandoned Dumnonia for more promising lands across the channel and Drustan was ecstatic.

"You have won me the rest of Dumnonia without shedding a drop of blood!" he told Arthur.

Arthur frowned. It had not come easy to him to turn his back on March and he did not like the idea of being the one to drive the wedge deeper between two men he would have as his allies. But there was little to be done. Pride burned too hot in the hearts of some men.

They rode for the southern coast to see what the situation was at Cair Dor. They found the harbour at the mouth of the Afon Fowydh swarming with people trying to get themselves and their belongings onto the few boats that were left. They seemed to be of the wealthier Dumnonian stock and there was much haggling doing on down on the jetties as men tried to outbid each other for safe passage for them and their families. A holy man wearing the hooded robe of a monk was preaching a sermon atop a hay cart, calling for all to repent their sins for judgement was upon them.

As Arthur and Drustan led their men to the top of the slope that led down to the harbour, many heads turned to gaze with worried expressions but, upon realising that they were Britons and not Saeson, they turned their attention back to the crowded docks and the holy man.

"What's going on?" Arthur asked of a nearby family who were trying to manoeuvre their way down to the quayside.

"King March has deserted us!" said the man of the family. "He has taken all of his warriors to Armorica. We are left open to the Saeson pagans in the east!"

"They are fleeing," said Arthur. "Fleeing before the battle has even begun!"

"This battle began long before any of us were born," said Menw. "But now these wretches have seen the last of the defences that have kept them safe for many years crumble; first Aurelianus and now March."

Arthur spurred Hengroen on and forced his way between the throngs of struggling families and their carts of belongings. "Hear me!" he cried. "Men of Dumnonia! Why do you flee?"

"Because the Saeson come!" cried out an elderly man further down the slope.

"Aurelianus is defeated and now our king abandons these shores!" cried another. "Armorica is the only safe place for us!"

"Your king abandons you yet still you seek his protection?" Arthur asked incredulously. "Why not remain and fight the Saeson?"

This was greeted with a grim ripple of laughter.

"As well fight the tides!" cried the man. "For Aelle will not stop until every farmstead and every fort from Cent to Din Tagel is under West Sais rule."

"The Saeson are but a small people on a big island!" Arthur persisted. "We outnumber Aelle's warriors ten to one!"

"But who is to lead us? Aurelianus is defeated, March is fled. Who will command our warriors? You?"

"Yes! I am Arthur, penteulu of Venedotia. I have driven the Saeson from Cair Badon where Ambrosius Aurelianus now trains new warriors for my teulu. We are five-hundred strong but we could be stronger, much stronger, if you would only stay and contribute your men and your horses."

"Why should they?" spoke another voice and Arthur turned and saw that the hooded monk atop the hay cart was none other than Abbot Petroc. "What can you, a pagan barbarian, offer that is anything better than waiting here for the heathen Saeson to come with their long knives?"

Arthur was momentarily lost for words. "I offer resistance," he said at last. "A fighting chance for Christian and pagan alike."

"But how can salvation be achieved by following an unbaptised man who worships false idols in the northern hills?" Abbot Petroc answered. "No, better that these people flee or remain to die at Sais hands than follow a heathen."

"This is madness!" Arthur said to Menw as the people continued their press to fill the boats.

"Madness born of fear," said Menw. "The Christians of the south have learned to look upon the older faiths with scorn and disgust. They are not as the Christians in the north who are still outnumbered and must recognise the faiths of others. Here, the old gods are already dead."

"How can I make them listen?" said Arthur. "Dumnonia will be emptied of the cream of its warriors ere Aelle reaches its eastern marches!"

"Gold will win hearts quicker than faith," said Drustan.

"Gold we don't have," muttered Arthur.

"But *his* kind hoards it as a squirrel hoards nuts." Drustan indicated Abbot Petroc.

"The church?"

"Aye. Gold clutters their altars as if they can buy their way into their god's favour."

Arthur said nothing. He remembered the little chapel on the windswept slope down from Cair Cunor where he had attended mass with his mother as a child. He had never thought of it as anything other than dismally humble. And yet, he remembered the simple gold chalice upon the spread white cloth that the deacon had poured the wine into and the silver platter he had broken the bread upon. If a wattle and daub chapel in Venedotia had gold and silver, what riches might these grander churches of the south contain?

He thought also of *Caledbulc* and the other treasures he had found in the temple to Sulis Minerva. Why was it that men thought the gods valued precious metals as highly as they themselves did? Was the forging of a precious sword in the name of a Goddess any different than breaking bread over a silver plate or pouring wine into a golden cup? These things were tools, surely? And what good were tools if they were never used? In that moment he made his decision. Just as he used *Caledbulc*, so would he use whatever the Christian churches had to offer in order to defeat their enemies.

They turned away from the harbour and made for the deserted Cair Dor.

The following day, they rode north to the granite moorland that straddled the centre of the peninsula. Here, amidst a cluster of outbuildings and workshops, stood the monastery of Abbot Petroc.

Monks in their black robes scurried indoors at the approach of Arthur and Drustan's approach. As they rode up the hill and into the compound, Drustan's men whooped and laughed. Arthur held his fist aloft and flashed a look at Drustan. This was not to be a raid.

He dismounted and strode up to the doors of the church which the monks were desperately trying to bolt. "We come in peace," he said. "Where is Abbot Petroc?"

He received no answer but the slamming of the church's doors.

"Abbot Petroc?" he called, his voice bouncing off the whitewashed walls. "I have come to discuss the defence of Dumnonia!"

There came the sound of bolts being drawn and the doors opened a little. Whispering could be heard and then the doors swung wide and the abbot himself emerged, hood drawn back, eyes steely with barely suppressed anger. "You ride into our home like a band of reavers and then demand to speak to about the defence of the kingdom?"

"I apologise for the nature of our intrusion," said Arthur. "But we are warriors and the kingdom is at war. I promise you that your safety and security is my top priority."

"Then what is it you come riding in here for? We are monks, not warriors. How can we help you?"

"I am glad you asked me that question, Father Abbot," said Arthur. "Because if we are to beat Aelle and his dogs, we must all band together and those with the most must, I am sorry to say, contribute the most."

"What are you getting at? We have taken holy orders and are sworn to poverty. What can we have that could possibly aid you apart from our prayers? Or perhaps it is a baptism you are seeking?"

"Not exactly," said Arthur and he pushed his way past the abbot into the sanctity of the church.

It was a modest affair; whitewashed walls gleamed in the sunlight that shone in through high windows. Plain wooden pews lined the nave and a rather impressive fresco of Christ on the cross lit up the apse in an explosion of colour. But it was the trestle table beneath the depiction of the crucified Son of God that occupied Arthur's attention. On it stood a golden crucifix, a chalice and a plate.

"Within the month," Arthur said to Abbot Petroc, "I shall travel to Armorica. There I hope to purchase near on two-hundred horses; fine stallions and brood mares from Gaul and Iberia and even as far away as Arabia. With these horses I will defeat Aelle and secure generations of peace for Dumnonia and many other British kingdoms besides. To do this, I require wealth."

Abbot Petroc followed his gaze to the trestle table. "Surely you don't mean…"

"Think of it as a loan," said Arthur. "With it you will be ensuring that the roof of this fine building is not torched, that the heads of your brethren will remain attached to their necks and that your god will continue to be worshipped here in this place instead of the Sais thunder god. What do you say, Father Abbot?"

The abbot rounded on Arthur with fire in his eyes. "Listen to me, you barbarous hound! I am not fooled by your manners and graces. I see you for what you are; a pagan marauder intent on stripping the houses of God of their treasures so that it may be spent on wine and whores! I know the ways of military men and any loan I might care to grant you would be spent before a single blow against the enemy is struck! You swagger in here as if you were anything better than them! How dare you! You may kill me and my brothers if you wish but know this; it will be God alone who will judge you in the end."

Arthur nodded. He had suspected that this would be the way of it and he found that he was glad. Abbot Petroc was a man of courage. He was willing to die for what he believed in and in that he found a sympathy for the holy man.

"The wealth of the church was given freely by the people to your god in exchange for their salvation, correct?" said Arthur. "You are the middle men, as it were."

"That is a rather cynical way of looking at it," said Petroc.

"Well, consider me and my warriors as sent by God to save you. Time to pay up."

Petroc's face burned red as Arthur's men pushed their way through his frightened brethren towards the altar. A sack was produced and the valuable items placed within.

"You will not get away with this," said Petroc in a low voice, the rage behind it barely controlled.

"You had better hope that I do," said Arthur.

As they mounted their horses outside, Drustan's penteulu Corbinal spoke. "What of the grain in the silos yonder?" He indicated three round granaries on the other side of the monastery's enclosure. "Far more than an order of monks require."

"Corbinal, you dance with the devil!" said Drustan with a laugh. "You are a credit to your people, if not your faith!"

"What good is my faith if we are all killed by the Saeson in the end?" asked Corbinal gravely. "Arthur has the right of it. We are God's avenging army and we need gold and grain more than these monks do."

Further outrage from Petroc and his brethren was ignored as Arthur commandeered a cart and loaded it with half of the grain from the silos.

"A profitable day," said Drustan as they rode away. "I've a mind that other churches and monasteries will yield similar fruits."

"This is but a daughter house of Petroc's first monastery," said Corbinal. "There is a larger place on the coast north-west from here. Abbot Petroc took over this community from Abbot Goran."

"And what happened to Abbot Goran?" Arthur asked.

"He moved deeper into Cornubia and founded a new monastery on the banks of the Afon Camel."

Arthur turned to Beduir. "Drustan and I have much to organise regarding our trip to Armorica. I want you to take your company first to Petroc's church on the north coast and then to visit this Abbot Goran. You can drop in on Abbot Piran's house on the way too. Give them the same message we have given to Petroc here. A contribution is needed to save Albion. Bring everything to Din Tagel. I aim to set sail before the next sabbath."

"My lord, I…" said Beduir, his eyes not knowing how to look Arthur in the face. He had been oddly silent during their visit to Petroc's monastery.

Arthur put his hand on Beduir's shoulder. "I know, old friend, I know. This cuts deep for you. But you must see that I am right. What use is your god if he demands his tribute and lets Albion burn for it?" He could see that Beduir remained unconvinced. It felt strange to have to comfort the big man who had been as an older brother to him and Cei for many years. "I have never begrudged any man his faith, you know that Beduir. Albion is large enough for many gods, including yours. Please understand that I am doing what I must to ensure that it remains so. All must bleed a little for the greater good."

Beduir finally found the courage to look him in the eye. "Yes, my lord. You can count on me. I will do what is required."

"Thank you, Beduir," said Arthur and he embraced his friend.

Over the following days more news reached Arthur that the great lords of Dumnonia were following their king's suit and selling up and moving south, seeking safe passage to Armorica.

"We have to do something to stop them from leaving," he said to Drustan. "Two-hundred horses are no good if there is nobody left in Dumnonia to ride them."

"How do you intend to convince them to follow you?" Drustan asked. "I have the backing of the Cornubians for I won them their independence from March. But the Dumnonians, they are hardly willing to follow a northern warlord and a pagan one at that."

Arthur thought long and hard on Drustan's words. That night at table, he called on Gualchmei. "You know most of the Christians in the teulu," he said. "Do me a favour and bring me the one who has the most skilled hand at painting."

"Why a Christian, lord?"

"I have a special commission I want to put his way."

The following morning Arthur and his men set out in a round-about circuit of the kingdom, heading for the holdings and forts of all the lords Drustan knew of. Arthur carried his shield hung from his saddlebow uncovered and freshly painted. On it, in bright yellows and blues was the image of a woman limned in light as if radiating it. On her lap sat an infant. There was much muttering and discussion of this in the ranks but Arthur refused to speak of the matter.

Every household and every settlement they visited told the same story. The wealthy were converting their possessions into easily transportable wealth and were heading for the coast with their families and servants. It was an exodus and many homesteads lay empty already.

The sight of Arthur and his mounted troops caused much distraction from the tasks at hand and Arthur found that he had a ready audience wherever he went. He gave them the same speech; championing the need for unity in the face of adversity, extolling the love he had for Albion and its hills and valleys. He told them that a home was nothing if it was not worth fighting for and promised them that there would be a dawn after the darkness if they could only withstand the night together. He told them of his teulu at Cair Badon, of Aurelianus, old as he was yet still eager to fight, and he finished by telling them of his plan to ship two-hundred fresh horses from Armorica; horses that could win them this war if they all agreed to remain and see it through.

There was opposition of course. Fear had worked its way into Dumnonia like a plague. They had all heard of the rising in the east, of Aelle and his great heathen army now unfettered since Aurelianus's defeat at Guenta Belgarum. It was said that even more Sais chieftains had joined with Aelle. How could anybody withstand such a force?

But there were some, and Arthur could see who they were as he talked just by the expression in their eyes. He could see a flicker of hope rekindled by his words and that gave him the strength and confidence to continue. If he could reach a few then the word would spread; Albion was worth fighting for. *Arthur* was worth fighting for.

They rested on the third day by the banks of a creek. While they watched the horses being watered Menw rapped his knuckles on Arthur's shield.

"An ingenious bit of political scheming," the bard said and Arthur could sense the disapproval in his words. "Pretending to be something you are not in order to gain favour."

"I pretend nothing," said Arthur. "I cannot stop people from seeing what they want to see."

"You are helping the Christians see what they want to see by carrying an image of their Virgin Mary and the infant Christ on your shield."

"Is that what this is?" said Arthur, feigning innocence as he glanced at his shield. "I thought it rather resembled Modron and Mabon."

Menw looked at him in silence, his eyebrows raised. Understanding dawned and a smile cracked across those weathered features.

"A mother and her divine child," said Arthur, "that is all that is painted on my shield. Why not let people make up their own minds as to who they are? Mary or Modron. Perhaps there is not so much of a difference between them."

"Modron is the mother of all," said Menw slowly. "Perhaps even of God. Your cunning extends beyond the battlefield, Arthur. I apologise. I misjudged your actions, but not your intentions I think."

"These people will find any reason to divide themselves," said Arthur. "I have just given them a reason to unite behind."

'Mother' was perhaps the one name all men held highest. For the pagans, she was the mother of the gods themselves and even the Christians ranked their Blessed Virgin alongside her holy son in glory. For Arthur's part, when he looked into the eyes of the woman upon his shield, he saw the face of the woman in the principia of Cair Cunor; the woman who had birthed him and been his guiding light all his life. She had abandoned her own life, putting all her hopes and dreams in the future of her only son. She had never given up on him and now here he was, the man the west looked to for protection. He would not be there if it had not been for her. Was there any figure he could honour higher?

Peredur

Silence reigned over the ruined town of Cair Gloui. Silence and fear. The sun beat down on its deserted streets, criss-crossing them with the shadows of broken monuments to a departed people. On every side stood the crumbling relics of a forgotten age when the town's people had flocked to the forum to buy and barter everything known to civilisation and the voices of the vendors had filled the air between the striped, colourful marquees. Now only dust travelled down those streets and the only chattering in the forum was of the crows perching on broken columns.

Peredur squatted, crow-like himself from his perch in the upper storey of the basilica and gazed down at the intruders as they made their way cautiously down the street below him. *Intruders*. As if this town in its entirety belonged to him. But that was how it felt. He had lived here in its ruins for days, seeing no one, speaking to no one.

He had explored and found much to occupy his time poking about in what had been the very lap of luxury for some and the squalid hell of poverty and desperation for others. He had slept in the pillared bedrooms of vast town houses and he had perused the wine shops and brothels, marvelling at the vulgar graffiti inscribed on their walls. He had found the burnt-out campfires of the Saeson who had camped here before Arthur had come down from his mountains and driven them back east. They had left little; broken mead pots, a few meagre stores and a couple of fairly fresh corpses of either whores or local women who had displeased them. Peredur had given them Christian burials on the town's outskirts amidst the overgrown tombs and obliterated inscriptions. Before long, boredom and loneliness began to set in and he started to imagine the little bells he had set on his traps ringing their tune in distant streets, signalling somebody's approach.

He had heard the bells ringing that afternoon and had crossed from rooftop to rooftop, his light feet not disturbing a single tile, bow in hand and quiver over his shoulder to track their progress.

There were three of them; warriors by the look of their garb and arms. They were a smidgen better than common farmhands pressed into service and a tad less gaudy than bandits. It was not beyond reason to expect that others might come poking around the ruined town perhaps looking for odds and ends the Saeson had left behind, but he was confident that he looked now upon three of Arthur's men. None of them were Cei though and he chided himself for feeling disappointed. It would be too much to hope for that Arthur's captain would come in person. He had left a message at the tavern on the road that led north and hoped that rumour would spread. He would have to send Cei a new message…

He let the men wander into the forum before he nocked an arrow to his string and aimed at the cobbles a couple of feet from them. He loosed and the arrow ricocheted loudly, making the intruders leap in fright.

Peredur ducked out of sight and made his way along the rooftop to the hole in the tiles he had crawled up through. Swinging himself over the edge, he dropped down into the darkness.

He could hear the ancient hinges on the basilica's tall double doors creak open as the three warriors let themselves into the darkened interior.

Boots trod the dusty stairs and frightened voices echoed in the cavernous interior as they climbed to the second story. Peredur waited in the shadows and noiselessly drew his father's sword from its jewelled scabbard.

Light streaming in through the broken window trellises illuminated the rooms and offices on the northern side of the building yet the landing was cloaked in darkness. He watched as the three men reached the landing and peered about, seeking out the hidden bowman. One of them barely stifled a cry as he spotted the figure standing in one of the rooms, a mere silhouette, limned in the dust-filled light of the afternoon.

They moved out of sight from the open doorway and crept up to the wall, one on one side of the doorway and two on the other. Peredur watched them closely. The one who stood alone nodded to his compatriots and they edged closer, tensing themselves as they prepared to enter the room.

Ah, thought Peredur. *The leader*.

The two warriors crept stealthily into the room and advanced on the figure. They raised their swords into the air and brought them down on the mannequin. There was a 'twang!' and the counterweight Peredur had hung by the door, tumbled down. The fishing net he had suspended from the ceiling floated down upon the two warriors like a gigantic spider and enveloped them in its web.

Peredur stepped out into the light which glinted off the length of his sword. The leader of the intruders spun around to face him, his frightened face pale in the gloom. He quickly recovered when he saw that he faced just one man and little more than a boy at that. He charged and swung high.

Peredur sidestepped the blow and the man was caught off balance. Peredur stuck his boot out and tripped him. As he went sprawling to the mosaic floor, Peredur tried to bat the sword out of his hand.

But the warrior was quick. He rolled. Peredur's sword point scraped the tiles. The man rose up and swung at his midsection. Peredur deflected it and the clang of iron echoed throughout the building. Remembering his uncle's insistence on footwork, Peredur fended off a furious series of chops and hacks from his assailant but refrained from counterattacking. *Wear him out*, he told himself, drawing upon every ounce of his patience. *He will soon falter.*

Falter he did and Peredur was ready for him. An undisciplined thrust, all the more uncontrolled by the man's tired arms, went wide and Peredur batted the sword aside with his own blade. The weapon slipped out of the man's grip and clattered to the floor.

The man gaped and swallowed deeply as Peredur tickled his chin stubble with his sword point. "It's your lucky day," he told the defeated man. "I am not going to kill you. You are Arthur's man, are you not?"

The man nodded and then wished he hadn't as he remembered the sharpened blade half an inch from his Adam's apple.

"He sent you to look for his grain, didn't he?"

"Cei did," said the man.

"Ah. Even better. I have a message I want you to carry to Cei. Tell him I have Arthur's grain here in Cair Gloui. Tell him it is his if he agrees to face me in single combat."

The man's face registered incomprehension.

"I want no tricks!" Peredur warned. "Just me and him. Wooden foils, I have no interest in killing him. If he beats me or if I beat him, then the grain is his either way. I just want to fight him. Do you understand?"

The man did his best to give an approximation of a nod.

"Then get moving."

Peredur picked up the man's sword and hurried off into the shadows.

Not two days passed before a host of riders approached Cair Gloui from the south. Peredur watched them from the rooftops and smiled at the fluttering banners and armoured warriors on horseback. Cei was making a show of it.

Good. The greater his pride, the greater his humiliation.

As he descended to street level he knew very well that he might be walking to his execution. They were under no obligation to give him a chance to prove himself. He had stolen their grain and they had every right to kill him for it. He prayed to God for the courage to see this through to its conclusion, whatever that might be.

The riders were in the process of dismounting to examine the town's outskirts as Peredur emerged from the great arch in the southern wall. Two dozen heads turned to look at him.

Peredur scanned their faces. Arthur seemed to be absent. He had no idea what the Venedotian warlord looked like but he hoped he was grander and more noble-looking than this lot. Cei was the only face he recognised. It was a face that had been burned into his brain; its arrogant smirk, its bull-neck and ruddy complexion mocking him in his dreams. Now that oafish face blinked at him in dumb fascination.

"Do you remember me, Cei?" Peredur asked, his voice carried by the swirls of dust on the stretch of road that stood between them. "Or am I just another insignificant face to you?"

"I must admit you have the better of me," said Cei. "Although there is something familiar about you."

"Perhaps it is my armour you recognise. It struck you enough to mock it in the arena at Cair Legion at any rate."

Cei's face broke into a grin. "Cair Legion! I remember now! The boy with the fancy armour! Is this what it's all been about? I offended you and so you stole our grain and sent out challenges from your hidey-hole in these ruins?" He threw back his golden, glistening head and roared with laughter.

"No more, Cei," said Peredur. "You laughed at me once but you will not do so again. Not after I beat some manners into your thick skull and prove to everybody here who is the better fighter."

"The boy runs mad!" said Cei, looking to his comrades. "Do you dare to challenge me?"

"Do you dare to refuse?"

Cei's face turned stony. "Fetch the foils," he said to a man beside him.

As the weighted wooden swords were brought forth, Cei strode out into the centre of the road to examine Peredur closely. "Last chance to back out, boy. Tell me where our grain is and I'll let you live."

"If you can defeat me in combat," said Peredur slowly, "the grain is yours."

Cei snarled as a foil was pushed into his hand. The second foil was tossed at Peredur's feet. He stooped to pick it up and Cei instantly attacked.

Peredur had expected as much and whipped his foil up to block Cei's downwards swing. Wood clacked against wood as they sparred back and forth, going through every parry and attack Peredur's uncle had taught him to expect. The gathered warriors watched on, slack jawed as their champion faced off against a stripling of a lad who was proving with every blow that he was more than he seemed.

"You've been trained since we last met," said Cei, a little impressed but far from worried.

Peredur ignored him and lunged deep only to find his foil batted away. He chided himself for giving in to his impatience. A brute like Cei had to be worn out before the killing blow was to be made. There was no other way.

He recovered his error with difficulty and brought his foil up just in time to block a savage chop to his neck. The sheer force behind Cei's sword arm knocked the tip of his foil back to connect with his cheekbone. Pain jarred through Peredur's face and the blood started instantly from his split cheek. He did not allow himself to be distracted and caught Cei's follow-up low.

Cei shifted his stance suddenly and Peredur realised that he was on the wrong footing. The foil whirled around to his other side and caught him just beneath the ribs. Peredur felt something deep inside crack, despite his armour and he cried out as the pain lanced up his side. He stumbled, tripped over his own feet and fell, consumed by the clouds of dust kicked up.

Arthur's men roared at their champion's triumph. Peredur squeezed his eyes shut, forcing back the tears of agony. He could not let this happen! He could not be defeated!

Biting down on the pain, he crawled to his feet. Planting the tip of his foil down into the ground, he levered himself upright. Cei stood with his back to him; an easy target. Peredur lurched into a loping gait and charged his opponent, foil raised.

"Watch it, Cei!" cried a voice from the crowd.

Cei whirled around, eyes white and goggling in his beet-red face. His sword arm snapped up to catch Peredur's foil mid strike. Cei's face turned from surprise to anger and he planted his boot in Peredur's chest and thrust him backwards.

Peredur reeled across the road and fell once more, the back of his helmet striking the cobbles. He coughed and rolled over, arms straining to lift himself.

"Stay down," Cei warned. "Or I'll put you down permanently."

Peredur ignored him and rose, fumbling at his chin strap. His helmet clattered to the road and he turned to face Cei.

There was an intake of breath from Arthur's men. Cei watched in disbelief and Peredur made his way towards him once more. He was all out of prayers. This was his make or break moment. If he gave in to Cei then everything was over for him. His oath to God, his promise to Angharad, his uncle's belief in him; all of it was for naught and he would go back to being that inept boy who had inherited his father's arms but not the right to bear them. Better to die here, right now.

He swung at Cei but it was a poor swing from an exhausted and bruised body. Cei knocked it back and slammed the edge of his foil into Peredur's unprotected left arm, bending him sideways with agony. His foil clattered to the ground as he involuntarily reached for his bruised arm.

Cei jerked his foil up into his face, snapping his head back with a sickening crack. At first Peredur didn't feel the pain. Then he felt a warmth spread over his face and a dull throbbing began. He was fairly sure that his nose was broken.

He collapsed flat on his back and the metallic taste of blood filled his mouth and he coughed, the motion making his ribs scream in agony.

He rolled over and spat blood on the cobbles. He forced himself to his feet once more. There was still some life left in him. His punishment was not over. He turned to face Cei.

An awful hush had descended over the crowd and Peredur could sense them willing him to stay down, to give up the fight. Cei looked at him with a pained expression.

"Please," said Cei. "Don't make me do this."

"Do it!" Peredur said and to his own ears his voice sounded garbled and moist. Blood ran down his chin and streaked his cuirass.

"No," said Cei. "I have won. There is no honour in this." He looked Peredur up and down as if in disgust.

"Damn you!" Peredur howled and he lurched towards Cei, fists up, ready to take him on with his bare hands.

Cei threw his foil aside and caught Peredur in an embrace that felt like it cracked a few more ribs. He hurled Peredur to the ground and pinned him down. He brought his face close to Peredur's.

"Enough!" he roared. "It is over!"

"Just kill me!" Peredur sobbed, the tears streaming down his face to mix with the blood that masked the lower portion of his face.

"Why?" Cei asked. "Why are you doing this? Just because I insulted you? Let it go!"

"I came to Cair Legion," said Peredur, "to join Arthur's teulu. I thought I was ready but you showed me that I was not. You shamed me but I know now that the shame was my own. I have trained, prepared myself for this moment, thinking that I could beat you and win my place in Arthur's following. But again, I have shamed myself. I am nothing if I cannot live up to my vow. Just kill me. Please?"

Cei swallowed as he took in his words. Then his face hardened. "The grain. Where is it?"

"Here," said Peredur. "In a stable yard covered with a canopy."

Cei stood up, not taking his eyes from Peredur's. Peredur did not attempt to rise. He lay defeated, broken, waiting for death.

"You stole that grain to lure me out here," said Cei, "so that you could fight me and win a place in Arthur's teulu?" He smiled. "Arthur has need of good fighters. In fact, the need for fighters is so great that perhaps he has need for fools too. Do you have any idea what you are asking? Do you know what we face, what brews in the east?"

"To stand with Arthur is all I want," said Peredur. "Then I can make my father's shade proud. Then I can meet God with a clear conscience."

"When I first fought you, I saw you for a half-wit and a weakling," said Cei. "Now, after our second encounter, I still think that. But by Modron's sweet arse, you have courage!" He extended his hand to Peredur.

Peredur looked at the offered hand, his mind roiling in confusion. Gingerly, he took it and Cei hauled him to his feet.

"As I said, Arthur needs fighters more than he needs lads with any sense in their skulls. Your technique needs more work but from what I have witnessed here, the Saeson could do worse for an adversary. And Arthur could do a lot worse for a follower. Now, show me where you have hidden this grain and I'll take you to Cair Badon where the greatest battle of our time is about to begin!"

Guenhuifar

"I thought I had lost you!" Guenhuifar's father raged. "I thought you were dead in a ditch, murdered by brigands or drowned at sea by whoever it was that you were chasing! How could you put me through this?"

"I am sorry, father," said Guenhuifar. "But I had to know. I had to find out before all tracks were covered over and Cadwallon went to war with Eternion."

They were sitting in the main room of the steward's hall. Guenhuifach sat beside her sister and shared in the tirade their father was heaping upon them for her part in the cover up. The ploy hadn't lasted long. Guenhuifar's quest had kept her from home far longer than either of them had anticipated and Guenhuifach had soon run out of excuses. As soon as Guenhuifar's absence had been revealed, Gogfran had frantically begged Cadwallon to send out search parties.

It was one of these search parties Guenhuifar had come across on her way back home. She had spent the night at Custenhinn's tavern, starving and weary beyond words. A hot meal, her old clothes on and a good night's sleep improved her spirit no end and she headed back west not knowing how she would explain all that she had learned.

"And the wife of Venedotia's penteulu too!" Gogfran continued. "I dare not think what Arthur would say if he knew what his wife has been up to!"

"Father…" Guenhuifar said. "I need to talk to Cadwallon. I have… much to tell him."

Her father sighed and gave up berating her. She was a grown woman now and there were some powers parents lost as the years went by. "He's a busy man these days. Etern is still a prisoner here. All of Eternion is marshalled on the border, poised to take Cair Cunor. I am glad at least that you remained here. With Arthur and the teulu gone, there will be little to stop them sweeping north and laying siege to Ynys Mon. We are on the brink of civil war once more."

"But that is why I must speak with Cadwallon!" said Guenhuifar. "It has all been a ruse! Etern didn't try to kill Owain. The assassin was set up."

"But what proof do you have, daughter?"

Guenhuifar fell into a frustrated silence. She had no proof. After all her questions, all of her hardship, what did she have to show for it all? She had found out many things but she was no closer to finding out who had tried to have Owain killed.

"None," she admitted. "But I have something else to tell Cadwallon. Something about his family... something about Anna."

"Anna?" her father and sister looked at her in shock.

"She had a son; a boy called Medraut who was the son of Meriaun. Had the civil war gone in Meriaun's favour, Anna would have become Queen of Venedotia with her own son next in line for the throne." She went on to explain all she had learned from Cerdwen.

When she was done, Gogfran left for the Great Hall, promising that he would secure an audience with the king for later in the day. Guenhuifar went for a lie down to compose her thoughts and rest her body. Guenhuifach stopped her.

"I have something to tell you," she said. "Something I couldn't tell father. Or anybody else for that matter. It concerns a patient of mine. They swore me to secrecy but I suppose none of that matters now and I just can't keep silent any longer…" Tears welled in her eyes.

"Calm down," Guenhuifar said. "This has obviously been weighing on your mind so you had better tell me."

"It's just that everybody trusts me with their secrets that sometimes I feel like they are building up and up inside of me and I shall explode."

"If this has something to do with the assassination attempt…"

"It… it might have. I just don't know!"

"Come," Guenhuifar said, taking her by the hands. They sat back down at the table. "Let us try and work it out together."

"Fine. You know that on occasion I help girls who have been a little careless with their lovers…"

"I was aware."

"Well, one girl came to me a few weeks after Calan Mai. She was a servant who was provided to King Etern to cater for his needs during his stay. Well, she had recently taken a lover and fell into an unfortunate way. She came to me for help and so I helped her. But she was frightened. The man she thought had loved her had used her. He had used her position…"

"For what?"

"He asked her to steal a ring from Etern's quarters. A ring that was easily identifiable as his. After the assassination attempt, when word got around that Etern's ring had been found on the assassin, she panicked."

Guenhuifar stood up suddenly. "How long have you known about this, Guenhuifach?"

"Only a few days. You see, the girl started to show after you had gone and came to me, most upset and told me the whole story. But it gets worse. Only a day after I spoke to her, her body was found on the beach, smashed to bits on the rocks. Everybody said it was an accident. She had been walking along the cliffs and slipped…"

"And you didn't tell anybody?"

Tears formed in Guenhuifach's eyes. "I didn't know who to tell! I was frightened that whoever had killed that girl would kill me if I spoke up! Oh, Guenhuifar! I missed you so much! I needed you but you were off being brave and doing your own thing. I wished I could be as brave as you but I just couldn't! I kept telling myself that you would be back any day now, but you were gone for so long!"

"All right. It's all right, Guenhuifach. We'll sort this out. Now, tell me, who was this girl's lover?"

Guenhuifach wiped away the tears. "Seraun."

"Seraun? Prince Maelcon's hound?"

"Yes."

Guenhuifar looked up at the rafters. *Now why would a pampered dandy like Seraun want King Owain dead? More to the point, why would he want civil war?*

She looked at her sister. "Guenhuifach, look at me."

Guenhuifach focused her teary eyes on Guenhuifar's.

"You are going to have to be brave now. I will be right beside you so we must be brave together. You are going to come with me and speak to Cadwallon this afternoon. We are going to tell him everything and get to the bottom of this."

Guenhuifar still had some questions and she wanted answers before her audience with the Pendraig. She knew that he would demand that Seraun be brought before him for questioning and she also knew that Seraun would lie through his teeth. They needed to be better prepared and she wanted to know all there was to know about Seraun. *There has to be a motive somewhere.*

The only connection she had to Maelcon's circle of friends was Nevin.

She found Nevin laughing with the wine merchant whose two sons were carrying the amphorae into the storage hut adjacent to the Great Hall.

"Nevin, can I speak with you a moment in private?" she asked.

"Guenhuifar!" said Nevin, more surprised by Guenhuifar speaking to her than in her reappearance after so many days gone. "Of course. Don't mind Belcho, he's got work to do, haven't you, Belcho?"

The wine merchant nodded, knowing he was dismissed, and ambled off to bellow at his sons to be cautious with the king's wine.

"Have you seen Seraun about today?" Guenhuifar asked.

"Yes, he's with Maelcon up on the walls, watching the bowmen go through their routines. They have both become so dreadfully dull recently. They only want each other's company, it seems."

"Any idea what they talk about?"

"Oh, I don't know. Another local slut, I expect." There was a hint of bitterness in her voice. "As if that servant girl who threw herself off the cliffs wasn't enough, Seraun's always got his eye on some other piece of trash."

"The dead girl was Seraun's lover?"

"Yes. He chucked me for her. Serves him right that she killed herself."

"But Seraun and Prince Maelcon have been acting strangely ever since?" Guenhuifar probed. "Like they had a secret, perhaps?" She did not like where this was going. *Did Prince Maelcon know?*

"Well something keeps them whispering to each other. I thought it was something to do with that brother of Seraun's. His sudden appearance had Seraun most unhappy and I don't blame him. Dreadful common type. The apple fell far from the tree in that one, and I think Seraun was a little ashamed of him. Still, he seems to have moved on now…"

"Wait a minute, what brother?"

"Oh, I suppose you wouldn't have heard, not being in *our* circle, of course. Some scruffy boy with a nasty way about him turned up claiming to be Seraun's estranged brother. Their mother, you see, had him out of wedlock before she struck gold by marrying Seraun's father. He was sent off to be raised somewhere remote. Anyway, he turned up out of the blue and there was an awful row. Seraun's mother came clean about her past and it was all hushed up. But Seraun was terribly embarrassed. He's always been too proud, you see, and this brother of his kept pestering him for money. He even turned up at the lys and Seraun all but died of embarrassment! He'd hate me for telling you about it but it serves him right for ignoring me the last few weeks." She pouted a little.

"And this brother of Seraun's has not been seen for some time?" Guenhuifar asked.

"No, he seems to have vanished. You'd think that would make Seraun happy but he's been as moody and inapproachable as a dog with a sore head recently."

Vanished. Guenhuifar was willing to be that Nevyn would recognise the dead assassin as Seraun's brother. Too bad that the corpse had long since been buried and its features turned to worm food.

So, Seraun had found a use for his new-found brother that would rid him of his presence for good. But there was still a key piece of the puzzle missing; motive. Why had Seraun used his brother's services and then had him murdered instead of just killing him in the first place? It was all far too elaborate just to get rid of an embarrassing family member.

Time had run out. The sun was setting over the thatch of the Great Hall and she could see her father by its entrance, waiting to accompany her into the Pendraig's presence.

She fetched Guenhuifach from the house. The poor girl was shaking but kept her head up and let Guenhuifar accompany her to the Great Hall.

Cadwallon's face was stern as they told him all they knew. First Guenhuifach told him about the murdered serving girl, then Guenhuifar related every twist and turn of her journey across Ynys Mon to the Isle of the Dead. She finished with what she had just learnt from Nevin.

When they were done, Cadwallon and Meddyf shared a look. Guenhuifar did not know what it meant but she feared they had trod close to treason by suggesting that Maelcon might have some knowledge of what Seraun had been up to.

"Bring Seraun to me," said Cadwallon. "And my son." He turned to Gogfran. "Take your daughters outside."

"Do you think the king believes us?" Guenhuifach said to their father as he escorted them out.

"Yes, I think so," he replied. "After all, what reason would you have to lie? Seraun, on the other hand, will have to do some very clever talking to discredit your stories. I must go, the Pendraig will require my presence."

He went back in and closed the side door behind him.

"Have we done the right thing, Guenhuifar?" Guenhuifach asked, her face wracked with worry.

"Of course we have," Guenhuifar replied. "We did the only thing. I just wish they would let us watch while Seraun is interrogated! I want to see him try to worm his way out of all this!"

The interrogation took two hours and despite Guenhuifach's repeated desire to retire home, Guenhuifar would not leave the vicinity of the Great Hall. With her ear pressed to the wood of the side door, she tried to catch what was being said but, apart from a couple of bouts of shouting, she could make out none of it.

Eventually, as the torches were being lit around the settlement, their father emerged, pale-faced and tired-looking.

"What happened?" Guenhuifar demanded.

"Well…" he said, clearly not sure how to begin. Then he sighed and spread out his hands. "It's all true."

"All of it?" Guenhuifar said. "He admitted it was him?"

"It was the dead servant girl that tumbled him. Several people saw them together at Calan Mai and when she turned up dead there was talk of foul play. But nobody knew she had been pregnant until Guenhuifach came forward."

"So Seraun gave Etern's ring to his brother and instructed him to kill Owain," said Guenhuifar. "Then he hired a second assassin from the Brotherhood of the Boar to wait in the woods and kill his brother as he fled."

"Tying up loose ends and ridding himself of an unwanted family member into the bargain," said Gogfran.

"But why?" Guenhuifar asked in exasperation. "Why start a civil war?"

"In his most desperate moment, when he knew he was about to be condemned, he attempted to shift some of the blame from his shoulders. He claimed that it was Maelcon who ordered the whole thing."

"Maelcon? But he is to marry Etern's daughter… oh!" As soon as she said the words, Guenhuifar realised.

"Yes. An arrangement he has always resented."

"But would he really throw the land into civil war just to get out of an arranged marriage?" Guenhuifach asked.

Gogfran father shrugged. "Prince Maelcon has never been a particularly moral boy but I must confess I had thought this beyond even him."

"What do his parents think?" asked Guenhuifar.

"Time will tell. All have been ordered from the hall while they have a long talk with their son. Seraun was dragged away to a cell and I have orders to release Etern and his family. Reparations will have to be made. The scars this has caused will take a generation to heal."

Peredur

At first, Peredur was distraught to learn that not only had Arthur moved on into Dumnonia but Cei was going to ditch him at Cair Badon and take the teulu south to meet up with him. Everyone had been going frantic during Cei's absence because Arthur had urgently summoned the teulu.

Caradog, whom Peredur learned was one of Arthur's captains besides Cei and Beduir, was marshalling the cavalry as they arrived.

"The auxiliaries are to remain here with Aurelianus to guard the town," he said. "We are taking cavalry only."

"Is there war in Dumnonia?" Cei asked.

"Not yet, but things are tense between the Cornubians and the Dumnonians. Arthur wants us there to keep a lid on things until he gets back."

"Gets back?"

"Aye. From Armorica. He's sailing from Din Tagel with Drustan to buy some horses. You're to go too. He said he doesn't want to travel to foreign parts without you at his side."

Cei nodded and made arrangements for fresh horses to be saddled and war gear to be prepared. He took Peredur into the town's basilica which had been converted into a base of operations. The nave was lined with weapons racks and the apse was occupied by trestle tables spread with maps and inventories.

An elderly man with a white beard and a military tunica descended the stairs. "Cei!" said the man in a voice that was hale and powerful despite his elderly appearance. "I'm glad you have returned. The grain?"

"Currently being unloaded into the town's granaries," said Cei.

The old man noticed Peredur at Cei's side. "Who's this?" The darkening of his face suggested that he already knew the answer.

"The lad who has been giving us so much trouble," said Cei. "His name is Peredur. He has been brought to heel."

"So I see." The man grimaced at Peredur's smashed nose and blackened eyes. His wounds had been treated with vinegar on the road but Peredur still ached in every part of his body.

"He wants to join the teulu, though he can't ride a horse for shit. Good with a bow, or so he claims, and his sword work isn't too shabby although in need of refinement. See what you can do with him."

"He'll have to join the auxiliaries. I'll see to it. You had best get going. My scouts report that Aelle is on the move, although slowly. He won't risk attacking until he has every possible ally under his banner."

Cei turned to Peredur. "This man is Ambrosius Aurelianus. Have you heard the name?"

"Yes," said Peredur. He had, albeit only recently. Aurelianus was the talk of the taverns and Peredur understood that he was something of a legend in the southern kingdoms. He gazed at the old man and felt that instead of meeting Arthur he had been handed over to an older legend of a different generation.

"Aurelianus is in charge here," said Cei. "Follow his orders. Train hard and who knows? Perhaps you will earn your place in the ranks."

Peredur could only nod as Cei went off in search of something to eat.

They departed that afternoon and Peredur watched them from the gatehouse. It seemed to him as if all his hopes and dreams were being carried away with those fluttering banners and jingling bridles, leaving only his battered and broken body – a mere shell – behind, drained of hope. He had been dumped here. Far from joining Arthur's company as a fellow warrior, he had been handed over to somebody else to be given guard duty or at best, a place in the shield wall if he ever saw battle.

Spring turned to summer as the days drifted past and Peredur found himself thrust into garrison life. Training occupied the first few weeks and he honed the skills Edlim had instilled in him. His bowmanship stood him in good stead and he was given a place on the walls by Aurelianus. He wore ring mail and an iron cap provided by the town's armouries. He kept his father's armour hidden in his quarters. It was an embarrassment. He didn't deserve to wear it, certainly not as part of the town's garrison in front of his lowborn comrades. He did his best to forget it just as he tried to forget his dreams. He had failed in his vow and had reached the furthest he could go. Garrison work was all he was good for.

Even so, every day he walked the walls he would look towards the south-west, hoping to see the return of Arthur and his teulu.

It was on a hot day as the afternoon was slowly receding to dusk that the first news of their doom came. Refugees made their way along the road from the east, driving wains and livestock, clutching small children and helping the elderly. They spoke of fire and death snapping at their heels. Aurelianus dispatched more scouts for his first had not returned and were feared dead. He also sent riders into Dumnonia to recall Caradog and Arthur's cavalry. Even if their chieftain was still in Armorica, they had need of whatever help that could be sent.

The scouts rode back that same day, pale-faced and their horses near broken with exhaustion. "They come!" were the words spoken from their dry, spittle-flecked lips. "Aelle and his horde march on Cair Badon!"

Aurelianus looked out across the hills that were silent beneath darkening skies. "So be it," he said.

The enemy arrived in the night and made camp in the ruins of an old hillfort that overlooked the town from the east. As Peredur watched from the walls the following morning, lines upon lines of men with their great round shields emerged from the trees, spears bristling. Bowmen, arrayed in clusters a hundred thick moved across the grassy slopes while captains and chieftains rode their horses beneath billowing banners depicting the animal sigils of a dozen Sais tribes. They forded the river north of the town and headed south towards its northern gate. A rumble as that of thunder reached the ears of those atop the walls and Peredur realised that it was not thunder, for the sky was clear and blue. It was the roll of drums, beating out a tempo to an ever-increasing war chant.

"God in heaven," said one of Peredur's comrades, whose name was Guto. "They come upon us before Arthur returns. What can we do against such numbers?"

"We have the town," said Peredur, trying to comfort him with a confidence he himself did not feel. "What can a thousand Saeson do against thick stone walls and barred gates?"

"Look!" said Guto. He pointed at several shapes making their way down from the hill. They were massive yet spindly as if fragile. Peredur was put in mind of spiders as large as houses, creeping across the fields.

"What are they?" he asked.

"Siege engines," said Guto, his voice grim. "The bastards have built catapults."

The significance of this rippled along the walls and there were groans and cries of dismay.

"Those things will rip holes through our defences," said Guto.

"And the enemy will seep in like an infection into a wound," said another.

They watched in dismay as the Saeson halted just out of bowshot from the walls and the great siege engines, built according to Roman designs, began hurling their loads at the towers and gates of Cair Badon.

The walls were thick as Peredur had said and the round stones of the catapults chipped away at the town's defences, showering the Britons with sharp chunks of broken masonry. They fell back from the northern walls and took cover within the town. Some missiles passed clean over the walls and tore into the buildings, smashing through tiled roofs, crushing anybody unfortunate to be caught underneath.

The enemy kept up the barrage throughout the day while groups of Saeson crept around to the east and west of the town carrying ladders and grappling hooks. Supported by clusters of bowmen, these groups tried to scale the walls and the Britons had their hands full trying to stop them. Spreading themselves thin, they desperately tried to cover every new stretch of wall the enemy tried to mount, all the while being shot at from the ground.

Peredur and the other bowmen moved along the rooftops and sent volley after volley down onto the enemy who fell back each time only to move further along and try at some point less guarded. It was exhausting work and a couple of times the enemy succeeded in placing a ladder against the ramparts and several Saeson reached the parapet which caused a great drive to hack them down and dislodge the ladder to halt the flow.

As dusk approached the enemy fell back. By the time darkness descended over the chalk downlands, the catapults stopped their barrage and hung slack.

Everybody was exhausted. The siege had lasted a full day with no respite. Behind the walls of Cair Badon, food was distributed and the Britons took stock of the damage and mourned their lost comrades.

They slept in their armour, finding whatever comfort they could in the ruins, awaiting the morning with heavy hearts. Even if Caradog had received Aurelianus's message, it might take him days to pull his troops out of Dumnonia. Who knew what the situation was down there? He might not come at all which meant that they were completely alone.

Peredur's exhausted body would not let him dwell on their fate for too long, regardless of how pressing it was. He slumbered until dawn broke over the shattered ramparts, promising a hot and hellish day.

The Saeson renewed their attack as soon as it was light and Peredur, his muscles aching and stiff, climbed the wall once more. They had all refilled their quivers with fresh arrows the night before but there was a limit to how many they had left. As soon as the last arrow was shot, they would have nothing to keep the enemy from the walls.

The siege engines focussed on the northern gatehouse and by noon both towers had crumbled to rubble. The gate still stood but now, with nothing the guard it, the enemy were free to bring their ram right up against it.

Aurelianus ordered everybody to fall back. The streets were barricaded with rubble and timbers and the basilica stood as the last bastion against the tide of death that washed around the town's walls.

Peredur sought out Aurelianus for further orders on where the bowmen should marshal once the Saeson broke through the north gate. He found him in the nave, on his knees before the bright painting of Christ. His sword was unsheathed and he rested on it, point down, its hilt and cross guard level with his eyes as if it were crucifix.

"Sir, there are no suitable rooftops for my men to cluster on. There are the basilica's balconies but they are on the eastern and western sides and are too narrow in any case to place a large enough contingent to do any damage."

"No," said Aurelianus. "The time for arrows has perhaps passed. We must meet them hand to hand in this place which is likely to be our tomb."

"The catapults will soon be in range. They could decimate this basilica without any Sais entering the town. Should we fall farther back?"

"What for? To die in the gutters with the southern wall at our backs? Better to die here, in the house of God, our swords in our hands."

"You..." Peredur began. "You sound like you have given up the fight, sir."

Aurelianus turned his head and looked at him in a bemused fashion. Then he smiled and slowly, with much effort it seemed, got to his feet. He sat down on a bench opposite Peredur. "You are young, lad, and it heartens this old soldier to see the boundless optimism in the face of death course through your veins. It is a good time to live. Perhaps it is a good time to die, and not wait until you are half-crippled and so old that none who now live remember you as a young man."

Peredur did not know what to say. The booming of the ram against the gate echoed in the cavernous chamber. All around them was death and ruin and yet Ambrosius Aurelianus, last of the Romans, was content to smile and talk of youth.

"Peredur, wasn't it?" Aurelianus asked him.

Peredur nodded.

"Tell me about yourself. What brought you to us? I never quite understood your feud with Cei, though, God love him, short as I have known him, he is no man to want for enemies."

"My father was the commander of Eboracum," Peredur began and Aurelianus's eyes lit up.

"Indeed? What was his name? I must have known him."

"Fabianus, sir."

"Is it true that Septimius Fabianus's son stands before me? You come from fine stock, young Peredur! Had we lived in more civilised times, your father would have been known as the *Dux Britanniarum*, guardian of the north. Although he came to the position long after the old Roman titles fell out of use. The last Dux Britanniarum fell in battle a generation before your father picked up the standard. He tried to hold back the darkness in the north just as I did in the south. I liked your father. He shared the same dream I did to re-establish what once was. Truly, I had never thought to meet old Fabianus's son!"

"He had many sons, and me last of all. They all fell with my father in a Pictish raid when I was but a babe."

Aurelianus's face saddened. "Aye, I remember it. It was a sad loss to all of Britannia. Courageous though he was, it was not enough to keep the barbarians on the other side of the Wall."

"My mother raised me in the wilderness and I knew nothing of war or the Saeson until I wandered too far one day and saw Arthur and his host marching south. I can't tell you what emotion that sight stoked in my soul. I knew I had to join them, even if it meant abandoning my mother and the only home I had ever known. I wandered far and had many misfortunes…" he broke off at this point, not sure how he should continue. The smashed and ruined face of Bevin flashed before his eyes. He had no desire to tell Aurelianus of his crime. "… but I did find an uncle – my mother's brother – who took me in and trained me. I could have remained with him but still the desire to wear my father's armour and fight side by side with Arthur burned in me too hot to ignore. So I left and made it my mission to fight Cei and prove that I was his equal. Cei had insulted me, you see, and my family name."

Aurelianus smirked. "Aye, Cei does have a habit of raising peoples' hackles."

"But when it came to it," Peredur went on, feeling the colour rise in his cheeks, "I discovered that I am not Cei's equal. I am just a boy, good with a bow perhaps, but I am no warrior worthy of Arthur."

Aurelianus regarded him in silence for a moment and then said; "Let me tell you something, Peredur mab Fabianus. You may be the son of a great man born in ignorance in the wilderness, but in Britannia's direst hour, you are *here*. You are here when so many others have fled, fled west, fled to Gaul, fled anywhere they think might be safe from the Saeson. You came here of your own free will and you have remained because you believe in Arthur. I was sceptical when that man came down from his mountains with his men. I had for so long given up on the Venedotians as a bunch of self-interested brigands who care only for stealing the cattle of their neighbours. But Arthur showed me something. He showed me that the old spirit of Britannia still burns and if it could burn in the heart of a Venedotian cattle thief then perhaps if might burn in a good many more hearts. It is that hope which is Britannia's salvation. I see the same hope and spirit burning in you, Peredur. The torches sputter and die but there is a spark which might kindle a new fire. That spark is carried by you and by Arthur and by all the young men who flock to his banner."

"But you yourself said that there is nothing we can do," said Peredur. "The Saeson are at our gates and there is no way out. When I approached you just now I saw you praying. Were you praying for a miracle?"

Aurelianus clenched his jaw and looked Peredur in the eye. "No. Listen, son. When I spoke of hope just now, I spoke of Britannia's hope. For us, you are right, there is no way out. But I am prepared to meet our enemies and feed the ravens with as many of their corpses as I can before I go to meet God. Our sacrifice here will be heard of across the island and it will kindle many more fires. Let us give Arthur the torch of our memory to carry onwards, to ignite hope in town and in field, until all Albion rises up once more and the Sais scourge has been entirely burned away."

His own words brought tears to his eyes but there was something else there; an emotion that had lain dormant for so many years that, now that death drew near, it demanded to be heard.

"You ask me what I was praying for just now?" Aurelianus said. "It was not for a miracle. It was for forgiveness."

"Forgiveness?" Peredur asked. "For what? You are a hero to every Briton."

"I have won battles, it is true, but my fight has not been entirely selfless." His eyes showed a deep sadness now and refused to meet Peredur's. "You have told me your story, now let me tell you mine. I have not spoken of this to a soul for many years but now that I know my final hour is upon me, I must do justice to the one I have wronged."

"I had a daughter, many years ago. I was little more than a lad myself; young to be the *Dux Britanniarum* and younger still to be a father. Too young, perhaps, too prideful. It was in those days that the Sais menace was but a small one in the south-east. Hengest and Horsa led them and they had entered my service at the insistence of the lord Vertigernus, head of the Council of Britannia. It was an ill-advised treaty born of lust. Vertigernus desired Hengest's daughter, you see but I did not find out until too late that Horsa desired my own. Our close association enabled them to carry on a clandestine affair."

"When I got wind of it and learned that my daughter would never give him up, I arranged for Horsa's assassination. The attempt failed but that is irrelevant. My daughter thought it had succeeded and that her father had slain her lover. She hanged herself from the stairs in my villa."

"Since that day I have been a man possessed by a demon; a demon fed on guilt and hate. I hated everything and everyone. I waged war after war on the Saeson, long after Vertigernus had died. My hate kept me alive, kept me fighting. It has consumed me and now I find myself at the end of the road with nothing to show for my life but my hate and my sword."

Peredur blinked. Aurelianus's honesty shocked him and the fact that Albion's champion had chosen to tell his secret to him – a boy he barely knew – both flattered and tore at his own conscience. "I too am driven by guilt," he said. "I killed a man. In cold blood. He was nothing but a common thief but he tried to steal my father's armour and so I bashed his brains out with a rock. Ever since that day I have sought to redeem myself but everything led me to failure. Now, here I am, a garrison soldier, too ashamed to wear my father's armour. I never will, not until I have earned it by honouring my father's spirit and earning God's blessing."

Aurelianus smiled and placed his hand on Peredur's shoulder. "It seems we both have much to make up for."

They listened to the booming of the ram on the north gate.

"Peredur, will you do something for me?" Aurelianus asked.

"Anything, sir."

"Go and put on your father's armour."

"Sir?"

"We are at the end of all roads, Peredur. Redemption must be claimed now or it will be forever out of our reach. Go and put on your father's armour and we shall pray together for God's blessing. Then, we shall die side by side and God can pass what judgement as He deems fit. We shall die for Britannia. And Arthur."

Peredur rose and left Aurelianus in the nave. As he hurried outside and down the street to his quarters in the arena, he could hear the slamming of the ram against the northern gate all the louder. It beat in his head like a heavy pulse. Aurelianus was right. All roads ended here. There was no more time.

He strapped on his armour and hurried back to the basilica. He passed many men cowering behind barricades, uncertain of how to meet their fate. That was something no man could dictate and he hoped they would all meet with good ends. He entered the basilica and crossed the nave, his footsteps echoing. Aurelianus rose to greet him.

"And now, Peredur..." he began but then stopped. Something had distracted him and he looked up at the high windows.

Peredur heard it too. Horns. Distant horns, but horns that blew with a vibrancy that drowned out the dull bellows of the enemy host.

Aurelianus and Peredur exchanged a look and then, without a word, ran to the staircase that led to the upper galleries.

From the windows facing south they could see a line of horsemen on the ridge, spears bristling, banners trailing. There were scores of them – hundreds even – arrayed in formation, row upon row, the sinking sun glinting off helms and spear tips as if they were made of fire. In the centre of the front line a banner was held higher than all the others. It was difficult to make out at this distance, but Peredur could see that it was red. *A red dragon.*

"Arthur," said Aurelianus, tears streaming down his bearded cheeks. "Arthur comes. God has heard us!"

Arthur

The chalk ridge looked down onto the western wall of Cair Badon. The horses, their flanks dripping from the recent fording of the river, shook their manes and whinnied softly as the teulu formed battle lines.

The river ran on their right flank and, rising like an ant hill on the other side of the town, was the hill upon which the enemy had made their camp. Between them stood nothing but carnage and ruin. Dust and smoke rose from the town and the whole northern face of it was little more then a pile of rubble.

The enemy swarmed around it like a black tide washing around a rock. The hut on wheels that housed the battering ram was pressed right up against the northern gate and it was flanked by bowmen who sent flaming arrows over the shattered walls into the town. Saeson with ladders followed the wall along and were trying at intervals to scale it, constantly beaten back by the Britons who defended the ramparts. It would not be long before they would gain a foothold on the walls and then the town would fall within an hour.

Arthur looked along the lines of his horsemen. That they should arrive now, just as the tide was about to turn, was nothing short of a miracle. He had made landfall at Din Tagel a couple of weeks ago. It had been a slow process unloading all two-hundred of his newly-acquired horses and leading them, one by one, up the path from the harbour and across the land bridge to the mainland but he had his cavalry at last. And as he had been fitting out every horse with a rider and his equipment, Caradog had received word from Aurelianus that Cair Badon was under attack.

Arthur's companies, now more than a hundred strong each, and Drustan's mounted Cornubians, made over four-hundred riders. Four-hundred against every Sais in the east or so it seemed. As Arthur looked down upon the enemy he found it impossible to arrive at an estimate of their numbers for they were a poorly disciplined lot who charged about in rag-tag groups, some keeping to the treelines where the catapults hurled their loads, some charging forward as if they planned to hew through stone walls with their swords.

No more. It is over for them.

"Beduir!" Arthur called. "You take the left flank, Caradog the right. Cei, you take the centre. I shall ride with you while Drustan brings up our rear. We shall hit them as a single blunt force. I want to move in a smooth curve to the left, wiping them from the walls like ants from our sleeve before we continue towards those catapults. Strike brands. We shall burn those things to the ground and when they are blazing, we shall turn towards the town's northern gate and hammer the enemy up against the walls."

His captains rode off to marshal their companies and Arthur urged Hengroen forward so that he stood apart from the teulu. He turned and spurred the white horse into a gallop, running the length of the line. The faces of four-hundred comrades, some familiar, some wholly new, gazed on him in wide-eyed expectation. They were scared, of course they were. He was too. But the sight of Cair Badon under such brutal attack, the last bastion between the west and utter ruin, ignited a determination in them, even if it meant their deaths.

"Comrades!" Arthur bellowed, making his voice travel as far as it could, urging it to be heard over the snapping of the banners in the wind and the distant war chants of the enemy. "Some of you have ridden with me from Venedotia. Some have recently joined me; Dumnonians, Cornubians, men from Guenta and even those local to this area. You all joined me because you believed that Albion was worth saving. Down there lies the greatest threat Albion has faced since the earliest Caesars landed their legions on its shores. They will not stop until every Briton is part of a new land; *their* land, ruled over by *their* gods."

There was much murmured outrage at this for he had struck at the heart of pagan and Christian alike. Many eyes looked to his shield and saw the face of the mother that was most precious to them. He had their hearts. Now he needed their courage. He drew *Caledbulc* and held it aloft. It was a fortuitous moment that the sun was making its descent into the west as they stood there on that ridge and its dying light caught the long blade and made it glimmer as if it was a blade of fire spat from the mouths of the two golden serpents on its hilt. There was an intake of breath as the last men of the west gazed upon Arthur, his body protected by the image of the blessed mother and his hand wielding a sword of flame that Albion's enemies would surely flee from as rats from a burning brand.

"Ride with me, my companions!" Arthur roared. "Ride for your freedom and the freedom of your grandchildren. Ride for Albion!"

It would take a true craven not to be stirred into action by Arthur's words on that day. A cheer arose from four-hundred throats and the whole ridge sang with defiance.

Arthur wheeled Hengroen around to face the besieged town. Still holding *Caledbulc* aloft, he kicked Hengroen into a gallop and began his descent. At first, he rode alone and then, in one glorious movement, four-hundred companions trod in his wake.

Peredur

From the western balcony of the basilica, Peredur and Aurelianus watched Arthur and his massive following charge down from the ridge, their rear ranks engulfed in the dust kicked up by the front lines. It was an awesome sight that brought tears to Aurelianus's eyes and made Peredur feel short of breath and heavy in the chest.

The Saeson had begun to attack the western gatehouse and attempt to scale the walls on either side of it. In one sweeping curve, Arthur led the charge along the foot of the wall. Spears punched out and swords and axes scythed downwards and the Saeson fell like wheat. They tried to run but there was no outrunning something that wide moving that fast.

Arthur's companies slammed into the bulk of the enemy on the northern side of the town, taking them completely unaware for their approach had been hidden by the town walls. They drove deep and hard, with no shield walls or organised groups of spearmen to hinder them. They were halfway into the enemy ranks when they began to falter. The enemy, recovered from the initial charge, were curling around their right flank and pressing in on their rear ranks.

"We have to aid them," said Aurelianus. "They are being enveloped!"

"How?" Peredur asked.

"We must open the western gate. I shall lead what few riders we have left."

"There aren't more than fifty horses left in Cair Badon!" Peredur protested. "You'll be overwhelmed!"

"Is Arthur not overwhelmed?" Aurelianus demanded. "Is he not willing to lay down his life to save us? How could you expect me not to return the favour? We may all die today but I will not die a coward!"

Peredur nodded. He knew that Aurelianus was right. He knew also that the old soldier was possessed of some wild and frightening desire Peredur did not quite understand. He felt that, victory or no, Aurelianus meant to die that day.

Aurelianus strode out of the nave and gave orders to his closest companions to saddle their horses and prepare to ride out. Each of them nodded, clearly frightened by the prospect but too desperate and unwilling to challenge their general.

"I need your help, lad," he said, turning to Peredur. "Clear the roads of our barricades so that we might pass through. Carry word to the western gatehouse that the gates are to be flung open at our approach."

Peredur saluted and ran off to do Aurelianus's bidding. There was but one barricade barring the road to the western gatehouse and, once he had kicked the group of bowmen guarding it into action, progress on its dismantling began in earnest. They seemed in awe of his fine armour which nobody in Cair Badon had seen him wear before and did his bidding without question.

He left them to it and ran on to the gatehouse. As he approached, he halted in his tracks. The heads of several Saeson were emerging over the parapet. In the wake of Arthur's charge, some of the enemy had wheeled back to renew their assault on the town.

Peredur counted five or six bearded warriors scrambling over the parapet, intent on opening the gates to admit their comrades. If those gates were opened too soon, the town would be lost despite Arthur's efforts. He turned around and bolted back down the street. The bowmen had succeeded in shifting most of the barricade.

"Pick up your bows!" he told them. "The enemy have the gatehouse! We must hold it for Aurelianus!"

They seemed less keen on this order but fell into line all the same and Peredur led them back up to the gatehouse.

When they got there they saw a group of Saeson trying to heave the gates open. As one, Peredur's bowmen nocked, drew and loosed, felling the group in a lethal spray of arrows. More Saeson were already clambering onto the parapet.

"We've got to knock that ladder down!" said Peredur. "Cover me!"

As the arrows whistled overhead, thudding into the unsuspecting enemy who tottered and fell, Peredur dashed up the steps. He made the rampart just as another Sais poked his ugly head over the parapet. Peredur drew his sword and swung it down at the point between the neck and the shoulder and winced as a gush of hot blood spurted across his knuckles. The man cried out, lost his grip and tumbled back down to where his comrades waited at the foot of the wall.

Peredur hurled his weight against the ladder and pushed it away, sending a couple more Saeson screaming.

Two more Sais remained on the wall and several arrows were sent from his comrades on the ground. They were cautious of hitting him and most went wide of the mark but one struck the Sais on his left. That just left the one between Peredur and the gatehouse.

The man was ready for him, brandishing a buckler and the long knife his people were known for. Peredur feinted and let the Sais overreach himself and then hacked through the arm at the elbow. The man screamed and clutched the bleeding stump before Peredur finished him with a blow to the top of the head.

Casting his body aside, Peredur ran for the gatehouse. He encountered another Sais in the first tower. This one was armed with an axe. He leapt back and narrowly avoided having his skull crushed as the axe head whistled within an inch of his scalp. Taking advantage of his opponent's offset balance, Peredur thrust his sword in between his ribs, causing the man to suck in a lungful in agony. With a rip he withdrew the blade and hacked at the man's knee, causing him to buckle under his own weight.

Peredur rushed out into the sunlight on the wall between the two gate towers and realised that there were no more of the enemy on the walls. He checked the other tower. The gatehouse was clear. He looked down the street that led to the basilica and arena and could see a column of horsemen galloping towards him.

"Aurelianus comes!" Peredur shouted to the bowmen below. "Get the gate open!"

As a couple of them ran forward to unbar the thick gates, he peered over the wall at the seething mass of Saeson on the other side and realised that Aurelianus would be riding into the jaws of death itself.

As the gates opened and the first of the Saeson began to spill in, unaware of the riders galloping down the road towards them, Peredur bellowed at his bowmen. "To the walls! To the walls!"

The Saeson who had entered the town suddenly saw Aurelianus and his followers riding hard towards them. In their terror, they dived for cover as Peredur's men hurried up the steps to the rampart.

"A volley!" Peredur cried. "As one! Down into the enemy!"

Aurelianus was close now. Blades cut down the Saeson who had entered the town. On the other side of the wall, more pushed forward, trying to rush the open gates. Peredur raised his bloodied sword aloft as the bowmen drew back on their strings.

He swung his arm down. A dozen arrows whickered down to land like hail on the enemies directly in front of the gate.

A cry from many throats arose as the black shafts pierced them. Men fell or scurried for cover, fearing a second volley. They were wary now and were less concerned with storming the gate than withstanding whatever its defenders could offer and cowered under their shields.

Peredur had opened a path between the enemy ranks and Aurelianus led the charge two abreast, through the gate and dived into the breach.

Arthur

The Saeson fled from them as they crossed the plain beyond the town's northern gate, spreading out and curling behind on both flanks. Arthur knew they would be doubling back and mustering on their rear but it didn't matter. All that mattered was pressing through and getting to those siege engines.

Some of the torches Arthur's men had carried had sputtered out in the mad charge but there were still enough burning brands to get the job done. As they approached, sparks whirled from cartwheeling torches as they were hurled, spinning end over end to land in the machinery of the catapults or to roll on the ground beneath them, scorching the grass. The wind was blowing against the enemy and it was not long before the catapults were roaring infernos.

Arthur wheeled Hengroen around to face the enemy host that stood between them and Cair Badon. As he had expected, the Saeson had joined ranks behind them, cutting them off from the town. The trail of carnage caused by their charge could still be seen like a scar across the battlefield. The bodies of the enemy lay strewn in a wide column that vanished into the distant ridges from where they had begun their descent. Many riders had also fallen and the shapes of dead or lamed horses blotted the ground. This had been a costly charge.

There was nothing for it but to see their plan through and try to press the enemy up against the town walls.

"Look!" cried Beduir. "Riders from the west gate!"

Arthur squinted and could see fifty-odd horses, their riders lashing their flanks, charge the rear of the enemy, gouging into their ranks. Leading the charge, he could make out a Roman helm cresting a white beard.

"Aurelianus rides out!" he exclaimed in a mixture of awe and desperation. "Press forward! We have them on two flanks! Push!"

It was a hard fight for they were still vastly outnumbered. Arthur spread his ranks thin and wide to try and encircle the host with Beduir leading the left flank and Caradog the right.

The ground was churned up into a hideous mess of blood, guts and mud that sucked and tugged at the horses' fetlocks. Gore streaked their shields and ran down their blades as they fought on, every foot of ground paid for dearly.

The enemy host was thinning now and Arthur could see the whites of Aurelianus's eyes over the bobbing heads and wavering spear tips of the enemy. The old man fought as a demigod, putting every ounce of his strength into the fight, hacking left and right, his horse foaming at the bit as it twisted its exhausted body and reared up to avoid spear thrusts.

The enemy knew who he was for they clustered closer to Aurelianus than they did to Arthur. They all wanted the honour of felling the greatest enemy to their kind since their ancestors had landed on these shores and as they hemmed him in, Arthur knew that the outcome was inevitable.

He cried out all the same as he saw the spear work its way around Aurelianus's defence. The leaf-shaped head punched through his cuirass below his armpit. Aurelianus screwed his face shut in agony as he reeled in his saddle, the shaft still fixed in his body. The Sais who had wielded it was quickly trampled under the hooves of Aurelianus's companions.

"To Aurelianus!" Arthur bellowed. "To the *Dux Britanniarum*!"

The Saeson, having struck their blow, seemed to lose the will to fight on and began to fall back out of the breach between the two mounted ranks. It was not long before the horns of their commanders on the far left flank began to bellow for a retreat.

The enemy drained from the battlefield like the tide being drawn out. There was no attempt to pursue on the part of Arthur's men. All were exhausted and knew too well how costly this victory had been.

Arthur dismounted and hurried over to where Aurelianus was being gently lifted down from his horse by Marcus and Claudius.

"Fetch Menw!" he shouted to Cei.

He knelt at Aurelianus's side and the old man's face looked so pale. There was a smile there and Arthur recognised it for he had seen in on many a warrior's face, the elderly usually, when their soul is so close to the edge that there is no longer any pain, just a feeling that a journey had reached its end.

"Arthur," said Aurelianus in a hoarse voice. "You are victorious."

"For now," Arthur said grudgingly. "And at such a cost!"

"Freedom is always costly. But we pay its price willingly. You have many battles ahead of you. I have fought my last one. Finish what I started, Arthur.

Keep fighting for Britannia. For Albion. *You* are now the *Dux Bellorum*."

The final words were all but whispered yet all around Arthur heard them. They looked from Aurelianus to Arthur and Arthur burned with grief. Aurelianus's face relaxed as his last breath passed between his lips and his hand went limp in Arthur's.

Many men wept. This man had been their saviour for so long that most could not remember a time when they did not know his name. Claudius and Marcus were inconsolable. Arthur's own men were merely stunned.

Men had come from the town, picking their way through the rubble to mourn at their lost hero's side.

"Take his body to the basilica," Arthur told them. "We shall follow once we are done mopping up here. You," he said to a leader of a group of bowmen in particularly fine armour. "What's your name?"

"Peredur, sir," came the reply.

"That's the lad I was telling you about," said Cei.

"Are you the one who retook the western gatehouse?" Marcus asked him.

Peredur nodded. "Along with these lads." He indicated the dozen or so bowmen at his back.

"That was well done," said Marcus. "We would not have got as far had you not sent a volley into the enemy just as we left the gates."

"The Saeson retreat to their camp on the hill yonder," said Drustan, pointing at the grey hump to the east of the town. "Their spirit is crushed and they will surely head back east."

"We pursue them," said Arthur in a steely voice. "Kill as many of them as we can. This will be a day forever remember by friend and foe alike. The enemy's grandchildren will learn to fear its memory. Mount up! Cei, you lead the centre. Where is Caradog?"

"He fell too," said Beduir, tears cutting clean lines down his smoke-blackened face.

Arthur squeezed his eyes shut. This was a sore day for the old guard.

"Gualchmei, where are you?"

"Here, sire!"

"You are now acting captain of Caradog's company."

Gualchmei nodded, showing no emotion. Arthur knew that he had wanted this for a long time but not under these circumstances.

Arthur turned to Peredur. "Find yourself a horse, boy. You shall ride with me."

Peredur's jaw hung slack. "I... I am no fine rider, sire," he began.

"There are many riderless horses," said Arthur. "And I will not storm that hill unless I have every saddle filled. Now, get to it, lad!"

Peredur looked suddenly ill, and then was unable to stop a smile spreading over his face before he ran off to do his bidding.

Aesc

The hilltop provided them with a full view of their destruction. The town gleamed in the fading light of the day, white and pure as if untouched by all they had thrown at it. The fields before its walls were littered with the dead; enough dead to scar a generation of their people.

Aesc turned from it and gazed at the wounded pouring into camp. Those who still had their lives and their limbs looked about in confusion, unsure of what was expected of them. The dream, Aesc could see, had died in their eyes.

"Look," said Octa, pointing down the slope. "They are preparing to give chase."

Down by the town, the Welsc cavalry were forming battle lines.

Aesc walked over to where Aelle was drinking deep from a water skin.

"You should give the order to strike camp now," he said. "If we act quickly we may be able to take the wounded and the baggage trains with us."

Aelle turned to him, incomprehension showing in his eyes. "Strike camp? What are you talking about?"

"The Welsc are mustering for an assault on our position. We must retreat."

"We have the high ground," said Aelle, his face resolute. "No. We stand here and fight them. Every last one of them."

"This battle cannot be won!" Aesc said. "We have lost hundreds of men and those who still stand are exhausted. We simply cannot withstand their cavalry!"

"Then turn and flee, coward!" Aelle bellowed at him. "Run home to your farms and your halls and all the things your father and uncle bought for you with their blood! Leave the fighting to those who have nothing and must lay down their lives so that their families might have a future!"

Aesc was shocked and not a little shamed at being called a coward in front of his own men. But what could he do? Fight Aelle? Aelle was possessed of something wild that drove him to extremes. There was nothing that could be done. He walked away.

"Father?" Octa said.

"Ready the men," Aesc said to him.

"Are we going home?"

"Not yet. We stand with Aelle but if this hill is lost then be ready to break ranks. I will fight for Aelle but I will not die for him."

Octa nodded and went off to ready the men.

The attack was three-pronged. The entire Welsc cavalry split into three companies and ascended the hill from the north, the west and the south. Aelle ordered every warrior with a missile in their hands to ring the crest of the hill and hurl everything they had down on the attackers. Arrows, javelins and even stones were cast down but it was too little to stem their approaching doom.

The enemy horsemen climbed at a steady rate, shields and bucklers raised to protect themselves from the missiles. It was Arthur's company that crested the hill first, or at least they carried the dragon standard with them. They came hard and fast despite their exhausted horses, so keen they were for vengeance.

Aelle stacked up the shield walls but it was little good. Most spears had been lost or broken in the previous battle and many warriors had but a knife to defend themselves with as they cowered behind their shields. The cavalry swept over and around them, swamping them.

Aesc ordered his thegns to surround Aelle, determined to show loyalty to the last but it was hopeless. Their defensive lines shattered, the Welsc came upon the camp in a wave of scything blades. Tents were trampled or torched, thegns in their finest mail and boar-crested helms were hauled down from their horses and butchered. It was over.

Aesc turned to Octa. "It is time to go. We must leave while we still have a chance."

Octa blew his horn and the Centish thegns disengaged and drew back to the eastern edge of the hill. Before they descended, Aesc turned in his saddle and saw the camp aflame and heard the victory cheers of the Welsc burning the air. A head was being carried on a pole and even at this distance, Aesc could tell that it was Aelle's.

The dream was over. The Welsc had made their stand. Just as his father had learned all those years ago. This island was simply too big. Aurelianus had been the one to teach them that back then. Now they had taken the same lesson from a younger warrior of a new generation whose name would now be a rallying standard for all of Britta, just as Aurelianus's had been.

That name was Arthur.

Guenhuifar

Seraun was hanged from a splay-branched tree on the outskirts of Cadwallon's Lys. A large crowd gathered to watch as he was hauled up by the neck, hands bound behind his back, to twist and dance for the best part of an hour before he was cut down and beheaded. Despite his parents' pleas, his body was not turned over to them and instead joined that of his brother in an unmarked plot some distance into the woods.

One person who was not at the hanging was Maelcon. It seemed that King Cadwallon and Queen Meddyf knew all too well what their eldest son was capable of and had little difficulty in believing him to be the mastermind behind the whole plot. There was no hope of covering it up. Seraun had gone to his execution cursing and blaming Maelcon with every step.

Guenhuifar felt bad for Meddyf. The queen had always seen the best in their son and that was a very small gem to spot. Time and again she had defended him for his many transgressions but there was no defending this. Punishment had to come and it had to be something permanent.

If Cadwallon had given up on his son and heir, then he had also given up on resisting his wife's Christian ambitions for the lad. Abbot Illtud was to have another student for his monastic school. Before the leaves on the trees began to turn to yellow, Maelcon was escorted south to begin his career in the church alongside the infant Gildas; two embarrassing heirs hidden away in the cloisters of learning.

Upon Guenhuifar's information, Cadwallon dispatched troops to expunge the Brotherhood of the Boar from the Isle of the Dead. Just as they had pushed the Gaels into the sea from that bleak and mysterious isle, so did they rout these new settlers and the isle belonged once more, to the dead.

The little colony of outcasts led by Cerdwen was also investigated and Medraut, bastard brother to the Pendraig (just as Arthur was), was brought to Cadwallon for his inspection.

The lad was frightened as he stood before the king in his Great Hall, and Guenhuifar pitied him. Here was another black sheep whose fate was now uncertain. There was talk of letting the boy live out his life with his grandmother but now that he had been presented to the king in front of all his court, such a dismissal would appear cold and heartless. But what, everybody asked, was to be done with him?

"I shall take him!" said Guenhuifar. "He shall be fostered in my own household, if you are willing, my lord."

"Fine," said Cadwallon, eager to resolve the matter. "He is after all, Arthur's nephew just as he is mine."

So it was decided and Medraut was ushered into Guenhuifar's keeping with promises of a life far finer than the meagre existence he had previously experienced.

Guenhuifach was quite taken with the boy and fussed over him and coddled him, promising to feed and clothe him as befitting a young prince. She took him indoors while Guenhuifar and her father watched from the gardens.

"Why did you take him in?" her father asked her.

Guenhuifar shrugged. "His family has made rather a habit of disregarding its base-born members."

"I wouldn't say so. Arthur has managed to rise to the position of penteulu."

"You know what I mean. He may be the penteulu but he had to fight so hard for that recognition and would have been forgotten had he not. I just couldn't live with the thought of Medraut wasting away on that bleak isle with that awful woman."

"Well, whatever your reasons, he is welcome at my hearth."

"Actually, I thought I might take him with me to Cair Cunor."

"Cair Cunor? You're not staying here?"

"Other hearths need tending, as people are so keen to remind me. Perhaps it is time I listened to them." She smiled at her father. The past few weeks had given her a courage to fight battles she had long dreaded. "I thought I might go and await my husband's return."

Peredur

The road north was bare of people and the warm afternoon glow of late summer hummed in the oaks and over the fields which had long lain fallow. The people would return in the aftermath of the Battle of Badon. Aelle was dead and the West Saeson and their allies had limped back east to lick their wounds. The Borderlands had been reclaimed.

Peredur rode a dapple grey and led a dun mare by the bridle; two fine horses from Arthur's new stock. They had been a gift to him from Arthur along with his blessing. Peredur had promised to return to Arthur's service at the end of the summer. Plans were being made to winter at Aurelianus's old hill fort further east to keep a check on Sais reprisals.

The siege of Badon Hill had been more of a massacre and Peredur still had trouble sleeping. He could rarely close his eyes and not see the terror on the faces of the enemy as they had crested the hill and ridden through their shield walls. He could hear the thudding of axe heads, spear points and sword edges into flesh and the screaming of the dying. Whatever notions he had of battle before that day were clean gone form his mind, instead replaced by the brutal reality men like Arthur lived with every day. Being a warrior, he had quickly learnt, was about mastering more than the use of arms. It required the mastering of fear, guilt and the ability to block out the nightmares that clawed at each and every one of them in the hours of darkness.

But he had done it. He had ridden alongside Arthur and had gained acceptance into the Teulu of the Red Dragon. He was one of them now. Although he was happy, it was not as he had expected and the journey that had led him into Arthur's esteem had marked him in more ways than one.

With the fading sunlight glinting off his father's armour and a song of victory and companionship newly learnt in the company of his new friends on his lips, he continued north. He would go first to his uncle's villa and then on to Angharad to fulfil the promise he had made her.

Arthur

Cair Badon's ruined forum thronged with people and not just soldiers. Over the past few weeks, traders, craftsmen and nobles, all with their families, had drifted into the reclaimed town. There was always business to be done wherever an army was camped. The appetites of fighting men for drink, food, whores and religious talismans was renowned and now that the Sais menace had gone, it was a lot safer to ply one's trade in the towns of the Borderlands. Besides, everybody wanted to see the mighty Teulu of the Red Dragon and its fearsome leader for themselves.

Arthur watched the heaving forum from a window high in the basilica. Word had reached his ears of the stories being told about him. There were even songs though Menw put them down as amateurish efforts by non-bards. He would compose a song of Arthur, he had promised; one that would truly do him justice.

Arthur cringed at the prospect. He certainly did not feel the picture of the fearless hero that was currently being painted of him. The Battle of Badon had had many heroes but most of them were dead. Cei had told him to just enjoy it for the people adored him. But that was Cei through and through. Enjoy the day and forget about tomorrow and whatever responsibilities it might carry. He had everything for the asking now; horses, supplies, loyalty. No king or chieftain of the south-west doubted him now. He was their hope. He was their *Dux Bellorum*.

The word evoked both pride and trepidation in him. That people should see him as Aurelianus incarnate was an honour beyond anything he had ever dreamt of. But with it came a terrible weight. Beyond all the victory celebrations and all the praise heaped upon him lay a simple, hard fact. He had won a battle, not a war. The Saeson were far from gone. He had inserted himself into a conflict that seemed to have neither beginning nor end. Who knew how many months, years he would spend fighting the Saeson? Aurelianus's words to him in this very basilica many nights ago rang in his head; 'I have been fighting this war for forty years.'

He missed Guenhuifar. He missed her so much that he could weep though he would never allow such a weakness in front of his men. No, he would force those feelings down, deep down into his gut, and continue with the business in hand. Then, one day, when Albion was safe at last, he would return to her. He just hoped that such a day might come before he was as old and grey and lonely as Aurelianus had been.

The teulu was currently preparing to ride east. They would make for Aurelianus's old fort and see what reparations were to be done there before winter.

"Arthur," said Cei from the doorway. "The men are ready. We should head out."

Arthur turned from the window and followed Cei down the steps to the nave. As they exited the building into the blinding sunlight a wall of noise hit them. Arthur stood in the shadow of the dragon banner which fluttered above them and the crowds in the forum went wild. His heart fluttering, he went to mount Hengroen who stood waiting for him, brushed and saddled by his grooms.

They rode off to join the teulu beyond the walls and a chant rose from the crowd, inaudible and disorganised at first but growing with intensity and synchronicity with every second as more and more took it up. It was his name; a word that meant more than a name to those who had lived in the shadow of the Saeson for a generation. It was a name that meant hope and peace and everything the Britons had dreamt of since the last Roman legionary had departed.

Arthur smiled as he and Cei rode through the gatehouse, the chant ringing in their ears;

Arthur! Arthur! Arthur!

HISTORICAL NOTE

"Then Arthur along with the kings of Britain fought against them in those days, but Arthur himself was the military commander (dux bellorum). His first battle was at the mouth of the river which is called Glein. His second, third, fourth, and fifth battles were above another river which is called Dubglas and is in the region of Linnuis. The sixth battle was above the river which is called Bassas. The seventh battle was in the forest of Celidon, that is Cat Coit Celidon. The eighth battle was at the fortress of Guinnion, in which Arthur carried the image of holy Mary ever virgin on his shoulders; and the pagans were put to flight on that day. And through the power of our Lord Jesus Christ and through the power of the blessed Virgin Mary his mother there was great slaughter among them. The ninth battle was waged in the City of the Legion. The tenth battle was waged on the banks of a river which is called Tribruit. The eleventh battle was fought on the mountain which is called Agnet. The twelfth battle was on Mount Badon in which there fell in one day 960 men from one charge by Arthur; and no one struck them down except Arthur himself, and in all the wars he emerged as victor."

Arthur's twelve battles listed in the 9th century *Historia Brittonum* (The History of the Britons) have sparked a treasure hunt among enthusiasts hoping to uncover more about Britain's shadowy 5th century war-leader and where he was active.

The first six battles possibly took place in Lincolnshire which was settled by Anglo-Saxons who took on the name 'Lindisfaras' (eventually becoming the Kingdom of Lindsey) after the Roman town of Lindum (Lincoln). There is a River Glen in

Lincolnshire but the rivers Dubglas and Bassas are too vague to identify with any confidence.

We are on firmer ground with the seventh battle which happens in the forest of Celidon. This is clearly a reference to the Caledonian Forest that once took up large swathes of the Scottish Highlands and pops up several times in Welsh stories and folklore.

The eighth battle at the fortress of Guinnion has several candidates ranging from the Roman fort of Vinovia at Binchester, to either of the 'Ventas' – Venta Silurum and Venta Belgarum (Caerwent and Winchester respectively). This entry is interesting for its reference of Arthur carrying 'the image of holy Mary ever virgin on his shoulder.' This resembles the entry in the Welsh Annals in which, at the Battle of Badon, Arthur 'carried the cross of our Lord Jesus Christ on his shoulder for three days and nights.' There may be some confusion as to what is meant here as the words for 'shoulder' and 'shield' ('scuid'/'scuit') in Old Welsh are easily confused.

There were three Roman legionary fortresses in Britain (York, Chester and Caerleon) and two of these (Chester and Caerleon) derive their names from the Latin *Castra Legionis*. This became Caer Legion in Old Welsh which was the location of Arthur's court in several of the Welsh tales. It is a matter of debate as to whether this (and the battle in the *Historia Brittonum*) referred to Chester or Caerleon.

While the Tribruit is probably the same as the battle of 'Tryfrwyd' mentioned twice in the Arthurian poem *Pa Gur yv y Portaur?* (Who is the Gatekeeper?) it has so far defied identification.

Geoffrey of Monmouth in his *Historia Regum Britanniae* (The History of the Kings of Britain) identified Agnet with Edinburgh (Din Eidyn) but there is little to confirm this. Some versions of the *Historia Brittonum* supplant Agnet with 'Breguoin/Bregomion' which could refer to Bravonium (Leintwardine in Herefordshire); the location of a fortified Roman *mansio* and baths which supplied nearby cavalry forts or Bremenium; a Roman fort at Rochester, Northumberland.

As well as the aforementioned entry in the Welsh Annals, the Battle of Badon is also referred to by the monk Gildas in his 6th century polemic *De Excidio et Conquestu Britanniae* (On the Ruin and Conquest of Britain). Gildas, who infamously makes no mention of Arthur, describes the victory at Badon as the culmination of a native resistance to the Saxons led by Ambrosius Aurelianus, a man of noble stock. The *Historia Brittonum* later names Aurelianus as 'king among the kings of Britain' but does not connect him to the Battle of Badon. Mynydd Baedan in Glamorgan has been put forward as a possible site, as have various places named Badbury ('Baddan byrig' in Old English). There has been more support for a site near the city of Bath. Although we don't know what the Britons called the Roman town of Aquae Sulis before it became the Saxon town of Bathum in the ninth century (Caer Badon is a popular guess) it does have several hills nearby that bear evidence of 5th century fortification.

It is probably unwise to take the list of battles as gospel. The *Historia Brittonum* is a collection of history, folklore and pure fantasy. It is possible that some of the battles credited to Arthur were in fact the exploits of later military leaders. Nor is the order in which the battles occur set in stone. It has been suggested that battle list is a Latin summary of a poem written in Primitive or Old Welsh and the names for well-known locations that once rhymed have now been corrupted to obscurity.

The characters Drustan and Esyllt in this book represent an early form of the Tristan and Iseult romance that enjoyed huge success in many different versions in the late middle ages. King Arthur has been linked to the tale since the beginning, appearing as a mediator between Tristan and his uncle King Mark of Cornwall.

The main characters appear in the Welsh triads (fragments of folklore preserved in threes) as 'Drystan son of Tallwch', 'Esyllt' and 'March'. Then there is the often-overlooked Welsh fragment called *Ystoria Trystan* written down in the 16th century. It is impossible to know if the oral tradition on which this was based predated the more popular continental versions but it does have some interesting differences, namely that the action takes place not in Cornwall but in the forest of 'Clyddon'. This is probably the same as the Caledonian forest mentioned in the battle list presenting us with the tantalising possibility of a literary echo of one of Arthur's battles.

Further strength for a northern origin of the legend comes from the frequent appearance of 'Drest', 'Drust' and 'Talorc' in the lists of Pictish kings and Tristan's fictional homeland of Loenois in the continental versions is also the Old French name for Lothian; a northern British kingdom (Leudonion in this book).

If the Tristan and Isolde story began in northern Britain, it is unclear why it was located in Cornwall by the French and Breton writers. In the 5th century, Armorica was gradually being settled by migrating Britons (hence its modern name 'Brittany') and these largely hailed from Cornwall. It may have been natural for them to place the tale in the part of Britain inhabited by their ancestors.

The tale of Peredur is largely taken from the 12th century Welsh romance *Peredur son of Efrawg*. As with Tristan and Iseult, there was also a continental version; Chrétien de Troyes's *Perceval, the Story of the Grail*. While *Peredur* was undoubtedly influenced by Chrétien's work, there are enough differences to suggest that there was a native British version which Chrétien used as his source. I have followed the Welsh version for the most part, stripping if of some of its more fantastical elements and conflating several characters for the sake of simplicity (for instance, I condensed Peredur's two unnamed uncles into one and named him after a third character – Edlim Redsword).

In this trilogy I have also conflated the traditional three sisters of Arthur; Morgen, Anna and Morgause. The sorceress Morgen, first mentioned in Geoffrey of Monmouth's 12th century *Vita Merlini* (The Life of Merlin), originally had no familial connection to Arthur, being merely a healer and chief of nine women on the isle of Avalon. Monmouth *did* give Arthur a sister in his *Historia Regum Britanniae* (The History of the Kings of Britain); Anna who was married off to king Loth of Lothian and became the mother of Mordred (Medraut to give him his earliest name). Later tradition makes Morgause the wife of king Lot and mother of Mordred (by way of an incestuous encounter with her brother Arthur).

That Morgause's name was originally written as 'Orcades' – the Latin name for the Orkney Islands – led the historian Roger Sherman Loomis to suggest in his essay *Scotland and the Arthurian Legend* that Morgause and Morgen were in fact one and the same (being something like 'Morgen, Queen of the Orkneys') before becoming separate characters in later tradition. I have used this theory in consolidating Anna, Morgen and Morgause into a single character; Anna of the Morgens, mother of Medraut.

Medraut plays a key role in the next book where Arthur's story continues towards its devastating conclusion. *Field of the Black Raven* which will be released later this year.

Printed in Great Britain
by Amazon